Frank Penny

&

The Mystery of Ludlow Hums

Happy Reading

Frank Penny

&

The Mystery of Ludlow Hums

Jeremy Elson

Eyrie Press

First published in 2018 by Eyrie Press

Cover image copyright © Glyn Bateman

ISBN 978-0-9932614-6-6

A catalogue record of this book is available
from the British Library.

Any resemblance to persons fictional or real,
living or dead, is purely coincidental.

To Treena and Finlay - my inspiration

The End?

Run. Run and don't look back.

Her lungs were on fire. Deep gulps of air choked her as she fled. Run, don't look back.

But she couldn't help it. She knew they were closing in on her; she could feel them at the nape of her neck, like a cold sweat, and knew they wouldn't give up until they'd caught her. Still she ran, faster than ever. But not fast enough, like a fox hunted by a pack of bloodthirsty hounds and exhausted from the chase.

She turned her head and glanced down, instantly wishing she hadn't as she watched the men moving swiftly up the slope after her. They were stronger and fitter and she didn't know how much longer she could keep going. How could she have thought it was possible to outrun them? Her horse stood at the foot of the hill, mane flapping in the breeze, lame. She'd had no choice but to leave him there and continue on foot. Beside the beast, she could just make him out. The tall, dark figure, standing, arms folded, while his men gave chase. She could see his long, dark hair and beard; the black scorpion on his red tunic was barely visible. The man with the orange streak in his hair. The man she truly feared. She imagined him watching, eyes wide with boyish expectation, with evil intent, knowing for certain she would be overrun and he would finally take what she had. How could she have been so stupid? How could she have trusted him? He knew she had managed to create the one thing he desired above all else, the most powerful of objects, known only in myth and legend. He would do anything to possess it and he knew that, unfortunately, only she stood in his way.

The pursuit had continued for miles. Across the border and into her homeland they had hunted her. Escape never looked possible but she had to try, try with every fibre, every sinew of her being, because, if they caught her, the outcome would not bear thinking about. They would spare her life, but her fate, and that of everyone else, would be worse than death.

Her breath was spent and they were closing in, fast. A dozen of them pursued her, swarming up the hillside like angry wasps whose nest she had kicked. Her bare feet slipped and scraped as she moved, as swiftly as she could, over the rocks that hid amongst the heather. Her fight for breath pulled in the sweet scent which would have been beautiful in any other circumstances, but which was now an unforgiving reminder of what she knew she was about to lose. She stumbled and fell, letting out a gasp. Quickly and instinctively she dragged herself back to her feet. *Keep going, don't look back.* But she couldn't go on much longer. Her legs were full of lead and she started to feel the fear, until now suppressed by her determination to avoid capture, rise up in every grain of her.

Her chest heaved, rocking like a ship in a storm. Despite her youth, she struggled to keep ahead of them. They were catching her. One woman against all of them was no fair fight, not that that ever bothered *him*.

She came to a point where the hill rose in a sheer cliff face, towering thirty feet towards the sky, laughing at her and the futility of her predicament. She clawed frantically at the rocks, trying desperately to find a way up, but the wet stone gave her no purchase and she lost her grip as it spat her back. Letting out a cry of desperation, she fell to the ground. She got up and tried again, praying that the cliff would be forgiving, that it would feel her distress and come to her rescue. It didn't. She looked up, knowing it was hopeless. A sob stuck in her throat - she was trapped. There was no way up, no way out.

Then they were on her, surrounding her like a pack of hungry wolves, their faces menacing, but wary. She turned, defiant, still fighting for breath, sensing their satisfaction at cornering their prey. The run across the moor and up the hill had taken all her strength, yet still her eyes darted quickly between the men, looking for a way out. There was none. She knew the hunt had come to an end - her fate was sealed. The men stopped, gripping their swords firmly; they too breathed heavily from the chase.

There was a pause; no one seemed certain what to do next. Then, one of them took a step towards her, carefully.

'Hand it over,' he said, beckoning with his fingers.

It was concealed under her cloak. They knew it and they had their orders to seize it and to give it to him, their master. She knew this was it; the time had come for her to make a choice – give it up, or destroy it. She reached in and touched the object. Its neatly crafted wooden shaft felt as cold as steel, as cold as death, as if it sensed this was the end, that the power it held was about to be given up to a new, dark master, to wield in unthinkable ways.

She thought back to happier times, of the man she loved, knowing she would never see him again. He'd known she was gifted. It was her curse, and it had brought her to this place, to her ultimate ruin. But she had never considered herself gallant, not until now, now that she stared into the monster's mouth. Devour or be devoured. Tears pricked her eyes and scratched her cheeks as they fell. She felt their saltiness on her lips, a reminder of how alive she was, but she knew there was only one way this was going to end. Destiny was a cruel master.

She gripped the object tightly with both hands and pulled it out from under her cloak. The soldiers looked on in wonder as they cast their eyes upon it. The object of legend. She was the one talented enough to have created it, and she also knew how to destroy it, aware that, if she did, it would also heave her into oblivion as an unwilling passenger. But it was the only way; she couldn't let it, and the incredible power in contained, fall into his hands. The consequences for everyone, and everything, would be unimaginable.

Her eyes leapt from one man to the next, and then a calmness came over her. Two of the soldiers ran to her, as if they knew what she was about to do. Quickly, she raised the staff high into the air.

'*Absolatum!*' she cried, and brought the tip down onto the ground with all the energy she had left.

There was a blinding light and a thunderous, ear splitting, explosion. Then ... nothing.

12 YEARS LATER

1

THE FARM BOY

'See you later, dimwit!' Phoebe's words had stuck in his mind all morning.

She'd grabbed her bag and headed out for school, throwing him the familiar insult without looking back, and was gone before he'd had time to think of a smart response. He wondered ... how much more irritating could she actually get? However much he tried, he was finding her harder to ignore, so there had been only one thing for it; he'd grabbed some sandwiches and headed up to the wildflower meadow to calm down.

* * *

His gaze followed the Brimstone as it fluttered from one flower to the next. The butterfly had a last slurp of nectar and moved on down the meadow, stopping here and there to refuel until it disappeared from view in the long grass.

After being wound up at breakfast, Frank had spent the morning relaxing in the shade of the tall oak, which gave him a glorious view of the farmland below. His dad's farmland. He could see the farmhouse away to the right, the array of familiar low stone buildings stuck among their surroundings like an old man's teeth and, in the distance, he could just make out the winding lane that led to the village, further on.

A small stream wound its way like a lethargic serpent gliding slowly along the length of the farm. Across the stream, on the other side of the shallow valley, his dad's sheep sought shade under the trees. Frank thought it was the most idyllic place on earth and felt he would never want to be anywhere else. Phoebe or no Phoebe.

He rolled over onto his back and closed his eyes, fingering the locket around his neck as the early afternoon sun beat down. He yawned and breathed in the peace and solitude.

He loved this place; he loved his dad's farm where he lived and worked - well, sort of worked - even though he was only thirteen. He loved the freedom he had to go off exploring on his own whenever he wanted. Not going to school had its distinct advantages.

He also loved the summer. The way nature grew their crops and heaved their livestock towards adulthood had always held a fascination for him as he'd grown up amongst them. But today was one of those days when he needed to get away on his own, away from the house, away from everyone. All the other kids were going to be off from school in two days and, although being home educated had its benefits, once the holidays started, his cousin, Phoebe, with her giggling friends, would very soon be around to take part in their most favourite pastime of all - annoying him all day long. Well, maybe it wasn't their favourite, Frank wasn't entirely sure, but it certainly ranked up there with gossiping about and poking fun at everyone and everything at school, and burying their heads in rubbish celebrity magazines. Definitely top three. Three teenage girls against him. Ugh! Why did they have school holidays?

He and Phoebe were the same age and had lived together in the same house for most of their lives, but Frank liked his own company and stayed out of her way as much as he could.

She was becoming a master of the constant smart comment, as if she sat in school thinking them up all day long so that she could come home and aim them at him, one by one. Her recent great witticisms included:

'Hey Frankie, is that a cow pat I can smell, or your breath?' or 'Melissa' —the dimmest girl in the school, apparently— 'wants to go out with you, but she thinks you're a bit thick.'

She'd come home the day before and said, 'We've been learning all about this mystic man who just lay in bed for a year, staring at the ceiling. Didn't know you were so famous, Frank.'

Each comment was followed by a self-satisfied snort. Yes, tomorrow would be his last day of peace and quiet for the next six weeks.

He had to make the most of today and tomorrow, starting with a nap. He listened to the grasshoppers chirruping as he started to snooze.

'Frank, you up there?' The lazy peace was broken without warning. It was Brigg, his dad's farmhand. How he'd failed to notice him coming across the meadow a moment ago was quite a mystery. Frank rolled over onto his front in the long grass, pretending he hadn't heard, and waited. In the warmth, his mop of fair, curly hair stuck to his neck with sweat. It never failed to surprise him that, no matter where he went, his dad or Brigg always seemed to know where to find him.

He stayed silent as he heard the heavy footsteps approaching, crushing the grass as they came. A huge shadow cast itself over him as if a rain cloud had unexpectedly appeared in the sky. Frank turned onto his back once more and opened his eyes. A giant of a man stood over him, sweat beading on his brow, hands on hips. Beside him sat Jip, a shabby looking collie, panting quietly with an oversized tongue lolling out of her mouth like a giant pink slug.

'There y'are. Bin lookin' f'yer all over – wen' t' yer tree 'ouse but shoulda known you'd be up 'ere. Didn' yer hear me callin'?' he said, wiping his forehead and breathing heavily.

Frank sat up. Brigg stood there beaming at him. He smiled back. Frank had never known a time without Brigg, strong as two oxen, gentle as two lambs. Brigg, who could turn his hand to anything. Brigg, who had taught him so much over the years, lessons Phoebe couldn't hope to learn in the classroom. Brigg, who had pulled him from the well when he was a small boy. Brigg, the big man who Frank loved nearly as much as his dad. He wore his usual pair of faded, scruffy, blue overalls which were ingrained with dirt from years of working on the land. He wore them like a second skin and Frank couldn't think of a time when he'd worn anything different. It was as if he must have a number of identical sets into which he changed each day. He was the most thickset and muscular of men - his short neck rose up like a tree trunk from his body - but he always had a smile on his kind, gentle face which bore the marks of hard work and belied his vastness. His hair was dark and unkempt, a bit like the black sheep that roamed the fields in the distance.

'What's up?' said Frank, yawning.

'D'ya know what the time is?' replied Brigg.

Frank had clearly lost track of time, which wasn't surprising given what a fine day it was and that he had been trying to put his cousin out of his mind since he had strolled up into the meadow after breakfast.

'Not tea time?' said Frank. He wasn't hungry, and he'd only just finished his sandwiches.

'Naw. It's time t' be roundin' them sheep up for shearin'. 'S'your turn if yer like,' said Brigg. Frank's face lit up. For a few weeks now, Brigg had been giving Frank lessons in how to handle Jip. He'd picked it up quickly and was getting so good at controlling her that, the day before, Brigg had said he could do it by himself today.

Frank hadn't wanted to do it in front of Phoebe the first time. He couldn't think of anything worse. He knew she'd want to watch with her friends, Heather and Jasmine, and they'd take it in turns to shoot clever jibes at him, trying to outsmart the last smart comment in an attempt to distract him and make him think he didn't know what he was doing. She couldn't do it herself so, for some reason that Frank had yet to discover, she had to try and knock anything that he did. Brigg had sensed this and Frank was thankful to him for allowing him to do it today, away from prying eyes.

'You should never worry 'bout what others think of yer. 'Cept yer dad maybe,' Brigg had told him when Frank had admitted his concerns. 'Always remember what you know in 'ere,' he'd said, tapping his temple. 'Just do what you know you can do, 's easy. Big old bloke like me don't say much, I know, but I know what I can do an' just get on with it, an' no one can tell me otherwise.'

Frank thought this was good advice. For a big lummox, Brigg was unerringly wise at times. Even so, Frank still didn't like Phoebe and her friends scoffing at him.

Brigg held out a hand. Frank grasped it and was pulled up as though light as a feather. He stood, still in the big man's shadow, a respite from the glare of the sun. He yawned again and stretched. Brigg leaned forward and put a giant hand on Frank's shoulder.

'Ready then?' he asked.

'Let's go and round up some sheep,' smiled Frank. 'Last one there's a steaming cow pat!' He shot off across the meadow towards the stream and the sheep on the other side, Brigg and Jip in hot pursuit.

The afternoon flew by in a frenzy of bleating and, before he knew it, the sheep had been rounded up and he and Brigg were leaning on the fence as his Aunt Rachel's harsh tone shot across the farm from the kitchen door.

'Frank, time for tea, get yourself in here now, please.' Her shriek filled the air. Jip's ears pricked up and she let out a whine. Frank sighed. He wasn't really ready to go in for the day, but with his dad in town he didn't want to upset his aunt.

He looked up at Brigg. He would have liked to stay to see how he sheared the sheep - strong hands to hold the animal, a delicate touch with the shears. But Frank knew he'd learn soon enough.

'Best be gettin' on,' said Brigg. 'Yer dad'll be 'ome soon. Don't wan' t' keep yer aunt waitin' now. I'm sure that cousin o' yours'll be scoffin' like a piglet already. Be nothin' left for yer if yer don't 'urry.' Brigg smiled down at him. Frank looked back and both burst into giggles. They laughed until their faces hurt and Frank knew it was time to say goodbye for the day.

'See you later,' said Frank as he turned toward where his aunt's voice had come from. He should hurry.

'Yep, we got that barn roof to fix tomorro',' said Brigg as he watched Frank walk away.

Frank turned and smiled back at him. 'Excellent!' he thought, and Dad would be there too. The three of them working together. Just the way he liked it.

He thrust his hands into his trouser pockets and walked quickly across the sheep pen, a slight spring in his step. He climbed over the wooden gate, landed on to the path that led to the yard and headed towards the farmhouse.

As he jogged across the wide flat yard in front of the house he scattered the few chickens that roamed freely around him. He smiled at them and they clucked back. Away to the left was the large five-bar gate that led out on to the lane. It was open, ready for his dad's return. He leaned against the wall outside the back door, eased his boots off and placed them upside down on the boot rack. The house seemed to groan with age. It was old, yet solid, and it was home, his home.

They generally lived a harmonious life on Tresparrik Farm. His dad had brought him up to be at ease around the outdoors and, from an early age, he had involved Frank in the farm. This had started with simple jobs like collecting the eggs and cleaning out the chickens, but, over the years, he had been allowed to help with more interesting things, such as milking and harvesting. Last year his dad had even let him drive the plough, under Brigg's supervision, although his lines had left a bit to be desired. Frank had learned so much and loved every minute, every single minute of his education.

They grew a few crops and kept some sheep, cows and pigs, and they had a good reputation. They sold their produce to the local traders and his dad even bartered some milk and eggs in return for other things like fruit and cloth. They also had a good-sized vegetable plot that they all loved to tend and most of their homegrown produce found its way into Aunt Rachel's mouth-watering recipes.

The door was open and led straight into the large kitchen. Despite the warmth of the day outside, and the heat from the range inside, the room was cool and the chill of the old stone made for a welcome haven from the sun. Two windows looked out onto the yard. The low, beamed ceiling gave the room a homely feel and the floor was cold flagstones. In the centre of the room, set with four places, stood a large oak table which always oozed the sweet smell of beeswax. A jug of water sat in the middle next to a vase of fresh wildflowers, picked by Aunt Rachel from the meadow that morning. Frank loved the vivid pink of the campion and the vibrant blue of the cornflowers. There was a large dresser at the side of the room, adorned with plain crockery, and a comfy looking armchair in the corner. From the ceiling there hung an assortment of copper pots and pans and, despite the array of utensils, the kitchen was always tidy and uncluttered. His aunt stood at the cooker stirring a bubbling pot of stew and humming to herself.

Frank had grown up here with his dad and his aunt and, of course, Phoebe. There were times when he wished it was just him and his dad and, even though they'd lived under the same roof for most of his life, he was still a bit unsure what his aunt thought about him. She was quiet and detached and she could be really abrupt. It was obvious where Phoebe got some of her ways. But Aunt Rachel looked after them all in a strange sort of way; she was nice to him more often than not and was really quite fair. When she had been short with him his dad just said to try and ignore it, that she really didn't mean it, it was just her way, and he had learned to do just that. Frank thought there was sometimes a sadness about her which she covered with a hard exterior, as if there was something she was hiding. Dad always said they needed each other around, like a proper family, so he was happy to accept her as she was. Certainly the stew she had been cooking up smelled delicious. He was ravenous after his success in the sheep pen and had caught its waft from the other side of the yard. His mouth had started to water and his stomach had begun to ache in anticipation of the tasty meal to come.

Frank walked up quietly behind her as she continued to stir. She turned quickly and dropped the spoon onto the floor in fright, hand darting onto her chest.

'My goodness, Frank,' she gasped. 'What do you mean creeping up behind me and scaring the life out of me like that!' She bent down and grabbed the wooden spoon. 'I've got a hot pot of stew on. What if I'd spilled the lot? Why don't you think!'

She brandished the spoon at him as if it were a weapon, pointing the end towards his chest. A drop spilled onto the floor with a thick plop. Frank was getting to the age where he knew he could get the better of her, but was careful not to overstep the mark; he'd certainly learned that the way to get what he wanted was to keep the adults in the house on his side, so he let Phoebe to take a more petulant approach to her mother. Certainly that was an advantage of having his cousin around.

He quickly reached a finger into the pot, dipped it in and licked the hot sauce off the end.

'Get your filthy hands out of my stew!' Rachel scolded, smacking his hand with the spoon.

'Ow!'

'You'll get more than "ow" if you don't get and wash your hands. Been touching Jip 'n' sheep 'n' all. Go on, now, I'm about to dish up.'

She scowled at him and her pale face twitched. She had her hair pulled back into its usual ponytail; wisps escaped the clips that held it to her head. She was younger than she looked. Frank sensed she was in the mood for an argument, but he wasn't so he wandered over to the sink and pumped the handle on the tap. Cold water came gushing out and Frank washed his hands and drenched his face. He felt the pleasure as his warm skin prickled in the refreshing surge. He hadn't realised just how hot and parched he had become with the exertion of the afternoon. Perhaps he should have stayed up in the meadow after all; the shade of the big oak there would have kept him cool. He leaned under the tap and drank thirstily. His aunt gave him a sideways glance.

'There's water on the table if you're thirsty,' she barked, and he heard her mutter 'No manners' under her breath as she began to spoon the rich stew into bowls. As if Phoebe had any, he thought.

Right on cue, the door to the side of the kitchen opened and in walked an olive-skinned girl. The door slammed loudly behind her. Aunt Rachel jumped again and turned, scowling at her daughter. Frank could see her holding back a rebuke.

Phoebe was much shorter than Frank but just as athletic and strong. Her long, dark hair, which was tied back, hung to her waist. Her features were the same as her mother's, unlike her complexion, which was more like her father's.

Aunt Rachel was married to his Uncle Simeon, a miserable stick of a man who always dressed in black and seemed to sneer at everyone and everything. He looked as though he had a constant bad smell under his nose. He worked away all the time. Where he was and what he was doing was a mystery to Frank, but, in all honesty, he couldn't have been less interested. He could only remember meeting the man on a handful of occasions when he visited his wife and daughter at the farm. Aunt Rachel and Phoebe would go off with him for a week each summer, normally to the beaches near the Furnace Marshes, in the south of Byeland. He'd ride his wagon in, pick them up, and head straight off without so much as a hello or goodbye.

But not having Uncle Simeon around seemed to be acceptable to everyone and having Aunt Rachel at the farm made for a better life. His aunt certainly seemed to have no complaints and Frank was sure the absence of his uncle was best all round and no one really seemed to miss him.

It was evident that his father detested his brother-in-law, although he was careful not to say anything around Frank. That was his way. 'You need to take as you find, Frank,' he would say. 'Don't let others make your mind up for you, even me, before you've got to know someone.' But he knew there was something about Uncle Simeon that his father disliked. Frank could only guess why the two of them didn't see eye-to-eye. He thought it was probably the way he treated Aunt Rachel, although she was certainly a strong-willed woman who didn't seem bothered by Uncle Simeon's indifference to her, as well as to everyone else.

His dad was evidently fond of his sister and, in the absence of a mother, Frank was certain the presence of his aunt in the house had been a good influence as he grew up. But she was no substitute.

Aunt Rachel and Phoebe had come to live with them when Frank was only a baby, just after his mother had died. She'd been involved in an accident, but his dad never talked much about that and Frank knew to avoid the subject as he grew up. For all the fun and laughs they'd had, there was sometimes an air of sadness about his dad. Frank knew he hid it well, but had come to read the signs. It was obvious he missed her. The only thing Frank had of her was the small portrait in a locket which he kept on a chain around his neck. His dad had given it to him when he was only seven. He'd taken it from around his own neck and given it to Frank on his birthday.

'Guess you're old enough to have this now,' he'd said. Frank had noticed the tear he shed as he'd taken it off and fastened the clasp at the back of Frank's neck. His dad had passed on the only image they had of her to him, and Frank now understood it must have taken considerable effort on his part.

From then on he'd never taken the locket off and he looked at the image every day. He daydreamed about her, imagining what she would have been like and, despite her not being there, he always smiled when he pictured their laughter in his head. His beautiful mum.

Phoebe, who had her head in a book, went straight to the table without so much as a glance or a grunt in either his or her mother's direction. She pulled out a chair, scraping it along the floor which made his aunt look around. She sat on the pink and white checked cushion.

'Must you make *so* much noise?' Aunt Rachel said in Phoebe's direction. She was obviously having a bad day. Frank gave Phoebe a mocking smile. In return, she wrinkled her nose at him and stuck her tongue out, taking care her mother didn't see.

Frank wiped his hands on the cloth and went to sit down opposite Phoebe. He pulled at the chair but it stuck. Phoebe had wrapped her foot around one of its legs. She let it go, causing that chair to scrape along the floor too as Frank struggled not to lose his balance.

'What did I just say?' shouted his aunt. Frank felt like telling her that it was Phoebe's fault, but, due to the mood she seemed to be in, decided against it.

'Sorry, Aunt Rachel,' was all he could say. He settled himself on the chair, curling his lip at his cousin, who sat there, looking down at the book she had brought in, a self-satisfied look of smugness stuck to her face. Another small victory in her seemingly eternal battle to wind him up.

Phoebe, despite years of schooling, seemed less and less interested in what was going on in the classroom and more interested in the world of fashion, music and gossip magazines. She would need frequent reminders to finish her homework, rather than look at the badly hand-drawn pictures that accompanied reports of the latest high-profile wedding, or a feature on how some baron from the upmarket Strondia Provinces had done up his massive castle. Frank, on the other hand, had never been to school and would constantly remind her about what she wasn't learning.

'What are you reading there?' asked Aunt Rachel, as she brought two bowls of the delicious stew to the table, along with a basket of crusty bread, freshly baked.

'Oh, we're doing the history of the ancient Luggans at school,' replied Phoebe, turning a page without looking up.

'The Luggans. Oh, yes, I remember reading about them when I was at school.'

'Yeah, we're learning all about life in a Luggan village - what they ate, the tools they used and all sorts,' said Phoebe, seemingly engrossed in the book.

'Great,' laughed Frank. 'That'll be of use to you in about, er, well, a gazillion years' time.'

Phoebe's expression changed. 'Shut yer face. At least some of us actually go to school' - she paused and looked up at Frank - 'while some of us just lay about the farm all day. Doing nothing.' She continued to study her book with a look of amusement on her face.

'Looks like your cousin's mistaking going to school with getting an education,' came a familiar voice.

Frank spun round in his chair to see a figure standing in the shadow of the porch.

'Dad!' he got up and ran to hug his father, who held the boy tightly around the shoulders and kissed him on the head.

'Come back here and eat your tea,' said his aunt, raising her voice only slightly. The presence of his father seemed to cool her temper.

'Leave the boy alone, Rach,' he said and shot her a smile. She looked back as if to say something, but thought better of it. She turned back to the stove and spooned up another large portion of stew. His dad always seemed to bring calm to proceedings.

Frank returned to the table as his dad walked into the kitchen. Lawrence Penny was tall and had to duck under the frame of the door as he entered. His short, dark hair was greying at the temples. He was well-built, but not heavy like Brigg. There was a strength and confidence about him, both physically and the way he held himself. He walked to the table and poured himself a glass of water. He drank it down quickly, poured himself another and set the full glass on the table.

'Hello, Phoebe,' he said.

'Hi, Uncle Lozza,' she replied, still thumbing through the book.

Lawrence went over to the sink and washed his hands.

'My, it's warm out there today,' he said to no one in particular. He sat at the table next to Phoebe and stretched his legs out wearily. Aunt Rachel put another two bowls of stew down and sat next to him. 'Thanks Rach,' he said. 'Smells gorgeous.'

'Just like me,' mused Phoebe.

'Yeah, you do smell like meat and potatoes,' laughed Frank. His father looked at him over his spoon and raised his eyebrows.

'What?' His dad continued to look at him. 'I know,' sighed Frank. 'If you can't say anything nice, don't say anything at all.'

His dad smiled. Frank could hardly remember any time during his life that his dad had raised his voice to him. That wasn't his way. Somehow he was just able to give him a look, as if waiting for Frank to recall an important lesson he'd learned over the years. Just like now. Sometimes, though, he just couldn't help himself and Phoebe had walked right into that one.

'Sorry Phoebs,' he slurped into his spoon.

'Saw Brigg at the gate, tells me you've been rounding up sheep this afternoon,' said Lawrence.

'Yeah, it was great. I managed to get them in more or less all by myself,' said Frank eagerly. His dad nodded approvingly. He was sparing with his words, but Frank always understood him from his actions and demeanour.

'Well that'll be *soooo* useful too,' said Phoebe in an attempt to get back at Frank. He ignored her. Even she would have to concede that what he had done was of far more use than knowing how some ancient settler scratched his bum.

'Last day at school tomorrow then, Phoebe,' said Lawrence, steering her off her confrontation with Frank.

'Yeah, can't *wait*.' She shuddered to overemphasize her relief that another year would soon be over. 'No more lessons, no more teachers. Hoooo-ray!'

'What!' said Frank. 'And no more "amazing history of the Luggans"!' They all looked at him and burst out laughing, even Aunt Rachel managed a chuckle.

'Okay, you win,' said Phoebe. 'Luggans equals major yawn. Mum, can Jasmine and Heather come round after school tomorrow please? We finish at lunch time; I said we could go down to the river for a picnic. *Please!*'

'There's some great dragonflies down there at the moment,' said Frank. Phoebe gave him a 'What are you talking about?' look, as if she would be interested in looking at dragonflies with her girlfriends. Frank could picture them just shrieking around, the way they did, splashing in the river and disturbing everything around them. Dragonflies beware. Perhaps those hornets would still be around, though.

Frank thought he'd stay out of their way. He would probably head to his tree house once they'd finished the barn roof. It was high enough in the ash tree to deter anyone who disliked heights and the way her friend, Heather, had started looking at him recently made him feel really uncomfortable. Yes, he'd be able to keep out of their way all day, if necessary.

'I suppose that'll be okay,' said Aunt Rachel. 'Mind they let their folks know, though.'

'Fab!' Phoebe grabbed a piece of bread and stuffed it into her mouth. At least she won't be able to speak for a bit, thought Frank. With a half-eaten mouthful, she then proceeded to force a spoonful of stew in. Frank grabbed a piece of bread as he thought there might be none left at this rate.

They finished their meal and the kids cleared up. Phoebe washed and Frank dried. The long summer evening turned to dusk, a lazy orange sky hung over the land and the farm hummed with tranquillity.

The four of them stayed in the kitchen, talking mainly about Phoebe's last day at school, how she couldn't see the point of going in just for the morning and how her teacher, Mrs Harper, would make them do work rather than let them just chat, although Frank got the impression that she and her friends just chatted their way through each term anyway. Their voices filled the homely space until late on into the evening.

Phoebe yawned. Frank did too and he stood up and kissed his aunt and dad goodnight. Phoebe did the same and they headed towards the stairs. Frank paused at the foot of the staircase and turned.

'Barn roof tomorrow, then?' he said to his dad, who looked over and nodded.

'Better get to bed then,' he said. 'Big day tomorrow.'

If only he knew how true those words would turn out to be.

2

The List

The next day started like any other. Lawrence was up first, as always, but he let Frank take his time. He believed in getting up when you were good and ready rather than having anything that would wake you up early. That was one reason why they had never kept a cockerel on the farm. Frank thought this was a great idea and it allowed him some freedom in the mornings, whereas Phoebe had to be ready for school each day at the same time, whether she liked it or not, which would normally make her very grumpy indeed and which amused Frank tremendously.

This morning, though, Phoebe didn't seem in any particular hurry and she was sitting at the table as Frank came through into the kitchen. *The History of the Ancient Luggans* had been replaced by a magazine which appeared to feature pictures of the recent wedding of a famous actor and his new bride. Frank could never see why anyone would be the least bit interested in the lives of people they didn't know. He found it so dull, but Phoebe seemed totally absorbed by each and every page. He preferred books on nature, or those that gave exciting accounts of the battles of Geraint the Lancebearer with his crimson crossbow or reported sightings of fabled creatures like the miniature winged horses of Curfulu.

His dad came in from the yard, ready for breakfast.

Aunt Rachel made sure they were all seen off with a bowl of porridge. Phoebe couldn't wait to get out of the door so that she could see out the last day at school and come home with her friends. She grabbed her school bag and headed out shouting, 'See you later!' as she left. Frank rolled his eyes.

Frank and his dad left soon after, heading across the courtyard to the barn where Brigg was already waiting for them. The big man grinned at Frank and they went to their work.

The morning passed quickly. As he had hoped, Frank spent it up on the barn roof in the glorious sunshine, watching and learning as his dad and Brigg repaired the part of the roof that had started to leak during the rains in the spring. Every so often his dad would show him how to fix a tile on and then let him have a go at fixing the next one. He soon got the hang of it.

They took breaks, taking water from the pump in the corner of the yard. Aunt Rachel made some cookies and brought them out with her delicious elderflower cordial which Frank had helped her make earlier in the year. It tasted like a fresh summer breeze.

When lunchtime approached Aunt Rachel appeared at the kitchen door. She shielded her eyes from the sun as she looked over to the roof where the men were working.

'Lawrence!' she shouted in her usual, sharp tone.

'Yep?' Lawrence stopped what he was doing and looked across the yard to where his sister was standing.

'Lunch in five minutes, okay?'

'Yep,' he said again and went back to his task, grabbing a final nail and hammering it home to fix the last of the morning's tiles in place. He looked up at Frank and Brigg and, with a smile, said, 'Nice work, chaps.'

They climbed down the ladder. All were hungry after the morning's labours and once again the smell of something tasty wound its way from the kitchen.

The three men paused at the barn door and looked up, admiring their work. Lawrence looked at Frank.

'You go on in, Frank, I'll only be a minute or two.'

'Okay, Dad.'

'And wash your hands, please.'

'Okay, Dad.'

Frank walked across the yard and took his boots off at the

kitchen door. He went in and sat down at the table to scratch an itch on his foot that had been troubling him for the last few minutes.

At that moment Phoebe burst into the kitchen, back from her last morning at school, her two friends nowhere in sight. She was gasping for breath. It appeared she had run all the way back from the village without stopping. In this heat! Frank thought she must either be really hungry or, more likely, just couldn't wait to get away from the place. But Phoebe rarely ran anywhere, so what was the rush?

She stood in the doorway, bent at the waist from exertion, hand on the door handle, panting and trying to get her breath back. Her mother and Frank just stared in her direction. Phoebe kept on panting until her breath slowed. She finally got enough puff back to speak.

'Mum! Mum! You will *never* guess what!' she gasped, chest still heaving.

'Goodness girl, what on earth is wrong with you?' said her mother, who was standing at the sink.

Phoebe staggered into the kitchen, breathing heavily, and put her hands on the table as if to steady herself. She noticed Frank sitting and scratching his foot and gave him an odd look, although she often did that, then turned once more to her mother.

'You'll *never* guess, Mum.'

'Yes, you said that,' said Aunt Rachel, who looked a little bewildered, even though she was used to her daughter's outbursts. 'So, do you want me to try and guess, which would be strange as you've said I'll not be able to, or are you just going to tell me?' She was typically straightforward.

There was the sound of hurried footsteps at the door and Phoebe looked around as her friends, Jasmine and Heather, bundled into the room. They appeared not to have been able to keep up with the more athletic Phoebe on the sprint home from school. They glanced in Frank's direction. More odd looks.

'You'll *never* guess what,' spluttered Jasmine. Aunt Rachel rolled her eyes, clearly getting irritated by the lack of information.

She stood there, drying a glass with a cloth. She eyed the girls and waited expectantly, deciding not to waste any more of her breath until one of them, preferably Phoebe, enlightened her further. The glass squeaked as she rubbed it. Phoebe got the message.

'It's Frank. It's Frank!' Phoebe spluttered, her eyes wide. She motioned towards her cousin.

At the mention of his name, Frank suddenly took more notice. He stopped scratching and looked up, his gaze darting from one girl to the next. What was that? What about him? All eyes seemed to be on him, where just a moment ago they were firmly fixed in Phoebe's direction. He looked to his aunt for some help and shrugged his shoulders, wondering what brainless story they were going to make up about him now. She looked back. Still the girls looked at him. The silence was deafening.

Aunt Rachel had had enough.

'Oh, for goodness sake, enough riddles, Phoebe. What *about* Frank?' she said.

'Yeah, Phoebe, what am I supposed to have done?' said Frank, beginning to feel slightly uneasy. He knew he hadn't done anything, and Phoebe had been at school all morning, but a strange feeling had began to work its way into his stomach for no apparent reason. Phoebe paused as if not sure what to say. She looked up at her friends, who nodded, eyes wide, urging her to finish whatever it was she had started.

'His name's on the list,' she blurted out, looking at her mother but pointing a long finger at Frank. There was a moment's silence as Phoebe waited for a response. 'Frank, his name's on the list.' Aunt Rachel looked as bemused as Frank felt.

'The list? What list?' she said. Frank felt suddenly relieved. Being on some list didn't necessarily seem like the worst thing his cousin could accuse him of, even if he had absolutely no idea what she was talking about. He thought she and her friends probably created their own stupid lists about all sorts of meaningless things, like 'Top ten boys you'd like to snog' or 'Top ten boys you'd rather snog a sheep before you snogged them'. The list of lists could be endless and he could be on any number of them.

'Oh, Mum, the list at *school* of course, you *idiot*,' said Phoebe.

Frank raised his eyebrows in surprise; he'd never heard her dare adopt such a tone with her mother. Aunt Rachel took a deep breath and held it, indicating that Phoebe had just overstepped the mark. She looked like she was about to burst, but then let the breath back out. A puzzled look appeared on her face. Her brow creased. There was a brief pause as the information Phoebe had just given her began to sink in.

'What did you just say?' she said.

'Oh, get with it, Mum.' Now Phoebe seemed irritated. 'Frank. He's on the *list*.'

The girls stopped staring at Frank and now all turned to Aunt Rachel. Frank felt that some kind of penny was beginning to drop with his aunt, which was more than could be said for him. He wished someone would get to the point, and quickly, so he could understand what was going on.

'Let me get this right. Did you say that Frank is on the list?' she asked.

Frank shook his head. This was like watching some appalling, second-rate comedy production down at the local theatre, although the joke currently seemed to be on him.

'Yes!' said Phoebe in a triumphant tone, throwing her arms up in relief as her mother finally seemed to get it.

The other girls nodded in support. Aunt Rachel stopped wiping the glass and set it on the worktop. More silence.

'Frank, our Frank, is on The List?' repeated Aunt Rachel, her expression turning to one of concern.

'That's right,' said Phoebe.

Frank felt like a strange bystander to this weird conversation about him, as though seeing it in a dream, even though he was sitting just a few feet away from both his cousin and his aunt and was very much wide awake. They seemed to have forgotten he was there.

'What list?' he piped up.

No one spoke. His feeling of unease went up a notch. Aunt Rachel went to say something, but Phoebe got there first.

'I'll tell him, Mum,' she said.

At last, Phoebe turned to Frank.

'There's a list that's always put up on the notice board on the last day of school,' she said. 'The headmaster puts it there. It gives the names of the students who are going on to, er' —she hesitated, choosing her words then, slowly— 'other things.'

'Yeah, I know,' said Frank. 'You've told me before. Like those who are leaving or going on to university. Those sorts of things. So what?' Frank had heard about this every year. Phoebe would come home and gossip endlessly about who was going to do what, as if they didn't all already know, living in a small community as they did.

Phoebe sat down at the table.

'Yeah, but the list is divided into different parts,' she said. She appeared to have calmed down, but still spoke quickly as if something might happen if she didn't get the words out fast enough. Frank waited for her to continue as her mother looked on. 'The first is for those students leaving to go to work, like Gethin, the boy from the butcher's.'

Frank nodded. He knew Gethin Rogers and knew that, whatever he did at school, he was always going to work in his dad's butcher's in the village. Pointless going to school then, Frank thought. Gethin's dad and his dad were good friends and Gethin, with his sausage-like fingers, was always destined for the family business. Nothing new there.

The room was silent as Phoebe continued to speak.

'The second,' she went on, 'is for those clever trevors going on to university. People like that brain-ache, Warwick Williams.'

'Like I just said,' nodded Frank. Warwick was perhaps the cleverest student the village had ever had. Sharp and erudite, everyone knew he would end up going to one of the top universities to continue his studies. Frank couldn't see the point. It seemed like just doing more school. He'd probably end up being a teacher so he could just stay in school for the rest of his life.

'So I'm on one of those lists?' quizzed Frank, scratching his head. 'Like I'm getting a job or going to uni?' But Phoebe hadn't finished.

'And then ... then there's the third list ...' her voice trailed off and she glanced around the room.

Frank looked surprised. He'd never heard of a third list before. Certainly Phoebe had never mentioned it, which was unusual, seeing as Phoebe talked non-stop about everything that went on in the school.

'Third list?' said Frank, waiting patiently to learn what all this had been about.

Phoebe looked towards her mother, as if she was unable to finish what she had started and wanted her to come to the rescue. She didn't, but just stood looking firmly at her daughter, hanging on her every word; she evidently knew what was coming, even if Frank didn't. Finally Phoebe took a deep breath.

'There are never any names on the third list,' she said. '*Never.*'

'Right.' said Frank, still none the wiser. Phoebe continued.

'The third list is for those students destined for' —she hesitated— '*greater things*,' she said, slowly and deliberately. 'Those chosen to go to' —she hesitated again— 'Excelsus Academy. And it's always - *always* - blank. Always.'

She stopped talking, but her words hung in the air. Her eyes fixed on Frank, waiting for a response but he didn't really get what she was saying. He guessed that was why he'd never heard of the third list. No names had ever appeared on it, so Phoebe couldn't spend hours gossiping about it. He shook his head and shrugged his shoulders.

'What?' he said, not really knowing what this was all about.

'Oh, catch up Frank,' she said, making a face. 'You're on the third list.'

The words hit him like his dad's bull charging down the barn door. He was momentarily speechless. Whatever Phoebe had just said, he was sure it had left him in a daze. He tried to gather his wits.

'I'm on what?'

'You're on the third list, dimwit,' she said, shaking her head and tutting in annoyance.

He looked at her two friends who were standing silently. Their eyes widened and their heads nodded in affirmation of what Phoebe had just said.

Frank didn't know much about Excelsus Academy. There was no need - he was never going anywhere near the place, or so he thought. But he did know that a place there was highly prized indeed, that it was a place only select individuals attended, those with special talents. He had none. It was obviously a mistake or, more likely, a childish, Phoebe-style prank of some sort.

'That's what I thought you said.' He didn't know what else to say. He looked at his aunt who seemed to have gone a shade paler than her usual complexion, if that was possible. 'But I don't even go to school, none of the school authorities even know I exist. Dad's always told me that.'

'Not to mention that you're not talented,' said Phoebe. 'Unless you call making wonky lines with the plough a gift of some sort.'

She snorted a laugh. Heather and Jasmine sniggered.

'That's enough, Phoebe,' shot her mother. Frank turned to his aunt.

'But I'm right, though,' he said.

'That's right.' Aunt Rachel wrung the cloth nervously in her hands. 'My goodness, what will Lawrence say?'

'Say about what?' Lawrence came into the kitchen, strode over to the sink and began to wash his hands, his back to the room. He looked around, smiling at the others gathered around the table, his mood chirpy from the morning's activities. He saw that everyone was now looking at him and noted the strange atmosphere and the expressions on their faces. His chirpiness faded and he became more serious.

'Hello, Heather, Jasmine,' he said, nodding in their direction.

'Hi, Mr Penny,' they both said politely. They fidgeted behind Phoebe, playing with the chair back, feeling now that they were unwelcome guests intruding on a family funeral. But even so, this was something they definitely didn't want to miss.

'So, what might I say something about? I think that's what I mean,' he said to the room, as he smiled and grabbed a towel. His eyes came to rest on Frank, who looked back with his mouth downturned and his palms turned upwards.

'Apparently my name's on some list at the school, Dad, whatever that means,' he said. He wasn't sure what to think.

'I've just said what it means,' Phoebe interjected irritably.

'Which list?' said Lawrence quickly, turning to Phoebe, his tone stern. Frank noted the look of concern on his dad's face.

'List Three, Uncle Loz,' she said, her voice waning. 'Frank's name's on List Three.' Lawrence stopped drying his hands and looked at his sister. She looked back and then to her daughter.

'This isn't some kind of joke, Phoebe?' she asked gently.

'Yeah, Phoebs,' said Frank. 'Not like it's the sort of thing you'd do.'

'No, Mum, I swear. I wouldn't make it up. Jas and Heather saw it.' She turned to her two chums. 'Didn't you?' They both nodded mutely in unison. 'The whole school saw it. Everyone knows, Mum.'

Frank's head felt like it was about to explode. Things seemed to be happening so quickly and everyone around him seemed to know more than he did. He was really confused. It appeared that he might not be the subject of some kind of schoolgirl practical joke as he had first suspected and that his name really was now associated with a place he'd only heard of in passing conversation between adults. He looked to his father for some clarification.

'So, Dad, Phoebe appears to be saying that my name is down to go to Excelsus Academy, right? Because it's on List Three.'

His dad looked at him. Frank could tell he was mulling over what to say. He had always been totally honest with his son and

Frank had come to respect this, even if his honesty was sometimes not that welcome.

'That would appear to be the case,' he said, nodding in Frank's direction. Silence in the room.

'So there's been some kind of mistake then, right?' Frank went on. 'Because the school authorities don't know about me.'

'There must be a mistake, Lawrence,' agreed Aunt Rachel, a level of concern in her look and her voice that Frank had rarely detected.

'Yeah, there must be,' piped up Phoebe. 'Cos Frankie doesn't even go to school, so no one would know to put him on the list cos he doesn't really exist. Well, you know what I mean, and he's not good at anything either, apart from laying about all day.'

Heather and Jasmine sniggered again.

'Anyway,' Phoebe continued, 'I know it's a bit unexpected and all—'

'A bit unexpected!' said Frank, acknowledging the understatement.

'Yeah, but if it's legit, you have to admit that it's pretty cool. I mean, Excelsus Academy. Wow! Heather's *really* gonna like you now,' she giggled.

'Shut up, Phoebs,' Heather whispered curtly under her breath, pushing Phoebe on the shoulder. She looked embarrassed. Phoebe laughed, but Frank just ignored them.

'That's enough, Phoebe,' said Aunt Rachel. She sat down next to Frank. His dad pulled out the chair opposite and went to sit down, but stopped himself. He looked thoughtful. Frank continued to look at him as he spoke.

'I think we should go down and check for ourselves,' he said to Frank.

'Can we come?' said Phoebe excitedly.

'I think just Frank and I should go,' said Lawrence, calmly but firmly. Phoebe looked deflated. 'Get your shoes on Frank, we'll go now.'

'But what about your lunch?' said Aunt Rachel. Lawrence just gave her a look. 'Silly question,' she said. 'I'll keep some warm for you. You can have it when you get back.' She shot Frank a smile, which he returned. With all that had just gone on, Frank had lost his appetite anyway. He went to the door and slipped on his shoes. Lawrence followed him.

'We shouldn't be too long,' his dad said and, with that, he placed his hand on Frank's back and ushered him out of the door.

3

THE SCHOOL

Lawrence opened the farm gate and they climbed into the trap. Frank would have preferred to walk. He always walked and Smithwood wasn't far, maybe fifteen minutes, but evidently his dad considered that speed was required. Lawrence checked that Frank was in his seat before he turned to the horse. He tapped at the reins and they set off.

He hadn't spoken since leaving the kitchen, but now he turned to Frank as the horse pulled them along the lane in the direction of the village and the schoolhouse, bumping on the rough surface as they went, hooves rattling.

'Well, this is all a bit strange, don't you think?' he said, his tone soft. He gave nothing away. Frank nodded. His mind was racing faster and faster. He knew that, when they reached the school, it would either confirm what Phoebe had said, or show that she was a mischievous layabout who needed a good punch from him. He still hoped the latter was true, although something told him it wasn't and the feeling made him both excited and scared at the same time.

'I still don't really get it, Dad,' said Frank. 'I've never been to school; no one has ever been on List Three, apparently - well, not in recent years anyway - and now somehow my name's there which means I've been selected for Excelsus Academy.' He paused as though checking he hadn't left anything out and waited for a response from his dad. He got none. 'Do you think it's a trick or a joke of some kind? I mean, from what I've heard, I thought Excelsus was only for some kind of talented person or if you're from a select background or something, and I'm neither of those things.'

Frank looked up, seeking some reassurance from his dad who turned his head to check the road. They passed the churchyard on the right, where his mother's grave lay, making Frank touch his locket for comfort.

'I'm not sure what to make of it at the moment, Frank.' he said. 'Let's see what we find up at the school before we start jumping to the wrong conclusions, yeah? If what Phoebe says turns out to be true, I'll tell you all I can.'

'Yeah, I suppose so,' said Frank. He knew his dad was right. They needed to have all the information rather than start guessing what lay ahead, especially as they only had Phoebe's word for it at the moment, but his dad did annoy him at times. He never seemed to get flustered, which Frank thought was a good thing but which he also found irritating. Frank knew he could get ahead of himself frequently and was sitting there thinking about what might lie ahead and what it might mean for him, feeling his dad should be doing the same.

'But what if Phoebe *is* right?'

'I said—'

'I heard what you said, Dad, but what if I am on the list?' Frank felt he needed to know what would happen if they found out Phoebe was telling the truth. He wanted his dad to tell him what he would need to do.

'Then we'll deal with it.'

Frank slumped back into his seat and folded his arms, frustrated. He would have to wait.

They turned left before the main street. It was early Friday afternoon and the assortment of small shops was bustling with locals topping up their provisions for the weekend. Everyone went about their business as though it were a normal day, which was more than could be said for the way the afternoon had developed at Tresparrik Farm.

Frank could see a lot of the kids from the school hanging around Mr Hartiman's sweet shop, chatting intently to each other, some slurping milkshakes in the afternoon sun. Frank could only think that the topic of conversation was all about him. What else would they be talking about?

St Barnabus School was just along the side street, tucked behind the row of shops on the main drag. His dad slowed as they reached the large, twisted, iron gates by which the students entered every morning and he pulled the horse to a halt by the few traps that were parked outside.

Frank had assumed, as term had now finished, that the place would be deserted, but there were a few teachers milling around the playground just inside the gates, talking quietly to each other. As they got out of their vehicle, Frank could make out their conversations, which were about the forthcoming six weeks' holiday. He noticed that all of them looked tired but relieved, smiles on their faces.

Lawrence tied the reins to the rail and patted the horse on the side of the neck. He turned to Frank.

'Come on then, let's see what all this is about, shall we?' he said. Frank nodded and they set off through the gates.

As the two of them walked across the large playground to the main building, no one took any notice of them. Frank relaxed when he realised they all seemed more interested in where they were all going to spend the break, rather than The List. He thought he might well be the topic of conversation on everyone's lips, that was why he'd been straining his ears trying to make out what was being said. He wasn't. Perhaps it had all been a big mistake after all.

St Barnabus was quite grand for a village school. Built in the same grey stone as the farm, it appeared large in comparison to the size of the village, although Frank remembered that the council had, in previous years, shut down some of the other schools in the locality, meaning that Phoebe's school now attracted pupils from a larger area, and it had recently had its number of classrooms extended to accommodate the influx. Phoebe and her chums had been up in arms that some pupils from their hated local rival schools were now at St Barnabus. She felt it would dilute the intelligence of her classes

- bring down standards - although Frank thought it would just give her more people to poke fun at.

The building was a single storey arranged in a square, with classrooms running all the way around. At the front there was an archway which led through to an inner courtyard. The whiff of lunchtime cabbage mixed with the dryness of chalk dust as the last school day ebbed away. Above the archway, embedded in the masonry, was the school crest – a ram with fierce-looking curly horns – with the words 'Dream. Hope. Aspire' etched around it. The courtyard itself was ornately cloistered around the edge with a green square of lawn in the middle. On either side of the archway, as they went through, were doors leading into the building and there, in front of them, under the cover of the cloisters, was a large rectangular notice board about six feet across.

They stopped and looked at each other, as if on the verge of some great discovery. Indeed, Frank thought they were. They just needed to take a few more steps and they would be able to read what was on it.

At first sight, the board itself looked ordinary enough. It was covered in an assortment of announcements and posters advertising local and school events. Frank noticed one for the end-of-term play in which Phoebe had played the part of the good queen in a story of greed and treachery. Not exactly typecast, he thought. There were also advertisements by holiday companies featuring drawings of relaxed-looking people lazing on some idyllic beach, sipping from a glass while their children ran into the sea. It didn't seem like anywhere Frank knew of. On the beach they went to, which wasn't often, it was nearly always windy and the sea rough.

It didn't take long for his eyes to focus on it. There, pinned squarely in the middle of all the other announcements, as if space had been cleared to make room for it, was a rectangular piece of parchment. It was much smaller than Frank had imagined, and, if it had been pinned in amongst all the other bits of paper, he would hardly have noticed its presence. But there it was. The List.

Frank scanned it quickly with excitement. As Phoebe had described, it was divided into three columns. The headings were printed, as if the document needed to be duplicated to put up in all schools across the country. At the top was the Byeland insignia; a golden eagle with wings spread, head held up, and formidable beak open as if calling out to the reader. In its talons was a scroll, bound by a vivid blue ribbon and, underneath the image, the words 'Freedom and Honour' were emblazoned.

Under the emblem the words 'By Order of the Department for Education' were printed and then followed the date, handwritten.

The headings for each column were also printed. Each heading simply read LIST ONE, LIST TWO and LIST THREE. Nothing more, as if anyone reading it would understand what they meant without further explanation. In each column were the names of students, beautifully handwritten in vivid azure ink. Frank wished his handwriting was as striking, rather than looking like a massive spider had danced across the page.

He noted the names in the first two columns. Gethin Rogers and Warwick Williams appeared as Phoebe had said, along with a few others. Some Frank recognised, others remained a mystery. Perhaps some were going further afield, finding careers in Rhaeder, the large town where Frank knew the academy was situated. It all felt very exciting, this annual posting that opened the door on the next chapter of people's lives.

Finally his eyes came to rest on list three. Under the carefully printed heading was one neatly written name - *Frank Penny*.

Frank's flesh immediately sprung into goose bumps and a strange tingle washed through his whole body. His heart thumped underneath his ribs, but he felt a sudden and unexpected sense of relief. There it was, in black and white (or azure, in this case). Confirmed. Phoebe hadn't been playing a stupid joke. At the discovery of his name on the list he had expected to feel differently, a bit shocked maybe, but he actually felt okay, now that he knew. He looked up at his dad who had been studying the notice board in much the same way.

'Looks like your cousin was right,' he said with his usual sense of calm.

'Yeah, fancy that, Phoebe telling the truth,' said Frank. His dad let out a slight laugh, which made Frank laugh too. He put a paternal hand on Frank's shoulder. But what now?

They stood there for a moment, looking at the piece of parchment. Frank just read his own name over and over, hoping that, if he did so, the writing might disappear. Or perhaps there was another boy in the school with the same name as him who he was blissfully unaware of. That would explain it.

His dad went to speak, but, at that moment, the door to their left opened and a rotund, dark-skinned man appeared. He was wearing a long black robe, edged with gold braid. On the left breast was the school crest, surrounded by delicately embroidered wool sacks sewn in red thread, and around the bottom was the school motto. The man had close-cropped, curly black hair which was thinning on top, but not greying, making him difficult to age. His shoes sparkled.

He took a step back in surprise on seeing the two of them. Then a big beaming smile lit up his face and his eyebrows shot up in joy.

'Oh, good afternoon!' he said. He seemed genuinely delighted to see them standing there. He thrust out a podgy hand, grasped Lawrence's and shook it vigorously, greeting him like a long lost friend. 'Oliver Jelly,' he said. 'I'm the headmaster here.' Frank immediately thought he was the jolliest man he'd ever met. His big brown eyes scanned Lawrence, moved to Frank and then back again.

'Pleased to meet you, Mr Jelly. I'm Lawrence, Lawrence Penny,' smiled Lawrence. Jelly continued to beam back as if absorbing the name. Then he was hit with the realisation of who they were.

'Mr Penny, of course.' He paused, the smile ebbed slightly and he glanced at the notice board. 'I had a feeling you might come down, but certainly not so soon. My word' —he looked up at the clock on the tower in front of him— 'five to two. School only finished less than an hour ago.'

44

'Phoebe,' said Lawrence, nodding.

'I should have guessed she would race home to tell you. I sometimes wish her brain was as fast as her feet,' he smiled. Lawrence smiled back. Frank stifled a laugh. Lawrence spoke.

'This is—'

'Frank.' Jelly finished the sentence for him, as if it wasn't obvious. He looked at Frank, his eyes scanning his face, which made Frank feel a bit uneasy, but he sensed the man was just a bit intrigued and didn't mean to be rude.

Frank held out his hand.

'Hello,' he said. Jelly shook it, although not quite as vigorously as he had his dad's, for which Frank was grateful, as he feared the big man might pull his arm out of its socket. It appeared to Frank that Mr Jelly exuded a happiness that was quite infectious and made those around him smile for no apparent reason.

Naturally, Frank had heard Phoebe and her friends talking about him and several of the other teachers. Nothing polite or kind, of course. They often referred to him as Smelly Jelly or Big Belly Jelly. Very original. If only the man knew, although he probably did. Frank didn't have to guess that cheeky students went with the territory if you were the headmaster of the school.

'So, you're our mystery man, eh?' said Jelly, looking down at Frank. 'Pleased to meet you.' He looked back at the small square of parchment pinned to the notice board and waved his finger in the air.

'Strange thing,' he said. 'The list was already up when I came down this morning, which is unusual. Never happened before. It's normally delivered by post for me to check and then I put it up. So that was a bit odd and, when I saw the list, you can imagine my surprise to actually find a name on List Three. Your name.' He pointed to Frank's name. 'I went through the names of all my students in my head and realised I didn't recognise it, but then, of course, I wouldn't, would I? I didn't even know that Frank Penny existed.'

Frank groaned inwardly. He was sure that was at least the third time someone had referred to his own non-existence that afternoon.

'I just kept scratching my head, wondering who you might be. None of the staff here seemed to know either. I've never known so much gossip and speculation in the staff room as there was this morning. It was only when I heard your Phoebe screaming the place down that I was finally able to find out.'

'How do you mean?' said Lawrence.

'Well, I was sitting in my office over there.' He indicated towards a small oak door to the right, opposite the one he had just emerged from. There was a small sign screwed to the door which bore the word 'HEADMASTER'. 'The notice board is right outside, you see ...'

His voice trailed off as a very short, red haired woman emerged from the same door he had just come through. Over her shoulder was a bag which looked like it was full of an assortment of education-related things, and she struggled to carry a pile of books awkwardly in both hands. A couple of pencils fell from the bag and, for a moment, Frank was convinced she was going to drop the lot so he moved back slightly in anticipation of the pile coming down in his direction. Jelly turned around.

'Oh, hi, Alice,' he said. 'Do you want a hand?'

She stopped, but still looked as if she was going to topple over with the weight of the books she held. Frank bent down, picked up the pencils and went to hand them to her. She gave him a look as if to say, 'How am I supposed to hold those?', so he thrust them into her bag. She smiled curtly. Frank assumed she was one of the teachers. She certainly had the look of a strict schoolmistress about her - and then there were the books. A bit of a giveaway. Given her stature and hair colour, he could only imagine what abundance of rude names she was given by Phoebe and all her friends behind her back. Then he remembered; she must be Mrs Livett, the Ginger Midget.

'No thanks, Oliver, I think I can manage,' she replied, unconvincingly.

'You off now?' continued the headmaster.

Alice nodded. 'Yep, be glad to see the back of this place for a few weeks. No more kids. No offence,' she said, twitching her head towards the school. 'Six weeks of freedom.'

It was obvious to Frank that she was itching to get away and was trying, badly, to hide the inconvenience of bumping into the headmaster. He wondered why you would want to work in place that you couldn't get away from quickly enough when the opportunity arose. It struck Frank as quite strange that someone would do a job that they didn't want to stay and do every day.

'Going anywhere nice?' asked Jelly.

'I'm going to spend a couple of weeks down at the sea,' she said.

'Sounds great. Have a nice break and see you in September,' said Jelly, conscious of her impatience and not wanting to keep her.

Alice adjusted the books in her arms once more, nodded towards the two men and Frank, and headed down the path to where the traps were parked. Then, through the door and in her wake, came a young woman, with a young man in a blue tunic. They both carried large bags filled with books and were talking quietly between themselves, organising their summer break as they walked. They briefly acknowledged Jelly with a 'See you soon', which he returned with a nod, and headed off to join the group of teachers that Frank and his dad had passed minutes earlier. The Great Escape, thought Frank.

The school suddenly seemed very quiet, as though the building itself was finally breathing a huge sigh of relief that everyone, children and adults, had left and it too could have a rest.

There was a silence. Jelly, whose gaze had been following the departing staff, looked thoughtful for a moment; perhaps he always looked like this at the end of the school year. Frank wondered if the headmaster, like his teachers, was also going away, or whether he would stay at the school for the entire summer, somehow bound to the place. Phoebe had said that he lived in the headmaster's quarters on the school grounds, so Frank assumed he didn't ever get away during the whole of term time.

Then Jelly seemed to remember he had been in mid conversation. 'I'm sorry,' he said, turning back to Lawrence. 'Where was I?'

'You were telling us how you heard Phoebs, er, Phoebe, from inside your office, there.' Lawrence indicated to the oak door, as Jelly had done a few minutes earlier.

'Oh, yes, so I was. Yes, I was sitting at my desk, going over a few end-of-term things, and all of a sudden I heard a girl shriek right outside my door. My, your Phoebe can make a noise when the moment takes her. Gave me a right shock, I can tell you. Even more shocking as my door is quite thick. Never normally hear a thing, so she must have made a hell of a noise. Of course, I didn't know what was going on so I rushed out. For all I knew one of my students was being attacked, but, when I opened the door, it was just Phoebe and that friend of hers.'

'Jasmine,' said Frank.

'Yes, that's right, Jasmine. And all Phoebe could say was "Oh my god, I don't believe it!" over and over again. Once I had managed to calm her down, she explained that the name of the person on the third list was her cousin. You.' He looked at Frank. 'She explained that you didn't even go to school. Imagine that. Here's me, I've been head of St Barnabus for ten years and always wondered, hoped really, that one of my students would get the nod from Excelsus. But no, not a sniff, and there have been some really talented individuals, let me tell you. And then, without any warning, there appears on the list the name of someone that doesn't even come here. Well I never.' He threw his hands into the air and stopped talking, as if allowing Frank and his dad to take in what he had just said.

'Phoebe said the list was always blank,' said Frank.

'That's right - *always*. I thought Warwick might be asked at some point, but it appears they overlooked even him. Bright lad, very bright indeed, sharp as a pin.' He looked and sounded proud. 'But obviously not Excelsus material, by the looks of it.' The look faded to one of dejection.

'Asked *at some point*?' said Frank. 'What do you mean?' He had thought that people would just go once they had finished school, a bit like going to university. It had been nagging him a bit that he was only thirteen and had years before he thought anyone his age would go.

'Yes,' said Jelly. 'You see, Excelsus accept students of all ages, although most are of secondary school age of course, maybe a bit older than yourself. It's thought that when a student is ready they get asked, and it's the academy that decides when that is. So the intake for September, when I guess you'll be going, will be of all ages.'

Frank listened and his dad nodded as Jelly spoke. Frank knew next to nothing about the academy or what went on inside its walls and was a little reluctant to learn too much from a man he'd only just met. He had the feeling that his dad would be able to tell him more, later.

'Anyway. Now, where was I?' said Jelly vacantly. 'Oh yes, well, it's a good job I found out who our unidentified boy was, otherwise—'

'Otherwise what?' interrupted Frank.

'Otherwise, I wouldn't have known who to give the letter to, would I?' Jelly said, beaming. He seemed to be enjoying the situation, as though it was some light relief at the end of term. Like he relished being involved in a drama to be played out at his village school where, Frank guessed, nothing different ever really happened. But the disclosure of a letter pricked his interest immediately. The clock struck two.

'Letter?' he asked, 'What letter?'

'There's a letter here from the academy,' said Jelly, looking directly at Frank. 'For you.'

4

THE LETTER

Frank was instantly excited. A letter. For him. All of a sudden he had a hundred questions. His dad seemed intrigued by this too.

'I guess we'd better see it then,' he said. They both waited for Jelly to respond. He seemed to dither, as though he'd been awaiting this moment all day. His hesitation surprised both Frank and his dad; it was as though time stopped for a moment while he considered an answer. He looked at them with a half-smile.

'Of course, of course,' he said.

Lawrence nodded him a 'come on then' look and Jelly took the cue. The large man pushed past them with a muffled 'excuse me' and took the few steps towards his study door. He cleared his throat.

It's in here, on my desk,' he continued.

Frank and his dad stood still. Still Jelly hesitated. He reached deep into his pocket and took out a big bunch of iron keys which clanged as he thumbed through them looking for the right one. There were at least twenty keys on the ring, all about the same size and shape, and Frank thought it must be a struggle to carry them around all day.

'Now, let me see ...' he mumbled to himself as he searched. 'Here we are.' He produced a large key from among the other large keys, placed it carefully in the lock and attempted to turn it. He couldn't. He tried it a couple more times and then pulled it out, grunting.

'Always getting this wrong,' he smiled, shaking his head. 'Been here ten years and still can't figure out which key opens my study.' He went through the keys again, this time more slowly.

Frank had to admit that they all looked the same and he

imagined Jelly standing at door after locked door throughout the school day, huffing his way through his collection of keys every time he had to use one of them, picking the wrong one time and time again. Frank felt like suggesting he label them, but, as Jelly now seemed a bit tetchy, thought better of it.

'This one,' he muttered, more in hope than certainty, selecting another key which looked identical to the first one. He slid the key into the hole and turned it. There was a heavy click. Success. Jelly seemed relieved as he turned the door handle and pushed. The old door creaked as it opened, revealing the headmaster's study beyond. Jelly strode in, robes flapping behind him, then, sensing the others hadn't moved, turned and beckoned them over. 'Come on then,' he smiled. 'What are you waiting for?'

Frank followed his dad into the room. What little light there was inside made it difficult to see at first, especially as it was quite bright outside. His sense of smell adjusted before his eyes caught up. The room smelled fusty, like the village's old library, with its leather chairs and large tables, where Frank had spent a lot of time when he wasn't on the farm - hours in fact. He just enjoyed looking at the books there, at all the stuff that interested him. It was the sort of smell he guessed you'd get used to if you were immersed in it all the time, as Jelly obviously was.

He soon became accustomed to the lack of light. The room was much smaller than he had expected. He had imagined a headmaster's study, where the serious work of planning and organising the education of his pupils took place, to be impressive, but this was just a small square chamber.

From what Frank could make out, the walls were oak panelled and dark, in an antiquarian way - well, what he could see of the walls anyway. Books and parchment were stacked in awkward piles all around. Tomes of all sizes, bound in an array of colours, stretched from floor to ceiling, some looking like they were about to topple over, making the room seem oppressive. On the walls was an assortment of portraits of men and women who, Frank assumed, were former heads of the school, although he couldn't make out the writing on the plaques at the foot of each picture because of the gloom and dust. The frames hung crookedly on wooden panels and looked as if they had done so for years. Frank had the urge to straighten one as he walked cautiously past it, but he resisted the temptation. People, once cherished, neglected and left to gather grime.

The floor was covered by a dusty old rug, worn in the middle from a multitude of student feet over the years, and frayed at the edges with age. It seemed to have borne a picture of a knight slaying a boar, but Frank could barely make it out, threadbare as it was.

At the far end was the room's only window; a small round beam of dust-filled sunlight radiated through the latticed pane and fell directly on the headmaster's desk, the surface of which was inset with green leather and illuminated by the shaft of light as it cut through the darkness.

The desk seemed large in comparison to the room. It was completely empty, except for a small envelope sitting in the middle. Frank thought this emptiness was very odd, given the state of the room in general, with all its clutter. It seemed like a calm oasis in the middle of a very turbulent sea. Perhaps that's how the headmaster had found it. Or perhaps he cultivated his small space to free him from the domination of his surroundings, once he'd shut himself behind his thick oak door to escape.

Jelly skilfully negotiated a few smaller piles of books and found his way to the other side of the desk. Frank and his dad edged slowly into the room and stood on the opposite side, careful not to bump into anything, as, if one pile went, Frank feared they may all collapse like a row of dusty dominoes.

They stood there in silence, Frank and his dad on one side of the desk, Jelly on the other. The three of them looked blankly at the envelope. Lawrence went to take it - it was Frank's after all. But Jelly suddenly made a grab for it.

'Thanks Mr Jelly,' said Lawrence in his usual calm manner. 'That's for Frank, right?'

The headmaster hesitated, as though he was being asked to give up something valuable of his own. He smiled and held out the envelope, but his grip noticeably tightened as Lawrence grasped the edge. Lawrence looked at Jelly, who let go, exhaling as he did.

Frank looked at the headmaster. He could imagine that years as a parochial teacher and then head of a village school had never brought him much in the way of excitement and he seemed unwilling to give up this moment, a moment that fate had handed him, which he may never see again. Frank sensed that his dad understood, and, although he could have been annoyed, he didn't show it.

Lawrence looked at the envelope curiously. He turned it over a few times in his rough hands, handling it gently, the way he did the newborn lambs each spring. The small cylinder of light from the window bounced off it, giving it a mysterious glow. He stopped and looked up at the headmaster, disappointment etched on his face.

'I see the envelope interested you more than I had imagined,' he said. Frank glanced at the envelope to see that it was flap side up and someone had obviously been trying to open it. Lawrence glanced sideways to where a kettle sat on one of the book piles, a small plume of steam snaking its way upward. Jelly gave him a guilty smile. This, at least, explained his hesitation outside the office.

'Are you kidding me?' said Lawrence, trying to hide the irritation in his voice. 'It's not yours to open, Mr Jelly. I would have thought better of you.'

Jelly gritted his teeth in embarrassment and looked down at the desk.

'I'm sorry, Mr Penny,' he said, looking back up. 'I have no excuse, I was just curious. A letter like that, from Excelsus Academy. Well, you don't get to see something like that every day now, do you? I just thought I would ... I mean I thought ...' his voice trailed off. He held out his hands in a gesture of defeat, somehow hoping his infectious joviality would help him get away with it. It didn't.

Frank looked on as his dad continued to scowl at the man, who shifted with discomfort, looking like one of his pupils that had just had a good telling off.

'When did this arrive?' asked Lawrence, turning the envelope once more.

'Same time as the list I should imagine, although this' —he motioned towards the letter— 'was pushed under my door. I never saw who was here, and so early.' Then Jelly said, 'Well, now you're here, why don't you open it?'

'What?' said Lawrence. 'So that you can see what it says too, I guess.' The headmaster beamed back at him transparently. Lawrence looked again at the small packet in his hands and held it out for Frank to take.

'It's addressed to you, son,' he said. 'Guess you're the one who should open it.'

Frank took it and, like his dad had done, turned it over a few times in his hands as if weighing it mentally. He handled it like a delicate flower that would break if he was too heavy-handed. A treasured possession.

Like his name on the list, the address was beautifully handwritten in the same azure ink. It said, simply:

Master Frank Penny
c/o St Barnabus School
Smithwood
Byeland

It had to have been written by the same person who had written his name on the list, unless everyone at the Department for Education had a Master's degree in calligraphy. No - it was definitely in the same hand. The envelope was stuck down with thick red wax. How Mr Jelly could have hoped to open it and reseal it without them realising it had been tampered with was beyond him. The wax had been stamped with a seal, which Frank could only guess to be that of the Department for Education. He looked at his dad, who nodded for him to proceed, so he took a deep breath, slipped his finger under the flap and pulled.

The seal broke with a satisfying click and the flap of envelope sprang open. Inside was a single piece of paper, carefully folded. Frank pulled it out and opened it up as the two men looked on, making him feel quite important. He wasn't used to receiving letters. He'd got a few in the past, mainly from Grandad Penny, who wrote to him a couple of times a year, and he got an unexplainable sense of joy at opening them when they came, but this was quite different. Nothing his grandad ever wrote would shape his future.

Frank scanned the piece of paper. Oddly, it had a different feel about it than the envelope, as if the two were somehow separate. It was written on vellum and possessed a quality to the touch. He soon realised that the letter had come directly from the academy itself, while the envelope was from the Department for Education. At the top was an impressive looking crest, which Frank took to be the insignia of Excelsus - a vulture, sitting, wings open. Underneath was the motto: *Fortitudine Peritia Virtis* – Strength Skill Virtue.

Frank felt like a child in a sweet shop.

'Well, my boy, what does it say?' said Jelly impatiently, wringing his hands in expectation. Frank gave him a glare. He certainly wasn't going to take any direction from the headmaster, a man he had only just met, yet who was now giving out orders to him as though he were one of his pupils, which he most certainly was not. Having warmed to the cheery man initially, Frank was now feeling irritated with his attitude and the look on his face obviously wasn't hiding his emotions. Jelly forced a smile. His dad read the situation.

'It's okay, Frank,' he said, as he shot a scornful look in Jelly's direction. 'You can read it out if you want to, but don't feel you have to.'

'It's okay, Dad. Felt like I was in school all of a sudden,' he remarked, looking directly at Jelly, whose beam faded on hearing Frank's comment. Point made.

His attention turned back to the letter. He focused on the page and studied it, scanning the words as if rehearsing before reading it aloud. It was written in a steady hand in dark black ink. The lettering was straight and unerring; he could sense the quality of it, a reflection of the establishment itself. He felt the eyes of the people in the portraits, hanging askew on the walls, on him, craning their necks for a better look and waiting with baited breath for him to recite out loud. Frank nodded, took a deep breath and started to read:

Dear Master Penny

It gives me the greatest pleasure to inform you that you have been selected by the New Entrants Committee to attend Excelsus Academy for the Gallant and Gifted.

As such, your current education will cease.

I can confirm that your learning here at the academy will start on Monday 7th *September and that you will be part of intake 821.*

Further instructions will follow, but you are required to confirm your acceptance, direct to the academy, by return.

Students should consider it an honour to attend our seat of learning, which has served the country for centuries and which prides itself on the highest of standards.

May I take this opportunity to welcome you to the academy and look forward to hearing from you in due course.

Yours sincerely
Aurora G Moonhunter
Principal
Excelsus Academy

Frank continued to look at the letter - he thought he had read the whole text in one breath and felt a little worn out. He had to admit to himself that, for all its importance, it was rather short. For all the fuss it had created, both at home and here, in the headmaster's study, he felt a little short-changed, as if the letter lacked any sort of relevant information as to what this was all about. He had expected, perhaps, for it to enlighten him as to why he had been selected. It didn't. Or maybe how they knew about him, a boy who had always been home educated and had never set foot inside a school. It didn't. Or to give him some information about the academy itself or what he was required to do there. It didn't. Admittedly it said that further information would follow, but the disappointment after the surge in anticipation was clear. Now that he was finding himself getting rather impatient for answers, all the letter did was simply throw up more questions.

However, two bits of the letter stuck in his mind.

The first was the term 'the Gallant and Gifted'. He was genuinely mystified by the use of these words, especially in relation to himself. He was a thirteen year old boy who had grown up and, until now, worked on his dad's farm. 'Gallant' and 'Gifted' were not words you could realistically associate with him or his surroundings. Not unless you would describe chopping wood or ploughing a field as particularly gifted, or disturbing a wasp nest in the woods and legging it for dear life as exceptionally gallant.

'Gallant and Gifted' sounded like someone exciting, someone other than him. This was all beginning to feel like a big mistake.

The other was the name - Aurora G Moonhunter, the principal of the academy. To Frank, it conjured up an image in his mind of a seriously powerful, yet mystical, person - in charge and not to be messed with. If he had to make up a name for someone in authority at somewhere like Excelsus Academy, then that was the exactly the sort of name he would have thought of. He wasn't sure whether it was a man or a woman. He assumed a woman. A tall stern lady in glittering silver robes, presiding haughtily over those learning under her watchful gaze.

He snapped out of it. He'd couldn't believe that he'd started the day helping mend the barn roof on the farm yet now, not a few hours later, he was standing in the middle of a dingy old office of a person he'd never met, at a school he'd never set foot in, thinking about an individual whose name he'd just read seconds ago on a letter he never expected to get, from a place he never thought he'd go to. It was all very bizarre indeed. Frank just wanted to get away from the school, go home and run to his tree house, where nothing and no one could disturb him, where he wouldn't have to think about anything that was going on, where he was in control.

'Is that it?' said Jelly, huffing his disappointment.

'That's it,' said Frank and handed the letter to his dad, who had been standing there allowing Frank to digest its contents. Lawrence's eyes darted over the page, as if just to confirm that Frank had indeed read everything. He said nothing. He looked at Frank and gave him a slight nod, then held out his other hand, indicating to Frank to hand him the envelope. Frank obliged. His dad folded the letter neatly and carefully slotted it back into the envelope. He placed the flap under the opening so that it stayed shut and handed it back to Frank.

'Put it in your pocket for now, Frank,' he said. 'We can discuss it on the way home, okay?' He looked reassuringly at his son, who instantly felt a bit better, especially as it confirmed that they could leave.

'Oh, no need to go just yet, we need to celebrate our new entrant to such an esteemed place,' said Jelly, seeming very eager for them to stay. Both Frank and his dad could guess that he only wanted to keep them there so he could play host to their private thoughts and plans. Eavesdrop to feed his appetite for more of the unusual situation that he considered himself part of. 'Well,' he continued, 'I admit you're not exactly *ours* in the truest sense of the word, what with you not being a pupil at the school, but you know what I mean. Please, have a cup of tea,' he pleaded, a wide smile lighting up his face, teeth twinkling.

'Hmm,' said Lawrence. 'Kettle's just boiled, has it?' He looked over to where Jelly's kettle still steamed lazily. Frank tried to hide a smirk.

'Thanks, Mr Jelly,' he continued, sincere in his gratitude, 'but I think we'll be off. You'll let us know if any other letters come, won't you.' It was a statement rather than a question. Jelly nodded.

'Of course, Lawrence,' he replied.

'Although I doubt if any will,' Lawrence went on. Without looking at Frank, he turned and went to make his way back to the door. In his haste, he seemed to have forgotten the closeness of their surroundings and his sleeve brushed awkwardly against a pile of encyclopaedias, heavily bound in green leather. The pile of tomes rocked one way, then the other and, just as they seemed to have steadied themselves, came crashing down in an almighty cloud of dust, making Lawrence sneeze repeatedly.

There was a moment's hush as the three of them held their breath. Frank looked on; he expected the next pile to be knocked down, setting off a massive chain of book toppling, but, to his astonishment, the large sets of hardback dominoes which lined the room stayed put. The others looked equally amazed.

Once the dust had settled, Frank quickly stepped over the mess and followed his dad towards the door, not wanting to spend another second in Jelly's stuffy room.

'Er, never mind,' said Jelly, exhaling. 'I'll tidy them up later.'

Lawrence opened the door and he and Frank left, leaving Oliver Jelly contemplating the events of the last few minutes.

5

THE JOURNEY HOME

Retracing their way back through the archway and across the playground, Frank noticed the faded chalk hopscotch markings on the hard ground. The small stones used to play the game were scattered all around and seemed so ordinary, unlike the way his day was working out.

The crowd of teachers that had greeted them on their arrival had dispersed. Frank knew they would now be heading home; most of them were from the neighbouring villages and would be preparing for their long-awaited holidays out of reach and as far away as possible from their disrespectful pupils. While he was going to be spending his next few weeks contemplating what to do, and what an invitation to Excelsus meant, they would be relaxing on the beach, visiting the city or having a worry-free time in many different ways. Not him.

It seemed hotter than it had earlier. Frank felt his brow beginning to break sweat and couldn't decide if it was just the weather or the thoughts that were now brewing in his head about the possibility of leaving home to go to a place he never dreamed he would ever be associated with.

They climbed back onto the trap.

'So what are you thinking, Frank?' his dad said as they started away from the school. He hadn't said much since they had entered the school gates, not even in Jelly's office.

Frank shrugged. After all that had just happened he was still very much at a loss, and he could only hope a chat with his dad would help ease his concerns. The trap rounded the right hand bend at the junction with the main street and headed on up the lane towards the farm. He kept thinking about the letter. It was only in his pocket, but he kept recreating it in his head. The lettering, the insignia, the name.

'I'm not sure, Dad,' he said. 'It still doesn't seem real. I still don't understand why I've got a letter and why I should have been invited to Excelsus.' Frank had the habit of picking through problems to try and make sense of things. He had that sort of mind - logical and inquiring. But this was different.

'Nor me,' replied his dad, twitching the reins in his hands and looking ahead.

'So I've been thinking, why don't we just write back and say we think they've made a mistake.' It seemed obvious to Frank that they had. He had no gifts, after all.

'Do you really think they've made a mistake?'

'No, I don't,' said Frank, remembering how the letter was addressed specifically to him.

'I don't think so either, not a place like that.'

'Yeah. No way. I can't believe a place like that would make such a big error, especially when it comes to inviting the right people. Or the wrong people in this case.' He smiled at his own joke. 'I mean, I wonder how many people actually go?'

'Not many,' said his dad. 'At least, I don't think so anyway.' Frank thought he answered too quickly, but let the notion go.

'So, if not many go, then they would have to have made a major blunder to get me mixed up with someone else. So, if we assume this is for real' —the words sunk in as he spoke them— 'then they really will be expecting me on September the seventh.' The date, which had stuck in his mind since he had read the letter out loud just twenty minutes ago in Oliver Jelly's office, didn't feel that far away all of a sudden. Even now he could sense it creeping up on him as if he were a bird being stalked by a very hungry cat.

The horse trapped on up the lane, which was wide and flanked by hedgerows that glittered vividly with an abundance of summer wildflowers.

'It's a pity Mr Jelly couldn't shed any light on things.' It appeared to Frank that someone, probably from the Department for Education, had turned up early, posted the list, pushed the letter under his door and left before anyone had ever known he was there. That, in itself, seemed odd. If they knew he existed, then they probably knew where he lived. It just added to the mystery.

'Do you think Mr Jelly has something to do with this, that he knows more than he's letting on?' asked Frank. Although he had initially warmed to the man, he had grown a little unsure of him as the meeting had gone on and had left his office with a different impression of the jolly headmaster.

'I don't think so,' replied his dad. 'He said himself that he didn't even know you existed and, if he keeps himself cooped up in that study of his, he'll be blissfully unaware of your cousin gossiping like she does. And even if he has heard her talk about you at school I wouldn't think he'd have paid much attention to the idle chit-chat of a thirteen-year-old schoolgirl. Goodness, can you imagine if he did that? His mind would explode with all the rubbish they talk about.' Frank laughed.

His dad became more serious. 'Do you want to go?'

The question was as direct as it was obvious and it caught Frank slightly by surprise. With all that was going on, he hadn't even considered whether he felt he wanted to actually go to Excelsus Academy or not; whether he should accept their misplaced invitation. It was dawning on him that the dream he thought he was in, back at the farm and then up at the school, had quickly become a reality. Now his dad had asked the question he felt his heart begin to skip as he thought of the possibilities that might be opening up to him. He chewed his lip as he considered his response for a moment.

'Do I have a choice?'

'Of course, you always have a choice. You know that.'

Frank thought again.

'I don't know, Dad. I don't really want to go. Not really. I mean, I love our life on the farm, you know I do. I learn so much, stuff you can't get from books, or any school. Look at me and Jip yesterday, for example. I don't want to stop doing that and I really don't see why I should.'

He surprised himself. He knew that he was being offered the chance of a lifetime, a chance to attend this great academy, a chance that others would give their lifetime's pocket money for. But he was feeling this was an opportunity he was not cut out for; he was neither gallant nor gifted, nor had he ever craved anything better than he already had.

'Sorry, Dad.'

'Oh, don't be sorry, Frank. It's fine. I've always said to you that I'd never expect you to do anything you don't feel comfortable with, or don't feel ready for. If this is one of those occasions then you don't have to go, of course you don't, and I'll support any decision you make. But perhaps we should see how you feel in the morning. Sleep on it maybe, what do you think?' Frank agreed that he needed more time to let the whole thing sink in a bit. It was a huge decision and, if he was even going to begin to contemplate leaving behind everything he'd ever known, he needed to find out more about the place.

'Okay, but if I don't want to go, you really won't mind?'

Frank knew his dad wouldn't. His approach to Frank was that, if he wanted to do something, he could do it all day, every day. But he knew there was little point making him do anything that he felt was pointless or beyond him. Frank would give up or lose concentration quickly if something didn't interest him. He always felt that school was probably like that. Phoebe was always bringing back homework on subjects that she couldn't care less about and, consequently, they went in one ear and out the other while her mind engaged with her latest magazine.

'No, I mean it. You don't have to go if you don't want to,' he repeated.

Frank felt reassured that, although he was feeling troubled, he would have the support of his dad. He put his fingers to the locket and rubbed the ornate fretwork that encased the portrait of his mother, wondering what she would make of all this, what guidance she might give him. He often imagined her, walking with her arm around his shoulders while she handed out her own brand of wisdom, or just sitting on his bed stroking his hair at night time. Although she wasn't there, it didn't make her any less real.

Frank had been dying to ask his dad more about the academy. Since reading the letter, it was a great imaginary building, set in the vast openness of his mind. Until that morning he'd never needed to give it a second thought, but now he couldn't think of anything else.

As with the establishment's principal, Aurora G Moonhunter, he had quickly created a picture of what the academy might look like, what went on there, and what the people who walked its ancient corridors might be like. It was an impossible task and, although he had meant it when he'd said to his dad that he'd rather not go, he couldn't help but feel a hard jolt of intrigue pulling him towards the vision in his head; an itch that might eventually need scratching. Frank was distinctly aware that, once something had pricked his interest, he could often find it difficult to resist the temptation to investigate further. He hoped that anything his dad could tell him would put an end to this fascination, but wasn't sure it would.

'So, what do you know about Excelsus?' he asked, trying to dampen the enthusiasm in his question.

His dad looked sideways at him, like he knew the question was coming. The horse was nearing the farm, so Lawrence slowed the trap to delay their return, as if he wanted the chance to answer Frank's question without either his aunt or Phoebe springing on them, eager to devour the news of their visit to the school. Frank could picture them waiting in the kitchen; Phoebe and her pals nattering like jackdaws, occasionally glancing out through the window that looked onto the entrance to the farm and squawking with anticipation. His dad then stopped the vehicle altogether, commanding the horse with a gentle 'whoa.' He turned to Frank.

'So, what do you know, Dad?' he asked again.

'Not much,' he said.

Frank studied his face. It bore the marks of hard graft out in all weathers on the farm. Lines radiated from the corners of his eyes and his forehead wore crinkles that shone with the sweat of the afternoon sun. His dark eyes were kind and comforting.

'What does that mean?'

'It means exactly that. Not much, but I guess you want to know what I do know?'

'Yeah,' he said excitedly.

'Well now, where shall I start? Well, as our new acquaintance, Mr Jelly, told us, each intake is made up of kids of different ages. What he didn't mention is that some are selected, like you seem to have been, but others actually pay to attend.'

'Wow, I bet that must cost a fortune. Why would they want to do that?'

'Because some folks find that paying for something, anything, is their way of owning or accessing what most of us can only dream of, even if they don't merit it, and education would be on that list. But the main thing is what the academy produces.'

'Produces?'

'Yes. That is, the reason why kids go there and what they become while they are there.'

'Phoebe said that List Three was for students who were destined for greater things,' remembered Frank. He hadn't really taken it in at the time she said it, but he now recalled what a peculiar thing it was to say. 'So what does that mean? What greater things can there be?' He was happy that being a farmer was the greatest thing in the world.

'It may sound strange, but the academy nurtures the special talents that its students have, or have the potential to possess.'

Frank looked a bit bewildered. Special talents? What was that all about? His dad noticed the expression on his face.

'Let me put it this way,' he said. 'Every country, including

Byeland, needs the right leaders to govern it. To guide its citizens, take great responsibilities like defending its borders from malicious outsiders, to predict the future or to be accountable to its people. Really important stuff like that. Naturally, each country seeks the best of the best and needs to nurture its talent to keep itself safe. If you think about it, it's obvious that you want the most able people to lead and you don't want any of your enemies to have an army of individuals so above average that it presents a clear danger to you. So what Excelsus does is take those who have special abilities and talents and cultivates them so they can fulfil these crucial roles and take a particular role in life; some obvious, like being on the council, some ... less so. Like a sort of destiny, but on a much higher level than the likes of you and me. Well, normally anyway.' He seemed to realise his choice of words wasn't very apt, given Frank's current circumstances.

Frank was intrigued. His dad's revelation that many who went to Excelsus then went on to fulfil certain important roles across the land fascinated him, not that he understood how this applied to him.

'But you said that some people pay to go. How can they claim to have any particular gifts or talents? I get it that some get chosen, but ... '

'Well, that's a good question. Some might call it breeding. There are families that have attended the academy for generations and so, if you come from a family where your father went, and your grandfather and so on, if you're from that type of family or background, some folk might consider it your destiny to follow in your ancestor's footsteps. Like a birthright. But that doesn't mean anything really. It doesn't mean you're able to fulfil what one might expect from an Excelsus graduate and that's where the system falls down. You can get the wrong people at the highest level making decisions that might affect us all. Imagine a less competent person or someone with the wrong morals governing a land. Quite worrying when you think about it. *If* you decide to go, you'll be there on merit. Very different that, very different indeed.'

'But remember, Dad, neither of us actually knows why I've been chosen, do we?'

'No. No we don't. But there will be a reason. There always is.'

There was a moment's pause, allowing Frank to absorb this new information. There was a slight breeze. The mane of the horse flapped quietly.

'How do you know all of this, Dad?' Frank asked, puzzled. He had imagined that, working on the farm for all his life, his dad would have been relatively sheltered from any detailed information on anywhere outside the immediate vicinity and he had rarely seen him with a newspaper. He was more likely to know about assorted low level celebrities from Phoebe's tea time chatter than the goings on at an academy in a town miles away.

'Well, your Aunt Rachel has a good friend, Polly, who owns a shop in Rhaeder, that's where the academy is, and your gran doesn't live that far away. Most people would be able to tell you what I've just told you.'

Frank recalled Aunt Rachel talking about her friend Polly, although he hadn't paid that much attention to the detail, other than that she ran a small tea shop and that aunt Rachel used to stay with her from time to time before she came to live on the farm. They were still good friends. He wished that he'd listened a bit more but, then, how was he to know that he would one day be part of the renowned Excelsus Academy intake?

As for his grandmother, he hadn't seen her in years and she was really a stranger to him. Dad had once told him that, since her daughter had died, she had become quite reclusive and Frank could only remember visiting her once when he was about five years old. She lived in a little house by a big lake. He remembered the house being small even though he was only very small himself. He had no idea that she lived close to Rhaeder and, therefore, close to Excelsus Academy. His dad didn't talk about her much, not, Frank thought, out of unkindness, but more because she just wasn't part of their lives.

His dad had thrown up more questions than answers and, while Frank was glad to understand a bit more about his invitation, he began to think it was a fascinating box, full of mysteries and intrigue. His main problem was that he had begun to open it.

His dad fell silent again. Frank felt that he'd had enough for now. Maybe he'd ask more later. He also thought he might venture down to the library and search for information on his own, as he liked to do when he discovered something that interested him. The library was where he'd taught himself to read, where he'd spend hours engrossed in books that sparked his interest. There was bound to be a whole section there about Excelsus in which he could immerse himself and spend the next few days learning more about it.

'Ready to go?' asked his dad, aware that Frank had stopped asking questions.

'Yeah. Although I'm not sure I can handle the third degree from Phoebs and her pals.'

'I can drop you off at the lower field if you want, you can get over to your tree house from there. Keep out of their way for a bit.'

Frank thought. 'No, don't worry. I'm starving.' He had just begun to realise that he hadn't eaten since breakfast and, although his adrenaline rush had yet to subside, he started to think of the smell of his aunt's cooking in the kitchen and heard the telltale sign of hunger as his stomach squeaked.

Lawrence loosened the reins and flicked them. The horse came back to life and walked slowly toward the farm gate.

6

THE VISIT

'I've got them, I've got them!' shouted Phoebe, rushing into the house. She had the broadest grin on her face.

'Got what?' asked Frank, who was sitting at the kitchen table thumbing through a book on pig breeds.

'Tickets of course. Numpty!' she said, pushing her tongue in to her lower lip and making a face in his direction, waving three pieces of paper in the air as she did so.

'Phoebs, there's nothing you could possibly have that I would be the slightest bit interested in,' said Frank, not looking up. She leaned over and waved the bits of paper under his nose.

'Tickets to see the Jesters,' she said, 'Whoopeeeee!'

'Oh, right!' said Frank, feigning interest badly. 'Like I said, there's nothing you could possibly have that I would be the slightest bit interested in,' he repeated, with a grin.

'You're just jealous,' huffed Phoebe. 'Or tone deaf. Or both.'

As if Frank couldn't have guessed. Phoebe had been going on about her favourite band of wandering minstrels for the last few weeks. She had thought and talked about nothing else since they announced the dates for their latest tour. Phoebe had been to see them twice before in neighbouring towns and managed to learn all of their songs but, this time, they were coming to Smithwood to perform at the local hall in the new year. Frank couldn't be less interested, especially since the news of his invitation to Excelsus Academy. He was indifferent to the howlings of a group of well-presented teenage boys even before this, but now his lack of interest turned to apathy. He'd rather spend the morning clearing dung from the cow shed than listen to Phoebe singing Jesters tunes. He didn't understand why they held such an appeal. The pictures of them that he'd seen on the wall of Phoebe's bedroom showed five young men with a wholesome clean-cut image, well-coiffed hair, unnatural smiles and matching fashionable tunics in an array of colours.

Phoebe seemed especially attracted to a band member named Dougal and had a number of pictures of him adorning her bedroom wall. He'd even seen her write 'P loves D', surrounded by a heart, in one of her school books. Obviously the chance of seeing her idol in the flesh, once more, was not to be missed and she had vanished in the early morning to queue up at the theatre to ensure she would get tickets for their show. She hadn't trusted either Heather or Jasmine with the task in case they failed, which, Frank thought, would probably have ended their friendship.

Phoebe had lost interest in his own dilemma since the Jesters had announced their tour dates, which suited Frank totally. He had wondered how he would get any peace to think about what he was going to do, with incessant questions from Phoebe irritating him at every turn, especially now she was home for the holidays. Having the vain and talentless Jesters to occupy her mind seemed like the ideal distraction, even if he'd had to hear about them each and every morning since.

When he'd arrived back at the farm after his visit to the school Phoebe and her friends weren't there. Only Aunt Rachel had been in the kitchen and she'd kept tactfully quiet, busying herself kneading dough, only asking if everything had gone all right. Frank had got the feeling that she'd banished the three squawking girls to Phoebe's bedroom to spare him the ordeal of having to answer their questions; a move he had appreciated.

Over the next few weeks he had been able to reveal what they had learned and, with the help of the Jesters, the subject had died down to a simmer, meaning the farm was back to relative normality. With Phoebe having the distraction of her favourite boy band, and of the preparations that she and Aunt Rachel were making for their customary week away with Uncle Simeon, Frank had found time to clear his mind. He had never felt so grateful for the solitary retreat of his tree house, where he'd found himself increasingly often, contemplating his next move amongst the finches and sparrows.

Despite talking things over with his dad, they were four weeks on from the eventful day at the school and he still hadn't decided what he was going to do. He was being unusually indecisive; while he felt a degree of responsibility to stay on the farm to help out, he knew that his dad and Brigg could manage perfectly well without him. He didn't like to admit it, but he would miss everyone if he went, even though he was intrigued about what he might learn at the academy. Would he find that he had some sort of gift? When he had first learned about the list, and then read the letter, he couldn't have been more intent on staying put. After all, the safety and security of the farm was what he knew. Having kept away from school all his life, and having come to realise that it would do him no good at all, why on earth would he want to change the way he learned things? The academy just didn't seem like his sort of thing.

His dad had said that he couldn't be at all sure that it would help nurture his free spirit or his wandering curiosity. Frank agreed and, as they had moved into August, he was leaning towards remaining at home.

He began to read a bit about the academy at the library. Although there appeared to be unpredictably little in their archives, he was able to find out that the place had been established around a thousand years ago by a man called Finestone Lamplight and, as his dad had said, its graduates went on to fulfil extremely important positions or, more intriguingly, some took paths that were shrouded in mystery. Interestingly though, Frank had found out that it wasn't always called Excelsus; the name had been changed from its softer, original, Hurtwood Centre for Alternative Learning. It had been named so by Lamplight when he founded it, but, he assumed, as time had gone on, a more catchy title had been required. The more he discovered, the more his interest was piqued and his initial indifference soon gave way to fascination and a growing desire to know more. He thought perhaps the time had come to explore the outside world more and what better an opportunity than going to a place like Excelsus Academy. But still he felt the attachment to his home. His mind was divided down the middle and nothing he seemed to do could sway him one way or the other.

* * *

Phoebe sat at the table humming Jesters songs. Frank was annoyed that he actually knew some of them. He'd done his best not to remember, although he had to admit some of them were pretty catchy tunes.

'Do you have to?' he said, annoyed. Phoebe just hummed louder.

Frank was about to put his fingers in his ears when there was the sound of hooves along the lane. They clattered loudly on the hard surface and came to an abrupt halt. Phoebe stopped humming and Frank gave an inward sigh of relief. The kitchen didn't afford a direct view to the front of the farm but, from the sound, it was obvious that there were several horses and Frank knew they had stopped at the farm gate.

They were accustomed to visitors, but the regulars from the village and neighbouring communities would always bring their carts up to collect their milk, meat or whatever they had ordered from the farm. Most of their friends would walk the mile or so up the lane. These visitors sounded very different. Hurried and urgent. Frank thought it didn't bode well.

He stood up and went to the window to get a view of the gate. He could just see it if he pushed his head against the pane of glass. Phoebe had the same idea and the two of them barged each other as they jostled for position to get a good look at the arrivals. His dad had been in the yard replacing a hinge on the milking shed door and Frank saw him stand up at the sound of the horses, looking towards the gate. He stood there, hands on hips. Jip barked.

'Who's that?' said Phoebe, nose pressed firmly against the glass so it misted when she breathed.

'No idea,' said Frank. 'Perhaps they're lost.' He knew this was unlikely to be the case. 'Or perhaps it's the Jesters' manager, come to get your tickets back from you in case you try and snog Dougal,' he chuckled. Phoebe aimed an elbow into his ribs.

Frank could see a short, round man dismounting his horse. He wore a bright green shirt upon which, to Frank's surprise and dismay, was emblazoned a familiar looking emblem - the vulture insignia of Excelsus Academy. The shirt was done up to the collar and it looked like the top button was about to burst open with the strain from his fat neck.

Before the man could enter, Lawrence Penny wiped his hands on his trousers and wandered over to the gate, looking at the stranger in expectation. The two teenagers watched from the window.

* * *

'Can I help you?' asked Lawrence, placing his hands on the top of the gate. The man stood on the other side. He wiped his brow, revealing a large sweat patch under his armpit. His thinning hair was combed over the top of his head, where it stuck down with perspiration. His jowls hung from his face like soggy brown slippers.

'Mr Penny?' he asked.

'That's me,' replied Lawrence.

'Good, got the right place then. Nice to meet you,' said the man, breaking into a smile and holding out a hand which Lawrence took over the gate. The men shook a greeting. Lawrence then looked at him in anticipation. The man got the hint.

'Oh, excuse me, where are my manners. Yes, of course, manners. My name is Briar, Briar Messenger. I'm from Excelsus Academy,' he said nodding enthusiastically in Lawrence's direction. At the mention of the academy, Frank's ears pricked up. He rushed from his position at the window, went out into the yard and walked over to the gate where the men stood.

As Frank had suspected, Mr Messenger wasn't alone. On the other side of the gate stood two large, muscular men. They wore expensive brown, military-style uniforms, the front of which bore the same crest as that on Messenger's shirt. They were fierce-looking and were armed with short swords. Frank had only ever seen anything like them before in books. Certainly no one in the village ever dressed like that, not even at the fancy dress ball that was held every year, in the spring.

Now that he stood face to face with someone from the academy he was intrigued, although the man looked more like he'd come from an all-night banquet.

'You must be Frank,' stated Messenger, looking to Frank and then back to Lawrence.

'You've come a long way then,' said Lawrence. 'Why don't you come inside for some tea and, er, bring your blokes with you if you like.'

'Thanks, they'll be all right here. We won't be staying long, but tea would be lovely. Any cake?'

'Who are they?' asked Frank as he continued to look at the two burly men at the gate.

'Oh, the academy likes to keep its people safe, so they insist a couple of their heavies come with me. Really not required in Byeland, although, I have to say, if I had to go to somewhere less, er, harmless I'd be considerably more grateful to have their company. For some places I'd take four men to be on the safe side.'

They made their way inside. Aunt Rachel seemed surprised to see the man come in with them. She wasn't accustomed to strangers in her kitchen. Phoebe had gone back to her chair and just stared at the new arrival as he puffed and sweated his way to the table.

'Rachel, this is Mr Messenger ... he's from Excelsus Academy,' said Lawrence.

'Pleased to meet you, Mrs Penny,' said Messenger cordially, nodding from across the kitchen. Aunt Rachel let the comment go.

'Rachel's my sister,' corrected Lawrence.

'Oh,' was all Messenger could say. He seemed to mull something over in his mind, but decided not to pursue that particular conversation. Lawrence came to his rescue.

'Have a seat,' he said. Messenger sank into the nearest chair at the table. 'Mr Messenger would like some tea, Rachel ... and some cake, if we have any.' Lawrence raised his eyebrows in his sister's direction, his tone amused. Messenger's expression changed to one of expectation.

'Oh, yes, cake,' he said.

Aunt Rachel produced a delicious-looking sponge cake from the cupboard. Half was missing as they had shared some at supper the night before. She poured three cups of tea and cut a generous slice. She put it on a plate and handed it to Messenger, who grabbed it and immediately took a massive bite out of the delectable sponge as if he hadn't eaten for a week. He began to scoff.

'Mm, wonderful,' he said, although his words were barely audible as he chewed greedily, crumbs sticking to his sweaty shirt. He swallowed with a hurried gulp. Aunt Rachel handed him a cup of tea and passed another to Lawrence, who took a sip and placed his cup on the table.

'Thanks Rach,' he said. Messenger took a huge slurp of tea and realised, too late, that it was very hot. He slapped the cup down and grabbed Phoebe's glass of water. He proceeded to gulp a few mouthfuls to cool his mouth down. He gasped. Those in the room looked on as if they were party to the feeding of the pigs. Messenger seemed to realise and put the glass and remaining cake down slowly, his breathing heavy. Phoebe looked like she was ready to explode with laughter.

'Oh yes, what must you think, where are my manners?' he said, still chewing the last of the cake. He looked at Aunt Rachel. 'Thank you very much, Mrs ...'

'Peth,' said Aunt Rachel.

'Thank you, Mrs Peth, delicious cake. Can't remember when I last tasted one so delicious. Yes, quite delicious.' Crumbs stuck to his face. He pulled out a bright pink handkerchief and wiped his mouth hurriedly, blowing his nose at the same time with an enormous snort. Phoebe looked at him wide-eyed and badly stifled a laugh, as did Frank. Lawrence shook his head slightly.

'Not eaten much on your journey?' asked Lawrence, with a smile.

'Oh no, on the contrary, I always eat well,' replied Messenger patting his ample stomach. 'I'm just a sucker for the sweet and sticky.' He put the handkerchief back into his pocket.

'So what can we do for you, all the way from Excelsus Academy?' asked Lawrence, cutting to the chase, as if he thought that, if the man stayed much longer, he might start to eat them out of house and home.

'Well, I'm a messenger, from Excelsus Academy, as I said outside, here on behalf of the New Entrants Committee.' His breath lightened.

'Sorry?' said Frank. 'You're the messenger, and your name's' — he paused— 'Messenger?' Phoebe stifled another laugh and appeared to be having trouble not descending into a massive fit of the giggles. Aunt Rachel shot her a look, but she still struggled to hold it in.

'Yes,' said Messenger matter-of-factly, not appearing to find anything even slightly amusing. He looked around as if to check if he was missing something. Once he was sure he wasn't, he patted his trouser pockets, delved into the left one and pulled out a crumpled piece of paper. Out of the other pocket he produced a pair of glasses. He put them on, unfolded the piece of paper and examined it, lips mouthing the words as he scanned, as if reminding himself of why he was actually there.

'Now then,' he said. 'Yes, anyway, our records show you haven't responded to the letter, to our invitation to attend our academy.' He looked up. 'So I've been sent by the New Entrants Committee to check to see if you have any, er, problems or questions, or perhaps your acceptance letter just got lost in the post?' His voice trailed off as he waited for a response. Frank wasn't sure whether to feel honoured or not; the academy had actually sent someone to see him just because he hadn't sent a reply to their invitation. Perhaps Mr

Messenger could help him clear a few things up.

'We just haven't responded, well, not yet. I'm still considering what to do,' said Frank flatly, shrugging. Messenger gave him an odd look as if Frank had just spoken in a different language.

'Considering what to do?' he said, screwing up his plump pink face.

'That's right. I still think there may have been some sort of mistake and—'

'Mistake? I don't think you quite understand,' interrupted Messenger, scooping up some more cake, clearly taken aback, his tone serious. 'No one has *ever* turned down a place at the academy. *Ever*, do you hear? And we certainly don't make mistakes,' he said with a tone of indignation. He looked at Frank. 'Are you really saying you might not attend? Is that what you're saying,' he said quizzically, eyes scanning Frank's face.

Frank was momentarily lost for words. He thought he'd given a straightforward answer and now he wasn't sure what to say. He certainly didn't want to upset the poor man, especially as he'd come a long way, but, on the other hand, surely he was entitled to take his time in making his decision, one which might alter the course of his life, and he certainly hadn't anticipated that the academy would send anyone to check up on him. There were still two weeks to go before he was meant to start. His dad spoke.

'Look, Mr Messenger. We really appreciate that you've come to see us, but it really doesn't matter that no one has turned you down before. What's important is whether Frank, here, feels it's the right thing for him to accept,' he said, 'and sometimes important choices take time to make.'

'The right thing! The right thing!' Messenger's voice rose an octave and his eyes widened.

'Yes, it's important to me that Frank has the right amount of time to make sure that going to Excelsus is the right thing for him. Wouldn't you agree, Mr Messenger?' Lawrence's tone was pointed.

Messenger sucked in a large breath and sat there open-mouthed, plainly dumbfounded, looking from Frank to his dad. He even looked for support from both Aunt Rachel and Phoebe. He found none. His mouth moved like he had something to say but was battling with the merits of actually saying it. He threw his arms around and his face started to redden like a ripe tomato - Frank thought the man was on the verge of a heart attack. Messenger exhaled at last.

'So, when do you think that might be?' he said incredulously. 'Goodness, have you no idea! The new term will be upon us before you know it and you can't just turn up unannounced on the first day and expect to take your place, not unless we know in advance. No, we have to know. There are preparations to make you know, yes, preparations. Don't think that running a place like Excelsus Academy is an easy thing. Hmm, easy, hmm.'

Frank didn't think that at all and he conceded that the man had a point. It slowly dawned on him that his hand was, now, finally going to be forced. That the decision he always knew he would have to make now needed to be made. His dad let out a breath, as if in resignation, and spoke again.

'Okay, Mr Messenger, I get your point and, in a way, I accept you're right. It's fair that we should let the academy know and perhaps we should have done so before.' He paused. 'Look, there's a really good inn on the main street just the other side of the village, The Four Peacocks. You probably passed it on your way through. They do some really great local ale, so why don't you and your guards head down there for a bit, while Frank and I have a chat? Come back in a while.'

Lawrence looked directly at the man, a look Frank knew meant Messenger had no choice. If he wanted an answer he'd have to do what his dad suggested, or leave empty handed.

Defeated, Messenger screwed up has face. He got Lawrence's meaning and, although it seemed that he wanted a more immediate solution, he conceded that this was the best he could hope for. They both stood up.

'Okay, fair's fair,' he said. 'I'll pop down for a swift half. Got to be careful, can't drink and ride now, more than my job's worth you know. I'll be back in, what, an hour?' He looked at Lawrence for clarification.

'I think that should do it,' said Lawrence. Messenger grabbed the last handful of his piece of cake, stuffed it into his mouth and nodded. With that, he bade them a farewell and headed out the door and down to the town, taking his guards with him.

As the sound of hooves faded, the room was quiet - all eyes turned to Frank.

'Interesting man,' said Lawrence.

'Better make another cake, Mum,' said Phoebe. 'Then we can all take bets as to how much he'll try and stuff in his face when he comes back. My guess is he'll scoff the whole thing.'

The four of them sat at the table. Frank realised that this was it. He'd put this off ever since the day he'd learned about his name being on the list. For all the talk and thoughts about it over the last four weeks, he'd known that there would inevitably come a moment when he would need to accept or reject the letter. A decision had to be made. He looked at his hands and swallowed.

'So, Frank,' said Lawrence, as if reading his thoughts. 'I guess it's time to make up your mind.' His dad and aunt looked calm and thoughtful. Phoebe just looked like she could burst with excitement, the Jesters now temporarily forgotten. Frank looked up at his dad.

'What would you do, Dad?' he asked.

His dad thought for a moment and then said, 'It would be very different from home education. More formal, proper lessons; not just doing your own thing.'

'Yuk,' joked Phoebe. 'Don't go, Frank, you'll have to learn all about the Luggans.'

Frank laughed. Lawrence smiled and went on.

'You know, your mother once said to me that to live a life in full you need to regret what you do, not what you don't do. That if you just do what you *can* do, you will never be anything more than what you are. She said you have to create yourself, feel all the shades, tones and variations of life and never wait a single moment before starting to improve the world.' He stopped, choked up. A tear came to his eye and he made no attempt to wipe it away. He was momentarily deep in thought. Aunt Rachel uncharacteristically put a hand on his. 'What she meant was,' he continued, 'we all need to get out and experience as much of life as we can and, sometimes, when we venture into the unknown, it's the only time we find out who we really are.'

'But what about the farm, and you and Brigg?'

'Sure, if you go, I'll miss you. You're my son. But, d'you know what, Frank? I can't tell you how much I would deeply regret not seeing you grasp each and every opportunity to live your life. There are times I look back and regret that I didn't do the same when I was younger and I look at you and the young man you could become and think that perhaps you should give this a go. I ache with sadness at the thought of not seeing you here every day, not eating with you around this table, not teaching you more things on the farm, your own classroom; but, as your dad, I know I shouldn't stand in the way of an opportunity that might give you so much more. If I said that you should ignore the invitation that's in front of you, it would be like me standing in front of a closed door, never letting you know what was on the other side, and that wouldn't be right. It's not the way I brought you up. Remember, you can always leave and come back any time, it's not a one way street, and I ... we ... will see you back here in the holidays.'

Lawrence put his other hand on Frank's and gave him a loving smile, which Frank returned. He looked into his dad's kind eyes and nodded slightly. He knew his dad was making sense. Even Phoebe seemed to be welling up with the emotion of the moment.

Over the last few weeks he had become more and more curious about what a future at the academy might hold for him. Yes, he'd miss his dad, Brigg and Aunt Rachel. If he was honest with himself, he'd even miss Phoebe. However, the initial shock of being on the list had slowly given way to excitement and interest and he had lain awake night after night thinking about himself and what it might be like at Excelsus. This was different; this would be him going out on his own for the first time, admittedly with the fall back of being able to come home whenever he wanted, or, as his dad had just pointed out, to drop out altogether. He knew his dad would support him if he did that, but also had a feeling the academy had never had anyone quit. Perhaps he could be the first? Would they send Briar Messenger again that time, or someone of greater authority? Perhaps Aurora Moonhunter herself?

The kitchen was quiet, as if the farmhouse itself was holding its breath, waiting for Frank to speak. Only the tick-tick-ticking of the clock broke the heavy silence. Frank drew a deep breath.

'Okay, Dad. I'll give it a go.' He leapt up and hugged him tightly. Lawrence held him even tighter, hands clawing the material at the back of Frank's shirt.

'Yaaaaa!!' shrieked Phoebe. She leapt up and ran over to hug both of them. 'Cor, Frankie, check you out! My cousin's going to Excelsus Academy! Wait till I tell everyone at school. This is *so* cool, Mum.'

'Well done, Frank,' said his dad, 'I think you've made a good decision.' Tears still welled in his eyes.

'I'll miss you, Frank,' said Aunt Rachel walking over and, for the first time as far as Frank could remember, giving him a huge hug. 'I think this calls for a celebratory piece of cake.'

The room suddenly seemed to explode into life, as if there were more than just the four of them in there.

'Just as well there's some left after Mr Pig Chops was here,' squawked Phoebe and they all laughed loudly. Even Aunt Rachel couldn't find it in her to tell her off.

They started to talk about preparations. On Frank's mind was where he would stay. The original letter had promised further instructions, which he guessed Messenger would have with him.

'Where will I stay?' asked Frank.

'Good point. I'm sure Messenger will have some ideas, but we ought to have our own plan. What about Polly, Rach?' said Lawrence, reminding them about Aunt Rachel's close friend, who lived nearby.

'Of course. I'll send a letter right away,' said Aunt Rachel. 'She'll be delighted to have you stay. You'll really like her.'

Messenger returned with his sentries about two hours later. It was apparent that he had enjoyed a bit more than a swift half and his guards accompanied him to the door of the kitchen this time as he swayed slightly en route.

'Hello again,' he said as he came into the room red-faced and smiley. He plonked himself down in the same chair, the aroma of beer and smoke filling the kitchen. He looked at the assembled faces, his eyes coming to rest where the cake had been. He gazed disappointedly at the empty plate, then swept the remaining crumbs into a pile, picked them up and shoved them into his mouth. Aunt Rachel gave him a disapproving look. He looked back apologetically.

'Well then,' he said. 'What have you decided to do, Frank?'

Frank took a deep breath. 'I'm going to accept the invitation to the academy,' he announced. The look on Messenger's face told that he was both relieved and delighted. Perhaps taking bad news back to the New Entrants Committee was not something he had experienced before and was probably a task he wouldn't have particularly relished.

'Good for you, my boy!' exclaimed Messenger, standing up and shaking Frank's hand. 'You won't regret it, no, won't regret it at all.' He reached into his breast pocket and pulled out a piece of paper. This one was neatly folded and bound by a piece of thin gold ribbon, unlike the scruffy piece he had produced earlier. He leaned forward and handed it to Frank. 'Further instructions,' he said in a low voice. He straightened up. 'Any questions?' he asked to both Frank and Lawrence, who exchanged glances.

'Not at the moment,' said Lawrence. 'Thanks.'

'Good, we'll see you on the seventh, then. Look forward to it,' said Messenger, clasping a hand on Frank's shoulder. 'The academy looks forward to it.' And, with his smelly beer-breath filling Frank's nostrils, he turned to leave.

As he strode towards the door he seemed to misjudge his route and hit his head on the side of the low frame. Frank winced, feeling the pain, but Messenger didn't seem to feel anything. He just stumbled back slightly, rubbing his forehead where it had collided with the doorframe and, without looking around, continued out of the door, leaving those in the room shaking their heads.

Frank had made the most important decision of his young life. He was off to Excelsus Academy in two weeks' time. There was no going back.

7

KNOX

Frank had been astonished to find out that the academy would send its own transport especially for him. The instructions that Messenger had left with him included a memorandum telling them that the Excelsus Student Bus would arrive at ten o'clock in the morning on Friday the fourth of September and would take Frank and his dad on the two-day journey from Smithwood to Rhaeder. It would even take his dad back to Smithwood once Frank had settled in.

The fourth seemed to arrive very quickly. Frank had been ready early that morning and had spent what had seemed to be an eternity looking out of the front window waiting for the bus to arrive, butterflies running riot in his stomach. He'd never really felt so excited, although he was nervous at the same time. His dad had been his usual calm self.

Right on time, a large enclosed coach, pulled by four jet-black horses, arrived at the farm. It was driven by an efficient-looking man called Knox. He turned the vehicle around proficiently in the yard, jumped out and loaded Frank's small suitcase into the luggage compartment.

The coach was of the highest quality, and, without doubt, the most ornate that Frank had ever seen. Coming from a small village, there really wasn't much call for opulent transport of this kind; it would have stuck out like a sore thumb. It was immaculately clean, both inside and out, for something that had just come on a long journey on a dry summer's day. Frank had expected it to be quite dusty, but it sparkled in the sun, as if Knox had stopped just down the lane and given it a good wash. The horses, likewise, were immaculately turned out and frothed at the mouth as they stood patiently.

Excelsus seemed to want to portray itsself in the best light possible and the appearance of coach and beasts definitely had the desired effect on Frank. The paintwork, decorated in the gold and blue colours of the academy and bearing the vulture crest, was flawless and the words 'Excelsus Transport' were meticulously painted on the side. But it was the size of the wheels that caught Frank's attention. They were enormous, unnecessarily so, as if they had been an afterthought of the design, or just made that way to convey power and status to the onlooker. Certainly Frank thought that you'd have to be very wealthy indeed to own something so fine, but he'd always been taught by his dad that such status symbols were empty and meaningless and to avoid their trappings. He looked at the peculiarity of the wheels and couldn't help but agree with him.

However, he felt just a bit important as he climbed aboard. Initially, Phoebe had stood there open-mouthed with an 'Oh my God' look, but this had rapidly turned into hyper-fidgety excitement as she tugged furiously at her own sleeves in an attempt to contain herself. Her new term started on Monday and Frank couldn't imagine how she would get through the weekend trying not to burst until she could relate the tale to everyone in her year down at St Barnabus. Aunt Rachel had been sensitive about Frank's departure and had made it clear that Heather and Jasmine were not welcome at the house that morning. Frank wasn't to be treated like some freak show to be ogled at by three baying young females; a sentiment that Frank had been very happy about.

Frank gave Phoebe an awkward hug. He'd never had to do that before and was glad that it might be another thirteen years before he might have to do it again. He went to say goodbye to his aunt and, before he knew it, she'd pulled him to her and held him tightly for longer than he would have imagined. She held his head in both hands, turning it up to her face.

'You take good care of yourself, Frank,' she said, looking down into his eyes. 'And, like your dad says, you can always come back.' Frank smiled. It was a genuine and rare moment of affection from her.

'I will,' he said, knowing that her friend Polly would keep her abreast of his news. 'I'll be back for the holidays.'

'I know.' She seemed truly sad to see him going, but she didn't shed a tear. That would have been a step too far. She gave him an affectionate kiss on the cheek before she let him go and Frank walked over to Brigg who was standing a few yards behind. He wore his usual grin, as well as his usual overalls. Although he was obviously fond of Frank, he didn't appear too upset to see him leaving; he was more practical than that.

'See yer then,' Frank said to him, giving him a smile.

'You show 'em wha' yer made of,' said Brigg clapping a big hand on Frank's shoulder. He had never been one to show much emotion and this occasion was no exception. But Frank could tell he was happy for him to be going out and exploring the wider world like a young lad should, spreading his wings. Frank assumed his dad had talked to him about it. Perhaps Brigg had once yearned for an opportunity to go beyond the farm. Perhaps not. He seemed completely happy living and working at Tresparrik in his own small world, where he could be his own master and no one would give him any trouble. Nonetheless, he had his own way of giving him his blessing and Frank, although he knew he would miss his giant of a friend, felt his approval.

* * *

Frank had visited his mother's grave the day before to say his goodbyes. Like he always did, he'd sat by the neatly engraved headstone and placed a bunch of wildflowers in front of it. It read, simply, 'Rebecca Penny'. He had opened the locket and brushed his finger over the image as though stroking her face, wishing for a moment that he really could touch her, that she could speak some words of advice and encouragement to him, that he could hear her voice, just this once. Just once. For a moment he'd pined for her, something that he had very seldom done in the past and, when he'd got up to leave, emotion had welled up inside and a few tears had dropped down his freckled cheeks and onto his shirt. He knew that, although he was leaving her there, she would be with him in spirit all the time he was away. The feeling was naturally reassuring. He'd looked back and said, 'Goodbye Mum, I'll be back soon. I love you.' He'd kissed the portrait, closed the locket and held it tightly as he'd walked back to the farm.

* * *

Knox opened the carriage door for Frank and his dad to get in.

'Best be getting off now, sir,' he said to them as they finished saying their goodbyes.

Lawrence nodded. 'Come on, Frank,' he said, then turned to Brigg. 'I'll be back on Monday,' was all he said; he knew he was leaving the place in capable hands. 'See you later, Rach, Phoebe,' he smiled. They smiled back.

'Give my love to Polly,' said Rachel.

Frank jumped up into the carriage. As he expected, the inside shouted quality; it was upholstered in a soft blue quilted material that felt more comfortable than his bed. He bounced up and down a couple of times, then caught Knox's look of disapproval and stopped. He noticed a small cupboard. Opening it, he found drinks and snacks, including a range of sweets and biscuits. Above the window was a magazine rack that held today's newspaper and other publications. All provided to make the traveller's journey more satisfactory. There were even pairs of eye shades and ear plugs in case he wanted a snooze en route. Frank wondered if Knox would periodically stop the coach in order to serve them some food, or if the Jesters would appear out of a secret cupboard somewhere to entertain them on the way.

Lawrence climbed in and sat in the seat opposite. Knox closed the door behind them, produced a clean cloth from his pocket and gave the door handle and the door a hard wipe before climbing up into the driver's seat.

Waving from the window, they took a last look at the farm as they headed down the lane.

* * *

They stayed the night at a luxurious inn, the Black Horse, on the edge of a small village. Again, it appeared that the academy had been highly organized and had booked the best room in advance. They had an evening meal of scrumptious game pie. They slept in the twin beds which were the comfiest Frank had ever experienced and spent the hour before bed talking about the day and the journey yet to come, his dad keen to make sure that Frank was still sure about his decision to go.

'You know it's not too late for you to change your mind,' he said, but, although he was grateful of his support, now that the day had come, Frank was eager to get to their destination and start his new adventure.

He slept well and, the next morning, suitably refreshed, they were treated to a full breakfast so tasty it would have given Aunt Rachel's a run for her money.

Frank wasn't sure where Knox had slept. Perhaps in the back of the bus given that the seats were so comfy. Perhaps in the room next door to theirs. But, in the morning, by the time they had finished their breakfast, he had the coach ship-shape and ready to go. He was as immaculately presented as his coach, which looked like it had just come out of the showroom and showed no signs of the dust and dirt of yesterday's travel. Perhaps Knox hadn't even gone to bed, but just stayed up all night cleaning the vehicle. He went to load Frank's case onto the bus once more and looked slightly miffed when Frank told him that he could manage it himself.

Lawrence had bid him good morning as he had emerged from the inn. Knox had acknowledged this with a slight bow, as if in the presence of royalty, but Lawrence had ignored the gesture which obviously made him feel uncomfortable. Then, when asked if it was time to go, Knox nodded as though he'd been given an instruction rather than asked a question.

So, they set off on the final leg of the journey. The coach pulled out of the inn, turned left and headed down the road that went through the village.

'How long until we get there, Mr Knox?' asked Frank enthusiastically, to which Knox replied that they would be there just before teatime, if the roads were clear. He kept his answers brief, not appearing to have any appetite to elaborate or make any form of conversation, as if schooled in the art of the efficient. Frank wondered why the roads wouldn't be clear. He couldn't imagine what particular obstacles they might encounter as there was very little traffic anywhere and they only seemed to pass one or two carts every hour, but thought better of asking Knox anything too taxing for fear of upsetting the man, who appeared happy to conduct his responsibilities with the minimum of fuss. To Frank, the journey seemed shorter than he had originally anticipated, which he thought was a good thing, considering he would be making it a few times each year.

* * *

Sometime later, after a smooth journey, they came to the brow of a hill. For the past hour or so, Frank had noticed an increase in the number of gulls circling above, which meant they were getting nearer to the coast and nearer to their destination which, he'd read, was by the sea. Then, Knox unexpectedly pulled the coach over into a lay-by and stopped.

Frank looked at his dad, who seemed just as mystified by the halt. Lawrence leaned out of the window as he heard Knox getting down the short ladder that led to his seat at the head of the vehicle.

'Everything all right?' he asked, although he was unable to see where the driver had gone.

'Yes, sir,' said Knox, not elaborating on why they had mysteriously stopped.

They heard his footsteps. A few minutes passed. No sound from Knox. All they could hear was the distant sound of the sea and the occasional cry of a gull. Lawrence sighed. He reached an arm outside, found the ornate handle, pushed it down and opened the door. He stepped out of the carriage, closely followed by Frank, and both of them looked around in a slow circle, mystified as to where Knox had gone. He was nowhere to be seen. Frank slowly scanned the land again and noticed his dad doing the same. Although they couldn't see Knox, in the distance, not too far away down the other side of the hill, Frank could see a large town emerging from the landscape. He drew a deep breath. It must be Rhaeder, the home of Excelsus Academy. They had arrived. Well, nearly. First they just had to find out what had happened to their driver. Surely they weren't expected to walk the final few miles?

Frank saw him first; he was walking back to the bus with a bucket of water. As he approached, he nodded his head at the two men in acknowledgement and simply walked past them. He had evidently taken the bucket over to the small stream that ran alongside the road before starting its gradual descent towards the sea, filled it and was returning to give the coachwork a bit of a spruce up. The edge of the road fell away sharply and Knox had been crouching down to fill the bucket, which explained why they hadn't been able to see him from where they were standing. Frank noticed that there was a large sponge in the bucket and looked on as Knox started to wash the carriage down with it. He also noticed that he had a large box full of cleaning equipment, including a brush, soap, a tin of polish and a number of drab-coloured cloths which appeared well used.

'Can I give you a hand?' Frank asked.

'No thanks,' replied Knox, 'I'm okay. Can't expect my passengers to help clean my wagon here now, can I?' It was the most he'd spoken all trip. 'Won't be long,' he continued.

Frank raised his eyebrows in resignation and watched as the man went about his washing. He worked quickly and methodically, like he'd done this a thousand times before, probably more. Frank couldn't help but wonder about the point of it all. Surely by the time they'd travelled down the hill and into the town, the thing would be dirty and dusty again? This was why he'd hardly ever seen his dad or Brigg clean the farm vehicles - the sparkles would only last a few minutes on the farm - but Knox was obviously a proud custodian of the student bus and took fastidiousness to a new, extremely high, level.

As he waited for Knox to finish his cleaning, Frank surveyed the view from the top of the hill down to the town. He could see the road running all the way to the outskirts, where small houses sprang up as the place took on an urban look. He stood there thinking how much like Smithwood it appeared, only bigger, and could just make out a wall that encircled the inner part of the town, thinking he'd soon get the chance to see it up close for himself. But it was what he saw away to the left that caught his eye. The cliffs and, then, the wide blue expanse of the sea. It was a beautiful scene. He could hear the cries of gulls and the crashing of the waves as they collided with the bottom of the cliff face, and then there was a fresh smell in the air that reminded him of the trips he and his dad had made to the seaside. The town extended to the cliffs and some buildings were perched precariously on the edge; it looked to Frank that, at any minute, some could easily topple into the water with an almighty splash.

Away from the cliff edge there was a small island, covered in trees. Frank could see the waves crashing on its beaches and also noticed that foam sprayed up as waves hit the sides of the cliffs.

In the distance, beyond the town, was a thick forest that clung to the land like a giant, bushy green beard. It extended up into the foothills of the high moorland, hazed in purple with clumps of heather. The late summer sun shone down and there was a cool breeze in the air. The landscape was still and, as Frank took in his surroundings, he was suddenly aware of a low rumbling noise from behind him. Quickly, it became louder. Then, out of nowhere, came a large black carriage. Before Frank was able to react, it sped towards him at high speed, the driver oblivious to anything that might be in his way. It was pulled by two athletic-looking dark brown stallions that frothed at the mouth like the water on the cliffs beyond as they effortlessly heaved the vehicle along the road.

Momentarily deafened by the harsh clattering of hooves on the road, Frank jumped to one side and stumbled as the carriage passed him. As he recovered his balance, he saw that it, too, had massive wheels. Stones scattered widely as it passed, peppering Frank. He regained his composure just enough to catch sight of someone at the window. It was a boy, not much older than himself. He just made out the angular shape of his face, long, dark, slicked-back hair and heard the mocking laugh as the boy realised they'd nearly run Frank over. Frank glimpsed a snooty-looking, blonde haired woman sitting next to him and looking bored. Then they had passed. At the speed they were going, the whole episode can only have taken a couple of seconds.

'Bloody road hog,' muttered Knox under his breath as he continued wiping the carriage, not seeming to pay much attention to what had just happened, as if it were a regular occurrence. He proceeded to check the bodywork for any new blemishes.

As the black carriage whizzed over the brow of the hill and headed down the road towards the town, Frank noticed a crest etched into the coachwork on its back. At the rate the vehicle was going it was difficult to see, but he could just make out the outline of a raven, its wings spread and silhouetted against the dark paint on the coach. It seemed to be making a statement all of its own, and one to which Frank took an instant dislike.

He noticed his dad walking over. He'd gone over to the stream to splash his face in the cool water and appeared to have missed the passing of the black carriage.

'Did you see that?' said Frank, eyes still following the vehicle as it continued towards the town. He could feel himself getting angry at the driver's recklessness and the apparent indifference of the passengers. Not a good sign. Lawrence followed his son's gaze.

'Hmm,' his dad replied. 'You'll probably find a different type of person here, Frank. Not like Smithwood.' He stood next to Frank and placed a hand on his shoulder. 'You know what, Frank?' he said.

'Remember to choose your friends here carefully.'

His dad continued to stare down the road in the direction of the town. It seemed like a succinctly put warning, which was unusual. Frank sensed that he knew he only had a little more time with his son before he had to return, alone, and maybe felt the need to impart some previously unspoken fatherly wisdom. He must have recognized that Frank was about to enter a new world beyond his control and, although he had been completely behind his decision to come to Excelsus Academy, Frank knew it must be difficult for him to now let go and allow him to find his own way in the world. His dad had brought him up without any formal education, equipping him with the tools and principles he hoped would be enough for Frank to manage by himself in a strange place. Frank hoped he had done his job well.

Knox finished his cleaning and stood back to inspect the carriage, which looked brand new, and they were soon back on their way. The road leading to the town was open and afforded them great views of their surroundings and Frank felt the undoubted allure of the location.

He had the feeling he was going to like it here.

8

THE TEA SHOP

They passed a few rows of houses, then Knox slowed the bus as they came to a wide archway that led into the main town itself. The arch was part of the high wall that Frank had seen from their vantage point up on the hill and appeared to encircle the entire town. Its presence gave Frank a sense of the age of the place. He knew the academy itself was centuries old, which meant that the town here probably was too and, as they passed slowly through the entrance, it was as if the ancient stone was swallowing him up, like he was actually stepping back in time.

Although there were a few people on the road going about their daily business, they didn't lift an eye to Frank or his dad, as though seeing Knox's resplendent Excelsus carriage was an everyday occurrence to them, the novelty of which had well and truly worn off many years ago. Frank could only reflect on what the people of Smithwood had made of his progress through the village the day before. Everyone had stopped what they were doing and stood and stared as they passed. They had seemed eager to see who was travelling in the carriage. Frank was aware that, thanks to Phoebe, Jasmine and Heather, the word of his decision to go to Excelsus had spread, so they must have known it was him. He had felt important, like royalty, and he couldn't decide whether this was a good thing or not. Being momentarily in the public eye gave him a feeling of exhilaration but at the same time he felt uncomfortable. Phoebe would have undoubtedly said that it was worthy of a picture in one of her magazines, but Frank couldn't help but think that being like that all the time, like some of those so-called celebrities, would be a bit of a pain.

Without looking up, men and women on the road parted to allow them passage down the road and further into the town. The streets were lined with an assortment of shops and businesses - butchers and lawyers, fletchers and cartographers, newsagents and tailors. Frank had never seen anything like it. As they passed by, he pressed his face against the window of the carriage and took in the colours, the characters and the sounds of his new surroundings. The noise level was now higher and the town was humming a familiar tune to the voices of its inhabitants. Everything was busy. It was a far cry from the unhurried peace and quiet of the farm, but he didn't seem to care. It was all so new and exciting.

Sitting next to him, his dad looked unimpressed. Frank thought that the years on the farm must have dampened any taste or enthusiasm he might have had for a big town but still couldn't understand his dad's indifferent expression. Frank wasn't even sure that his dad had been here before, although he had a suspicion that he might have, sometime in the past. If he had, he'd never mentioned it.

They wound their way through the narrow streets and it wasn't long before Knox brought the horses to a halt outside a row of shops. Frank peered out of the window. He could see the line of buildings, each three stories high and so rickety they seemed to tumble from the sky. He guessed they were built a long time ago. They looked very old indeed; time had warped and twisted the timbers into an odd array of shapes, like someone had just randomly piled bits and pieces of junk on top of each other, giving the impression that the structures could fall on them at any minute.

Frank checked the signs that hung outside. First there was a barber's, next a shop that was selling second-hand goods in aid of wounded wild animals, and then what looked to Frank like a lawyer's office, judging by the fancy looking sign with a black quill on it. At the end of the row was a jolly-looking small-fronted tea shop bearing the unimaginative sign 'Polly's Tea Shop'.

Knox jumped down from his driver's seat and opened the door to the carriage. Frank yawned as he and his dad stepped down to the pavement. He was glad the journey was over. The sound of a small bell clinking made him turn his head towards the shop from which a plump woman, about the same age and height as Aunt Rachel, emerged. Her wavy red hair was tied up in a loose bun above her pale freckled face and she grinned widely at them as they stretched after the journey. She wore a gleaming white pinafore, the cleanliness of which would have pleased even Knox. Or maybe not.

'*Law—rence!*' she shrieked, elongating his name in an exaggerated way. She held both arms out and waved her hands, walking over to give him a welcoming hug and a big kiss on the cheek. 'I can't believe it's you, my darlin'.' She squeezed him tightly. 'Oh, it's really lovely to see you.' She meant it. 'It's been too long.' She let go her embrace and stood back, looking him up and down with a big smile.

'Yes,' replied Lawrence, nodding. 'Too long, and it's great to see you too, Pol.' He smiled warmly. Frank had had no idea what to expect, but the fact that he was going to be staying with Polly meant he knew he needed to like her. He did, instantly, especially now he'd seen that she and his dad obviously got on well. It was a good sign. She looked at Frank.

'And hello, *gaw-geous*, you must be Frank,' Polly said earnestly, giving him the once over.

'Pleased to meet you, Polly,' he said, offering his hand.

'Oh, none of that nonsense! Come and give me a hug.' She pulled Frank in and gave him a proper squeeze. She smelt like freshly cooked doughnuts and was squidgy like a large bap.

'Tall, like your dad,' she said, letting him go and regarding him again. 'Should've guessed you would be.'

Frank smiled. He knew he'd be okay with her; she had a homely and welcoming look and her eyes twinkled with kindness.

She looked back to Lawrence. 'How was your trip? On the road for a couple of days, you must both be starving,' she continued. 'Oh, just listen to me going on, as usual. Enough of my silly chat, I've got a shepherd's pie in the oven, best you two come on in and get comfy, it'll be done in a few minutes. Oh my word, isn't this wonderful.' She kept throwing her hands up into the air in a flurry. She was full of beans and obviously delighted to be welcoming them to her home.

She looked back at Frank. 'And, if I might say so, my shepherd's pie is the best in the town.' She turned to Knox who was unloading Frank's suitcase from the carriage. 'And what about you Mr ... er ... '

'Knox, ma'am' he said, dully.

'Yes, what about you, Mr Knox? You must be hungry too, looks like you could do with a good portion. I'm sure I've got enough to go around if you want to join us.' Frank hoped he wouldn't.

'No, you're okay, ma'am,' he said, polite and short as always, 'I should be getting the bus back to the academy. Looks like it could do with a clean before I knock off.' He licked a finger and ran it along the front wheel arch as if wiping away a smear. Frank did a double-take towards the man who had given the bus a wash down not half an hour before. He realised he shouldn't have expected anything else.

'Well, if you're sure,' said Polly.

'Yes, thank you all the same, madam.' Knox looked at Frank. 'Where shall I put your bag, sir?' he said.

'Oh, just leave it there please,' said Frank pointing to the ground in front of him 'I'll take it in.' Without a word, Knox put the bag down. 'And thanks for getting us here safely, Mr Knox.'

Knox paused and looked at Frank, which he had rarely done all journey. Up until now he had avoided eye contact, yet now he regarded the young boy as if he wasn't used to getting thanks and was slightly taken aback at the compliment Frank had just paid him.

'Just doing my duty, Mr Penny,' he said with the faintest of smiles, and he held his gaze for a moment before turning to Lawrence. 'See you tomorrow, then, sir,' he said, referring to the return journey. ''Bout ten?'

'Thanks, Mr Knox,' said Lawrence. 'I'll be ready.'

With a nod of the head, Knox climbed back on board, gave the horses a light tap with his whip and headed off, presumably, thought Frank, in the direction of the academy and the nearest hose pipe. They watched as the school bus disappeared round the corner.

'Well, come on in then,' fussed Polly, shooing them towards the door, her animated arms like windmills. Frank picked up his bag as she ushered them into the tea shop, shut the door behind them and turned the sign to 'CLOSED'.

Given the small size of its front, the tea shop was surprisingly large inside, extending back into the building to a long counter, on which stood an array of half-finished cakes and nearly empty baskets of yummy-looking pastries. The room was filled with tables covered with red and white checked tablecloths and on a large blackboard was written a whole list of what the shop had to offer. Under the headings 'Something Sticky?' and 'Something Hot?' there was the promise of a whole host of tasty treats: apple turnovers, iced buns and teacakes; hot and cold drinks; and savoury items such as pasties and sandwiches. The whole room smelled of sweetness and wholesome baking.

Polly led them through and into a large room at the back, which served as her kitchen and dining room. Frank felt the pangs of hunger as he caught the waft of the shepherd's pie bubbling in the oven. Sitting on a couch on the far side of the room was a girl, younger than Frank, while a short, round man with a bushy beard and glasses sat in a comfy-looking armchair, reading a newspaper: the *Broadsword*. A small wire-haired terrier sat on the couch next to the girl. They all got up when the three of them entered the room and even the dog seemed anxious to greet them.

The man threw his newspaper down, strode over and shook Lawrence's hand.

'Lawrence, my dear fellow,' he said. 'My goodness, you haven't changed a bit.'

'Just what I thought, Norris,' said Polly. 'Just as handsome as the last time I saw him. Oh, listen to me. Now up to the table you lot; I'll dish up. Don't want your food ruined now, do we? Maddy, give me a hand, sweetheart.'

The man introduced himself to Frank as Norris Quigley, Polly's husband. He ushered forward their daughter, Madeline, who half-stood, shyly, behind her dad, nervous to have a couple of strangers in the house, especially as one of them was going to be staying under their roof as a guest. Tinks, the dog, huffed and sniffed his usual canine welcome up and down the bottom of the visitors' trouser legs. Norris spoke to Lawrence like an old friend and they were nothing but welcoming to Frank, who quickly began to feel very comfortable in their company.

They talked about their journey, and the odd Knox, as they ate. Frank learned that Polly had known his aunt since they were at school together and had moved to Rhaeder when she married Norris, who worked as a senior manager in the main administrative offices of the council, situated in a grand building in the town square. Frank wasn't sure if his job was important or not, but he seemed to take it very seriously. Polly had bought the tea shop three years ago and they had all lived there ever since.

'I could tell you a few things about what goes on around these parts,' said Norris, earnestly. 'Shouldn't say, really.' Frank caught his dad's eye. Both of them smiled as Norris proceeded to tell them a few funny stories about his work, which Polly and Madeline appeared to have heard a dozen times, and the afternoon soon turned into evening. The dish that had contained the shepherd's pie lay empty in the sink. They'd all had a second helping, and, while Lawrence and Norris drank Norris' homemade beer, Polly gave Frank and Maddy her own elderflower cordial, which was refreshing and delicious. Maddy kept glancing at Frank and sat as quiet as a mouse that had lost its squeak.

Frank got the feeling he was going to like staying with the Quigleys. He'd spent an entire evening in their company and the fact that they hadn't even once mentioned his being invited to Excelsus Academy or bombarded him with questions about how and why he was going there endeared them to him even more. It was like they were interested in him, rather than why he was there.

Polly got up from the table and beckoned to Frank.

'Come on then, gorgeous, I'll show you to your room,' she said. She lit a lamp and led him up two rickety flights of stairs to the very top of the house, where two doors led off a narrow landing.

The first led to a small bathroom, the other to what was going to be his bedroom. The room was light and airy and, in the corner, under a large window that looked out onto a small green rectangle of park across the road from the shop, was a comfy looking bed. He could also see the rooftops to the surrounding buildings. More exciting for Frank was that the window was above the level of the town wall which, even in the dusky sky, meant he could see across to the surrounding countryside and the sea beyond. At home he loved his bedroom as he could see the rolling fields all around, but this was certainly a contender for best view.

There was a chest of drawers and a small bedside table with a candle lamp on it. A pair of red flower-patterned curtains hung at the window. Polly set her own lamp down on the bedside table and drew the curtains.

'There we are,' she said. 'Small, but well-presented. A bit like me.' Polly laughed at her own joke.

'It's perfect Polly,' said Frank. She looked at him, her face kind.

'We'll look after you Frank, don't you worry,' she said. 'Your Aunt Rachel and your dad mean a lot to us. Like family.'

'I think I'll be fine here,' said Frank.

'Well of course you will, we'll see to that, and you let me know if you need anything.'

'I will.' Frank liked her. She was naturally motherly and charming; although he got the impression she could be tough when the moment took her.

They went back downstairs and, after a cookie and a glass of warm milk, Frank said his goodnights and went to bed.

9

THE FAREWELL

He slept soundly. The bedclothes were fresh and pressed and smelled of iced buns, so much so he wouldn't have been surprised if he had woken up eating his pillow.

Early the next day, a delicate aroma of sweet pastries had risen all the way to Frank's room and woken him, but he'd drifted back to sleep easily.

When he finally decided to get up and go downstairs, everyone else was sitting at the table, chatting.

'Sleep well?' asked Norris, as if he had to ask. The previous day's travel had made Frank weary and he'd lost track of the time. 'Come on Pol, we're all starving.'

Although she had already been up for hours baking for the day's trade, Polly still rustled up some pancakes which she served with lemon, sugar and syrup.

'Get that inside you, you'll need your strength on your first day tomorrow,' said Polly with her now familiar forthrightness. Norris sat reading his paper while Polly, Frank and his dad made small talk as they ate. Maddy sat quietly, stroking Tinks.

Frank had no idea what the time was, but knew that Knox would be impressively punctual and, probably having washed the student bus down at least twice, would arrive at ten on the dot, and then his dad would be going back to Smithwood, leaving Frank in the strange town to start at the academy on his own the next day. Saying goodbye would not be easy.

As Polly cleared the breakfast plates away, Frank caught her trying to get Norris's attention. Norris had become engrossed in an article about a man who claimed he had invented a flying machine and was oblivious to her attempts to break his concentration. Finally, she cleared her throat loudly. Still no response.

'Norris,' she hissed. He looked up.

'Yes dear, what is it?' She gestured with her head for him to leave the room. Norris looked at her with a look of total puzzlement. She gestured even harder, which made him look even more confused and Frank felt a giggle rise in his throat. 'What's wrong with your neck, Pol?' Norris asked, then suddenly seemed to realise what she meant and put his paper down on the table.

'Oh, yes ... er ... is that the time? I should be...taking the dog for a walk. Perhaps we should all go. You up for it Maddy?' he asked, unconvincingly. Lawrence sensed his discomfort and stepped in.

'It's okay, Norris,' he said, 'Frank and I should get some fresh air.' He looked over at Frank who nodded. They both stood and headed out of the shop leaving Polly scowling at Norris, who looked as if he might get a good telling off.

They walked the few yards over to the park and sat on a well-crafted wooden bench. They heard the clock strike a three quarter chime for a quarter to ten. Neither of them spoke for a while.

'You okay, Frank?'

'I think so, Dad,' replied Frank; a nervous feeling had started to appear in his stomach at the realisation that his dad would soon be going. 'I'll be okay. Polly and Norris seem really nice.'

'They are. I couldn't be leaving you in better hands.' Lawrence nodded as he spoke. 'I won't be far away.'

'I know.' He reached over and held his dad's hand. His dad squeezed it gently and placed his other hand in Frank's, clasping it lightly. Frank realised he'd been looking forward to coming here for the last couple of weeks, but hadn't given any thought to the moment when he would actually be left alone. Well, not exactly alone, but without those with whom he'd grown up his whole life. Breaking free, now it was upon him, was a daunting prospect and there was a part of him that felt like jumping back in the carriage with his dad and heading home to continue his life on the farm.

'I'll miss you, Dad,' he said, a lump coming to his throat. He felt the prickle of a tear in his eye.

'I'll miss you too. Don't know what Phoebe's going to do without you to wind up.'

'She'll probably wind you up instead.'

'Oh, she does that already. No, I suspect she'll be extremely miserable. Your aunt and I will have to put up with more Jesters tunes and her imagining that Dougal as her boyfriend.'

'Yuk,' laughed Frank. 'I think I'm going to be sick.' They both laughed and then stayed silent for a while.

'You know, it's a strange thing for a father to see his child growing up and spreading his wings. I always hoped you'd find a way to get out into the wider world. Don't get me wrong, there's nothing wrong with the farm, but I had always hoped for more for you and, now, here you are. I'm really proud of you, Frank. Excelsus Academy has got itself a top, top student.' He paused. 'But, Frank, if I could give you just one piece of advice.' Frank felt his tone grow more serious. 'Remember what I've always told you.'

Frank thought for a moment. His dad had told him so many things over the years, both words of wisdom and all manner of practical things. Lawrence looked at his son. 'Be your own person and do your own thing. Remember, the most courageous accomplishment is to think and act for yourself, and sometimes the price of conformity is that everyone likes you, except yourself.'

'That's at least two pieces,' teased Frank.

'Okay, two pieces then,' said Lawrence with a smile.

Frank remembered; his dad had said these things to him many times and the fact that he chose to repeat them now meant that they were, perhaps, the most important pieces of advice he had given and they took on a deeper significance, maybe borne out of the fact that Frank was now going to encounter new things, people and experiences which were beyond his father's influence. He felt he had to remind him to be the person he had become and not to be swayed or tempted by others who didn't hold the same values or principles. If being home educated had taught him anything, it was that being an individual was worth ten who followed the crowd.

'I will, Dad,' he said. 'You know I will.'

As he said it the clock struck ten and, unerringly, there was the sound of horses' hooves along the street as Knox slowly drove the gleaming school transport towards the tea shop.

Frank and Lawrence watched as he pulled the horses to a halt across the street. They stood there chewing on their bridles.

Father and son looked at each other. Lawrence nodded to Frank and stood up, Frank followed and they walked back towards the tea shop and the waiting carriage, Lawrence with his arm around his son.

Knox nodded a hello as they approached. Polly, Norris and Madeline appeared at the door and they said goodbye to Lawrence in turn.

'Don't leave it so long, you handsome man,' joked Polly as she flung her arms around him.

'I've got no excuse now, have I?' said Lawrence, wincing under the tightness of her embrace, despite his size, 'Seeing as Frank's staying here. I don't want to forget what he looks like.' Polly let go and held him by the arms.

'Oh, go on with you. He'll be back home before you know it. Now, you have a safe journey home and don't forget to give my love to Rachel and Phoebe.'

'Don't worry, Polly, I won't forget. You just look after my son.'

Lawrence turned to Frank and gave him a tight hug which Frank returned in measure.

'Time to go then,' he said.

'See yer then, Dad,' said Frank. 'I love you.'

'Love you too, son. See you soon,' said Lawrence, his voice breaking slightly. 'Try and get to see your grandmother and don't forget to write.'

With that, Knox, who had been waiting patiently, opened the

door of the carriage. Lawrence climbed in and pulled the window down. Polly stood behind Frank and placed a compassionate hand on his shoulder as they all waved. Then, efficiently as you like, Knox tapped his whip against his horses and Frank watched as the gleaming carriage carried his dad off, around the corner and out of sight.

Even though he was sorry to see his dad go, Frank was determined not to feel sad. He knew he had his dad's blessing. He also knew that he wanted Frank to find his own independence. He thought he'd prepared him well, as if he had brought him up knowing a moment like this would come.

'Cup of nettle tea, Frank?' asked Polly, breaking the silence. 'Or how about a cheese straw, fresh out of the oven?'

'Thanks, Polly,' said Frank politely, 'but if it's okay with you, I'd like to have a wander around the town, clear my head a bit.'

'Good idea,' said Norris. 'I'll show you around. I'll get my jacket.'

'That's okay, Norris,' said Frank, 'I'll be all right by myself.' He wanted some time alone and, although he knew Norris meant well, he could imagine what sort of tour guide he would be. Norris looked surprised.

'Of course you will,' said Polly. She glanced at Norris. 'Of course he will, Norris. I'll put a few things in a bag for you, okay Frank?'

'That would be kind,' said Frank, thinking of the delicious smells that had awoken him that morning.

'But you don't know your way around!' exclaimed Norris, as though the town would eat him if he dared venture out alone, 'I wouldn't let Maddy walk around by herself.' Maddy blushed at the mention of her name.

'I'll be all right,' said Frank, 'I'm okay at finding my way around places.' He looked up at the sun. 'You're on the south side of town, and that clock tower's the tallest thing I saw on the way in. I'll find my way back, no problem.' Norris was taken aback, but looked more than a bit impressed at the youngster.

'And if you don't,' said Polly, giving Norris a look, 'there's a map in the main square with all the street names on it. We're on Murgatroid Square. You'll find us on that. Now you be sure and have a good look around.'

She disappeared into the shop, reappearing a few moments later holding a large chocolate muffin and a gooey pastry. Frank grabbed his shoulder bag, into which he had already placed a flask of water, and took the pastries, placing them carefully into the bag.

'Thanks, Polly, I'll see you at lunch time then,' and, with that, he took off into the town, leaving Norris looking a bit bewildered.

Frank had been keen to get familiar with his surroundings since they arrived. After the morning's events he thought a good stroll around the town to gather his thoughts would be a good idea and, as it was a mild day, he wasn't up for staying indoors, even though he thought that the Quigleys would have made a fuss and made him feel very much at home.

As it was Sunday, the streets were quiet compared to the flurry of activity he had witnessed the day before. All of the shops were shut, but that didn't stop Frank peering into their windows and looking at their signs to see what sort of things they were selling or services they were offering. Among the more interesting was a shop selling old books and maps, which bore the sign 'Amos Darkman – Antiquarian Bookseller' and Smithers Apothecary, whose window and shelves inside were laden with odd-looking jars and bottles of all shapes and sizes, filled with strange-coloured liquids and powders. Then there was Eldirissi's, purveyor of exotic spices, from which wafted the aromas of far-off places. A few people were out walking, but no one seemed to notice him as he ambled confidently along the roads. No one acknowledged him, even though he smiled as he passed them - it was as if people were happy to stay anonymous and unengaged, unlike the small village where he lived, where most people would stop and chat.

The town had a certain charm and an old feel about it. The main streets were wide and clean, with narrower side streets at right angles; some were no wider than alleyways and didn't look like the sort of place you'd venture down alone. A few were dark and gave Frank the creeps.

Soon enough, Frank came to a large square and guessed it must be the centre of the town. It was cobbled and enclosed on all sides by shops and businesses; baskets of vivid pink fuchsias hung from posts, set at regular intervals around the edge of the square. Apart from the shops there were more official looking establishments such as a large branch of Chetto's Bank, and Pearce & Sons, the expensive looking lawyer's. Both occupied impressive but austere looking buildings, as did Ivy & Bradshaw, a smart looking accountant's. But the place was dominated by a striking, gothic-looking building, fronted by several stone pillars. At the apex was a stone circle that bore an eagle crest. Frank knew it could only be the administrative centre of the council where Norris worked, and wondered what went on inside.

The centre of the square was paved and, as Polly had said, right in the middle, bordered on each side by wooden benches, was a wooden plinth that looked like a large table. Painted on the top was a street map; he went over to it immediately.

The map showed a detailed plan of the town. There was a big red spot in the middle which bore the legend 'You Are Here', as if it wasn't obvious. Frank scanned the diagram and mentally traced the route he had just walked, but he was really looking for something else - the reason he was here, the location of Excelsus Academy.

He couldn't really miss it. In the north west corner of the town was a building that was easily the largest on the map and seeing it made his heart beat faster. It extended outwards beyond the city walls, across to the cliffs and the sea. Frank stared at it. Not much more than a month ago he would never have thought the place would feature anywhere in his life, and now he was less than a day away from walking through its front gates as an invited student, someone supposedly gallant and gifted. Whatever that meant. He was still unaware, frustratingly so, as to how and why this was happening to him at all, but he was absolutely determined to grasp the opportunity firmly with both hands. He felt he owed it to both his mum and his dad, but, most of all, to himself.

Frank placed a hand on either side of the map and leaned in, staring down at the image, looking for the quickest route. He reached into his bag, pulled out the chocolate muffin and took a big bite. Crumbs fell down his chin and onto the map. There was a long straight street that led diagonally from the square directly to the front of the academy - Iron Lane. He lifted his head and looked in the general direction of the lane. He took another mouthful of cake and a swig of water and headed off, itching with anticipation of his first look at the building which was likely to be his home for the next few years.

As he turned into Iron Lane he quickened his pace and broke into a jog. The street was much longer than it had seemed on the map. Immediately, Frank was struck by the different feel he got from this area of town. It was lined with shops selling much higher quality goods than he had experienced so far during his walk through the town. There was a bespoke tailor and a milliner, at least three art galleries, and a swanky-looking tea shop with far better exterior décor than Polly's. Frank could tell that this particular part of town was set apart from the rest, as if you would only come here if you had a certain social status or wealth; even the people who were ambling down the lane looked differently-dressed and gave him superior looks. Frank wouldn't have been surprised if there had been a workshop that made huge vehicle wheels like the ones on the student bus. He thought how everything these places sold was the same as similar shops in the town, but that you would have to pay more to get it, and why would anyone want to do that?

He realised he had slowed his pace and stopped to look into the window of a shop that bore the sign 'Halberd-Stokes & Co – Jewellers to the Rich and Famous'. He caught his own reflection, and then the face of a tall, dark-haired man with thick-rimmed glasses staring back at him through the glass. The man had a pompous look and made a gesture with his head as if to tell him to clear off, so Frank moved on. Finally, he came to the end of the road. The space opened out before him into a vast marble plaza and he found himself staring across at what could only be described as the incredible frontage of Excelsus Academy.

Across the plaza, staring down at him, was the head of an enormous stone bird of prey: a vulture, its mouth open, crying out silently, its neck extended, and its eyes trained menacingly on the square. Its wings were outstretched in a huge mantle that cast a wide shadow in the late morning sun; it looked so real, like it could take to the air at any minute or, worse, pluck someone from the street. It seemed that the winged beast was set as a guardian and a symbol of huge power. It was certainly impressive and Frank stared in disbelief.

The giant stood on the townside bank of a wide river that cut the academy building off from the rest of the town and the only way to cross was via a wide, stone bridge that passed underneath the statue, as if the beast dared you to cross. On the other side of the water was the façade of the academy; tall, white and modern, it gleamed spectacularly behind its winged sentinel. Gold and blue flags flew from poles that extended from the building. Impressive was an understatement - he'd never seen anything like it before. Frank could see men up on the walls, patrolling the perimeter and prowling along the walkway. They were dressed in blue uniforms, military-style, and, for some reason, Frank imagined that they were armed, which he found very odd as, after all, it was only an educational building. He walked into the plaza itself to get a better view.

Frank thought it was unusual that the academy was cut off by the river. He would have thought the river would have run through the centre of the town, but it seemed that the place had been intentionally separated from the rest of Rhaeder, perhaps to give it an air of mystery. Whether old Finestone Lamplight had meant it that way when he founded the academy was anyone's guess.

Frank's gaze followed the men up on the wall. Back and forth they walked. One stopped and shielded his eyes from the sun to survey the plaza below. His stare fixed on Frank, who was immediately under no illusion that he ought to move on.

He took a final look at the entrance to Excelsus, realising that he would be entering through the large ironclad doors the next morning and, not wishing to loiter further, turned and headed back down Iron Lane and to the comfort of Polly's. He'd be back tomorrow. He was ready for Excelsus Academy.

10

THE ACADEMY

Frank didn't sleep well. The image of the great stone vulture guarding the entrance to the academy stuck in his mind and gave him a feeling in his stomach like an over-generous helping of Aunt Rachel's rhubarb crumble. He couldn't really tell if it was the bird of prey itself that gave him the butterflies or just that he was starting there the next day. Either way, he felt he could have done with a better night's rest.

He pulled the curtains open and looked out on to the town. The street below was busy with people going to work and children heading off to school. An ordinary day - for most.

Frank sat on the edge of his bed and brushed the hair from his eyes. He re-read the instructions that Messenger had left with him during his visit in the summer - 'Arrive at the academy at ten o'clock.'

Polly was delightfully reassuring at breakfast. She made sure he had a good helping of porridge topped with raisins and honey and gave him a large glass of dandelion punch which Frank was happy to gulp down, despite feeling a little heady from his restless night. Norris sat at the end of the table, presiding over a plate of bacon and eggs, reading his newspaper and letting out the odd grunt and huff. Frank glanced at the headline on the front of the *Broadsword*, which referred to some new transport law that the council was thinking of adopting. He couldn't see the detail but, after his close brush with the raven-clad carriage during his journey, he hoped it would be to impose greater taxes on those that drove vehicles with massive wheels - badly. Another headline caught Frank's attention - it read,

'ACADEMY UNDER GUARD?' He wondered what it might mean and whether it related to Excelsus. He thought it was strange, but he had other, more pressing, things on his mind that morning. Maddy, who hadn't really said much to him since his arrival, sat opposite him eating her breakfast. He caught her occasionally looking in his direction, as if still unsure what to make of their new guest. She ate like a sparrow; her small pale features creasing as she slowly chewed every mouthful. Frank wasn't sure what to make of her; he was used to the teasing and the smart, infuriating comments of Phoebe, who didn't seem to give him a moment's peace. Maddy was very different indeed.

Out of the blue she said, quickly and nervously, 'Hope it goes well today.'

He smiled gently at her. 'Thanks,' was all he could say. She blushed.

'You'll be fine up there, my boy,' said Norris, lowering his paper so he could eye Frank over his spectacles. 'Mind them posh kids don't get under your skin though.' Frank wasn't entirely sure what he meant, it sounded a bit like a warning.

'Posh kids?'

'Oh, Norris,' said Polly who was fussing around the kitchen clanging plates as she tidied up. 'Don't start talking such nonsense.' She tutted disapprovingly but Norris just ignored his wife and continued.

'Yes, those that pay to go. Feel they own the place sometimes. Don't let them push you around. Not that you look like the sort to get pushed around, if you know what I mean.' Frank didn't.

'You just ignore him,' interjected Polly, 'Norris gets these ideas in his head. You'll be fine, darlin'.' She gave Norris a tight-lipped look and shook her head at him in annoyance.

'Oh don't get me wrong,' said Norris, chewing on a piece of bacon. 'Most of them are fine; it's just some of them that give the rest a bad name.'

'Bad name,' muttered Polly. 'Like I said Frank, just ignore him.'

'Just saying, just saying. You know what I mean, Pol,' continued Norris, looking around at his wife, who didn't look like she knew what he meant at all. 'Not that we see them much over this side of town. They like to keep to the other end, around Iron Lane and the like. Those fancy shops and cafés, not half as good as what you get in here and charging twice the price for it. It's a bit more, well, *well-to-do* over there, but we get them in here occasionally and, like I said, they think they own the place, demanding this and that without a please or thank you. "Manners cost nothing" is what my Dad used to say. Get it from their parents they do, in their fancy carriages with wheels the size of giant dustbin lids. Can't even drive the things properly. Scared our Maddy here once, they did.'

'Oh, Norris,' said Polly, 'I don't know what's got into you this morning.' There was a moment's silence. Maddy looked coy and reddened slightly at the mention of her name.

'And another thing,' Norris went on, waving a piece of bacon on his fork. 'Strange place, that academy. A bit ... mysterious, if you get my drift.' Again, Frank didn't. 'Had a strange feeling about the place ever since we moved here, haven't I Pol?' he looked across to her for support but just got an irritated look back. 'Just saying. Of course, it's right on the other side of town from us, but the council's keeping an eye on the place, let me tell you.' He stopped himself. 'Or perhaps I shouldn't tell you,' he said, popping the bacon into his mouth and lifting his paper up in front of his face as if to continue reading. Frank got the impression he'd revealed a bit more than he should have.

'That's enough, Norris,' scolded Polly.

'Just saying,' he said. 'That's all. Just saying.' He dropped his paper quickly, looked at Frank and gave him a wink.

Frank still didn't know what to make of his comments. He understood that people could be selfish and unkind, but, like his dad had taught him, he was happy to take people as he found them and not prejudge. As for the academy being a strange place, Frank had no idea what he meant and just gave him a vacant smile. He hadn't wondered too much over the past few weeks exactly what kind of people he would meet there. He assumed they would be much like himself, although Norris's words made him think that they might not be at all. Perhaps he should have thought about it a bit more, maybe asked his dad, but one thing was for sure - it was a bit late for questions.

Norris left for work and Maddy for school. The town clock struck, telling Frank it was half past nine. He got up from the table and slung his small bag over his shoulder. The instructions from Excelsus had been clear: he didn't need to take anything with him for the first day, everything would be provided. It gave a list; he was to receive new shirts and trousers, exercise books and writing materials. Excelsus would have other items, such as telescopes for Astronomy and comfy cushions for Meditation. Interestingly, it added that students were not allowed to bring their own weapons, and definitely no dogs. Polly gave him a fresh muffin.

She had offered to walk with him, but he politely refused. He was confident enough to go into new situations alone, although this was undoubtedly the most daunting one he had ever found himself facing; even more daunting than the first time he'd stepped alone into the arena at the local agricultural show with Pickles, his dad's prize pig. He'd had to drive the uncontrollable beast around the ring in front of hundreds of people. He had managed it, sort of, even if the animal had headed straight for the tent where they had been judging the biggest vegetable competition, and the confidence it gave him had stayed with him since.

The walk seemed shorter than the previous day. He soon passed the council building in the central square and was nearing the end of Iron Lane once more, coming face to face with the winged beast of his previous night's dream. The vulture looked as impressive as it had the day before - growing familiarity hadn't diminished its impact - and Frank stood and stared again.

The scene was very different from the quiet of Sunday morning; there were many more people around, who he assumed were the general townsfolk going about their business. But what caught Frank's attention was the long cavalcade of carriages lining up in an attempt to negotiate the crossing, both ways, over the bridge that led to the entrance of the academy. Frank could hardly believe it; there were dozens of them, like a plague of bluebottles, all of them immaculate, each one pulled by high-class, well-bred horses and all sporting the huge wheels which Frank now understood was a mark of the owner's status. He stood and watched as each driver pulled and cajoled his horse and carriage among the others, jockeying for position in the queue to get over the bridge and drop off their occupants at the entrance. He was amazed that they avoided knocking into each other, and thought someone could easily topple over into the river if they weren't careful. The carriages were painted in a variety of colours: yellow, red and blue traded positions before his eyes like the smear of an artist's palette, but one in particular caught Frank's eye. A large black landau stood out from the rest, the dark embossed raven, wings spread, etched into its back. The same one that had nearly run him down a few days before. A frown creased his brow as he watched it fight for position in the mêlée.

He surveyed the chaotic scene for a few moments. As the carriages emerged from the other side of the bridge and back onto the main plaza, they barged their way uncompromisingly through the local traffic without any consideration for those around them, not even looking where they were going. He noticed some of the local people throwing up their arms, agitated, exasperated. Frank could imagine their relief that this only happened at the beginning and end of term, and not every day.

He grabbed hold of his bag and headed across the plaza towards the bridge, weaving his way between the traffic that had slowed to a near standstill. Some of the drivers gave him angry looks. He was pleased to find there was a pedestrian walkway along one side of the bridge; otherwise he would have had to have taken his chances amongst the spokes and hooves. The wings of the great stone vulture cast their shadow over him as he crossed, and the rush of the river below made him quicken his step.

Then, at last, he stood at the bottom of the wide marble staircase that led up to the grand entrance to the academy. High up on the wall, the flags flapped in the light morning breeze. Boys and girls of all ages were getting out of the carriages that continuously pulled up outside. Each large carriage seemed only to carry a single child, which made him wonder at the chaos all of this had created and why the individuals couldn't walk to the place on the first day, just like he had, or share the journey. He imagined that, like himself, most of the students would live a good distance away and would therefore be staying in the town while they attended, so wouldn't need a lift here today.

The surly driver of a red carriage barked at him to get out of the way as he pulled up in front of the building, even though Frank was standing on the pavement. Frank gave him an indignant look and moved to one side. The driver climbed down and opened the door to the carriage. A girl emerged, immaculately dressed and wearing a blue shirt bearing the Excelsus insignia. She walked straight past Frank, ignoring him and not thanking the driver who simply shut the door, climbed back up, and made off back over the bridge. The spot he had just vacated was quickly filled by another vehicle and the ritual repeated over and over again.

Frank took a deep breath as he walked up the wide marble stairs to the huge, open, ironclad oak doors, and went through into a vast semi-circular entrance hall, from which led a dozen corridors, set at even intervals around the far wall. Light spilled into the room which was white, modern and expensive-looking. The floor of freshly polished wood was dominated by the Excelsus vulture symbol, inlaid in black and surrounded by a simple yellow and purple pattern that encircled the beast.

High on the wall, directly in front of him, was a large portrait of a seated middle-aged man with dark hair and a long beard. Underneath was a small sign that read '*Finestone Lamplight, Distinguished Scholar and Founder of this Academy*'. Other, smaller, portraits hung from the wall and, year by year, the names of the academy's top students were engraved into the masonry alongside their intake number, but Frank hardly noticed them in the cacophony. A large notice board also hung on a wall to the side and at the entrance to each passageway were positioned a number of stands to which were pinned notices on bright yellow parchment indicating where students were to go for first-day registration. A tall man dressed in Excelsus robes and holding a clipboard sauntered around the entrance hall directing any students who appeared to need help. The whole space echoed with first day bustle.

Frank's attention was grabbed by a number of different breeds of dog that dodged and wove themselves through the criss-crossing legs of the students and headed into the corridors before him, each of them carrying books, rolled up scrolls or pieces of paper in their mouths. Very strange indeed, thought Frank, wondering what they were doing. He doubted that Excelsus catered for gallant and gifted canines, but nothing would have surprised him.

He glanced around and soon spotted a large sign with a black arrow on it. It read 'NEW ENTRANTS (INTAKE 821) - THIS WAY' and pointed down one of the long corridors that disappeared into the depths of the building. As his gaze followed the direction of the arrow, some students barged past him on the way to their own registration. Frank clasped his shoulder bag, took a deep breath and headed off down the passage.

It seemed to go on for ever. He walked quickly, but not so fast that he couldn't take in some of his surroundings. The walls were wood panelled and there was the sweet, heady smell of beeswax that reminded him of the kitchen table back at home, indicating that the place had only recently been polished ahead of the start of the new term. Frank pictured a group of Knoxes, brandishing cloths and brooms, giving it the once-over every day, keeping it spotless. What light there was came from a few skylights in the high ceiling. Portraits of past professors hung from the walls; they were all clean and squarely positioned, very much in contrast to the images that

Frank had seen in Oliver Jelly's office at St Barnabus. Very different indeed. He passed a few doors which had name plates screwed squarely on to them at head height. They bore what Frank assumed were the names of some of the current professors. He read a few - 'Professor Huxley' and 'Professor Hobbs' - and began to wonder what they did and whether they would be part of his education here.

The students thinned out and he was aware that he was approaching the end of the passageway. He looked behind him; two girls were heading his way. New entrants too, he thought, as, at last, he came to a door. Pinned to it was another sign which read 'NEW ENTRANTS' REGISTRATION'. This was it. He went to put his hand on the doorknob when he was suddenly aware of the presence of a small dog at his feet. It was like it had appeared out of nowhere and was now standing to the side, waiting patiently for him to open the door. He looked down at it and it gave him a furtive look back.

'Hello,' he said, wondering if it too, was a new entrant. The dog just continued to stare up at him. Undeterred, Frank grasped the ornately-carved, round doorknob and, taking a deep breath, pushed it open. It creaked loudly as it swung open, so loudly, in fact, that it made him grimace. The dog shot through ahead of him.

To Frank's surprise, the door opened out onto a wide circle of lawn, which was banked on three sides with rows of benches, set back a way, so that they looked down on the doorway through which he had just come, like a small outdoor arena. There was a large canopy to one side, drawn back to allow the area to be basked in sunlight. He noticed a number of students already sitting on the benches. Some sat in groups while others just sat by themselves, fidgeting nervously with their shirtsleeves. Some looked in his direction, curious as to the identity of the next newcomer. From a brief glance, Frank noted that most of them were about his age, although a few were a bit older. The quiet purr of chatter filled the air.

An officious looking woman sat at a table in the middle of the lawn. Her greying hair was tied in a tight bun, through which was lanced a long peacock feather; a pair of studious-looking half-moon spectacles were perched on the end of her long nose. As the door closed, it creaked and groaned like a howling wolf. Frank grimaced an apology, but then realised this must have happened every time someone had come through it. He saw the dog disappear through an open door to the side of the lawn.

Frank took a few steps towards her, expecting her to beckon him over, but she kept looking down at the papers on the table in front of her and didn't acknowledge him. He stood there for a few seconds and, when she still ignored him, he cleared his throat. Still no reaction. Finally, he walked forward and waved his hand under her nose, but not too close, which made her look up.

'Oh,' she said, gripping the edge of her glasses as if to get a better view, 'I didn't hear you come in.'

You have to be kidding, thought Frank; the door had made enough noise to awaken the dead. She would have to have had pig poo stuffed in her ears not to have heard it. Frank opened his mouth as if to say something but felt his first words inside the academy ought not to be rude ones. Instead, he smiled and she beckoned him over to the table as the door opened behind him with a loud screech and the two girls, about his age, came through.

'And you are?' the woman said, sternly as Frank looked behind him.

'Sorry?' said Frank, who hadn't heard her above the noise of the door. She stared at him, looking slightly miffed. Frank noticed she was dressed primly; her tweed jacket bore the Excelsus crest.

'Name?' she said in a slightly raised voice. 'Please.'

'Frank Penny.' She continued to look at him, there was a silence.

'You'll have to speak up young man,' she said, 'I'm a little deaf.' You're telling me, thought Frank, trying not to smile at her statement of the obvious.

'*Frank Penny,*' he said again, this time a little louder and slower. He wondered how long it had taken to process the new students who were already here; perhaps the process had started yesterday. The woman muttered his name under her breath and ran the tip of

119

her pencil down the piece of paper she had in front of her. Frank realised it was a register of those starting at the academy today. He noticed there were only about twenty names, a small select group, and thought that, if this was the intake from all the lands around, including Byeland, then there weren't very many who had been selected, just like his dad had told him. He wondered what special gifts these people possessed, or perhaps, like himself, they had none.

'Ah yes, Frank Penny, there you are,' she said, putting a cross meticulously by his name. Without looking up she asked, 'And where are you staying during term time?'

'Polly's Tea Shop, on Murgatroid Square,' he said as loudly as he dared, fearing that he might be there all day if the old woman asked him to repeat himself each time he answered a question. She looked up and peered at him over the rim of her glasses, looking him up and down, inspecting the way he looked and how he was dressed.

'Hmm,' she said in an interested tone. 'Meritter.' She paused. 'Very good.' She returned to the register, writing the address of the tea shop in the box next to Frank's name. 'Thank you, Mr Penny, if you'd like to take a seat please.' She indicated with her head for Frank to sit on the benches so she could deal with the girls who had followed him in. Frank nodded.

'Thank you,' he said, not sure if she would hear him.

Meritter? Frank wondered what she had meant, and how, just by looking at him, she was able to make some sort of judgement. He stepped to one side and looked around, deciding where best to sit, but, instead, felt the urge to go to the top of the grass bank to see what was beyond. He ran up the grass between two sets of benches, sensing the eyes of his fellow new entrants follow him as he did so. He stood at the top of the bank and looked around as he heard the two girls yelling to the woman that they were the Maddison twins, Honeycomb and Peppercorn. The area opened up into a beautifully-manicured wide patch of grass; well-tended trees were evenly spaced around the grounds and a wall ran around the entire area. There were a number of iron gates which led out into the fields and woodland beyond. The gates had uniformed men standing in front of them, as if guarding the way in and out, and more men wandered the walkways on top of the walls. He panned round slowly, feeling the guards returning his gaze. Watchful.

He was suddenly aware of a murmuring behind him and then a loud, sharp, voice of a man.

'You boy!' it snapped. Frank turned around, wondering who the remark was aimed at, then realised it was meant for him. He froze momentarily.

'Yes, you, up there.' Frank stood still, not sure what to do; all eyes were on him. A man had appeared in the lawned circle below, hands on hips, and was now looking up at where he was standing. As Frank stood there the man took a few strides forward so he was half way up the bank and stopped a few yards away from Frank. He was smartly dressed in professor's robes, edged with blue and gold. His dark hair was flat and meticulously parted at one side and he had a thin moustache. He had a serious look about him and, by the way he looked at Frank, he was in no mood to be crossed.

'What's your name?' he demanded.

'Frank,' said Frank. 'Frank Penny.'

'Well, Mr Penny, didn't you hear what Mrs Parsons said?' he indicated to the woman who had taken his registration details and who was now clearing up her papers from the table. All the new students must have arrived. Frank thought it comical that he was being asked if he had heard Mrs Parsons, when she plainly struggled to hear anything herself. But the situation didn't warrant a smile - the professor was evidently annoyed.

'I don't know what you mean,' said Frank. The man's temperature seemed to increase a notch. Frank kept calm; he certainly wasn't going to be pushed around on his first day and, although he had learned to respect authority, he also knew that respect had to be earned.

'When Mrs Parsons tells you to take a seat, it doesn't mean go on a grand tour of the grounds, does it!' A group of boys sniggered behind the professor, who turned and glared. Immediately they stopped. He turned back to Frank. 'Well?'

'Well what?'

'Why aren't you sitting down?'

'I just wanted to look around,' said Frank, frankly irked by his attitude. The professor just continued to look at him. 'I'll go and sit down now, shall I?' Frank continued.

'That seems like a good idea,' said the man. Frank felt his eyes follow him as he shuffled on to the nearest seat. He put his shoulder bag down at his feet. It dawned on him for the first time that this was going to be different from home; that, in the confines of the academy, he might not be able to just do what he wanted.

The man, bubble seemingly burst, turned and strode back to the front, robes flapping as he went, all eyes following him. Frank noticed that an older student had followed the man in and was now standing a few paces behind him. The professor turned and a hush washed through the gathering as he addressed the assembled students.

'Good morning,' he said, 'and welcome to Excelsus Academy. My name is Professor Lanks and I am the Head of Intake for this year.' Great, thought Frank, he'd only been here for ten minutes and already he'd got up the nose of the man who would be in charge of them. 'If you have any problems or issues, or need any help with anything at all during your time here, then please feel free to ask me, my door is always open.' He paused. The students, full of attention, smiled back at him, 'I will be charting your progress through the academy and, whilst some of you will be more familiar than othes with what goes on here, be under no illusions that attending Excelsus brings with it great opportunity and responsibility for you all—'

At that moment the door opened again. There was a collective shudder as the hinges shrieked like banshees. Lanks, mid-sentence, stopped talking and turned; the look on his face showed he was clearly annoyed at the interruption.

Through the door came a tall, elegant woman; her long,

wavy, pink and blue hair hung to her waist. She was dressed in a golden robe, which was edged with blue zigzags and covered in tiny sequins that sparkled like a thousand stars in the sun. Among the sequins were delicately embroidered celestial objects that appeared to move on the material as if floating in their own galaxy. Lanks's look of annoyance changed instantly. He smiled broadly and took a small step backwards and to one side with a slight bow, ushering the woman to the central spot where he had just been standing. The woman glided across the grass. She had a hypnotic air of confidence and authority about her and a silence instantly fell over the gathering.

Frank, like the rest of the students, was captivated. He knew instantly who the woman was, even though he'd only read her name once. Aurora G Moonhunter.

AURORA MOONHUNTER

She was exactly how he had imagined her to be. Her face was long, her cheekbones accentuated her features and, even at the age of thirteen, Frank was able to discern that she was a very beautiful woman indeed.

She stood calmly at the head of the gathering, her presence radiating around the students. She had their absolute attention.

She looked at Lanks who still stood to the side.

'Can you get that door fixed,' she said calmly, but with an air of authority. An instruction rather than a request. Lanks nodded. She turned to the assembled students and surveyed them one by one as if trying to gauge the quality of her new charges. The arena went ghostly quiet - everything, including the grass itself, was holding its breath. Frank could have heard a pin drop. She walked forward a couple of paces.

'Good morning, students, and may I welcome you all to Excelsus Academy.' Her voice was soft and mellifluous. Hypnotic. Frank was as mesmerised as the rest of the gathering. It was as if she had immediately acquired a celebrity status amongst all the new students there, even though he didn't think she would ever have appeared in any of Phoebe's magazines.

'Most of you will be familiar with our work here and the learning that you will undertake, so that each and every one of you can achieve your potential and be assured of exceptional opportunities beyond your education. However, some of you may not be so aware.'

Frank definitely considered himself in the latter category. He even imagined that Moonhunter looked in his direction as she said it. He glanced around at his fellow students for the first time and noticed a few nodding.

'But, rest assured,' she continued, 'you are all here because we feel you are destined for greater things, to become some of the elite individuals for your respective lands. Most of you have, up until now, been learning the usual subjects at school' —Frank smiled inwardly - not him!— 'and we will continue with some of those where they are considered of benefit. But the rest of what you will learn here will be very different. Excelsus is about finding your special skill or skills. After all, this is the Academy for the Gallant and Gifted. Some of you will already know where your talents lie, but there will be others amongst you who will need to discover this and it is our job here at the academy to help you do just that.'

That sentence pricked Frank's interest. He'd still been looking around, a little distracted, but realised he ought to be giving her his full attention and her remarks made him sit up. Special talents? What on earth could she be referring to? What sort of talents? Was he some sort of undiscovered high-quality blacksmith, or perhaps a yet-to-be-trained master weaver? He guessed that the possibilities were endless, but he doubted he had any particular ability - if he had he was sure he would have been aware of it. After all, he had been brought up on a farm; he didn't think he was here to study for a diploma in advanced cow milking.

Moonhunter continued, 'The journey to achieving your potential may be long and might not be easy, and at Excelsus we demand the highest effort.' She paused. 'I know that most of you are from what would be considered as more fortunate backgrounds' — Frank noticed she looked at some of the better dressed people in the arena and smiled. They smiled back expectantly. He assumed these were the students whose parents paid to send them here— 'and that you feel that might afford you some special privileges, or that coming from a more influential family may give you some sway here. Let me tell you that it won't. Everyone here is considered equal.' The smiles on the faces quickly vanished, replaced with disgruntled expressions.

'I appreciate that it may take some of you some time to understand, but understand you will, and with understanding comes the beginning of the fulfilment of destiny.' She looked from face to face as she spoke, her eyes resting briefly on each one of them, somehow making them all feel special. Her charisma swallowed them up. 'Destiny may be a matter of chance, maybe we are all tied to it. We all have a choice of which road to walk down. It is in your moments of decision that your destiny is shaped. I simply wish you all to read the signposts correctly.'

Frank's head started to spin. He didn't really understand what she meant. What sort of destiny could he possibly have? Perhaps the signs on his road should just point back to Tresparrik Farm, or say 'Nowhere In Particular'.

'Now, Mr Lanks will be your Head of Intake. I see he has already introduced himself.' Lanks smiled and nodded in their general direction, as if he had been paid a compliment. 'He will take care of any immediate questions that you might have.' She looked around and everyone seemed to nod in acceptance. Frank was still trying to work out what all of this meant to him. It seemed that the others there either knew what they were there for, what their so-called special abilities were, or just blindly accepted what they were being told and would work out the rest as they went along in blissful ignorance. Those two options weren't for him. He'd been brought up to enquire if he was not sure about things and, after Moonhunter's address, his head was immediately filled with questions.

Moonhunter went on. 'Welcome once again; I wish you a happy and enlightening time here.' She turned to go and the older student, who had entered with Lanks, jolted into life and scampered over to open the door for her. The silence was suddenly broken.

'Excuse me!'

It was if someone else had spoken the words instead of him, or as if he'd said them in his head rather than out loud, and, as he uttered them, Frank immediately felt he might have made a mistake.

Moonhunter was about to disappear through the door but his

voice stopped her in her tracks. She snapped her head round and looked at him, her expression unchanged, still calm and difficult to read. She knew it was him that had spoken and Frank realised he had his hand up - a bit of a giveaway. Her look, although benign, withered him and he slowly dropped his hand. Naturally, everyone had turned in his direction. Most had worried expressions on their faces, probably concerned about what might happen to their new fellow classmate.

Frank stayed silent. He wasn't sure what the fuss was about; he certainly hadn't felt reticent about asking her about what was on his mind. After all, he only wanted some answers, but now the questions he was going to ask slipped from his mind and a lump appeared in his throat.

Moonhunter continued to study him. She turned and faced the arena and then, to Frank's surprise, she lifted her right arm and pointed all five of her slender fingers in his direction. She held them there and closed her eyes. Frank thought he might have imagined it but he felt a tiny jolt pass through him. At the same time, Moonhunter's multi-coloured hair and her gown appeared to pulse a deep crimson, the colour of blood. But he might have imagined that too. After a few moments, Moonhunter opened her eyes and dropped her arm.

'Frank Penny,' she said over the silence. His name hung in the air as she eyed him with apparent interest. Then she turned back and continued through the door and out of sight.

Frank was gobsmacked. There were around twenty new entrants sitting there. They'd never met and the only contact they'd had was her signature on the bottom of the letter he'd read in Jelly's study, weeks earlier. There was no way she could have possibly known his name unless she was the luckiest guesser in the world, which he doubted as, if initial impressions counted for anything, there was no way she struck him as the sort of person who would make herself look foolish with a wild stab in the dark. She'd just said his name and walked off, leaving him both intrigued and bemused, as well as feeling a little uncomfortable and embarrassed.

He was aware that the others were still looking at him. Those sitting in groups whispered to each other. Frank felt himself turning a bright shade of red. Luckily, Lanks was his surprise saviour.

'That was our principal, Aurora Moonhunter,' he said, breaking the trance that had descended on the group. Thankfully for Frank, everyone turned back to look at the front of the small arena and nodded in Lanks's direction. 'I think you'll all find her very fair … unless you get on the wrong side of her that is.' He looked pointedly at Frank.

Lanks picked up a pile of papers that was neatly stacked on the table. 'Now, students; first, here are your timetables.' He walked up and down the steps, handing them out 'And here is a map of the building. You'll need to get used to the academy layout quickly, otherwise you'll get lost … quickly.' The students immediately started to study the diagram that Lanks had just handed them.

'Now, I see some of you already have your academy shirts.' He looked around, eyes stopping on a number of the students sitting in the rows in front of Frank. For the first time, he took stock of the people he was to study with. He saw that, unlike himself, quite a few of them were smartly dressed. He wore his usual dark brown trousers and light brown shirt, the sort of scruffy stuff he always wore when he was at home. Practical, nice and comfy, he'd never needed anything else and his instructions had said that any clothing would be provided. Most of the students, however, were in black trousers or skirts and wore smart blue shirts that bore the now familiar vulture emblem of the academy. Obviously, these people knew what to wear on their first day and had already purchased their academy outfits either in the town or from wherever they had come from. Frank was pretty sure that the lack of any names on list three at St Barnabus meant there was no shop in Smithwood that stocked anything like that.

Lanks went on. 'Those of you who haven't, can you make your way to see Mrs O'Flynn at the kit store where you'll be provided with a supply of uniform items and other things. It's important that you wear a uniform at all times during your stay here. As for the rest of you, our head boy, Ralph Jackson, will be happy to talk to you about life here at the academy and answer any questions you might have.' Lanks indicated to the older student who had been standing unnoticed behind him. The boy nodded. 'You'll see that the timetable begins with Professor Algernon's Astronomy class after lunch at one o'clock, so you are free to familiarise yourselves with the academy until then, and you will need to find the canteen at lunchtime. You'll see the common room is situated right next to it. Now, so that you don't disturb the other students, I suggest you take a walk around the grounds.' Lanks indicated towards the area over the back of the seating, where Frank had ventured earlier. 'Unless you've already done so,' he said, looking at Frank.

Frank had been distracted by a couple of crows mobbing a buzzard overhead. He was aware of the others getting up and starting to disperse but he stayed seated as the well-dressed among them shuffled past him to the top of the arena and disappeared from view. He stood as the final few passed by and, as he did so, he found himself face to face with a familiar-looking boy. Frank recognised him immediately. It was the boy he'd glimpsed briefly through the window of the raven-clad carriage which had nearly taken his toes off a couple of days before. The boy, who was about the same height as Frank and maybe a year older, was followed by a fierce-looking girl and two other boys – one was large and gorilla-like, with a big forehead, the other slight, blond and well-groomed. The boy from the carriage had long, black, swept-back hair, well-coiffed, and a chiselled chin. He stopped talking to his accomplices and looked Frank up and down, eyes full of distaste.

'Something the matter?' he spat in a rich, well-heeled accent, curling his lip. His pals all looked at Frank and sneered. Frank said nothing; he just looked back, unimpressed. The boy looked him up and down again. 'Why are you dressed like a beggar?' he laughed, flicking the lapel of Frank's shirt, the other three laughing with him.

It was obvious to Frank who the leader of this little gang was, but he kept his silence - he could sense trouble. It was his first day and the last thing he wanted was any sort of altercation, especially the way things had already started.

'Looks like that bloke we saw sleeping in the gutter last night,' said the clean-cut, blond boy.

'Yeah, but not as well-dressed,' said the girl as they all laughed. Frank smiled disarmingly, but this only seemed to rile the dark-haired boy.

'Best not forget your manners when you're around me,' he said. 'Know your place. Know what I mean?' Frank just continued to return the boy's look, unflinching, still unimpressed. The boy didn't seem to know how to react to this; he just looked at his friends, shifting uncomfortably.

'Look, he's got a locket round his neck, like a right girl,' said the gorilla. The dark-haired boy sneered and went to snatch it. As quick as lightning, Frank grabbed the boy's wrist and held it firmly, making his hand grasp at thin air. The boy made an involuntary gasp as he sensed Frank's strength and, for a moment, looked extremely shocked. Frank's quick reflexes and strength seemed to catch him off guard - Frank could feel him try to push against his grip, but to no avail. It was then that Frank noticed the unusual emblem embroidered on the inside sleeve of the boy's shirt, just by the wrist. It was a black scorpion, stitched perfectly within a red circle, with the number 821 neatly sewn underneath. He glanced quickly at the other three and could see that they also had the same monogram sewn neatly onto their shirts.

'Everything okay here?' came Lanks's voice from the back of the group.

'Yeah, sir. I was walking past, minding my own business, talking to Chetto here, and this boy just grabbed my arm, didn't he?' The dark-haired boy indicated to his friends to agree with him. They all nodded and mumbled to back him up. Frank shook his head incredulously.

'Well I suggest you ungrab Mr Emerald's arm,' said Lanks, pointedly. Frank held on for a moment longer and then let go, not breaking eye contact. Emerald pulled away quickly and rubbed his wrist, at the same time trying to act as if he was okay.

'Well, Mr Penny, you've certainly made an impression on your first morning here.' Frank looked at Lanks, whose expression was one of disapproval. Emerald smirked.

'Yeah, well you can take an instant dislike to some people,' said Frank, looking at Emerald. Lanks appeared to ignore him and turned to the small gang.

'Now, run along you lot,' he said to Emerald and his gang of three.

'I'll see you again, Penny,' spat Emerald, giving Frank a last look before he sloped off with his pals in tow. Frank didn't respond. He'd always made a habit of avoiding speaking to people he didn't like unless he really had to.

'I suggest you head off to the kit store before you get into any more trouble,' said Lanks.

'Who was that?' asked Frank.

'Oh him? That's Icarus Emerald, comes from a *very* wealthy family. His father and grandfather attended the academy, as did generations before that I don't doubt. The academy is very grateful to have his father as a benefactor. I'm sure you and he will get on very well, eventually.' An interesting comment. Frank wasn't convinced. He chose his company carefully and already didn't like the sound of Icarus Emerald one bit. 'Mind you,' Lanks continued, staring in the direction in which Emerald had disappeared. 'Perhaps some people need taking down a peg or two.'

The arena was now deserted, except for Frank and the professor.

'Why did Mrs Parsons call me a meritter?' asked Frank.

'Oh, that's just the term some use for those students who are here purely on their ability, or potential,' Lanks replied.

'You mean we don't pay?'

'Exactly.'

'What about Icarus Emerald?'

'Not quite the same,' said Lanks after a brief pause. Frank assumed that Emerald must be a fee payer, especially judging by the way he was turned out and the magnificent coach he had arrived in.

'But I only gave Mrs Parsons my address,' said Frank. Lanks gave him a strange look but said nothing. Frank let it drop - it didn't matter.

He looked at the map Lanks had given him. 'Now, how do I get to the kit store?' he said to himself.

Lanks eyed him for a moment. 'Well, I should let you find your own way really, but, seeing as it's your first day, I suppose I can help,' said Lanks.

'Oh, don't worry,' said Frank, 'I'll find it easily enough, I'm good with maps and I'm sure you're busy enough.' But, to his surprise, Lanks let out a loud whistle.

'Bertie!' he shouted back towards the academy. Frank looked to where Lanks had shouted and saw a small highland terrier appear from behind the side door and come bounding up the terrace towards them. It was the same dog he'd met earlier. It stopped just a yard or two away, tongue hanging out, looking like a loaf of bread with ears. His eyes were fixed on Lanks, awaiting his next instruction.

'Kit store,' Lanks said to the dog. Bertie turned and headed down the terrace and towards the oak door. Lanks turned to Frank. 'Best not keep him waiting,' he said. 'Gets a bit distracted if you don't keep him on his toes.' He gave Frank a limp smile. Frank wasn't sure what to make of Lanks or, indeed, Bertie. He assumed he was to follow the dog who would lead him to where he wanted to go. Odd.

He adjusted his shoulder bag and headed down to the door, where Bertie waited patiently for him.

'Oh, and Mr Penny,' Lanks called after him. Frank turned and shook his mop of hair out of his eyes, 'I'll be watching you.'

Frank paused, then turned and opened the door, taking care not to open it too far in case he woke the dead, and ran after Bertie who had shot off down the corridor.

12

THE INVENTOR

Despite the bad start, Frank was happy with the way his first day had passed. He'd followed Bertie to the kit store where he'd been supplied with five brand new Excelsus shirts and trousers, all bearing the now familiar vulture crest and his intake number, but lacking the scorpion monogram he'd seen on Emerald's sleeve. He'd never seen a design like that before and knew it must mean something, otherwise why would it be there? It was as if he belonged to some sort of exclusive club and, even though Frank had taken an instant dislike to Emerald, he had to admit to himself he was intrigued.

Frank had taken time to study the timetable Lanks had given them. There was plenty that piqued his interest, such as Weapons and Combat Theory, Falconry, Survival Skills, and Wild Nature which hinted at the unknown. Cunning and Dexterity sounded highly unusual. Then there were those subjects that that made him sigh: Meditation, and History, in all its forms, sounded so dull that Frank thought he would struggle to stay awake during the lessons.

After their introduction to Astronomy, when the ancient Professor Algernon had explained they would be studying the mystical elements of night sky, which Frank thought sounded very interesting, the later afternoon lesson had been taken by Professor Markowitz, Myths and Legends master, who whetted their appetites with tales of flying horses and mystical maidens, making them sound more real than legend. Frank loved her animated descriptions of the beasts and strange people that featured in the stories and wondered if, in fact, there was more to the tales than just fantasy.

He was happy to keep himself to himself. He was comfortable in his own company and had always tended to keep a distance in larger groups. Some took this as shyness and always seemed to blame the fact he was home educated, but the fact of the matter was that he just liked to weigh things up before getting involved with something. He'd gone to the common room and chatted briefly to a boy called Eric, who was from a small village in the north of Byeland and whose family ran an arrow and sword making business, but Frank didn't feel it was right to ask why he was there, or if he had any particular gifts.

He'd managed to avoid Emerald and his entourage and at the end of the day he left the academy with a spring in his step. He walked across the bridge, under the gaze of the massive vulture, and headed across the plaza to Iron Lane. As he crossed the marble pavement his attention was caught by the row of shops to his left. There was something odd about the frontages, something out of place. He couldn't put his finger on it at first. Then he realised that one of the shops stuck out like a sore thumb. In the midst of the high class couture and up-market businesses there was a run-down, scruffy-looking shop front that looked entirely at odds with its surroundings, like a very poor relation amongst its well-heeled neighbours.

Frank was drawn to it like a moth to a flame, curious as to how such a place could exist in this part of town. He had begun to understand the look Mrs Parsons had given him when he'd said he was staying at Murgatroid Square. It was apparent that Iron Lane was the better end of town, whereas Polly and Norris appeared to live in the less salubrious part. That must have been why she could tell he was a meritter and not a fee payer. Frank couldn't care less about the shops with large price tags or the pompous-looking people who worked in them and looked down their noses at others. But this place was different. He couldn't help asking himself what this ramshackle old shop was doing staring down the throat of Excelsus Academy, and what went on inside.

He wandered over and stood looking at the large front window.

He could hardly see through it because of the dirt and grime that stuck to the glass like a thin film of toffee. There was a large crack at the top of the window which was stuck over with tape. He looked up at the sign above the shop for a clue as to what the place was, but it was so worn and faded it gave nothing away. He cupped his hand over his eyes and leaned against the window to get a better look inside. His view wasn't clear but he could just make out a large table in the middle of the shop, rows of shelves to the side and objects hanging from the ceiling, like the pots and pans in Aunt Rachel's kitchen. He could hear a faint grinding noise coming from within, but the place seemed deserted. He wondered if anyone ever actually went in. Well, thought Frank, if no one else does, I certainly will. He moved to the door and pushed it open.

There was the tinkle of a small bell, just like the one in Polly's shop. Frank went in and was immediately hit by a burning smell that cut through the dust and dirt that seemed to coat everything in sight. The table Frank had seen from the outside was much larger than he had first thought and on it sat an odd looking metal object. The grinding noise seemed to be coming from underneath the table. The floor and shelves were covered with strange-looking things of all shapes and made from different materials, the like of which Frank had never seen. An array of tools hung in rows on the wall. It was cluttered and jumbled and he was instantly spellbound by the place. It was a hundred times more interesting than anything he'd seen before.

He reached over to a dresser and picked up a roughly-beaten metal object, shaped like a long cone and with straps on either side. He turned it over in his hands and walked further into the room.

'Hello?' he called.

There was a loud bump from beneath the table and the grinding noise stopped.

'Ow, damn and blast it,' came a voice and then, from behind the table, a figure stood up, rubbing the top of his bald head. The man stood there for a moment looking around, as if he wasn't quite sure he had actually heard anyone speak. Then he saw Frank, still toying with the odd object he had picked up.

'Hell's teeth!' he said, taking a step back.

The man's bald head was surrounded at the edges by bushy grey hair, which also grew out of his ears. A pair of round, wire-rimmed spectacles were perched on the end of his nose and he wore an oily pair of overalls which had seen better days, but not a laundry.

'Hello, er ... can I help you?'

Frank looked at the man. 'What's this?' he asked, holding up the metal object he had been inspecting, not really sure what else to say. The man regarded him oddly.

'What's what?' he replied nervously.

'This,' said Frank, pointing to the thing in his hand.

The man seemed stuck for words. He removed his glasses. 'Oh, that. Yes, well, just something I knocked up, like most of the things you see here,' he said, waving an arm around the room. 'Why on earth would you want to know what it is anyway? No use to you.'

'Just interested,' said Frank, undeterred. He got the feeling this man was a bit of an eccentric, but if he'd made the objects in the room, like the one he had picked up, then he was impressed, not to mention fascinated.

Frank put the object down and considered picking up something that looked like a long pair of tweezers with blades set at right angles to the ends. The man watched him like a mouse watches a cat.

'Can I help you, young man?' he repeated, picking up an old cloth and proceeding to wipe his hands, although Frank thought it would probably make his hands even dirtier, judging by its condition. 'It's just that I don't get many people coming into my workshop. Well, as a matter of fact, I never get *any* people coming into my workshop.' He smiled to himself as he stood scratching his head and fiddling with his overalls. He was kindly looking and Frank detected a warmth about him.

'I just saw your shop and thought it looked kind of, well' - Frank searched for the right word - 'different,' he said. 'Different to the others, I mean.'

'Oh yes, dare say it does. Most folks just ignore me now, but if you're new around here it can look a bit ... different, as you say,' the man said.

'Oh, I meant it in a good way,' said Frank. 'Interesting, I guess; that's why I thought I'd come in and just have a look.'

The man seemed to perk up a bit. 'Well, I'm glad you think so,' he said with a smile. 'Atticus Blackburn at your service,' he said, looking at Frank, then at the cloth with which he'd been wiping his hands. He gave Frank an embarrassed look.

'Hello, Mr Blackburn. I'm Frank. I've just started at the academy across the road.' Blackburn peered at him above his glasses. His eyes narrowed.

'If you don't mind me saying, you don't seem like the normal sort of youngster the academy gets over there,' he said, his tone guarded. Frank shrugged. He wasn't quite sure what Blackburn meant and he was more interested in what went on in the workshop.

'What do you actually do here?' he asked.

'Good question, Frank,' said Blackburn. 'Sometimes ask myself the same thing. I suppose you could call me a ... well, let me think ... yes, a maker of odd things.'

Frank looked at him quizzically.

'Maker of odd things?'

'Yes,' said Blackburn. 'Take that thing you were holding when I ... er ... ' - he rubbed his head as if reliving the bump - 'yes, well, that thing.'

He walked over and picked up the object Frank had been holding a moment earlier. Blackburn regarded it, as if it was something new to him too, then held it up.

'I met a man who told me he used to always burn his beard on some long candles he had in his home. So I made this device to go over his beard to stop him going up in flames every time he needed to use them.'

Frank could see now that the long cone would fit over a man's beard. Blackburn made a play of showing how the two straps were meant to fasten onto the ears, but didn't quite finish the demonstration.

'What's it still doing here, then?' asked Frank politely.

'Unfortunately, I never saw him again.'

'Why, what happened?'

'That evening, he was at home seeing to his stove, or so I'm told, when he tripped over his cat. So, in order to avoid getting singed as always, unfortunate man accidentally dropped his candle into a large container full of paraffin and ...' His voice trailed off. Frank got the picture. 'Whole house went up; all they found of him were his leather boots. If only he'd waited a day or two and used my device, he'd still be alive today. There was a silence. 'Still, can't help some people can you,' he smiled.

'So you're an inventor, then?'

'That's it, well, that's one way of putting it. Others might say I'm a little eccentric, a bit of a tinker man, but I don't bother them and they don't bother me and so it goes on.'

'Wow,' said Frank. He'd never met an inventor before and this man seemed to be surrounded with hundreds of objects he had made. Frank was unable to tell if any of them were finished or working, but the thought of having a mind that could create these things was fascinating to him.

'And can you invent anything?'

'Oh, I don't really know, perhaps just about anything. I get asked to make things by people who know what I can do; otherwise, I just fill my time fiddling around. A bit like today.' He glanced down at the table and the as yet unrecognisable object that lay there.

'Your shop isn't like the others around this part of town, is it?' said Frank. Blackburn smiled.

'I get what you mean,' he said. 'Some would say it's a bit of a boil that needs lancing. There have been plenty of times when the locals have tried to move me on, even tried to buy my shop off me. Offered me a king's ransom, they did. But, no, they'd probably turn it into a swanky bistro thing, or some hoity-toity interior designer's.' He screwed his nose up at the thought. 'And that's the last thing the town needs. So they can keep their money. Yes, I'm a bit different, I suppose, but sometimes a place needs that, don't you think?' Frank thought so. 'So I'm happy to stay here, wind them up a bit if you know what I mean, eh!' Frank smiled. An interior designer wouldn't know where to start in here, he thought.

'Don't let me keep you,' said Blackburn.

'Oh, it's okay, I've finished for the day. I was just on the way home, well it's not really my home.'

'And where might that be?'

'Polly's Tea Shop, on— '

'Murgatroid Square,' said Blackburn with a wide grin. 'Yes, I know it well. You might say I even know Polly, although casually acquainted would be a better description. Well, I have lived here all my life so I should know, shouldn't I? Finest pasties in town.'

Frank nodded and looked around. There were different tools and contraptions scattered around and, at the rear of the workshop, the coals on a forge of sorts glowed bright orange. The room ticked with the pace of an assortment of clocks and other gadgets. This was his sort of place, weird and wonderful, full of creativity and ideas.

'Do you fancy some nettle tea before you go?' asked Blackburn. 'I've got some brewed on the forge back there.'

'Okay,' said Frank and followed him to the rear of the workshop where a battered old copper kettle and a large chipped floral teapot sat on a small hotplate on the edge of the coals. There was one mug on the side and Blackburn fussed around looking for another. He found one in a cupboard and took a look inside. Frank assumed he was checking for anything growing in it and thought he might be disappointed if there wasn't, in case it was some great new discovery.

'Ah ha, that looks okay,' he said to himself. He took a cloth, picked the teapot up by the handle and poured two mugs of hot, yellowish-green liquid. There were two dusty and battered old armchairs at the side of the forge. The upholstery was tatty and scarred with burns and scorch marks so they fitted in perfectly with their surroundings. A large ginger cat sat comfortably on one of them, eyes closed, oblivious to the presence of the two men.

'Come on now, Cicero,' said Blackburn, chivvying the cat off the seat. The fat ginger feline opened its eyes and looked back at the man as if to tell him to get lost. It closed its eyes again and went back to sleep.

'Ah, typical,' sighed Blackburn. 'You sit there Frank, my boy.' He indicated to the empty chair. Frank hesitated, conscious that his nice new shiny uniform was about to meet its doom, but, not wishing to appear rude, sank down into the chair which, despite its shabby appearance, was very comfy. Blackburn perched himself carefully on the edge of the other chair, not wishing to disturb the slumbering orange ball of fuzz.

Frank sipped his tea, but stopped and nearly choked on a mouthful as snow started to fall steadily from the ceiling of the workshop. He sat there open mouthed.

'What the—'

'Oh, damn nuisance,' said Blackburn. 'You just ignore that, Frank. Just comes on sometimes. I was working on a watering machine months ago and the thing, well, blew up, and some of the formula ended up on the ceiling, there. Ever since, now and then, it just starts. Don't worry; it'll stop in a moment.' Frank just stared, wondering if he was about to be caught in a blizzard, but, as quickly as it had started, the snow stopped, leaving a dusting of white on Blackburn's workbench.

'So how are you enjoying the academy?' asked Blackburn.

'Well, it's only my first day, but, so far, so good.'

'Not like your old school, I guess?'

'Oh, I've never been to school.'

'No?'

'No, I'm home educated. I was brought up on my dad's farm.' Blackburn looked surprised, but impressed.

'Well, good for you, Frank,' he said. 'Bet you learned a hell of a lot more than in a classroom. Can't say school did me much good. I preferred being out with my dad, doing interesting things and just, well, you know, mucking around with ... er ... stuff like this.' He cast a finger around the room. 'Know what I mean?' Frank knew exactly what he meant and smiled. Perhaps he'd stumbled on a kindred spirit. Blackburn continued. 'Missing your mum and dad?'

'My mum's dead, but I miss my dad a bit,' Frank took another sip.

'Oh, sorry to hear that,' said Blackburn sincerely.

'That's okay; I was only a baby when she died. I keep a picture of her in my locket.' Frank took the chain in his fingers and showed it to Blackburn who smiled and nodded.

'Well, good for you. Best place to keep a picture of your mother, right by your heart.'

'How long have you been an inventor?' he asked.

'Oh, forever and a bit, as my old dad used to say,' laughed Blackburn.

'Was he an inventor too?'

'No, he was handy though and he was an interesting man, my old dad. Helped to modernise the academy in his day. Spent years over there. I've still got the blueprints somewhere from the work he did. Knew all that building's secrets, he did.' Blackburn tapped the side of his nose with an index finger and gave Frank a wink. He shifted on the edge of the chair.

'Secrets?' said Frank, all ears. 'What secrets?'

Blackburn looked at Frank as if he might have inadvertently given something away. 'Ah, nothing really, just kidding you, but a building as ancient as that is bound to have things to hide, don't you think?' Frank wasn't sure what to think. He thought there were lots of old buildings around the place that were just that - old buildings. Why any of them would harbour any secrets was beyond him; they were just bricks and mortar after all. Blackburn changed the subject.

'No, been here years, before this part of town got all grand. Shame the old local businesses had to go. Nice bunch. Most of them have moved across town now, but, as I said, I'm staying put. Good view, don't you think?' Frank looked over at the grime pasted window through which it was hard to make out anything and couldn't but beg to differ. He could just make out the stone vulture through the glass, but not much else. 'Must say that nothing much escapes me in here,' Blackburn went on. Frank thought just the opposite - that everything would escape Blackburn's attention, unless it pressed itself up against the window - but he nodded anyway.

Frank finished his tea. He felt he ought to be getting back to Polly's. She might be worrying about him on his first day. He stood and put his mug on the side.

'Thanks for the tea, Mr Blackburn,' he said and slung his bag over his shoulder, ready to go.

'Hell's teeth, is that the time?' exclaimed Blackburn, 'I should be getting on with my latest ... well, yes.' He stood and went to a drawer, in which were different sized metal cogs. He picked up a handful, sorted through them and shoved a selection into his pocket, discarding the rest. As Frank got up, Cicero gave him an indifferent look.

'Nice to meet you,' said Frank as he went to go. 'Do you mind if I call in again? I'd love to see what you're doing.'

Blackburn looked delighted.

'Yes, of course you can, and thanks for calling in, Frank, you're welcome any time.'

13

HARDCASTLE JONES

Frank largely enjoyed his first few weeks at Excelsus. Despite the fact that, while growing up, he had come to see a more formal and structured education as something he didn't think was worthwhile, he found some of the subjects, such as alchemy and astronomy, very interesting, even if his desire to learn more about them ran at a faster pace than that of the professor or the other students. This he found eternally frustrating. He would just be getting into a subject, asking loads of questions, when the lesson ended and it was time to move on to something he really wasn't interested in - like history - and his interest had to wait days to be revived. What sort of way was that to learn, Frank had thought. No wonder Phoebe wasn't that bothered with what she was being taught at St Barnabus, if she was made to study things that held no attraction, just so she could get some meaningless qualification. His first experience of a prescribed education was very different from the freedom he'd had at home and he'd written to his dad to let him know how he was getting on. But, whatever his early impressions, he felt he had to give it time to make sure he didn't jump to any hasty conclusions.

He started to discover a bit about why some of the other students in his intake were there. A friendly, dark-haired girl called Meredith Tulip told him her dad was fluent in twenty-seven languages and worked in some important department in the council, and that she hoped to do the same. Jamie Dobbs, a skinny-looking boy who sniffed all the time, as if he had constant hay fever, was the son of an army officer and said he came from generations of soldiers, although Frank thought he looked as if he would struggle to even pick up a sword, let alone swing one in combat. Some, including the Maddison twins, who kept themselves to themselves and seemed to whisper endlessly in lessons and whenever he passed them in the corridor, appeared very secretive about their backgrounds, and Frank didn't feel comfortable asking anyone, directly, about their exact gifts, just in case he had to admit that he didn't have any.

He also found out, from Professor Lanks, that everyone would be studying all the subjects on the curriculum for at least two years, when they would then begin to take specialist tutoring in the subject that they were gifted in to become proficient in their particular skill. Frank felt like pointing out that Excelsus might be teaching him for a good deal longer than that, given he had no skills worth noting, and imagined himself as a thirty-year-old, sitting at a desk next to a ten-year-old expert alchemist, looking and feeling more than a bit stupid. Still, at least there were no exams.

He'd begun to find his way around the warren of corridors. Some were austere and oak-panelled, some were stone, while others were smooth, white and modern. Frank assumed the stone walls were the older parts of the building and that Blackburn's dad may have had a hand in some of the more up-to-date looking parts. He'd also become used to avoiding tripping over the array of dogs in all shapes and sizes that seemed to endlessly walk the corridors running errands for their masters, skipping through the legs of the students as they went about their business.

At the end of that morning's Alchemy class, in which Professor Truelove, an engaging and lively teacher, had given them an introduction to the art of turning ordinary earth into a mild coffee, she asked him if he would return a couple of books to the library. Her golden retriever had developed a painful limp, so needed to rest, and Frank was happy to help, so he stayed to collect them at the end of the lesson.

He headed out of the room in the direction of the library, passing a large pair of ornately carved deer that sat at the end of the corridor. Alchemy had been the lesson before lunch, so the corridors were busy with students who had finished their morning studies and were now heading to the canteen to eat. Frank had got into the habit of eating early and then heading outside to make the most of the air which, due to the academy's proximity to the coast, was clean, crisp and fresh. He was happy to escape the confines of the classroom and felt at ease just sitting underneath a tree and reading, or exploring the grounds. He'd even ventured up on to the walls where he had a great view of the forest to the rear of the academy and an even better one over towards the sea. The river that separated the academy from the town wound its way a few hundred yards beyond the academy walls and disappeared off a high cliff in a torrential cascade. The waterfall spat and frothed as it dragged the calm water kicking and screaming to the sea below. In contrast, delicate rainbows rose calmly into the sky above the torrent. Frank saw it as a thing of beauty, but not to be underestimated.

On his way to the library, Frank approached one of the staircases that led up to the walkway at the top of the academy walls. Behind the staircase, Frank noticed, was a door that was slightly ajar. As he passed, he became aware of voices on the other side and there was something about the sound that made him stop. It sounded to Frank that there was some kind of altercation, even though the voices seemed somewhat muted, as if whoever was talking didn't want to be overheard. He also thought he recognised one of them.

He stopped and listened.

'Come on, Bones, hand them over or I'll have to get Woods here to convince you to give them to me,' said one of the voices.

'Yeah, hand them over, you heard what he said,' said another voice, its tone menacing.

Frank put the books down and pushed the door open. He knew who he would find, even before the light from the corridor illuminated the inside of the small store cupboard. Emerald.

There were three boys somehow crammed into the tiny room. Emerald stood just inside the doorway while one of his sidekicks, who Frank recognised as Sebastian Woods, the heavyweight thug, held another boy by the lapels. The boy had sunk back towards the shelves that covered the inside walls, which made it look like Woods was holding him up. His shirt puffed out as his weight strained against Woods's grip.

As Frank pushed the door open he cast a shadow across the small space. The voices stopped and all of them looked in his direction.

Emerald spoke. 'What do you want, farm boy?' he said, giving Frank a scornful look. Frank said nothing. He looked at the boy who was being held up. Dishevelled and thin, he shot Frank a wide-eyed, grateful look back. Frank remembered something his dad had told him - that it is important to stand up for yourself, but even more important to stand up for someone who can't stand up for themselves.

'Interrupted something, have I, Emerald?' Frank said after he had taken a moment to absorb what was going on. He looked directly into Emerald's eyes. Emerald twitched.

'Sod off and mind your own business, Penny. Haven't you got a cow to milk or something?' he hissed.

'Yeah, run along now,' said Woods in a menacing tone.

Emerald shot his friend a look. 'I'll deal with this,' he said. Woods immediately looked sullen at the reprimand. Emerald turned back to Frank. 'Don't you have somewhere to go? Be a good chap and close the door behind you.' Frank ignored him, he knew a bully when he saw one.

'Good job I took a detour,' said Frank, 'seeing as you don't exactly look like you're making a new friend here.' Emerald's face creased into its usual sneer but he looked unsure as towhat to do next. Frank reasoned that he wasn't used to anyone standing up to him and he certainly wasn't going to let him get the better of either him or the wimpish boy he and his friend had in their clutches.

'What do *you* know?' said Emerald, still looking like he wasn't sure what to do. 'Perhaps me and Woods here were getting acquainted with ... er ... him,' he nodded in the direction of the boy who was visibly more relaxed at the thought of Frank coming to his rescue.

'If this is you getting to know someone, perhaps you'd prefer to take your chances getting to know me?' said Frank calmly, throwing down the challenge to Emerald.

'Don't push it, Penny; you don't want to mess with me. My father would have you run out of here faster than you could say sheep dip.' His sidekick sniggered.

Frank wasn't impressed. The moment Emerald had hidden behind the veil of his wealthy and powerful father, he knew what sort of individual he was dealing with.

'I've wrestled bigger hogs than you, Emerald,' Frank said. 'I'm sure your mates would love to see you tied by the hands and feet, face down in the dirt where you belong. You run to your dad if you want to, but leave him alone.' He pointed to the boy. Emerald ran his hand through his swept back hair as if considering his options and looked around the small room.

'Come on, Woods,' he said finally. 'Let's leave these two losers to it.' Woods let loose his grip on the boy he was holding. The boy evidently wasn't expecting this to happen so soon and fell back against a pile of boxes, sending them toppling on top of him.

'Ha!' laughed Emerald. 'Serves you right, you snivelling little worm. Perhaps I'll see you later.'

'Don't count on it,' said Frank. Emerald turned to go. Frank stepped to one side of the small doorway to allow the two boys to vacate the room.

'Huh. Farm boy,' Emerald muttered and pushed his way out, making sure he barged Frank in the process. Woods followed and the two of them disappeared into the busy passageway.

The inside of the room fell silent and Frank turned towards the boy who was still awkwardly trapped under the boxes, arms outstretched. He took a couple of paces, grabbed one of his hands and yanked him upright with a single pull. The boy brushed himself down.

'Thanks, mate,' he said, full of gratitude. 'Not sure what I'd have done if you hadn't come in like that. Emerald and his cronies. Bunch of idiots if you ask me.' Frank smiled. He'd seen the boy in his classes but hadn't paid much attention to him. He was quiet and nondescript, perhaps the sort of person that the likes of Emerald found easy prey. The boy smiled back.

'I'm Hardcastle Jones,' he said, still dusting himself off. 'My friends call me Cas.'

'Frank Penny.'

'Yeah, I know,' said Cas. 'You're the one who had a little run-in with Moonhunter on the first day. I remember that.' He sounded impressed but Frank wasn't grateful for the reminder. He'd forgotten about that little episode and hoped others had too.

'Oh, that,' was all he could say.

'Yeah, cool. You don't want to be messing with Moonhunter.'

'I wasn't messing with anyone,' Frank retorted.

'Sorry, didn't mean to ... well, it was cool anyway.'

Frank looked at the boy. He was about the same height as Frank, but he was lanky and his clothes didn't fit. They hung on him like a scarecrow, as did his unkempt, dark hair which drooped around his pale face. He didn't appear like the sort who could look after himself in the hands of someone like Emerald and Frank felt a degree of pity for him, while, at the same time, feeling pleased with himself that he'd stood up to Emerald.

'I'm taking some books back to the library for Professor Truelove, then I was going to get some lunch. You can come along with me if you like.'

Cas looked pleased.

'Okay,' was all he said. They stood for a moment, then Frank picked up the books from where he had left them and the two of them headed off in the direction of the library.

* * *

'So, what was Emerald after?' asked Frank, as they sat down in the canteen with their plates of liver and bacon. Frank gave a nod to

Eric as he sat alongside.

'Oh, he wanted me to give him these,' said Cas, reaching into his pocket and pulling out a crumpled, brown paper bag. He offered it to Frank, who peered into it. All he saw were some small, round black objects that looked like sweets.

'They look like sweets,' he said matter-of-factly, looking up at Cas.

'That's because they are,' said Cas with a hint of a laugh. 'No fooling you, Frank.' Frank was puzzled.

'I don't get it.' He had assumed that someone like Emerald would be after something valuable, not an old bag of confectionery.

'They're liquorice toffees,' explained Cas. 'Want one?' Frank loved liquorice toffees. He reached into the bag and took one. He squeezed the small round object and popped it into his mouth.

'I still don't get it,' said Frank as he chewed, his words becoming slightly muffled as the sticky toffee welded itself to his teeth. 'Why on earth would Emerald want to rough you up over a bag of toffees? Although I must admit, they are pretty tasty.'

'Probably because he can. I don't think he needs an excuse to pick on someone like me,' said Cas in a resigned tone. The thought of someone just picking on this boy because it amused him annoyed Frank. 'I had a bag of these on the first day and he and his gang came up to me and demanded one each, just like that. I thought if I let them all have one they'd leave me alone, but then he's been on my back every day since, wanting them all. Seems to want me to give him my whole supply. My gran makes them. She also gave me some sherbet lemons and pear drops, but these are the tastiest and she gave me a pretty good stock for my stay here. I thought I'd have to give all of these to Emerald - before you came to the rescue, that is. Thanks.'

'Well, let's hope that's the last time you'll have any problems from him,' said Frank, warming to Cas.

'Wowzer, that would be good. I hope you're right. Thanks Frank,' he said sincerely.

'Don't mention it. Creeps like that get right under my skin.'

'You're not afraid of him?' said Cas, finishing his toffee and tucking into his dinner while it was still hot.

'Pah, not likely. As I said, I've dealt with meaner and nastier looking farm animals than him. My dad's farmhand, Brigg, taught me not to worry about that sort of thing, he'd say to just ignore things. "The nightingale doesn't stop singing when it hears the annoying knocking of the woodpecker", or something like that.'

'What does that mean?'

'No idea,' replied Frank and the two of them laughed at Brigg's expense. 'Goodness, these really are delicious. Good job he didn't get them off you; I wouldn't've wanted to miss having one.'

'Not sure it's a fair swap,' said Cas. 'You get Emerald off my back and I give you a toffee.'

Frank tried to laugh but found his teeth had momentarily stuck together.

'Anyway, I think he might be missing something himself,' Cas said mysteriously. Frank creased his brow, curious at the comment. Cas reached into his pocket, again, and pulled out a comb and a mirror. He dangled them in the air.

'What ... where did you get those?'

'They're Emerald's. I managed to relieve him of them in the store cupboard back there.' said Cas with a mischievous look on his face.

'How did you manage that?' asked Frank, somewhat impressed that Cas had managed to take them from Emerald without him noticing. Cas seemed to consider his response.

'Well, let's just say I have a talent towards the ... light-fingered,' he replied furtively.

Frank's hand instinctively went up to his locket and he was relieved to find it was still in place. Cas noticed.

'Oh, no need to worry, Frank, I would only pick the pocket of a git like Emerald. You're safe,' he laughed. Frank breathed an inward sigh of relief and managed a smile. He had a feeling he and Cas were going to get along.

'So, what, you mean you can' - Frank chose his words - 'lift things from people without them knowing?' He didn't like to use the term 'pickpocket' as it seemed to him like accusing Cas of being a sneaky thief.

'Sure, well, most of the time. I'm sort of an expert, although I have been caught before. Luckily, I've always got a good excuse. It's a family thing; call it our special talent if you like. You could say I come from a long line of pilferers, but sleight of hand appears to be in my blood and it's a kind of a gift, I reckon.'

Frank understood. Gallant and gifted. He was unsure whether coming from a long line of thieves was good gift to have, but the Cunning and Dexterity lessons began to make sense.

'So is that why you're here?' he asked, now quite intrigued by his new friend's ability.

'Yeah. Well, I think so. My dad was here, so was my granddad, and my older brother's still here. Our talent, if you can call it that, goes back generations, so I guess that's why I've been selected. To hone my skill.' This was the first time Frank had discussed with anyone, in detail, the reason why they were here, especially because of his own lack of any particular ability.

'So what does your dad do now?' he asked, remembering his dad had told him that students went on to serve their land in different ways, using the talents they had, and he was curious what benefit a master of sleight of hand might bring. Cas seemed to consider his response again.

'D'you know, I'm not really sure. He's never told me. I have asked him, but he never seems to give me a straight answer.'

'Oh' said Frank. 'Where does he work?'

'I don't know that either,' said Cas. Both boys laughed.

'Well, who does he work for?' said Frank, still chuckling.

'Oh, I do know that; he works for the council. But it's a bit secret, like he's doing some sort of undercover work or something. Now you mention it, it seems a bit cloak and dagger, but I've never thought anything of it.'

'Perhaps he's a spy,' Frank speculated.

'Or an assassin,' joked Cas.

'Yeah, using his skills to creep up on his chosen target.' Frank made a throttling gesture with his own hands and pretended to strangle himself. Cas chuckled loudly, causing other students, who were busily eating their lunch, to look round at them. Both boys became conscious that they were being looked at and quickly went back to eating their food.

'So you're here on merit.'

'Yeah, we're not the richest of families.' Frank had noticed the state of his trousers earlier and, although he had a new shirt, like his own, it looked like he was dressed in hand-me-downs. 'Not like the likes of Emerald and all of them,' Cas went on.

During the first week Frank had begun to notice that nearly all of the students in his intake seemed to be well turned out and realised that it was likely that they came from different backgrounds to him. Cas was an obvious exception. He questioned in his own mind whether this was the intention of Finestone Lamplight when he set the place up all those years ago. He thought that the founder of the academy would have meant this opportunity to be open to everyone who had the right abilities, rather than the right bank balance or the right connections. Frank felt that the sands had shifted in the direction of those with money.

'So what about you?' asked Cas. 'Why are you here?'

Now there was a question.

'I've no idea,' said Frank lamely. He went on to explain the circumstances surrounding his attendance at the academy. He talked about being home educated, The List, and the invitation he'd first read in Jelly's office back in Smithwood. Cas listened to the story intently. As Frank told it, he realised it all seemed so long ago. He'd only been at Excelsus a few weeks and it already felt like his new home. Even better, now he appeared to have made a friend, one he felt comfortable with.

'But there *must* be a reason,' said Cas, 'there's always a reason. Dad told me.'

'So I'm led to believe,' said Frank. 'It's obvious in your case, but I'm yet to find out. I'm sure I will, somewhen. Remember what Moonhunter said on the first day, that some of us have yet to find out what our talents actually are? Well, that's certainly me, for sure.'

'Perhaps Moonhunter knows,' said Cas. 'Let's go and ask her.' His eyes were wide and mischievous.

'Get real,' said Frank. 'There's no way I'm going to knock on her office door and ask her anything, not after what happened on the first day. Did you see her robes change colour when she looked at me?' Cas hadn't.

'Something odd about her if you ask me,' Cas said. 'Maybe she'd turn us into frogs if we were too cheeky.'

'Yeah, then tell us to hop it,' laughed Frank.

They were suddenly aware that the canteen had become quieter. The usual hubbub on the long tables, where the students sat to eat, had died to a whisper, and the noise of cutlery clanking on plates had momentarily stopped.

Cas looked up and nodded to Frank, who was just putting a mouthful of broccoli into his mouth, indicating to look behind him. Frank turned around and saw why the room had quietened. Two of the uniformed men that normally patrolled up on the wall had entered the room and were scanning around as if they were looking for something, or someone, amongst the throng of students. Both were tall and very official looking. They still had their caps on and, even though their faces were shaded, Frank could see they looked serious and focused. There was an air of nervousness in the room.

Frank studied their uniforms, but couldn't immediately make out any distinguishing emblems to indicate where these men were actually from. Then, as one of the men turned, he saw he had a badge sewn onto the blue fabric of his left sleeve. Within the brown hexagon was a simple red α. But it was the weapons hanging from their belts that caught his eye. Each man bore a short sword and what appeared to be a small type of dagger, together with a length of rope. One had a bow slung over his back. Frank started to get an uneasy feeling which seemed to spread across the room as the other students started to whisper to each other.

'Check out those swords,' whispered Eric. 'They're Silver Swifts, the best. Not your run-of-the-mill weapons.'

The men had been followed in by Professor Nobleman, the Deputy Head, who was scowling. He stood at the door as the two uniforms walked slowly around the far side of the room, across from where the two boys sat. Frank couldn't take his eyes off of them.

'Is this really necessary?' the professor said to the two men, who just ignored him and went about their business. One of them produced two long thin objects, which looked like smooth sticks, from a loop on his belt. One of the sticks had a sort of purple gem stone at the end. He attached them at one end so they formed a triangle with the man's hands, pointed end facing away from him as he held the two free ends. He pulled out a small bottle containing a yellow liquid and dipped the gem stone into it. Then, in an odd display, he pointed the device towards one end of the canteen and started to move it in a slow sweeping motion around the room. The students looked on, collectively holding their breath, but not knowing why. Frank could see them looking carefully under the tables and thoroughly examining the area as they moved the gadget along its arc. They even glanced at the faces of the students. One of them looked at Frank who didn't know where to put himself. He turned back around and noticed that Cas was looking equally as uncomfortable.

After what seemed like an eternity, they finished their impromptu search. The man holding the stick device took it apart and placed the two parts back in his belt. He turned to his colleague and gave a slight shake of the head. The other man gave a short nod and turned to the professor, who had been looking increasingly agitated throughout the performance.

'Nothing here. Sorry, sir. Thanks for your trouble,' he said and they both left the room. As soon as they had gone, the whole canteen erupted into a cacophony of voices, all speculating on what they had just seen.

'Okay everyone,' said Nobleman above the noise, 'settle down. Classes start in ten minutes. Make sure you're not late.' No one seemed to hear him. They were all distracted, and understandably so. Frank and Cas went back to their lunch as Nobleman passed them.

'Who were those men, professor?' asked Frank. Nobleman stopped and looked down his nose at Frank.

'And just what do you think that has to do with you, Penny?' he said. Frank got the distinct impression that Nobleman regarded him with look of distaste, but had no idea why.

'Well ...'

'Well what?'

'Nothing.'

'You just concentrate on your lunch, and your studies, and keep your nose out of things that don't concern you. Understand?' Frank got the message and went back to his lunch. Nobleman lingered on his shoulder for a moment and then walked on, muttering under his breath.

'Who were they?' said Cas. Frank gave him a 'no idea' face, shrugging his shoulders.

'I've seen them up on the wall,' said Frank, 'I just sort of assumed they were here to look after academy security, but then I read something on the front of the *Broadsword* about the academy being under guard. There must be a connection.'

'D'you think?' said Cas. 'But isn't that a bit odd? If you think about it, this is really just a glorified school. Who needs security for a bunch of kids?' Frank understood the point, but didn't have an answer. He had to agree it was odd, but they were new entrants and what could a couple of young boys do about it? He toyed with the notion that either they just had to accept it, or maybe try and find out a bit more. His natural instinct led him to the latter.

'Perhaps we should ask Lanks,' ventured Cas.

'Maybe, if we can find him,' said Frank.

'Yeah, if we haven't been bored to death by then by Double History.'

Frank thought of Phoebe and wondered if he was about to encounter the Luggans, again, in all their irrelevant glory.

14

THE ALPHAEN

The bell rang for the end of the day. Frank and Cas were weary from Double History and had been handed a load of homework on the Chocolate Makers' Rebellion of the last century. Lanks was nowhere to be found and they just wanted to get away for the day.

They spilled out with the rest of the students, walked across the bridge and entered the plaza under the hooked beak of the vulture; it was then that Frank had a sudden thought.

'Come on,' he said to Cas. 'I know someone who might be able to tell us a bit about those guys up there.' He indicated towards the top of the academy wall, where more blue-uniformed figures stood and watched. He picked up speed and headed off across the square with Cas in tow.

The door to Blackburn's workshop was shut. The faded sign on the door was turned to 'CLOSED'. Frank peered in through the grime, but couldn't see anyone. He tried the door. To his surprise, it opened and he wandered in. The pungent odour of sulphur filled his nostrils as he made his way through the dusty room. Judging from the smell, Blackburn must have been doing some sort of experiment, although it was hard to tell, given that the place was in a right mess. Frank coughed loudly as the air hit his lungs and he put his hand over his mouth.

Frank had made a habit of calling in to see Blackburn, who was happy to show him what he was working on and explain some of the bits and pieces that were scattered around the shelves in the workshop. The two of them had become friends and Frank was happy to confide in Blackburn who, in turn, would let him into some of the finer secrets of being an inventor.

As he made his way further into the workshop, he was conscious that Cas hadn't followed him. He turned around to see his new friend still standing at the door, peering timidly in. The look on his face was one of uncertainty.

'You alright?' he asked, still coughing.

'Phwoar,' said Cas, catching the eggy odour. 'Who's done one?' Frank laughed. 'Whoever it was, they obviously couldn't stand it, seems they've scarpered. No surprise there. Anyway, what *is* this place?' Cas was looking more nauseous by the second,. Frank had to admit to himself that the smell was a little overpowering and quite understood why Cas hadn't wanted to follow him in.

'It belongs to Atticus Blackburn - he's an inventor. He's been here forever, so he's bound to know a bit about what goes on over there.'

'Cool,' said Cas slowly. 'But only if he's invented something to help him see through his windows. Are you sure he won't mind?'

'Won't mind what?' came a voice behind Cas, who, startled, pressed himself against the door frame as if trying to hide, badly.

Blackburn walked past him, oblivious to his presence, and continued into the room, where Frank was standing. Despite having appeared to have replied to Cas just seconds earlier, he still seemed unaware that both the boys were there.

He stopped and stood there muttering, patting his pockets.

'Ah, there you are,' he said with a smile, and produced a key from his trouser pocket. He turned around to the door and jumped back in surprise as he saw it was open and Cas was standing there.

'Hell's teeth!' he exclaimed at the sight of the boy standing in his doorway. 'What ... who ... how did you get in?'

Cas just stood there, squashing himself even further against the door frame, lost for words. It was apparent Blackburn thought he had locked the door on his way out.

'The door was open,' chuckled Frank, coming to his rescue.

At the sound of the voice behind him, Blackburn jumped again and did a pirouette. His eyes centred on Frank.

'What ... oh, Frank, my boy, it's you. Well, thank goodness for that, thought I was being robbed.' Blackburn's demeanour calmed noticeably. 'How did you get in?' he asked again.

'The door was unlocked,' replied Frank. Blackburn held the key up and looked at it, then turned to the door, gave it a quick stare and returned his gaze to the key. He looked up at Frank, raised his eyebrows and sighed, then put the key back in his pocket. He made a grunting noise as if annoyed with himself.

'Forget my own head,' he muttered. 'Nettle tea anyone? I'll put the kettle on shall I?'

Frank smiled at the old man.

'By the way, this is Hardcastle,' he said, shooting a glance at his friend in the doorway, who was visibly more relaxed. 'But you can call him Cas.'

Blackburn turned and regarded Cas over his glasses.

'Well, come on in.' He beckoned Cas into the workshop. 'Any friend of Frank is welcome here.'

Cas smiled and ventured slowly into the room. As he went to cover his mouth and nose with his sleeve, he started to cough. Frank followed suit, causing Blackburn to look slightly worried.

'Hang on a tick,' he said. He opened a cupboard and pulled out a bucket that was half-filled with a bluish sandy substance. He plunged his hand in, grabbed a handful and tossed it up into the air. The sulphur-filled atmosphere cleared instantly, leaving no trace of the smell or the sand Blackburn had just thrown. The two boys stared at each other in wonder.

'Yes, well, should have done that before I popped out,' said Blackburn apologetically. 'Sorry about that, just something I'm working on that went a bit wrong this afternoon. I had to go and see Mr Smithers, the apothecary, to get some more of this.' He held up a large vial, containing a clear liquid, which he stood carefully on the worktop to the side of the room. 'Now then, nettle tea, wasn't it?' he said, rubbing his hands on his overalls as he moved through the room towards the forge where the battered kettle sat.

As Frank pulled up a third chair and the boys sat down, he remembered he had some cookies that Polly had given to him that morning, and which he had neglected to eat at lunchtime due to all the excitement in the canteen. As the kettle boiled, he reached into his bag and pulled them out. Blackburn poured the water into the teapot, gave it a stir and proceeded to produce three cups of nettle tea.

'Oh, they look good,' said Blackburn eyeing them up. 'Polly make them?'

Frank nodded and offered them around. Cas and Blackburn took one each. Cas took a bite and crumbs fell onto his shirt.

'Nearly as delicious as my gran's toffees,' said Cas, making Frank smile.

Blackburn sat down. 'Well, nice of you to drop in,' he said and sipped his tea. 'And to what do I owe the pleasure?'

Frank went to speak, but Cas beat him to it.

'We wondered if you had noticed those uniformed men over at the academy? The ones in blue up on the walls, looking like they're patrolling the perimeter all the time.' Blackburn looked up from his tea, gaze moving from boy to boy.

'No,' he said quickly and returned to his drink, still looking at them over his mug. Both boys looked at each other, instantly deflated.

'You know,' urged Frank. 'The ones you can see over there, they wear matching blue caps.'

Blackburn looked at him again.

'No,' he said once more. Sip.

'But surely you must see them when you come in and out of the shop,' said Cas.

'Yeah,' said Frank.

'No,' repeated Blackburn with a slight shake of the head. Frank looked disappointed; he'd felt sure Blackburn would know something. He had told him that he didn't miss anything, so he was slightly miffed that his plan to find out more appeared to have quickly come to nothing.

He thought for a moment and, grabbing a pencil and a piece of paper from his bag, quickly drew the symbol he'd seen on the sleeve of the men in the canteen. Cas and Blackburn looked on as he sketched.

'They have a badge on their sleeve that looks like this,' he said, holding out the drawing for Blackburn to see. Blackburn took an unexpected gulp and went into a spasm of coughing, spraying tea over himself. Frank thought he was going to choke.

'You okay?' he asked, as the coughing subsided. Blackburn regained his composure, grabbed a handkerchief from his pocket and wiped his mouth.

'Are you sure?' Blackburn said, putting his mug down on the hotplate next to the kettle and taking the picture from Frank. He studied it closely, looking from the image to Frank and back again.

'Positive,' said Frank. 'Both the men we saw had the same badge here. He indicated with his index finger a point on his upper arm where the badge had been fixed to the uniforms. He looked at Blackburn to make sure he knew what he meant. Blackburn continued to look a little distracted.

'They're Alphaen,' he said, with a serious look.

'What's an Alpha hen?' said Cas.

'Alphaen,' repeated Blackburn slowly.

'Okay, one of them, then.'

Blackburn didn't respond. Instead, he got to his feet and walked to the front of the shop. Frank watched him as he made his way to the window. Blackburn, still holding the handkerchief, gave it a lick, wiped a patch on the glass to clear the dirt and stood staring across to the academy for a moment. Cas and Frank exchanged glances. Blackburn appeared uneasy. Something had caught his attention and he appeared to duck away from the window, as if to avoid being seen. He was obviously looking at the top of the walls and the men on patrol.

'Well I never. I must admit I hadn't noticed them,' he said after a while, still looking across the square at the academy. 'I can only think they've been here just since the beginning of term. I'm sure I would have noticed them if they had been there longer. Goodness, I must get my eyes checked.'

Or your windows cleaned, thought Frank. Blackburn lifted his glasses off his nose and proceeded to inspect them, as if they had somehow failed him. He turned back to the boys, knocking over a metal pot full of pencils in the process. There was a clattering as they fell to the floor, but he just ignored it.

'Well I never,' he repeated. 'What on earth could they be doing here?'

Frank and Cas just stared blankly at him.

'So who are they, these Alphaen?' asked Frank, who felt it was odd that they had appeared to have a marked effect on the inventor.

Blackburn put his glasses back on and started to wander back towards the forge where the boys were sitting, cradling their mugs.

'They're specially selected fighters. Elite soldiers,' replied Blackburn after a while.

Frank and Cas looked at him in astonishment.

'Yes, I guess that's what you'd call them. Council's top fighters, quite unusual to see them up there.' He indicated towards the academy walls. 'Quite unusual to see them anywhere, as a matter of fact. Normally they're kept for undercover duties. Covert, you might say. Most of them are made up of ex-pupils from here, dare say.'

Gallant and gifted, thought Frank, as Blackburn's words sunk in.

'Well, they don't appear to be doing a particularly good job at being undercover,' said Cas.

Blackburn got the joke and chuckled as he slumped back down into his beaten old chair. Dust was flung into the air, but no one seemed to mind. Cicero, who had been keeping himself warm under the forge, jumped up onto his lap, purring as Blackburn tickled him behind his ear.

'No, it doesn't seem that they are, which is even more strange. It's like they want to be noticed.'

'Wowzer,' was all Cas could say.

'That doesn't make sense,' said Frank. 'Why on earth would several of the council's elite troops be walking around Excelsus Academy in broad daylight?' The revelation had certainly got Frank's mind spinning. 'After all, the academy's just a school, right? So why would they be there? What could be so important?'

Blackburn thought for a moment.

'When did you see them close up?' he asked.

Frank and Cas recalled the events of that lunch time, how the two men had barged into the canteen in full view of everyone and proceeded to act as if no one was there at all. Frank described the strange device with the jewelled tip that one of the men had coupled together and swept around the room as if looking for something.

'Searching, you reckon?' asked Blackburn, stroking his chin. 'Hm?'

'I'd say so, wouldn't you, Cas?' said Frank, turning to his friend for support. Cas nodded.

Blackburn stared into space, as if thinking.

'I wonder what would bring them here?' he muttered to himself. 'What could be so important?'

He was quiet for a long time.

'Hums,' he said to himself, quietly. 'Perhaps it's Hums.'

'Hums?' said Frank and Cas together, then Frank said, 'What's a Hums when it's at home?'

Blackburn seemed momentarily lost in his own thoughts as he looked towards the window and shifted in his chair.

'No, it can't be,' he continued to mutter to himself. 'Perhaps... no, no it can't be.'

'Can't be what?' said Frank. 'What's a Hums, Blackburn?'

Blackburn came to his senses and looked at Frank with a smile.

'Not *what*, Frank,' he said, 'but *who*. Hums is a person, a man.'

Frank looked at Blackburn, fascination spreading through him.

Were these so called elite agents here at Excelsus to look for a man? If so, why? It seemed so exciting.

'Hums is a person?' he said. 'Who is he then?'

'And why would Byeland's crack troops be looking for him across the road?' said Cas. Both of them looked at Blackburn, desperate for answers.

'I wish I knew,' said Blackburn, bursting their bubble. Cas looked a bit disappointed.

'But you know who this Hums is?' said Frank, not wanting to let Blackburn wander off the subject.

'Oh, but of course I know, everyone around here knows, or should I say knew, Ludlow Hums. Goodness me, quite a story at the time. He was the younger brother of old Wordsworth Hums. Now, Wordsworth used to be the caretaker at the academy. He was there for years, yes, years and years. Endearing fellow, lived over there all his life, practically, and his brother had an old cottage up in the woods. Then, one day, must be ... oh let me think ... about two years ago now, he and Ludlow had a falling out and the story goes that Ludlow killed his brother.'

'Killed him?' said Frank, wide-eyed. 'Wow, what happened?'

'Threw him into the river and poor old Wordsworth went over the waterfall. Drowned.'

'Wowzer,' said Cas. 'Why did he do that?'

'Well, I'm not entirely sure. You see, Ludlow was always a bit of a reprobate, always thieving or involved in some scam or other. You know the sort. Dishonesty followed him around like a puppy and not many people liked him. Very different to his brother, who got on with everybody. Rumour has it that he was being watched by the council, that he was up to something and they were on to him. I don't really know, you know how folks gossip, but some reckon that whatever he was doing - did - it was quite serious. Seems either he asked his brother for help, or Wordsworth found out what he was up to, but didn't want to get involved, the two of them had some sort of falling out and ... splash!'

'How do they know it wasn't an accident?'

'Someone saw it happen. Saw Ludlow push him in.'

'So what happened to Ludlow?' asked Frank.

'Disappeared. Vanished into thin air. No one's seen him since.'

'So no one knows where he is?'

'No. Some say he might have fled to somewhere far away, some say he went into hiding, some say he went over the waterfall to his death with his brother. I really don't know, and, to be honest, I'm not that interested.' He scratched his head. 'Come to think of it, I'd just about forgotten about Ludlow Hums until I thought of him just then, if you see what I mean. My guess is that most other people have too.'

'If I was Hums, and I'd done something really bad like that, I'd have wanted people to forget about me too,' said Cas. 'Fancy killing your own brother.'

Frank had to agree. He'd often said he'd wanted to kill Phoebe, but he knew he never really meant it. He took a bite of his cookie, then had another thought.

'So he could still be around here somewhere?' he said with a hint of excitement. 'That's why the Alphaen are here?'

'Oh, I wouldn't think so. If you were on the run, why would you hang around the place where you lived and worked? Chances are someone would spot you sooner or later, especially if you were so well-known. And where would you hide for two years, eh? Although that might explain why those Alphaen are sniffing around, and when you said they looked like they were searching for something, it just made me wonder too.' He paused. 'The object, it sounds like a quaero stick.'

'A what?' said the boys in unison.

'A quaero stick. It's a rather interesting device that helps in the search for lost things, including people,' said Blackburn.

'Doesn't look like it works, if they haven't found him in two years,' scoffed Cas.

'Oh, it works alright,' said Blackburn. 'But only over a certain range, about twenty yards or so. I should know; I invented it.'

Frank raised his eyebrows. He thought Blackburn might have wanted them to be impressed, but his tone was just matter of fact and unassuming, as though inventing something that useful was an everyday occurrence.

'Really?' said Frank, amazed.

'Of course, quite a straightforward device really. You dip the jewelled end into a special solution which contains the essence of something the person you're looking for used to wear, point it around the place, a bit like you described those chaps were doing in the canteen, and it will seek them out.' Blackburn did an impression as if holding an invisible object like the one the Alphaen had used. 'One hundred percent effective.' Cicero shifted on his lap.

'How?' said Frank.

'Well, the jewel will start to glow when it detects the presence of the person. Then you know they're not far away. It'll glow brighter as you get nearer. Simple really.'

'And it actually works?' Cas said.

Blackburn gave him a look as a slight reprimand.

'Sorry,' said Cas, as if realising he might have offended its inventor.

'They must have thought he was hiding in the canteen then,' said Frank.

'What, in amongst the liver and bacon?' laughed Cas.

'You're assuming it's him they're after,' said Blackburn. 'That was just me thinking out loud, remember. No, I can't believe it's Hums, not after all this time.'

Frank knew they were just guessing, they didn't really know why the Alphaen were in the academy, but his interest levels had moved up a number of notches after talking to Blackburn. He began to wonder how they could find out more. Blackburn seemed to read his thoughts.

'I wouldn't go looking for trouble, Frank,' he said. 'Leave them to do whatever it is they're doing. Best way. If it is Hums, they'll find him soon enough and, remember, he's a murderer.' He looked up at the clock. 'Goodness, is that the time? I must be getting on with my work, boys, if you'll excuse me.' He pushed himself up, grunting as he did and being careful to plop Cicero back onto the chair which he had nicely warmed. The cat turned round a few times and promptly went back to its snooze. 'It's good to see you, Frank, and nice to meet you, Cas.'

The two boys stood and Blackburn ushered them to the door.

'Thanks for the tea,' said Cas.

'Make sure you call again, you're welcome any time.'

'See you soon,' said Frank as they left the workshop.

As they walked away he turned to Cas. 'What do you make of that?'

'Not sure, but something's going on over there,' said Cas, looking over to the academy building. Frank followed his gaze. The walls were deserted. Frank wondered where the Alphaen had gone, and whether or not they were looking for the missing killer, Ludlow Hums.

15

BYELAND'S MOST WANTED

Frank had started to have a strange recurring dream. He would be standing on the edge of a wide square courtyard, just looking from side to side. The courtyard was surrounded by a high stone wall and, in the middle, was an ornate bronze sundial on a tall stone plinth. To the left was a fretworked iron gate. He always had the feeling there was someone there, but, however much he looked, he couldn't make out anyone in the dark. But this was unlike any normal dream; the strangest thing of all was that when he woke he could still see the images vividly, no matter how much he rubbed his eyes. Even though he knew they were in his mind, it was like he was actually there, peering through the darkness, despite the fact that he was underneath his comfy bedcovers in Polly's attic room.

He'd settled into Polly's so well it was like he'd been there for months. He'd got used to them as a family. Norris would sit and tell them what he was doing - or not doing - at work, while Polly kept him in line. They let Frank come and go as he pleased and he occasionally helped in the teashop, although Polly said it was important for him to make sure his homework was done. Maddy just kept quiet most of the time.

Frank loved the mornings. Polly always fussed around them with her usual bubbliness and Maddy normally helped her prepare breakfast. He'd watch the two of them; Polly giving Maddy directions, helping and encouraging her when she needed it. Sometimes Polly would go up behind her daughter and put her arms around her, catching her by surprise, making the two of them giggle. Frank would hold his locket tightly as he felt the warmth between them and his own pangs of sadness, seeing the two of them so close and thinking of how he might have been with his mother, had she been alive to see him grow up.

The revelation at Blackburn's workshop, and the discussion about Hums and the Alphaen, preyed on Frank's mind for some time, especially the way Blackburn had reacted to the Alphaen's presence. He was mulling this over at the kitchen table one morning, while tucking into his toast and Polly's homemade marmalade, when he remembered something Blackburn had said when he was talking about the missing Ludlow Hums. He remembered him saying how he was wanted by the council, Norris's employer. He finished his mouthful and looked up at Norris.

'Norris?' he said. Norris looked up from his paper. He'd been absorbed in a story about cuts to the Byeland transport budget and how it might affect the building of a new road linking two of the major towns in the country.

'Yes, Frank,' he said, glancing back down to his article.

'Do you know anything about Ludlow Hums?' he ventured, wondering how Norris would respond.

Norris lowered his paper which landed in the buttered toast he had in front of him and peered at Frank over his glasses.

'Hums? Well of course I know about that *crook*,' he said, raising his voice as he said the word 'crook' as if to emphasise his viewpoint.

'Norris!' said Polly at the kitchen counter, where she and Maddy were in the process of kneading a fresh batch of dough for some sausage rolls. 'You know you shouldn't cast aspersions. Don't you listen to him, Frank my dear; gets these things in his head sometimes, does Norris.' She looked at Frank before giving Norris a frosty glare. 'Don't you Norris?'

Norris reached over to his plate and grabbed a half-consumed piece of toast. He took a bite.

'Aspersions,' retorted Norris with his mouth full, toast crumbs spilling out into his beard. 'No aspersions of any sort, Pol. You know as well as I do that Hums was ... is ... whatever, a complete crook -

and a murderer.' Polly pointed a flour-covered finger in his direction as some kind of warning. 'Just saying, that's all, just saying.'

He turned back to Frank, and Polly went back to her kneading.

'Byeland's most wanted, Frank,' he continued, lowering his voice. 'Byeland's most wanted. Yes, strange business that was, hmm. Killed his brother. Poor old Wordsworth, decent fellow, goodness only knows how he came to have a brother like that. Chalk and cheese those two. Not really sure what went on but the council should have sorted it out before ... well ... before ... you know what I mean. Shouldn't say too much, really.'

He raised his paper back up in front of his face. Frank didn't have a clue what he meant. It was if Norris had spoken for a few minutes without actually having said anything. Frank understood from Blackburn that Ludlow Hums had thrown his brother into the river, but not why, so decided on a different question to try and clarify things.

'What was he meant to have done?' he asked, hopeful that that would provide a more straightforward answer.

Norris lowered his paper once more and thought for a moment, glancing in Polly's direction as though fearful she might scold him again.

'Well, since you ask, he stole a casket containing the Liberation Seal, greedy good-for-nothing. Yes, stole it right from under the nose of Aurora Moonhunter herself, and, when Wordsworth found out, they had a set-to and Ludlow killed him. Can you believe it! Of course, no one could at first. Of all the things to do. I'm sure nothing like that would ever have happened when Hector Baggus was there.'

'Hector Baggus?' interrupted Frank.

'Oh, he was the principal at Excelsus before Aurora Moonhunter was appointed. Decent chap, Hector. Don't think he ever got over what happened with the whole Hums thing even though he'd already left the place. He and Wordsworth were great mates you see, but he couldn't stand Ludlow. Not surprised. Whole thing seemed to break him up a bit so he decided to move away. He was a good head up there though. Bloomin' Hums, huh! All of that caused nothing but trouble up at the council, let me tell you, Frank, and muggins here, being the head administrator over there,' he thumbed in the direction of the council offices, 'suddenly had a pile of work to do as big as a horse's backside.' He huffed and went back to his paper once again.

'Mind your language,' scolded Polly.

'So what's the Liberation Seal?'

Whatever it was, it sounded extremely interesting. Norris, sensing that he wasn't going to be allowed to finish what he was reading in peace, closed the newspaper, folded it and placed it on the table. He took another piece of toast and spread some marmalade on it. He leaned in towards the table and lowered his voice to a whisper as though he didn't want to be overheard, even though there were only the usual four of them in the room.

'The Seal,' he said, 'is ... was ... whatever ... the most valuable object that Excelsus Academy owns. It is said it belonged to old Finestone Lamplight himself and was used in the building and opening of the original academy centuries ago. Made of solid gold, so they say, an object of supreme beauty, fashioned by the finest craftsmen in the world. Never seen it myself. No. It was kept under lock and key in the principal's office until that thief made off with it. Daresay he's sunning himself on some tropical island somewhere on the proceeds as we speak, along with his conscience, if he has one.' Norris huffed his disapproval. 'People speak of the Seal as if it's some kind of talisman for the place, that no good will come of its disappearance,' he huffed again. 'Load of old nonsense,' he scoffed loudly, his voice rising from its near whisper of a few moments ago.

'Norris,' came another reprimand from Polly, who gave him an even harder stare. He looked at her apologetically and quietened once more.

'Yes,' he went on, clearing his throat. 'Folk think of it as a lucky charm, but we all know, those of us at the council that is, that Hums, having lived the life of a scoundrel all his days, scheming and thieving, no money, just wanted it to line his own pockets, as usual. Probably been melted down and sold on as gold bars now for all I know and, as I said, he's not been seen since, so my guess is he's living the high life, rich as a king, lucky so and so. Wordsworth must have thought he would be implicated, that they were somehow in it together. My guess is that's why they had the falling out and Ludlow ended up throwing him in the river.'

Frank's eyes grew wide as Norris told the tale.

'But I thought Wordsworth was just the caretaker,' he said.

'He was. Goodness, you seem to know a bit more than I would have thought,' said Norris, giving Frank a surprised look. He went on. 'Well, that's just it you see, that's why the suspicion fell firmly at Hums's door, what with his brother being the caretaker; he had access to all parts of the academy, keys to every room, there at all hours. Story goes that Hums and Moonhunter didn't see eye-to-eye, that she was going to replace him even though he was part of the furniture. Not sure that would have worried old Wordsworth, due for retirement, but if his brother had his eye on the Seal he would have needed to take his chance. So, one night, Ludlow got hold of his brother's keys, went to Moonhunter's office, opened the cupboard where it was kept in a casket and made off with it, never to be seen again. Moonhunter turned up the next morning to find the thing gone and, as you can imagine, merry hell broke loose.'

'Mind your language,' Polly said, not turning round.

Norris rolled his eyes and shifted his position. His chair made a loud squeaking noise which made Tinks, who was lounging in an armchair, look up.

'By the time they'd searched the place, they found both the brothers missing,' he went on. 'They checked Wordsworth's office. Neat and tidy - just like Hums, always meticulous - but no sign of him. They went up to the house in the woods. No sign of Ludlow either. Nothing. Turned the place over, they did, but they'd just vanished.' His voice was all mystery now. 'Moonhunter ordered another search of the grounds and they found Wordsworth's cloak and boots up by the river, just before the waterfall.'

'So that's why they think he might have fallen in and drowned?' said Frank.

Again, Norris looked at Frank with interest. 'Pushed in, you mean. Murdered, more like. The brothers had been seen arguing by the river that evening and someone saw Ludlow push Wordsworth in. One of the professors saw it, now that I recall. The next morning, when they found the caretaker missing, they looked for Ludlow and found him gone. It didn't take long to put the pieces together, especially with the Seal missing. Thief. They never found Wordsworth's body, but he wouldn't have survived, not a man of his age.'

'What do you mean?' asked Frank. Up until now he'd drawn his own mental picture of Wordsworth and Ludlow Hums, but wasn't sure exactly if he was right.

'Oh, Wordsworth Hums was an old man, been at the academy for years, as I said, part of the furniture. His brother was a little younger than him.' Norris paused and looked around at the sideboard behind him. 'Hold on, I think I've still got a picture of them both somewhere.' Frank became excited - a picture! His eyebrows shot up as he waited expectantly.

Norris got to his feet and opened one of the sideboard drawers. He muttered to himself as he looked.

'No, not in there,' he said to himself as he pulled out an old pair of socks and a pack of crumpled old playing cards. He took a look at them and stuffed them into his pocket.

He closed the drawer and pulled open another. Frank could see it contained an assortment of old papers and opened envelopes, unimportant mail that had appeared to have been stuffed in there over the years.

'Ah, this is more like it,' said Norris with a tone of optimism.

He fumbled through the papers and then stopped He pulled out two pieces of paper which looked surprisingly smooth and unspoilt, given where they had been sitting for the last couple of years. He held them aloft triumphantly and turned back to face Frank.

'There you are,' he said, talking to the pictures.

Norris sat back down and pushed the pictures across the table to Frank, who put his hand on them and dragged them over so he could see them properly, turning them around so they were the right way up. Both images were of old men. He looked at the younger of the two. Ludlow Hums had a bush of white hair and a distinctive long, crooked nose. He had a naturally dishonest look about him. His immediate thought was that if this man was sunning himself on a beach somewhere he'd better make the most of it, and quickly, because, judging by the image, Frank thought he must be about a hundred years old. He looked more carefully at the piece of paper and saw that it was actually a wanted poster. The word 'WANTED' was emblazoned across the top in large black letters and then, underneath, it said 'By order of Byeland Department for Crime and Justice', together with the familiar Byeland eagle crest. At the bottom was the promise of a reward of 1,000 gold crowns for the apprehension of Ludlow Hums. Frank couldn't help but wonder why, if he was still at large, nobody had caught him. He looked like he'd stand out in a crowd and Frank thought there was no way he could walk particularly fast, let alone run anywhere.

Older still was his brother. Frank studied the picture of Wordsworth Hums more closely. Staring back at him was the gnarled and weather-beaten face of a very old man. His distinguishing white hair was sticking up at all angles like he'd just been hit by a lightning bolt and his gentle-looking eyes were sunk into his skull, overshadowed by his enormous eyebrows that hung on his forehead like the wings of an albatross.

Frank looked from one image to the other, wondering if simple greed had really brought the two of them to blows, ending in the death of the elder brother.

'Do you think he's still alive?' asked Frank after a while. 'Ludlow, I mean.'

'Oh, I wouldn't know really,' replied Norris. 'As you may know, some say he might have followed his brother over the waterfall, up by the academy there, but, if he did, they never found any trace of him either, no body or anything. Perhaps the weight of the Seal dragged him to the bottom of the ocean and he's still there.' He laughed. 'My guess is he's living out the rest of his days somewhere fancy.'

'But the council's still looking for him?' said Frank, intrigued. 'Even after all this time?'

Frank thought perhaps he had let slip a little more than he should have, but Norris didn't seem to catch on. So far Frank hadn't mentioned that he knew a bit about the Alphaen just in case it was all meant to be secret, even though Norris was bound to know about them, being high up in the council's administrative section in Rhaeder.

'And what makes you say that?' asked Norris.

Frank thought quickly.

'Well, I mean, if someone had stolen something so valuable and killed his own brother, it's not the sort of thing you just give up the chase on, don't you think? Especially if you weren't sure if he was alive or not.'

'I think you're right,' said Norris who looked at Frank as if he'd said something he shouldn't have. 'Although I shouldn't say really, no, I shouldn't really, and I'm sure that if he is still around, and I'm not saying that he is, you understand, they'll track him down somehow, got their best people on it, although it has been two years or more, so they'd better get on with it. Yes, Miss Moonhunter and the academy will want their trophy back and the people of Rhaeder will want to see Hums behind bars, that's for sure. But I shouldn't say, really.'

Frank knew from what Norris had said he shouldn't say that his instincts were probably right. That the council had sent a number of their elite force to the academy because they thought that Ludlow Hums might be there. He couldn't wait to tell Cas.

16

TWEEDY

Frank was suddenly woken by one of his strange dreams. They'd been getting more frequent, but this one was different, unlike anything he'd had before.

In the dream, as usual, he was staring out from the shadows onto the courtyard. This time, however, although it was the middle of the night, the moon was full and shone brightly which meant he could make out much of the detail. The sundial was illuminated and it sparkled as it cast a shadow over the grass. The grey stone walls glistened quietly in the stillness.

To his left, the iron gate opened with a squeak and a hooded figure of a man hurried in. In previous visions he'd not been able to see anyone. The figure closed the gate behind him carefully and headed swiftly across the courtyard. As he did so, something fell from his pocket and into the small bushes to the side of the gate. He stopped and looked behind him, as if sensing he'd dropped something or expecting someone to follow him in. He seemed edgy and nervous. Frank couldn't see the man's face, but noticed he was carrying a small sack in one hand.

There was a noise. Footsteps. Hurried. The scene cut back to the gate where two more figures were approaching. He looked back to where the hooded man had been standing and, strangely, he was no longer there. He had vanished.

The gate swung open once more and the two men strode purposefully across the courtyard. They stopped and looked around, expecting to find the hooded man. After all, there was nowhere for him to go.

One of the men was tall and menacing; the other was shorter and appeared subordinate. The tall man had long black hair and a pointed beard. He wore a dark cloak and, underneath, a scarlet tunic upon which was a black scorpion emblem. The same symbol that Emerald and his sidekicks had on the sleeves of their Excelsus attire. He started to pace; he was obviously seething over the missing man. He wandered over to the far wall and appeared to inspect it a few times with his hand, looking like he was checking it for weakness, as if the figure they were pursuing had walked right through it. He kicked the wall hard several times with the sole of his boot and mouthed some obscenity, then walked back to the other man, and, as he passed, gave him a clip around the head for no apparent reason, still agitated. He continued to walk and approached where Frank was looking from, so that his face was in full view, then stopped. The man's face was dark and cruel and he had a distinctive orange streak in his hair above his right ear. The image was so vivid; it was as if the man had a window into Frank's mind and his eyes bore into him as he dreamed. Frank could see every line and blemish on his face. He narrowed his eyes and flashed his perfect white teeth that shone in the moonlight as his face creased into a threatening smile. It was a face of sheer evil.

Frank woke up with a start, sweating, eyes wide, panicked. He jumped to his feet and gasped, feeling the terror, but, to his discomfort, the image of the man didn't disappear; it stayed there, clear as day. Frank rubbed his eyes quickly to try and erase the evil-looking face, panic rising, but still it stuck in his mind. It was as if the man was standing right in front of him, in his bedroom, as real as Frank himself. The dream had become a nightmare. Frank struck out a hand, fearful that he was actually there and he should knock him away. He felt his breath quicken and his heart race; he clawed at the curtains, pulling them open, then returned his hands to his head, squeezing his temples to try and get the image out of his mind.

Then it was gone. Frank sunk back down on the bed, panting.

He lay down, eyes open, fearful that if he went back to sleep the face of the man with the scorpion emblem, and the dread, would return.

He met Cas at the bridge before lessons and told him about his experience during the night.

'Don't worry, Frank, it was just a dream,' said Cas sympathetically, offering him a pear drop.

'A nightmare, actually,' corrected Frank, taking one.

'Yeah, okay, but I get them occasionally,' said Cas. 'Normally they involve me trying to pickpocket a clown and ending up falling into his bottomless pocket. Terrifying.'

'But it was *so* real,' said Frank for the umpteenth time. 'And the scorpion crest, what was that all about?'

'Your mind's just probably trying to figure out what type of hair gel Emerald wears and it's seeped into your dream.'

Both boys laughed and headed off to the academy, although Frank was still troubled by the images.

The morning started with their first lesson in Practical Falconry, taken by the humourless Professor Huxley. He was the resident falconer and, although they'd had some theory lessons regarding handling wild creatures from Professor Furze, Frank had been looking forward to this one since he had found out they would be doing it and was eager to get hands on with whatever hawks and falcons they had in the academy.

He'd handled a peregrine falcon before when one of his dad's friends had come to the farm to rid them of some annoying pigeons that kept getting in to the feed store. He was instantly captivated and went about learning as much as he could about the art. He wished that he could have convinced his dad to let him keep one, but he said they had enough animals to deal with and perhaps to wait until he was older.

The students gathered in the grounds at the back of the academy. Huxley stood in front of them. He was a stocky man, not much taller than Frank, and had a shaved head. Frank thought he looked for all the world like he'd be better wrestling bears than teaching the gentle art of handling hawks. Perhaps that was to come.

'Now, students,' he started in his deep voice, 'has anyone here had any experience in handling birds of prey before?'

Emerald's arm shot up. Frank decided not to put up his own hand; he was happy keeping quiet.

'Mr Emerald?' said Huxley.

'Yes sir,' said Emerald in his posh voice, preening his hair. 'My father owns a number of the finest gyrfalcons in the land. I've handled them a lot. He's often taken me out hunting. Seen those birds tear rabbits and pheasants apart, guts everywhere.'

He spoke as if relishing the picture he was creating, looking around at the other students as if everyone should be impressed. Frank wasn't. It was typical of Emerald, who failed to see any of the beauty of the bird and was just focused on the kill. Huxley didn't look too interested, he just nodded.

'Anyone else?' he asked.

'I held an owl once,' piped up Meredith, looking a little unsure.

Emerald gave a derisory snort. Huxley just nodded again. No one else ventured a comment.

'Now then, I've got three birds to show you this morning.'

It was then that Frank noticed three birds of prey across the grass, tethered to their perches.

'You'll all get a chance to hold one, even fly one, but if everyone can be quiet and calm until they get used to you, that'd be lovely.'

Huxley walked them over, stopping far enough in front of the birds so not to make them nervous.

'Now, remember what I told you, no sudden movements. You need to respect the bird, then she'll respect you,' he said as the students moved silently and carefully over, stopping a few yards in front of the trio of birds, which stood motionless on the roosts.

'A little closer,' said Huxley.

'Not very active,' said Emerald, stepping forward to try and touch the buzzard, which made a quick lunge for his finger. He retracted it in the nick of time, fright etched on his face.

'What did I just say?' scolded Huxley as the bird settled. Emerald looked sheepish.

'Careful Emerald,' said Cas. 'You know they're partial to a nice bit of rat.'

Frank laughed, as did some of the others.

'Watch your mouth, Bones,' said Emerald, clearly narked. 'I'm sure they'd love a bit of you too.' He stood back towards his cronies Chetto, Woods and De Villiers. 'And you, Penny, if they can stand the smell of horse manure,' he spat.

'That's enough, boys,' Huxley interjected, still looking annoyed at Emerald's attempt to touch the bird. Given his size, Frank didn't think he was the sort of man you should upset, despite his normally calm manner.

'Now,' he continued, placing a large leather gauntlet over his left hand, 'I'm going to get one of these ladies off her tether and show you her a bit closer up so you can learn about the anatomy.'

He stepped over to the middle bird, a magnificent looking red kite.

'This here is Tweedy,' he said and undid the tether from its perch. As he reached down to allow the bird to jump on to his glove, the kite suddenly started to beat its wings furiously in what looked like an effort to escape the professor. Huxley looked astonished and troubled as he fought to keep the bird under control.

The students looked on, not sure if the man needed any help. The kite squawked and pecked at him, so much so that he eventually had to let go and the bird instantly soared into the air with a heavy beat of its wings. Huxley looked flabbergasted; he had seemed to have a well-drilled routine and had obviously not expected a bird to try and escape from his control, let alone succeed. His eyes followed the kite as it circled around the edge of the grounds. The students, equally surprised, did the same, as if the bird held them under some kind of hypnotic spell.

The kite wheeled around three hundred and sixty degrees and headed back towards the group of assembled students. It swooped expertly within an inch of their heads, squawking as it glided efficiently in the air. Some of the students shrieked and ran to one side; some, including Cas, dived to the ground. The bird turned again, looking as it was coming in for another pass. Only Huxley and Frank were left standing. Then something unexpected happened.

The kite slowed to a stall as it came within a few feet of Frank and, to his astonishment, landed effortlessly on his shoulder. It was larger than he realised, but he wasn't afraid. It flapped its wings once, turned to face the front and sat there, alert, watching the crowd of students. Frank felt his skin burn furiously as the powerful talons gripped him. He winced, but, at once, the bird appeared to loosen its grip. Huxley quickly took off his gauntlet and placed it on Frank's hand; the bird hopped down to its more familiar position and sat there on Frank's fist, looking like nothing much had happened.

'Wowzer,' said Cas.

The others got to their feet and started to recongregate. Emerald had dived onto a mole hill and emerged with a long streak of dirt which ran from the top of his head right down his front. Frank just stared in admiration at the kite, then looked at Huxley with enquiring eyes. Huxley seemed genuinely shocked, but relaxed a little as he picked out another gauntlet from the box on the floor and went to take the bird from Frank.

'Come on, Tweedy,' he said, but, as he tried, the bird just pecked at him. He tried again but still the bird resisted, immovable from Frank's hand.

'Well I never,' said Huxley, scratching his head in amazement. 'I've never seen anything like that before, not in all my years. D'you know Penny, it can take months of hard work to man a bird of prey, but this! Young Tweedy here seems to have taken to you straight away. Extraordinary, I wouldn't have believed it unless I'd seen it with my own eyes.'

Frank shrugged, but was transfixed by the feathered beauty now sitting silently and patiently at the end of his arm. The other students looked on. Soon a hum spread over the gathering as they started whispering to each other, amazed at what the kite had just done. Without any tuition, Frank seemed to have become the proud master of the striking Tweedy. He sensed that Huxley wasn't sure what to do next. He rubbed his chin.

'Seeing as she'll not come to me, best you take her back to the mews for now,' said Huxley. He pointed to an iron gate in a wall behind a row of trees. 'It's just through there. You'll see an enclosure with her name on it, just open the door and pop her in, that's the way. You go with him, Jones.'

Frank nodded and the two boys headed over to the gate with the bird of prey.

'That was awesome!' said Cas once they were out of earshot of the rest. 'Did you see the look on Huxley's face?'

Frank nodded.

'And Emerald, he'll need to get one of his servants to give him a good clean up when he gets home, no way he can comb that out.'

The two of them laughed. They reached the gate. A sign hung on the wall to the left which read: 'MEWS – AUTHORISED PERSONS ONLY.' Cas opened the gate, which squeaked as he pushed it. He went in and Frank followed.

One side of the courtyard was lined with enclosures and perches, on which sat a variety of hawks and falcons, some looking nervously in their direction as they entered. Cas went ahead, walking slowly, looking for Tweedy's empty run. He turned and noticed that Frank hadn't come with him. Looking back, he saw that Frank was standing stock still by the gate.

'You coming?' he called. 'I think it's this way.'

But Frank just stood there, rooted to the spot. He was staring at the bronze sundial that stood in the middle of the quadrangle. Cas could see he was transfixed.

'You alright?' he asked.

Frank didn't answer immediately.

'Cas, this is the place,' he said at last.

'What place?'

'My dream, the evil looking man.' He looked at Cas. 'This is the place.'

Tweedy fidgeted slightly on his glove. Cas was lost for words. Frank took a few steps and looked around again. He walked to the sundial. Tweedy sat motionless as he ran his other hand over its smooth surface.

'It was like I was actually here,' he said seriously.

'But you weren't. You were in bed and woke up, you said so yourself, it must have been a dream, like you said.'

'I know.' Frank was struggling to make sense of things. 'I know.'

'Then you can't have been here,' said Cas.

Frank shook his head, then he walked towards where Cas was standing, looking purposefully into each enclosure as he did. He strode past Cas, who was watching his friend with interest, until he came to an empty pen about halfway along the wall. He stood facing it for a second, looking it up and down, and then turned around to face out towards the courtyard. He turned back to the pen. Frank did this a couple of times.

'What's up?' said Cas.

'It was from here,' he said. He looked meaningfully at Cas. 'Cas, it was from here, this is the exact view that I had in my head. The *exact* view.'

'Frank, it was just a dream,' reiterated Cas, beginning to feel a bit worried that Frank was starting to sound a bit ridiculous. 'Are you going mad?'

'No, it was definitely as if I was watching what was going on over there,' he pointed to the courtyard, 'from here.' He held his hands up as if indicating his field of vision from his position.

'And take a look at this,' said Frank, looking towards the pen, which was fronted with sturdy wire.

Cas walked over. A small sign hung over the empty enclosure. It read, simply, 'Tweedy'. Frank stared at Cas, who creased his brow as if trying to work out what Frank was thinking. He took a deep intake of breath. They both looked at the hawk, which still sat easily on Frank's hand, staring back at them, head cocked, then back at each other.

'What?' said Cas, not having the slightest idea what Frank was trying to tell him.

'I couldn't have just dreamt of somewhere I've never seen or been before, from somewhere I've never stood, could I? That's not possible and, yet, this is precisely like I saw it. It was too vivid Cas, too real to be a coincidence.'

'What are you trying to say?' said Cas, looking totally confused.

Frank hesitated. He didn't want to appear irrational in front of his friend, but he was now convinced why he could recall the detail of the vision he'd had, so intricately.

'Promise you won't think I'm going bonkers,' he said to Cas, who smiled and nodded. 'But I think I was seeing this,' he indicated the scene before them with a sweep of his free hand, 'from inside the cage here.'

'But that would mean— ' Cas stopped mid-sentence.

'That I saw the whole thing through Tweedy's eyes.'

Frank knew it sounded stupid when he said it and he expected Cas to burst into fits of belly laughter, but his friend didn't seem to find it funny at all.

'I think you're going bonkers,' he said. 'You think you were seeing the whole thing through the eyes of a bird. Yep, definitely crazy.' They both looked at the bird as if it might give them some answers. Frank was about to say something when a voice came from their left.

'Everything alright in there?'

It was Lanks. He was standing at the gate staring haughtily at the two boys. Bertie hung around his ankles, panting. What was he doing there?

'Yes,' said Frank. He wasn't sure if Lanks had heard any of their conversation and immediately feared the complications if he had. 'Fine thanks.'

Lanks's expression didn't alter.

'Can't you read?' he said, pointing to the sign on the outside of the courtyard.

'We were just putting Tweedy back for Professor Huxley,' replied Frank, wondering what Lanks could have possibly thought they were doing seeing as he had a large hawk gripping his hand, although it occurred to him that Lanks might have believed they were trying to make off with it.

He opened the door to the enclosure and placed Tweedy inside. She hopped from his gloved hand to a branch inside and sat there quietly, preening. He and Cas stood there shuffling nervously, both hoping that Lanks would leave them to it. No such luck.

'Well?' said Lanks, sniffing.

'Well what?' said Frank.

'Well, bird delivered, shouldn't you be getting back to your lesson?'

Lanks didn't look like he was about to leave them to it.

'Although,' he continued, 'it seems to me that you and Jones there are ... up to something.'

Neither Frank nor Cas spoke, even though Frank thought their silence might give them away. He certainly didn't like Lanks's tone and thought it a strange coincidence that he had suddenly appeared at the gate, as if he'd been following them. Lanks's lips tightened into an expression of annoyance at the lack of response from the boys.

'Well, on your way then, boys. I'm sure Professor Huxley will be wondering where you are.'

'Yes, Professor,' said Cas.

Both boys desperately didn't want to break their discussion about Frank's dream, if it was a dream at all, but Lanks just stood there, arms now folded, waiting for them to vacate the courtyard. Frank sighed in resignation and led Cas to the entrance and towards Lanks, whose eyes followed them at every step.

As Frank reached the professor, Cas dropped back slightly and bent down to tie his bootlace. Bertie sniffed them as they passed.

'Mr Penny,' Lanks said, making Frank stop and turn. 'Anything you want to tell me?'

Frank didn't reply.

'Anything?' he repeated.

'No,' said Frank. 'Everything's fine.'

He turned and walked back to Huxley's lesson with Cas. Everything was far from fine.

17

GABRIELLA ASARO

At the end of the day, Frank and Cas ran to Laskie's, the vibrant malt shop that they had come to frequent. Since the morning's events in the mews, they had been bursting to discuss Frank's visions further. Afternoon lessons in music and meditation had seemed to go so slowly that Frank thought they might never get away. Music had seen Professor Nobleman, who taught the subject as well as being deputy head, demonstrating an assortment of ethnic drums which he had banged for so long it had given Frank a headache.

They turned the corner by the Blushing Lemon tavern and burst through the door. The shop was busy, mainly with students, not only from the academy, but from the other schools around the town, all of them wanting a retreat from the day's studies. The square wooden tables were filled with children of all ages and there was quite a queue at the counter where Mr and Mrs Laskie were working hard to keep up with the steady trade. Frank and Cas fidgeted as they stood in line, both eager to talk about the mews.

Finally it was their turn.

'Okay, boys?' said Laskie, his accent thick, his brown teeth smiling behind his greying goatee.

'Yes thanks,' said Frank.

They ordered a couple of rhubarb shakes, which Mr Laskie frothed up in a matter of seconds. He handed the boys the two tall sundae glasses full of delicious-looking pink, milky liquid and Frank paid. They looked around the store, searching for somewhere private where they could continue their conversation. The room was full of raucous noise from the throng of people. A group of older boys was getting up from one of the cushioned booths in the corner of the room, so they quickly headed over to the spot to prevent anyone else claiming the seats. The older boys had barely moved out when they reached them and gave Frank and Cas harsh looks as they barged past. They slunk into the safety of the booth, sitting either side of the table, and leaned in to prevent anyone from overhearing their conversation.

'So what do you think?' Frank asked Cas, who had a look of bewilderment etched on his face.

'I still think you're flippin' nuts,' said Cas, although his voice held a hint of amusement.

'But let's assume for a minute that I'm right,' said Frank, keen to pursue his theory.

'Okay, if you must, but this *is* nuts, right?' said Cas, shaking his head.

'Maybe, but, on the assumption that what I saw wasn't a dream, okay, it can only mean one thing,'

'What?'

'That what I saw actually happened, that I saw that cloaked figure come into the mews and disappear and then those other two come in. That they were all there, they all exist, especially old Nasty Face.'

Frank shivered at the recollection of the dark image that he had seen in his head the night before, teeth gleaming, orange streak in his hair, eyes wild.

'Can't argue with that,' Cas replied.

'So, the man that came in first just disappeared. There's no way out of the mews other than the gate we went through, not that I saw anyway. Did you?'

Frank's voice was brimming with excitement; he had tuned out the noise in the shop and was totally focused on their conversation.

Cas considered this for a moment, shook his head and, with a sigh, reached into his bag.

'I guess I can't argue with any of it,' he said, 'especially as I found this.'

Frank watched as he pulled his hand out, placed a small book on the table and pushed it towards Frank, who stared at it as if it were about to leap up and smack him around the face.

'Flippin' heck Cas, where did you get that?' he said, incredulous.

Cas hadn't mentioned anything about it and his revealing it now made Frank instantly excited.

'You forget, I'm learning to be a master sleight of hand,' said Cas with a twinkle in his eye. 'I remembered you told me about something falling from the man's pocket in your dream and, as we were coming out of the mews, I spotted this in a small shrub in the border by the gate.'

He pointed at the book.

'Luckily, Lanks seemed to be more interested in you, so I managed to palm it when I was pretending to tie my lace and he wasn't looking. Easy peasy. Still think you're a bit nuts though.'

Frank picked the book up carefully as if it might break if he were too clumsy. This confirmed everything he had been thinking, that it wasn't a dream after all. That he had seen the man enter the mews. That he had seen him drop something and that something was a book, the book that was now sitting on the table, occupying the centre of their attention. That the man had also disappeared, although where and how was still an unanswered question. But then, horrifyingly, it also meant that the dark man with the long black hair and scorpion emblem was very real and probably lurking somewhere near the academy. His heart started racing at their discovery, about what it might signify, but he also felt a sense of trepidation. He was unsure why he was uneasy, although it might have something to do with the evil-looking face that had startled him awake.

Frank inspected the book. At first he thought it looked old, antique even, but, as he examined the ornate leather cover and binding, he realised, by the lack of marks and the crispness of the pages, it had been produced relatively recently.

It was small, just bigger than the palm of his hand, like a

notebook. He opened it and immediately noticed that the first page had been ripped out. Of the remaining pages, of which there were only about twenty, the first few were blank but the rest were covered with a mass of lines, ink splodges and strange-looking symbols. Some had odd purple flecks around the edges. Flicking through the few pages, he had no idea what language it was written in, if in fact it was a language at all, so unusual were the markings. He closed the book and turned it over in his hand and, as he held it between the thumb and fingers, he was struck with a sense of wonder. What was all this about? How were this strange little book, his visions and the dark man connected? He looked at Cas, who just shrugged.

'Search me mate,' he said, reading Frank's thoughts. 'I had a quick look earlier when old Chandra was going on about mindfulness and, what was it, the extinction of the fires of detachment, but it means less to me than that lesson even. Could be the scribblings of a two-year-old, for all I know.'

Frank agreed. The contents looked random and far from coherent and could well just be someone's sketch book.

'Perhaps we should show it to Professor Burdock, he might know,' said Cas.

Professor Burdock was the Languages master who spoke with a slight stutter and bored them senseless muttering about extinct ancient tongues.

'If it's written in some old language, he may well be able to help.'

Frank thought he had a point, but was reluctant to let anyone else in on their new find just yet.

'Or maybe we should just try and find out ourselves,' he said, 'I'd be a bit fidgety about telling anyone else until we know a bit more. What do you think?'

Although he had always managed to be resourceful, this might be a bit beyond him and he wasn't really sure they could it do by themselves. They sat in silence for a minute, both thinking of what to do. Frank's mind led him back to the vision in the mews and he went over the details again and again, trying to put together what was happening and make some sense of it. Cas noticed that Frank had become preoccupied.

'Frank, you all right?'

'Yeah, sorry, I was just thinking who the figure was in the courtyard, the one who dropped the book and then promptly disappeared,' said Frank, coming back to life, 'I was wondering if it was someone from the academy, someone we might have seen before, but I can't think who.'

'You don't think it was Ludlow Hums do you?' said Cas, thinking of the missing thief and the Alphaen.

'No way, this man was quick. Hums is a zillion years old. There's not a chance it was him, not unless he was on wheels. No, it wasn't Hums.'

Frank was sure it couldn't have been the wizened old murderous villain he had seen in the wanted poster that Norris had shown him; surely he would have walked with a stick or something. No, definitely not. It had crossed his mind that this was connected in some way, but that just begged yet another question amongst all the new questions that the day had thrown up.

'So I wonder who it was then?'

'Me too, but whoever it was is now missing a children's doodle book.'

Frank smiled. He put the book back down and they fell silent for a moment, sipping their shakes. They had no ideas. They had no answers.

Laskie's was still busy. More students had come in and trade was brisk. Frank occasionally heard Mr Laskie's voice rise above the din, announcing that an order of hazelnut steamed pudding or aromatic berry slush was ready. It was standing room only. A couple of the students in their intake, a sturdy girl called Willow and a bright looking boy called Bernard, looked into their booth for somewhere to sit. They said hello, but moved on when Frank and Cas failed to invite them to sit down, getting the message that they wanted to be alone.

Cas shook his head, not for the first time.

'The more I think about this, the more ridiculous it becomes,' he said. 'I mean, for starters, how can you see through the eyes of a hawk? Who does that? It's absurd.'

As Cas said it, he realised that he'd been a bit louder than he had intended and they looked sheepishly around, worried that he might have been overheard.

Although the shop was humming with students, Frank heard the scraping sound of a chair being pushed back at the table next to their booth. He thought nothing of it, but then, from around the corner, came a teenage girl in an Excelsus shirt. She was boyish, even though she had long, wild black, hair which hung in unkempt ringlets around her face. Her wrists were heavy with ornate bangles which she wore along with other weighty jewellery. She was kind of scary looking. Frank thought she certainly looked like she could handle herself. But most striking of all were the beautiful tattoos up her arms and the piercings in her ears, nose and eyebrow. She stood out, bohemian and anti-establishment. He'd never seen anyone like her and was immediately both intrigued and wary at the same time. Smithwood had its characters, but no girls like this, he was sure of that.

The two boys sat and watched as she pulled up a chair and sat at the end of their table, full of confidence. Both were speechless. She gave them both a smile. Frank removed the book from the table and put it into his bag, away from her prying eyes. He had a feeling that he knew what was coming.

'See you tomorrow, Anya.'

She turned to the girl she'd been sitting with, who got up from the table, nodded towards her and made her way out of the shop. Then she turned back to Frank and Cas.

'All right boys?' she said mischievously, flicking her dark locks away from her face. The boys didn't know what to say as their uninvited guest adjusted her position and made herself comfortable.

'Do you mind? This is a private conversation,' said Cas, but Frank got the feeling she was there to stay; she just had that sort of look about her and something reminded him a bit of Phoebe.

'Sorry,' she said. 'Couldn't help overhearing, even in this place. Anyway, if it's private, then you should learn to keep your voices down.'

She smiled and Frank shot an annoyed look at Cas, who grimaced.

'What did you overhear exactly?' said Frank, anxious to find out how much she had actually heard and, more importantly, if Cas had let one of their cats out of the bag, whether she was the kind to keep a secret.

'That one of you seems to have found a familiar,' she said, eyes moving from one boy to the other, silently weighing them up.

Frank felt himself twitch nervously managing to turn it into a nonchalant shrug to avoid giving himself away.

'A familiar what?' said Cas quickly. He looked at Frank who, this time, gave a proper shrug.

'Not "what". A familiar,' repeated the girl.

'Yeah, I heard what you said,' said Cas, his tone a little mocking. 'So what's that?'

'Well, perhaps I shouldn't tell you if you're going to be like that,' she said, sitting back with a smug look on her face.

She waited. Cas and Frank looked at each other. This girl seemed to know something they didn't, but she didn't appear too bothered if she told them or not, which would definitely be their loss. Cas spoke.

'Okay, sorry,' he said. 'So, what is it then, a familiar?'

The girl's tone lightened.

'It's an animal through which you can see.'

She said it so matter-of-factly that Frank almost missed its significance and thought he was going to fall off his chair when he realised that, if this unique-looking girl was to be believed, what he thought was impossible a few hours ago now appeared to completely possible.

'How on earth do you know that?' said Cas.

'My mother's got one,' she said, again very factually.

'Your mum's got a hawk?'

'No, it's a cat.'

'A cat?'

'Yeah.'

'Right. First a hawk, now a cat. Is everyone going completely barmy?' Cas threw his hands into the air, but the girl seemed undaunted. Frank got the distinct impression she was relishing the situation.

'Oh you can be partnered to any animal. At least, I think you can.'

She looked at Frank, who had kept quiet, weighing her up as she spoke. He liked her attitude; she was sparky, mischievous and definitely not lacking in confidence.

'Right, thanks, don't let us keep you,' continued Cas, turning to Frank for support.

The girl just ignored him and continued talking.

'But it's very, *very* rare; I can't tell you how unusual it is. I can only think of a handful of people my mum knows who have one, and they're *much* older than you. Certainly I wouldn't expect to get one for years yet, and it's probable that I won't even get one at all. See what I mean?'

Frank was beginning to get the picture and, even though at first he'd been sceptical of what she'd been saying, it was now dawning on him that she knew exactly what she was talking about.

'What do you mean, "expect to get one"?' said Cas.

'Well, normally, only really advanced sorcerers have one at some time or other, so I should think I'll get one if I'm anything like my mum,' she said nonchalantly.

'Sorcerers?' Cas realised he'd raised his voice again. This time, much to his relief, no one seemed to notice.

'Look, are you just going to repeat everything that I say?' she said.

'Well, only when you go on about talking cats and sorcery.'

'I didn't say anything about cats talking, that's a different matter altogether.' She raised her pierced eyebrows.

There was a moment's silence, then the three of them just burst out laughing at the strange conversation they were having. Frank couldn't help thinking how utterly bizarre it all sounded. It was like something out of one of the comics he used to read when he was younger, something completely made-up and far-fetched that it could only have come from the mind of the fantasy writer of his favourite characters. They quietened and looked at each other, oblivious to the hubbub behind them.

'What's your name?' Frank asked, breaking his silence.

'Oh, you do speak, then.' She flashed a smile in Frank's direction. 'My name's Gabriella. Call me Gabby. You guys join this year?'

'Yeah,' said Cas. Frank nodded.

'Thought so. I'm in the intake above yours. Anya and I joined last year. She's from the same village as me. We're best buddies.'

She flicked her head in the direction of the girl who had just left.

'So, who's the lucky one, then?' asked Gabby keenly. 'The one with the hawk as a familiar?'

'That'll be me,' said Frank, noticing the number 820 on Gabby's shirt and feeling a little less guarded. 'I'm Frank. Frank Penny. This is Hardcastle Jones.' He nodded over to Cas.

'That's a strange name,' said Gabby, cheerily.

'At least it's the only thing about me that's strange,' he replied. 'My friends call me Cas.'

'So I'll call you Cas, then,' she said with a hint of cheek. Frank suppressed a chuckle.

'I guess so,' said Cas in resignation. Gabby turned to Frank.

'Well let me tell you something, Frankie.' For a moment she sounded just like Phoebe. 'Having a familiar is a gift; it must have

been passed down to you somehow. What do your parents do?'
Frank hesitated.

'My dad's a farmer,' he said, 'and my mum died when I was young.' He didn't think that sounded like a recipe for teaming up with a beady-eyed red kite.

'Oh, sorry, I didn't mean to ... well, you know.' Gabby sounded genuinely apologetic and looked sympathetically at Frank.

'That's okay,' he said. He changed the subject back to his visions. 'So you think what I saw through the hawk was actually happening?'

'Yep, a hundred percent. You weren't dreaming, it's called an apparamal,' she said and sat back in her chair.

The boys looked at each other.

'So what did you see through your hawk?' Gabby looked at Frank, her look demanding an answer.

Frank, who didn't lack confidence himself, admired her forthrightness; she certainly wasn't shy in coming forward. The question was, could he trust her? He looked as Cas, who shrugged, so, with a deep breath, he told her the detail of his vision. Gabby listened, enthralled, and when he'd finished she looked at them and blew out her cheeks.

'Wow, you guys certainly know how to get a girl's interest,' she laughed. 'But you have to learn how to control it, Frank,' she said, seriously. 'You don't just want visions popping into your head without warning, do you?'

Frank shook his head, although he was not sure what he was meant to do to control these strange images.

'So,' Gabby continued, 'we have a strange disappearing man - or woman - and two men in hot pursuit. Sounds fab!'

Frank wasn't so sure it was at all 'fab', although he had to admit her enthusiasm for their situation was definitely rubbing off and he could sense she was genuinely interested and that she might want to help them.

Gabby went on, 'What did you say the weird-looking bloke was wearing?'

Frank wasn't sure he'd explained the man's appearance in that much detail, so he described the scorpion emblem that had adorned his tunic and watched as Gabby's expression went from the intrigued to the hostile. She gave a snort of contempt and sat back, folding her arms. He was certainly surprised at her reaction, as if he'd unwittingly insulted her.

'What's up?' he asked.

He noticed the tattoos on her arms again. Delicate depictions of rosebuds and daisies interlaced with stems of thorns. Unusual.

'That's the crest of Kzarlac,' she snarled.

'Who?' said Cas, who was slightly taken aback at the ferocity of her response.

'Not *who*, dummy, *where*.'

Cas and Frank looked at her blankly and Frank shrugged his shoulders in ignorance.

'Oh, come on boys, haven't you done geography in school?' snapped Gabby.

'Never my favourite subject,' said Cas. 'Never really listened.'

She looked across to Frank in anticipation, a cross expression on her face that Frank wasn't sure was aimed at them or this Kzarlac place, where ever that was.

'I'm home educated,' said Frank. 'Not sure what use knowing about some far off country would be on my dad's farm.'

Gabby huffed. Frank had been interested in faraway lands, and often wondered about what went on beyond the confines of Smithwood and Byeland, but he suddenly felt that perhaps he should have a greater breadth of knowledge of other places, of kingdoms and countries.

'Well it's a horrid place,' said Gabby. 'Hateful people.' She started to well up and averted her gaze as a tear came to her eye.

'How do you know?' asked Frank.

'Let's just say me and my folks have some history there, so we came to live in Byeland when I was a kid. I don't know much about it really.'

She paused as if mentally recollecting events in her mind.

'But check you out Frankie - home ed and a familiar. Right man of mystery, aren't you!' She had reverted back to her cheeky self.

Her observation gave Frank an odd feeling. Back in Smithwood, he'd been very nondescript indeed, and even up until now, during his time at Excelsus, had thought himself totally uninteresting, but, suddenly, he was being cast as someone mysterious and exciting by a girl he'd only just met. He had to admit that recent events had exposed a new aspect to his life at the academy. Strange visions, seeing hawks, a missing villain, a drowned elderly caretaker, a stolen Seal, three cloaked figures in the middle of the night and the chilling face of a man from a place he'd never heard of. Norris had said there was something mysterious about Excelsus and Frank now had to agree.

'So are you a fee payer?' asked Cas.

'Are you *kidding*?' said Gabby, as if she'd just been called something nasty.

'Just asking,' said Cas, awkwardness creeping into his voice as he realised he'd made a bit of an error.

'Do I *look* like a fee payer?' she leaned her head to one side and stared at him, eyes wide.

'Not really,' he admitted.

'So you're a meritter too, like us,' said Frank, somehow pleased that she was like them, that, although they had all arrived in this place from different backgrounds, they all shared some sort of common bond.

'Yep. So's Anya. She's my one and only friend here. We have a right laugh. She's a seer, or trying to be, so she probably saw the invitation coming.' Gabby laughed at her own joke.

'A seer?' said Frank. 'What's that?'

'Oh, you know, visions, predicting the future. That sort of thing. She thinks she's no good at it, but I reckon she'll do okay. Trouble is, she's got really pushy parents.'

'So why are *you* here?' asked Cas.

'I just told you, dummy. I'm from a long line of sorcerers on my mother's side, so my family has been coming here for generations.' Cas looked glum, his attempt to redeem himself after his last comment had backfired.

'Mine too,' he said, in an attempt to find some common ground.

'So, you can do magic?' said Frank.

Gabby shook her head. Frank looked at Cas who shook his head as though Frank had uttered a rude word.

'Get real, Frank, there's no such thing as magic. You can't just swish a stick around in the air, say a few words and expect something to happen. Spells and that sort of stuff's just in kids' books. Sorcery is a skill and takes a lot of time and effort to perfect. It's an art. But I didn't really want to come,' continued Gabby. 'It's all very well that my family has a long tradition, but I don't see why I have to do it too. I'm thinking of leaving; it'll be the winter holidays soon and I might tell my mum that I don't want to come back. She'll understand, I think. And I reckon Anya wants to leave too; she gets bored easily and, let's face it, most of what we do here is just plain dull. That's school for you, don't you think?'

'Leave?' said Frank. 'But I didn't think that anyone left once they started.'

He thought back to Messenger's visit to the farm when he had made it clear to Frank that no one had ever refused an invitation and he also seemed to recall that it was very rare that anyone ever left. Frank thought of the moments he'd considered turning down the academy in favour of staying at home. Given how events were turning out, he wasn't sure if coming had been a good thing or not.

'Let's just say I don't really fit in up there,' said Gabby.

'I guess you look a little different,' smiled Frank.

Gabby shrugged. 'It's not just that,' she said, 'I get annoyed by a lot of the teachers and they think I'm a bit disruptive. I was in Wisley's Remedies class this morning and he started mixing burdock with vinegar to heal bunions. Thought he was talking a lot of old rubbish, so I told him. Didn't seem to go down too well. I also got on the wrong side of Lanks yesterday.' She laughed, not bothered by her attitude.

'He's our head of intake,' said Frank. 'But I'm not sure what to make of him.'

Frank explained their encounter at the gate of the mews.

'I think he's an idiot,' huffed Gabby. 'They all are.'

Frank wasn't sure he agreed, but sensed that Gabby had some issues with authority.

'Yeah, he seems to be keeping an eye on Frank since he upset Moonhunter on the first day of term.' said Cas.

'Wow, you upset Moonhunter! Be careful Frank, she'll turn you into a mouse and that cat of hers will gobble you up.' She made a motion like a pouncing cat, then sat back and laughed loudly. Frank wasn't sure what she meant, but both he and Cas couldn't help but laugh with her.

At that moment a couple of older academy boys walked past and looked into their booth. The three of them immediately looked up at them and gave them a 'go away' look. The boys moved on. Gabby flicked her hair away from her eyes again.

'So why are you here, Frank?' she asked. 'History of familiars on the farm?'

Frank shook his head and shrugged as Gabby looked at him intently.

'No, I don't think a sheep would be too useful like that, do you? So I've no idea why I'm here.' Frank realised he hadn't thought about his invitation for a while. 'I'm just normal. Not sure that being gallant and gifted applies to me in the slightest.'

Gabby narrowed her eyes.

'There's always a reason, Frank. Surely you know that by now.'

'Yeah, so I keep getting told.'

'So, you think you're ordinary? Well, let me tell you, Frank, what if others know something about you that you don't?'

'Like what?'

'No idea, but I tell you what, though,' she said. 'You guys are suddenly making being here a bit more interesting. Perhaps I'll stay for a bit longer.'

18

THE HISTORY

Frank and Cas had the joy of History. Gabby's brief mention of Kzarlac had made him wonder if, or how, it was connected to their discoveries of the book and Hums, so Frank decided to ask Professor Huffie. He didn't feel he could ask Gabby any more, given how upset she appeared when she started talking about it. He found the reaction at odds with the strange and confident girl who had joined them at Laskie's.

As the class settled, Frank said, 'Professor, can you tell me about Kzarlac?'

The room fell silent and there was a murmuring from Emerald and his friends.

'If you like,' said the professor. 'But there's not much to tell. I'm surprised they didn't teach you a bit at your old school, Penny.'

Before Frank could answer, Emerald piped up, 'He didn't go to school, sir. I'm surprised he can even read and write, let alone know anything about Kzarlac.'

A wave of laughter spread across the classroom. Frank thought about a smart retort, but let the comment go.

'Thank you, Mr Emerald,' said Huffie.

He turned back to Frank who was waiting expectantly. The jowly professor had a large moustache which he had the habit of licking quickly between sentences. He looked back to Emerald. Frank now knew, from the insignia on their shirts, that Emerald and his lot were somehow connected to Kzarlac. He guessed that was where they all hailed from, like some sort of club, a little gang.

'So, what can I tell you?' Huffie said to himself He paced around the front of the classroom scratching his head and chin in equal measure, looking down at the floor. 'Kzarlac, land of the black scorpion, is a ... powerful nation, you could say.' Frank could tell he was choosing his words carefully. 'But I believe they have a strong identity, having come into being many years ago. Some might say that they are quite a strong-handed, hostile country. Their history is certainly one of aggression and they undoubtedly have a questionable record on how they treat some of their people.'

He stopped, nodding to himself. Frank looked vacantly at the professor. He'd used a lot of words but he hadn't really said anything specific, as if he was being deliberately evasive. Frank wasn't about to accept his vagueness as any sort of answer.

'So why would people dislike Kzarlac? A lot?' said Frank, recalling Gabby's reaction to his description of the black scorpion emblem.

'No one likes them,' interjected Honeycomb Maddison.

It was the first time Frank had heard her say anything audible in a class, or speak to anyone, except to her sister, who nodded vigorously.

'My dad reckons they're a nasty bunch,' said Eric, the weapon maker's son. 'He's had some business dealings with them in the past and says he wouldn't go back there after the way they treated him.'

The class became noisy as a number of the students mumbled their agreement and started speaking to each other as if they all suddenly had an opinion or experience of the matter. Huffie went to speak, but, before he could, Frank heard a familiar voice.

'It's obvious, isn't it,' Emerald jumped in. 'Other people and countries are so jealous of us, that's why they don't like Kzarlac.' Frank noted the use of the word 'us', confirming what he thought.

'Jealous!' Cas said, 'What, of a load of posh boys with dodgy hair?' The class laughed.

'Say what you like, Bones,' snapped Emerald, 'There's only one place you should be if you want true leaders, tough enforcers and real discipline. Not any wishy-washy losers, like Byeland.'

Emerald didn't seem bothered by his choice of words. Frank noticed some of the students in the class giving him derisory looks, but they didn't say anything.

Emerald had stopped short of declaring that he and his cronies were somehow superior to everyone else, but he certainly left Frank with the feeling that he considered all of those not from Kzarlac as second class citizens. Frank looked over at Emerald, who huffed a sneer back at him. There was a very frosty atmosphere in the room. Professor Huffie clapped his hands, regaining the room's attention.

'Okay, perhaps we should move on? Can't dwell on things that are of no concern of ours in this room,' he said.

'Now, if you could all open your books to page one hundred and ten, we'll continue on the origins of the collapse of the Nozertium Empire.'

No concern? thought Frank. How wrong could he be? It was a big concern for him. He looked at Cas, who was shaking his head. Emerald looked smug, as if he'd made some sort of important point that elevated him above everyone else. Frank was disappointed he'd not learned more, or anything for that matter, although the exchange had confirmed what he'd thought about Emerald and his gang of yes men. He knew now that their monogrammed shirts had been specially produced in Kzarlac to mark them out from the others, like some sort of badge of honour. Well, Frank wasn't impressed one bit and his contempt for Emerald and where he was from was growing considerably, not least because of the way his new friend Gabby had reacted, and he was sure there was more to her story.

* * *

As they left the academy at the end of the day, Frank heard footsteps running up behind them. He turned to see Gabby. She was with another girl, who Frank recognised as her friend from their encounter at Laskie's.

'Mind if we join you?' said the other girl as they fell in line. She was dark-skinned, with long, straight hair that was as black as the night. She wore thick-rimmed glasses, which she pushed back on her nose. They made her look kind of geeky.

'You must be Anya,' said Frank.

'Yep, that's me. Gabby's told me all about you guys.'

'She has?' said Cas, turning to Gabby.

'Alright chaps?' she said, with a wide grin on her face.

'Yeah,' said Frank. 'Although I'm a bit frustrated. We tried to find out a bit more about Kzarlac, but ended up discovering nothing.'

'Who did you ask?' said Anya.

Frank told them about the exchange in the History lesson and Gabby screwed up her nose.

'Not surprised. Old Huffie, waste of space; wouldn't tell you much more in case he upset the Kzarlac faithful, if you ask me. Anyway, don't try too hard,' said Gabby, 'you'll find nothing but a world of pain. Any more apparamals, Frank?' she said, changing the subject.

Frank glanced at Anya, then back to Gabby.

'Oh, don't worry, I tell Anya everything. What are best friends for?'

'Don't worry, Frank. Your secret's safe with me,' Anya said reassuringly.

Frank looked at Gabby, who nodded. He relaxed. 'No, not sure when the next instalment will be coming out,' he smiled.

The four of them strode across the bridge; the river flowed quickly under them as they headed out onto the plaza.

'Impressive, isn't it?' said Gabby turning and looking back at the great stone vulture. Frank nodded his agreement. He had become accustomed to the menacing stare of the enormous raptor and had even come to consider it a thing of beauty.

Frank looked out across the plaza and wondered if Blackburn, with all his knowledge and invention, might know something about Kzarlac and the mystery man. He was sure that if they could find out more about him they might start to connect why he was here to the strange events that had unfolded. He stopped and turned to the others.

'Anyone fancy a quick tea before we go home?' Cas knew what he was thinking.

'Sure,' he replied. 'Good idea.'

'Tea? Where?' said Anya.

'Why don't we just go to Laskie's? I quite fancy a shake and a cake,' said Gabby.

'Yeah,' said Frank. 'But Mr Laskie doesn't seem like the sort who might be able to help us,' and before Gabby or Anya could complain he led them across to the tatty-looking workshop on the other side of the road.

The four of them entered Blackburn's. He was talking to a rather tall, studious-looking man who was dressed in a garish multi-coloured shirt with a bright green waistcoat. The man had the shiniest bald head and small pointy ears. The two of them were laughing.

'Hello, Frank, Cas and ...'

'This is Gabby,' said Frank. 'And Anya.'

'Goodness, you'll soon be bringing the whole academy over here,' laughed Blackburn. 'See if you can find enough chairs. Tea's just brewed. I won't be a minute.'

He turned back to the tall man and continued his conversation.

'No apple shakes, then,' hissed Gabby.

Frank laughed and led them to the back of the room. The two beaten old armchairs were empty, so Anya and Gabby threw down their bags and sank into them. Frank found a small upholstered stool on the other side of the forge, on which Cicero was dozing. He scooped the cat up and moved the stool to where the others were sitting, placing the dazed animal on his lap. The cat looked around in indignation and promptly went back to sleep as if nothing had happened.

Cas stood and poured the tea, but his attention was caught by a line of small flasks that were sitting on the worktop next to him. They contained an orange liquid, flecked with slowly moving blue streaks.

He put the teapot down, picked one up and gazed into the fiery fluid. It had a strange look about it, as if it were alive.

The men finished their conversation and the man in the gaudy shirt got ready to go.

'And to what do I owe the pleasure?' asked Blackburn turning to the students as the other man grabbed his coat which, fittingly, was a tasteless shade of mustard.

Blackburn noticed that Cas was holding the small bottle.

'Ooh, careful with that, young man,' he said holding his hand up in alarm, as if to stop Cas doing something silly.

'What is it?' asked Cas curiously, still peering through the glass into the animated fluid in the bottle. 'Doesn't look like anything I've ever seen before.'

'No, I daresay it isn't. Just something I've been working on for a while, meant to put them away,' he said.

Cas still had a questioning look on his face.

'Can't seem to get the formula right,' continued Blackburn. 'If you give it a very slight shake ...'

He signalled a slight shaking motion with his hand. 'Gently, mind.'

Cas shook the flask gently and the bottle promptly emitted a bright incandescent light. Cas looked amazed, as did the others. They expected the light to vanish as quickly as it had appeared, but it continued to glow. Cas put the bottle back on the worktop where the light blazed out across the room.

'Wowzer.'

'Yes, not bad, this batch, light shines for about twenty minutes, normally, so I'm getting there. The problem is that if you shake it just slightly too hard the bottle tends to, er, well, explode a bit.'

'Explode a bit?' said Frank. 'How can something explode "a bit"?'

'Okay, explodes a lot, yes, I'm afraid so. Not much use is it, an exploding light? Not really. Can you imagine waking up in the night needing to go to the, er, well, you know? You grab your bottle of, this'

—he indicated to the bottles on the side— 'you give it a shake and the thing blows up in your face.'

He paused and looked at them. Then they all burst into laughter. If that was the case, Frank had to agree it wasn't Blackburn's best, but he could see it might have potential.

'Just need to work on the formula,' said Blackburn earnestly. He reached for the brightly lit flask, inspecting it for a moment before placing it back on the side.

'So,' said Blackburn. 'Is this just a social visit? No problem if it is, always nice to see you ... four.'

He looked softly toward Gabby and Anya.

'Well, we were wondering if you know much about a place called Kzarlac.' Frank asked.

Blackburn's expression changed and the tall man stopped, arm halfway down a sleeve of his coat.

'Of course. Why? Don't they teach you anything about it over there?' His brow creased into a frown.

'Well, I did ask Professor Huffie, the History teacher, but I felt he was a bit, well, vague,' said Frank.

Cas nodded.

'Didn't really tell us much,' he said in support.

'Really?' said Blackburn, his response more blunt than questioning. He paused. 'What makes you ask?' he said, inspecting the four of them.

The other man watched on with interest.

Frank thought for a moment, wondering how to approach the subject without giving too much away.

'I saw an insignia on one of the boy's shirts, a red circle with a black scorpion on it.'

Frank felt best not to make reference to the attire of the odious man he'd seen in his vision, he thought he should keep that from Blackburn at the moment and it didn't seem relevant to his need to find out about Kzarlac.

'Oh?'

'Yes, I mentioned it to Gabby and she said it was the mark of Kzarlac.'

Frank looked over to Gabby, who nodded. He noticed Anya cast a sympathetic look in Gabby's direction.

'That's right, black scorpion, no secret, but you don't get much talk of that place around here,' he said with an air of warning in his voice.

'Why not?'

'Damnable place,' said Blackburn. The tall man next to him smiled and nodded.

'That's what Gabby says,' said Anya.

'Told you,' said Gabby, looking at Blackburn. Although she had said it was a horrible place, she hadn't elaborated on why.

'So you know?' said Blackburn, eyeing Gabby with interest.

She shifted uncomfortably in her seat.

'Yeah, my folks used to live in a place called Prismia,' she said, not going into any more detail.

'Oh, right, say no more then, that'll explain a lot. Explains your tattoos.'

Blackburn looked at her arms and back again, raising his eyebrows. Gabby instinctively rubbed her forearms.

'Glad to see you're alive,' he continued mysteriously.

Frank looked at Gabby. Glad to see you're alive? he thought. What a strange thing to say. He'd also caught the reference to her tattoos, which he hadn't even thought needed an explanation, but which Blackburn's comments had given some sort of significance. However, now wasn't the time to deviate from the subject of Kzarlac.

'Well, it's a good job you called by when you did. My friend, Mr Halnaker, here, is somewhat of an authority on the subject of Kzarlac.'

The tall man bowed slightly at the introduction, his head gleaming in the light from the jar.

'Magnus Halnaker,' he said.

The four children smiled and nodded at him.

'And, let me tell you, sometimes the history they teach you in school is just the history they want you to know,' he continued mysteriously, a twinkle in his eye.

'What do you mean?' said Frank. 'History's just ... history, isn't it?' Frank remembered that Brigg always used to say that what's gone is gone, and you couldn't change the past.

'Unless you're Huffie, then it's just dull,' said Cas.

'Well, there's a lot that's gone on that they don't teach you, that's for sure. Perhaps they don't like you to know,' Halnaker continued. 'The Byeland–Kzarlac issue is probably one of them, unless things have changed, which I doubt.'

'Huh?' said Frank.

Cas looked blank. Anya looked intrigued. Gabby looked uncomfortable. Blackburn poured himself a mug of tea and offered one to Halnaker with his eyes; the tall man declined with a raise of the palm.

'D'you think I should tell them, Atticus?' Halnaker said to Blackburn in an amused tone.

Blackburn kept pouring his tea.

'Well, like I said, seeing as you're a bit of an authority on the matter, Magnus, I don't see that it'll do them any harm. Might learn something, don't you think?'

'Yes, please tell us,' said Frank. Halnaker, who was still standing at the workbench where Blackburn had been crafting some wooden object, sifted some wood shavings through his fingers. He stopped, pulled a stool from under the table and sat facing the four children. He clasped his hands together, interlocking his fingers, and placed them on his knees. Blackburn returned to his bench but stood there, listening.

'Hm,' he mused. 'Where to begin? At the start I should think.'

All four leaned forward in anticipation.

Halnaker began.

'Way back in time, many centuries ago, the land in which we live now was ruled by a chap called Albin. Very popular he was; the sort who was fair, wise and treated his people well. Before his time there was always a lot of in-fighting because there were no rules as to who would succeed the king. So, being the kind of person he was, he decided it was time to have things written down, get his house in order, so to speak, so there would be no more problems when he passed on. So, he passed a simple law that stated how the land should be passed from generation to generation and, when he died, these rules were to be followed. They were called the Settlement Transcripts.' Halnaker's eyes gleamed as he told the story. 'When he eventually died, the land was passed down to his eldest child, Antares, in accordance with the transcripts and he continued in his father's ways until he passed it on to his eldest child and so it went on.'

'That seems straightforward,' said Frank. 'Each king passes the responsibility to his eldest child. You'd have thought they'd have done that before.' Halnaker nodded.

'Straightforward, yes, you might think that. Straightforward that is … until you get an unexpected problem,' said Halnaker. He flashed his eyes and paused for effect. Frank's eyes widened, expecting the punch line.

'What sort of problem?' said Gabby, puzzled.

'Well, some generations later, the land eventually passed to a man called Kester, whose wife, Vega, gave birth to twins, a boy and a girl. Joleyon and Lashka.'

'So why's that a problem?' asked Cas.

'Well, you see, if you have a rule, no, a law, that states the land is to be passed on to your eldest child, what do you do when you have no eldest, hmm?'

'Which would be the situation if you had twins,' Frank interjected. 'They're both the same age.'

'Very good,' said Halnaker. The foursome thought for a moment.

'You'd make them joint rulers?' said Anya.

'Well, not a bad suggestion, young lady. That would be sensible, maybe,' said Halnaker.

'No,' said Gabby. 'You can only really have one person in charge otherwise it makes things difficult.'

'What about Byeland?' Cas piped up. 'The council isn't just one person, there's, what, fifteen of them?'

'Yeah, and it takes ages to get anyone to make a decision, or so my dad says,' retorted Gabby. 'They're useless.'

Cas looked taken aback and gave Gabby a grumpy look. He slumped back into his chair, sulking. Anya supressed a giggle.

'You see,' said Halnaker. 'Not as easy as you might think, and this presented Kester with a conundrum that no one had needed to consider before, and that wasn't covered in the original transcripts.'

Halnaker paused again, mentally searching for his words.

'The unfortunate thing was that Kester was not exactly as wise as some of his ancestors.'

'Why, what did he do?' asked Frank.

'He did what he thought was right at the time,' sighed Halnaker. 'Which we all do, I guess. He decided that, when the time came, the land should be divided in two to be passed to his children.'

'That seems okay,' said Frank. 'Fair, I mean.'

'Maybe, but then it depends on who you're putting in charge.'

'You said his children were put in charge,' said Gabby.

'That's right, but what if one of them was no good? A rotten apple?' Halnaker mused.

He left the question hanging for a second.

'What do you mean?' asked Frank.

'Well, Kester loved his children equally, as most good parents do, so he thought he had no need to be concerned about simply giving his two offspring half each. But what he failed to recognise was, while his son was the image of his father and his forbears, fair and reliable, his daughter, goodness me she was a different matter altogether - dark, sinister and a rather nasty piece of work, according to the story. Insanely jealous of her brother who, apparently, had a much better relationship with their parents. Kester, apparently, had no idea. He either couldn't or didn't want to see the bad in his own daughter, or, as some people thought, she fooled him, fooled everybody, right up to that point.'

'Wowzer,' said Cas, sipping his tea. 'Makes me and my brother look like we get on like a house on fire.'

'Me too,' chipped in Anya.

'So you see, when their father died, his wishes were followed, despite some quite robust protests from the elders in the land, and there was a lot of unrest amongst the people. But, eventually, the land was split down the middle, hewn in two by the hack of the legal axe. Half to be ruled by the son and half to be ruled by the rather terrifying daughter.'

'And those lands became Byeland and Kzarlac,' said Gabby.

'Exactly,' said Halnaker. 'The mountains became the natural border - a divide. The two new rulers, who, it turned out, had never really seen eye-to-eye when they were being brought up, all of a sudden became sworn enemies. From centuries of peace, harmony and prosperity, everything was suddenly thrown into chaos. Mayhem ensued, the border was closed and families were torn apart.'

He shook his head as though he had recalled events that had only just happened. 'Such a shame, such a shame.'

'But that was a long time ago, right?' said Cas.

'True enough, but the divide still exists to this day. Years have gone by and the two lands have had to live side by side. But Kzarlac, it seems, has always had some unspoken designs on Byeland.'

'You mean to reunify?' said Frank.

'Well, some might see it that way, especially those from Kzarlac, but, in my opinion, more of a hostile and conquering power would be a better way of putting it.'

The thought of some nasty power wanting to take over his homeland sent a shiver down Frank's spine. He would never have thought such a thing could happen, but the fact that a place like the one Halnaker had described even existed, let alone bordered Byeland, gave him an uneasy feeling, especially as he knew someone from Kzarlac was sneaking around the academy.

'But they've never, er, tried anything like that?' said Cas. 'You know, the hostile part, and the conquering.' He hoped Halnaker would quell any fears he had about aggressive neighbours.

'No, in fact they have never tried which, given Kzarlac's history and reputation, seems a bit of a mystery and I can't say that anyone knows why, or how, the two lands have lived in relative peace over such a long time.' A puzzled look appeared briefly on his face. 'But, one thing's for sure, they definitely have it in them and they've given other lands an awful lot of problems.' He cast an obvious look at Gabby who nodded, her expression serious. 'So, Byeland and Kzarlac are uncomfortable neighbours and each side makes no secret of the fact that they despise the other.'

Frank considered this for a moment, and then remembered he'd been thinking of the insignia on Emerald's shirt, the black scorpion of Kzarlac.

'So, how come there are students from Kzarlac here at the academy in Byeland?' he asked. He found it odd that they would be allowed to attend by either side, given the hatred that appeared to exist between them.

'Good question,' said Halnaker, 'and one simply explained by the fact that Excelsus is the best, the elite, and there is this unspoken, but tenuous, agreement that students from Kzarlac can still come, like they did when the lands were united. Seems that Kzarlac hasn't yet been able to establish anything like Excelsus in its own territory. Perhaps that's a matter of time. So, for now, you have to put up with Kzarlac students over there. I wouldn't be surprised if the powers that be in Byeland use it as an opportunity to see what sort of people Kzarlac are sending, sussing them out so to speak, and perhaps hoping they'll stay and work for them rather than returning home.'

The various clocks in Blackburn's workshop struck four. The jumble of rings, and a cuckoo, caused Halnaker to look round.

'I must be going,' he said. 'Nice to meet you all. Hope you enjoyed your history lesson!'

He got up from his stool and bade them farewell. As he headed out of the workshop he stopped to talk to Blackburn, who had returned to his chisel at the workbench.

The youngsters looked at each other.

'Well, that explains a lot, I think,' said Frank.

'Yeah, like bully-boy Emerald and his Kzarlac chums,' said Cas. 'It figures that they're from somewhere like that. He seems to have a right superiority complex if you ask me, and now I know why.'

Frank nodded his agreement.

'And that man you saw—' Cas continued.

The words were out of his mouth before he realised what he'd said. Too late. Frank gave him a painful elbow in the ribs.

Halnaker left, closing the door with a tinkle of the bell. Blackburn, who had been listening to Halnaker's history lesson, suddenly perked up.

'What man?' he asked, looking up from his work.

Frank had hoped he hadn't heard and cursed under his breath in Cas's direction. He couldn't backtrack without being untruthful, something his dad had always steered him away from, so, after a moment's thought, he decided to give a little information.

'Oh, that. Nothing really. I saw a man wearing a tunic with the scorpion crest on it; I guess he must be visiting the town or something.'

'Really? No, well, that would be very unusual Frank. If someone was spotted wearing the Kzarlac crest in the town I'm sure I'd have heard about it by now, would've caused a proper stink. Where did you see this man, then?' asked Blackburn.

Frank knew he should tread carefully. He liked Blackburn a lot but didn't really want to tell him about his connection with Tweedy in case he thought he was a bit odd. So he told Blackburn he had simply noticed him in the street, being careful not to reveal everything.

'Goodness,' he said, returning to his chiselling. 'So what did this person look like?'

Frank recoiled at the thought of the man that had appeared

in his vision. He shivered visibly as he went on to give Blackburn a description of the man's long dark hair hanging around his face, the dark eyes, and the bright teeth that had morphed into an evil smile. As he spoke, everyone in the room hung on his words; Gabby, Anya and Cas seemed to be silently urging him on.

When he had finished, Blackburn just nodded silently, then Frank remembered a final detail.

'Oh, and he had a funny orange streak in his hair, about here.' Frank ran his finger through his hair on the right temple.

Blackburn's chisel missed its target and landed noisily on the workbench where he was working, making a deep gouge mark in the wooden surface. He stumbled at the slip, lurching forward and knocking over a pile of nuts and bolts that had been placed in a tottering tower on the edge of the table, nearly doing himself an injury in the process. The four students jumped at the unexpected clatter.

'Damn and blast.' His finger went to his mouth and Frank realised he had somehow managed to cut it.

Blackburn sucked at it furiously to stem the bleeding. Once he had regained his composure he turned to Frank.

'What did you say?' he said, as if unsure what he had just heard.

'The man,' said Frank. 'He had an orange streak in his hair, about here ... '

His voice trailed off as he saw Blackburn's face turn a shade paler. He stared into space as if Frank had inexplicably stunned him. The students waited.

'Dagmar,' he whispered slowly.

The room fell deathly silent. The four students studied Blackburn, who had stopped what he was doing and was now in a state of suspended animation.

'Who's Dagmar?' they asked in unison. They broke the silence carefully, eager for Blackburn to enlighten them, but he didn't reply. It was as if someone had flicked a switch and turned him off. He just stood there, frozen. Frank couldn't tell if he was alive or dead and looked at the others for some indication as to what they should do next. They shrugged. Cicero snoozed.

'Are you okay?' asked Anya. Blackburn came back to life, slowly, as though thawing himself out.

'What? Yes,' said Blackburn, distractedly. 'Dagmar. Hell's teeth,' he muttered. His finger continued bleeding.

'Here,' said Gabby, reaching into her bag and pulling out a small leather pouch. 'Let me help.'

Frank and Cas watched as she produced a small, shiny, bright red and black patterned, oval-shaped stone from the pouch. She walked over to where Blackburn was standing.

'Give me your finger,' she said.

Blackburn complied and Gabby held the stone over the wound, waving it gently from side to side. She spoke what sounded to Frank like a short incantation, concentrating hard as she did so, while the others looked on. To Frank's amazement the gash immediately healed. Gabby curled her fingers around the stone and returned to her seat, a look of satisfaction on her face, leaving Blackburn standing there, examining his finger which had been seeping blood not seconds before.

'What did you just do?' asked Cas in astonishment, pointing his finger and looking at Blackburn and then back to Gabby.

She picked up the leather pouch, without looking up.

'Oh, it's just a Sano stone, or a healing stone. Most sorcerers have one. Didn't you know that?'

'Excuse me for asking,' sighed Cas.

Blackburn looked impressed but didn't say anything. Frank was just amazed. Gabby had described the object as if it were something ordinary, like a ball of string, but he was under no illusions about the intriguing world he had begun to enter.

'But his finger just stopped bleeding when you waved that stone over it,' said Frank.

'Of course it did,' said Anya, looking puzzled at Frank's remark. 'That's what it's for.'

217

'Yes, clever little thing, don't you think?' said Gabby, popping the stone back into its pouch, then into her bag.

'Does it work on everything?' Frank asked.

'Yep, most cuts, wounds, breakages ... '

'Breakages, wow,' said Frank. 'Like magic.'

Gabby huffed. 'I told you, it's *not* magic. There's no such thing. It takes a lot of practice and patience, not that I've got much of that. It's a skill, and probably not one I can learn much about over there.' She flicked her head towards the academy.

'Okay, I get it,' said Frank.

He was fascinated. A stone, no larger than a plum, which could simply heal without touching. He would have to talk to Gabby about it later, but at the moment he had something else on his mind. He turned back to Blackburn.

'So who's Dagmar?' he asked again.

He needed to find out about the man who had haunted him since his vision, to learn what he might be doing there, and Blackburn evidently held the key.

'Dagmar Dag,' said Blackburn, sitting himself on the stool vacated by Halnaker, and myopically inspecting his finger. 'Trouble, that's what he is, yes, trouble from head to toe. Probably one of the wickedest people you could wish to meet. Kzarlac's finest you might say.' Sarcasm laced his voice. 'The sort of person that shouldn't be skulking around Excelsus Academy, that's for sure.'

'So what's he doing here?' asked Frank.

'Good question. I wouldn't like to hazard a guess, but there'll definitely be a reason. Someone like Dagmar wouldn't venture all the way here from Kzarlac unless there was something in it for him, something very important.' He looked at the four of them, tight-lipped. 'And mark my words; he'll be up to no good.'

19

THE LIBRARY

Since he had first stepped foot in the library, Frank had wondered at the fine architecture and the large room had become his favourite place in the whole academy. Sunlight from the fine late autumn day shone through the large glass-domed ceiling that dominated it. The dome spanned a wide, wooden floor space which was covered by a large carpet. There were a number of staircases, each leading up to a mezzanine level; it circled and overlooked the main room on all sides and was lined with bookcases. The main floor was decked with a number of long tables, at one of which sat Frank and Cas. More bookcases lined the walls.

At other tables sat a number of students, heads buried in their books, and a few staff were moving from shelf to shelf, replacing books or getting one out for the dogs that arrived, periodically, with notes from their masters. The dogs sat and waited patiently for the librarians to retrieve the books from the shelves, then took them gently in their mouths and headed off to the four corners of the academy.

Although it had seemed very strange at first, Frank was used to this by now and was even getting to recognise which dog belonged to which professor. He'd also got to know which to avoid. He gave an especially wide berth to Nobleman's particularly nasty looking pinscher, which growled at him every time he encountered it. Even the library staff seemed wary.

Frank and Cas were recovering from the rigours of Remedies, a subject that Frank had discovered he wasn't cut out for since he'd nearly poisoned Professor Wisley by adding ground up hedgehog bones, instead of their spines, to his elementary cough medicine. Along with Gabby and Anya, they'd been puzzling over the events of the past few weeks without really knowing what to make of them. They had been trying to fit the pieces of the jigsaw together.

So far, they had learned that a frightening-looking man by the name of Dagmar was prowling around the grounds of the academy during the night, apparently chasing someone who seemed to have the ability to disappear into thin air, and that the council had a number of their elite people sniffing around the place, also looking for something or someone.

Perhaps the Alphaen were trying to track down Dagmar. That made sense to Frank. Knowing that you had a *persona non grata* from Kzarlac here in Rhaeder was certainly something you'd call in the Special Forces for, he thought. But then, Blackburn had an idea that some old bloke called Ludlow Hums might have something to do with it because of the missing or stolen Seal which Excelsus and Moonhunter wanted back, not to mention that he had been seen pushing his brother into the river. Frank knew he needed to find out more. He'd even thought about asking Norris, but he and Polly had been so kind and hospitable that he didn't want to run the risk of making them feel he was up to something.

One thing was for sure - the whole situation had made him more curious than he had ever imagined he could be away from Smithwood. The whole place now seemed flooded with conspiracy and he was determined to find some answers.

He'd also thought seriously about going to see Moonhunter with what he had found out, but there was something niggling him about her that he couldn't exactly put his finger on and he had a feeling that she couldn't be trusted. He suspected Lanks might have something to do with it all, especially considering the way he'd spoken to him at the mews gate and the fact that he appeared to be following him everywhere. He'd even toyed with the notion that Lanks was employing Bertie as some sort of canine spy, but had to admit to himself that sounded ludicrous and, on reflection, thought he was probably imagining it.

He'd be heading home for the holidays soon and he wondered what he would tell his dad, or whether he even should. He knew he would give him the benefit of his advice, but, then again, Frank felt he should be trying to solve things by himself. He also felt his dad might worry if he thought Frank was involved in something that was beginning to look more and more sinister. It was all very confusing.

He was glad to be able to share things with Cas, and, now that Gabby and Anya made up their little group, he thought the four of them would make a good team. Cas, although a bit of a scaredy-cat, was amusing and had some really mean pilfering skills, whereas Gabby was sassy, unafraid and seemed full of fascination and surprises. He wasn't sure what to make of Anya, yet, but she was obviously from their side of the tracks and seemed pleasant enough. The fact that Gabby trusted her was good enough for him.

Frank pulled out of his bag the small book that Cas had found in the mews. They hadn't really paid it much attention since that day, the day they'd met Gabby for the first time in Laskie's, and Frank had almost forgotten about it, having shoved it in his bag to avoid Gabby seeing it before they were sure about her.

'What do you think we should do with this?' he said to Cas, who picked it up and thumbed quickly through the unfathomable pages.

'Dunno,' he replied. 'Perhaps we should think more about who might have dropped it.'

'But we don't have a clue who that is, do we?' said Frank.

Cas just sighed and looked blank. 'I thought we could look in the *Brosters Encyclopaedia of Foreign and Ancient Languages*, just in case it's in there.'

Frank looked at the hefty tome of a reference book sitting beside them that he'd retrieved from the languages section earlier. It was at least ten inches thick.

'Are you kidding?' exclaimed Cas. He put the book down on the table and pressed his forefinger into its cover. 'If that's a language in there, then I'm a farting fox and I'm not spending two years looking through *that*.' He pointed to the enormous book next to Frank, who laughed. Cas looked like he was about to say something else, when a head popped around the side of a bookcase.

'Hi, boys.' It was Anya.

'Hi, Anya,' said Frank. Anya sat next to Cas, looking tired and dejected. 'You okay?'

Anya puffed out her cheeks and yawned. 'I guess so. It's just I've been given even more extra work to do by Lanks. Remedial Runes.'

'Really, why's he done that?'

'Oh, I'm used to it. My mum and dad never think I'm trying hard enough so they write and ask if I can have extra tuition. Great, eh? As if it'll do any good.' She sighed and looked mopey.

'What do you mean?'

'Well, I suppose Gabby's told you that I'm going to be a seer?'

The boys nodded.

Anya continued, 'I know that's what my mum did, and my gran, but it just bores me to death. My sister's become an explorer and my brother's a healer, which sound much more exciting.'

'Why don't you tell them?'

'I have, lots of times, but they don't care. They think that giving me more homework and extra lessons will somehow make me more interested, but ...'

'It just makes you dislike it even more,' said Frank.

'Yeah, that's right.'

Frank had seen Phoebe get so bored and uninterested at some of the things she was asked to learn that it just went in one ear and out the other. Sometimes she couldn't remember what she'd been taught that afternoon, which appeared a waste of time and effort on everyone's part, whereas he had been able to learn what he wanted, when he wanted, which seemed like a much better idea.

'It's not even like I'm any good at it, either,' continued Anya. 'It's like when I was really young and my parents wanted me to learn the piano, when I didn't. Not that I had much say in the matter. I had to sit for hour upon hour, plonking on the keys and never getting any better, but they never got the message. I hated it so much, now I start to sweat at the thought of Nobleman's music lessons. So, remedial Runes it is, until I get better. Who knows? I'm meant to be able to sense things before they happen, but I can't. I've even got this crystal to help me. Do you want to see it?'

The boys both nodded. Anya reached into her bag, pulled out a small glass ball and placed it on the table. Frank had never seen anything like it before.

'Does it work?' he asked, peering into to sphere.

'Dunno. Probably. I'll let you know when it does. To be honest, I don't really care.' She laughed and Frank could tell she wasn't bothered if the glass predicted her future or was hung up as an attractive ornament. She took her glasses off and inspected them.

'Funny, really,' she said. 'I'm meant to be a seer, but I can't see ten feet in front of me without these.' She waved her glasses at the boys and laughed at her own joke. The boys smiled back.

Frank felt a little sorry for Anya. She was sufficiently gifted to get an invitation to Excelsus, but was struggling to find her way. He thought she lacked confidence, and it didn't look like this was likely to be rectified any time soon by the stern and demanding Lanks, or by some apparently pushy parents. She didn't really seem to care if she did well or not. Maybe, like him, she didn't actually possess any abilities, which made him glad she was part of their group.

Frank felt a hand on his shoulder and turned to see Gabby.

'Thought I'd find you here,' she said.

'I was just failing to predict anything, again,' said Anya, with a slight grin. She put the crystal back into her bag.

'It's not your fault, Anya,' said Gabby. 'It's all these dumb teachers. You just need more confidence.' She looked at Frank and Cas. 'Don't you listen to her; she's cool and I know she'll be a great seer.' She looked at Anya. 'Well, maybe. Maybe not.'

Both the girls laughed. Gabby sat down, her eyes excited. 'Anyway, you guys plotting something?'

'No,' said Frank. 'We were just wondering what all this stuff with Dagmar, the disappearing man and the Alphaen was all about.'

'And what have you concluded?'

'That we don't have the foggiest idea.'

'Oh, well, Anya and I'll join the club then,' she said.

'I thought you had,' said Frank, affirming that they were all now members of the same, small gang. Both girls smiled and Frank thought perhaps they felt a bit of belonging, where before they may not have, here at the academy.

Gabby noticed the small book that had been sitting on the table, disregarded since she had joined them. For a moment Frank had even forgotten it was there.

'What's that?' she said, looking curious, reaching over. 'Do you mind if I have a look?'

'Go ahead,' said Frank. 'It's just a book we found.'

He picked it up and handed it to Gabby who took it gently and, just like Frank had done when he first handled it, turned it around to inspect its leather cover. She opened it. Her eyes widened as she flicked the pages over quickly, back and forth, her bangles clinking as she became visibly more excited. Frank's foray into the pages had yielded nothing but a lot of head scratching. Gabby took her time, appearing to absorb herself in the gobbledygook the boys had found. Frank and Cas sat there looking at each other, wondering what to make of Gabby's intense interest.

'This isn't just a book,' Gabby said finally, excitedly, not taking her eyes off the pages. Her dark curls fell across her face and she brushed them away impatiently so she could continue looking at the book, flicking through it for the umpteenth time. Still she was immersed in it.

'What do you mean? said Cas. 'Looks just like a book to me, you know, pages, a cover, writing.'

'Yes, but it's not just any old book. What do you think, Anya?' Gabby showed the book to her friend, who leaned in as Gabby turned the pages once more. Anya shook her head. Gabby continued, 'It's written in some kind of enchanted text, even I can tell that.' She looked up.

'Gosh. You're so clever,' said Anya.

'Why didn't you show it to me before?'

The boys just gawped. Enchanted text! Frank wondered if his stay at the academy could get any more bizarre and felt his excitement rise. The scary girl from a family of sorcerers had just made things more interesting.

Keeping his voice down, Frank asked, 'Can you read it?'

He hoped that she could. He loved a puzzle, but he was beginning to realise that there was no way he and Cas would able to work this one out alone. They definitely needed help and, just as he thought, he and Cas, together with the painted, pierced and tousled Gabby and the discouraged, carefree Anya, were beginning to work well together.

'No way, boyzee,' said Gabby. 'This is *way* too difficult for me.' Frank tried not to look disappointed.

'Perhaps if you paid more attention in class?' said Cas.

Gabby glared at him, making him shrink back into his chair.

'Don't be a dummy. This isn't something they'll teach me here, not yet anyway. Maybe never. It looks very complicated, and it will certainly not be in *that*,' she said, pointing to the large volume of *Brosters* that Frank had beside him.

She sighed and closed the book. No one spoke; both Frank and Cas were dejected. They'd had high hopes that the book which the hooded figure in the mews had dropped would at least yield some clues as to who he was and why he was being pursued by the two men from Kzarlac. But knowing that it was written in some strange magical language made Frank conclude that it would take a lot more than the academy library to unlock its mystery.

'Where on earth did you get this?' she said.

Frank explained that he had seen the man in the mews drop something, but Cas interjected to tell her that he had retrieved it from the bushes. Both girls looked impressed. Cas looked chuffed.

'Wow, so it's connected in some way to all of this?' said Anya.

'Not just in some way,' said Cas. 'Perhaps directly, perhaps it holds the key, who knows?'

They sat and stared at the book. Unassuming as it was, it had just taken on a new significance - a new piece of the puzzle that they seemed to have no way of solving.

'It's missing a page,' remarked Gabby.

'Yeah, we noticed,' said Frank. 'Looks like someone's torn it out.'

'I wonder why someone would do that?' said Gabby.

Frank hadn't really thought about it before, but, now that Gabby mentioned it, he had to admit it was a bit odd. Someone had ripped out the first page, in a hurry by the looks of things, whilst leaving the rest of the book untouched. Gabby was right - why would someone do that? Was it significant? Certainly he began to think it might be important. Gabby looked thoughtful.

'Look, you boys have no idea what it says, have you?' she said.

'None,' admitted Frank.

'Are you kidding?' said Cas.

'Neither have I,' said Gabby.

'Have you got an idea?' asked Frank, sensing Gabby was formulating something in her mind.

The girls looked at each other, then back to Frank.

'We know someone who might,' said Anya.

'I was thinking,' said Gabby. 'Why don't I show it to my mum and see what she says? She's bound to know, well, I expect so. I'm heading home for the holidays, I can show her then.'

Although he'd been initially guarded, Frank liked Gabby. She was straightforward, gutsy and independent, like himself, but even more so. Just as he had been brought up, he was prepared to take her as he found her and, even though she was strange in her appearance, to take his dad's advice and not judge. The fact that she'd offered to help meant he felt he could trust her. Perhaps this was misguided, but he was prepared to follow his instincts, and you can't judge a book by its cover, he thought, not missing the irony.

'Look, thanks anyway, but I'm sure we can find out by ourselves,' said Cas, looking to Frank.

But Frank had a different idea. 'No, it's okay. Gabby, why don't you show it to your mum? See if she can help us,' he said.

Cas didn't appear happy. 'Frank, are you mad? You're prepared to give her our book? What if she makes off with it and we never see her, or the book, again?' The astonishment in his voice confirmed he wasn't happy with the idea. He looked at Gabby who gave him a reproachful look, as did Anya, but Frank understood his misgivings.

'I guess we'll just have to trust her, won't we?' he replied, giving her a smile.

She nodded her approval.

'And anyway, what's the alternative, Cas? I don't really feel like showing it to any of the professors. Blackburn doesn't seem like the sort who would know and I'm certain Polly and Norris, and even my dad, wouldn't have a clue. If Gabby's mum is a decent sorceress, like Gabby says, then perhaps she can help, and we need all the help we can get.'

Cas sat back in his chair. He thought for a minute.

'Hmm, perhaps you're right,' he said with a tone of resignation. 'And I am a farting fox, remember.'

Both he and Frank burst into laughter, leaving Gabby and Anya with mystified looks on their faces.

'That's settled then.' Frank picked up the book and handed it back to Gabby.

'Look after it, and don't lose it,' he said, 'and make sure you bring it back.'

'Thanks Frank,' said Gabby sincerely. 'I won't let you down.' She put the book in her bag and tied it tight. 'I'll take it home and see if mum can shed any light on it. Oh, and I'll cast a charm to alarm my bag, so no one tries to get it.'

She looked really pleased that the boys had decided to trust her.

'Perhaps you could look into your crystal ball and let me know it'll be okay?' Cas said, looking at Anya.

'You're funny,' she said, with a smile.

The library had become busier. A librarian walked past heading to the far end of the room, followed by Professor Chandra's old, arthritic-looking wolfhound. The woman had to stop every few steps to allow the hound to catch up. She huffed. The four of them lowered their voices so they wouldn't be overheard.

'We were thinking about the man who dropped it,' said Cas, referring to the small book that Gabby now had in her possession. 'If only we knew something about him, it might provide some sort of clue as to what's going on around here.'

'You don't think it was Ludlow Hums?' asked Gabby.

Both boys shook their heads.

'No, like I've said, the person I saw was light on their feet,' replied Frank. 'But what I don't get is who is looking for who, or what. We know that Hums is meant to have stolen something valuable, killed his brother and then disappeared, that may explain why the Alphaen are here, but not Dagmar.'

'I was thinking—' said Cas.

'Careful,' joked Gabby.

Cas ignored her, '—about who might have let Dagmar into the grounds of the academy. I mean, the gates are always locked and we have Byeland's finest patrolling the walls.'

'Then either he would have to have a set of keys, or someone's helping him from the inside,' said Anya. Frank looked thoughtful, as did Gabby.

'You know, you've got a point there,' he agreed.

'I bet it's Lanks,' said Cas.

'That wouldn't surprise me,' retorted Gabby. 'He takes us for Runes. I'm not sure what to make of him and I'm pretty sure Professor Nobleman, my head of intake, doesn't like him that much.'

'Not my favourite person either. He's such a miserable so-and-so. Like he wants us to learn all the time,' said Anya.

Gabby raised her eyebrows. 'That's why we're here,' she said, with a tone of exasperation.

'What about Emerald?' said Cas.

Frank thought that was a definite possibility, especially now he was aware of the Kzarlac connection, and he reckoned that Emerald was just the sort to be caught up in this sort of thing. They knew his dad had money and influence and, given that Dagmar had apparently only just started creeping around the grounds at the same time Emerald had started at the academy, it seemed more than just coincidence.

'That wouldn't surprise me either,' he said.

'Who's that?' asked Gabby.

'Who?'

'Emerald, I've heard you two mention him before.'

'Oh, just some posh twonk in our intake, comes from Kzarlac.'

Just as Cas said it, right on cue, Emerald and Woods came into the library. They headed down the row of tables where the four of them sat, knocking Frank's chair as they passed. Frank, as usual, ignored them, which just appeared to annoy Emerald.

'Watch where you're going,' said Cas. Emerald and Woods stopped.

'Don't talk to me, loser,' he hissed, running his hand through his hair.

Frank clocked the Kzarlac emblem as he did so.

'What are you two doing in the library anyway? Thought you had to be able to read to be in here.'

Emerald looked at Gabby.

'Who's your new girlfriend, Penny?' he spat.

Frank continued to ignore him but Gabby got to her feet and took a step towards Emerald. She looked like she was about to punch him. Frank hoped she would. As she squared up to him Emerald flinched automatically, his expression changing to one of alarm. He took a couple of steps back and bumped into Woods who struggled not to lose his balance. Frank couldn't suppress his amusement as Emerald went from being his usual bluff self to a timid mouse.

'Got a problem?' she said, full of force.

'The only problem he has is finding a barber who'll take his haircut seriously,' said Frank, looking up at Emerald. 'Just leave us alone, Emerald. Go and annoy someone else.'

Emerald looked from Frank to Cas, then to Anya, then back to Gabby, who still stood there, face like thunder. He looked as if he didn't like the odds.

'Peasants,' he muttered and stormed off, Woods scampering in his wake.

'That,' said Cas, 'is Icarus Emerald.'

'Idiot,' said Gabby, watching Emerald as he retreated to the other end of the library. 'Typical of the sort who come from Kzarlac. We've got some in our intake and they're all the same.'

'You can spot them a mile off; think they own the place, or hope they will do, one day,' said Anya.

'Don't let him wind you up,' said Frank as Gabby sat back down. 'It's really not worth it.'

He had no time for the likes of Emerald, but he knew the one thing Emerald liked better than anything was to get a reaction. He was, however, intrigued as to why Emerald was there. He'd never seen him, or any of his cronies, in the library before, which may just have been a matter of timing, but, nonetheless, he thought it was a bit out of character.

His gaze followed them down to an area that bore the sign 'Maps', where Emerald disappeared behind a bookcase, leaving Woods standing there, looking around. He caught Frank's eye and quickly looked away.

'What's he doing?' said Frank.

'What do you mean?' said Cas.

'It looks like Woods is keeping guard while Emerald has ducked down behind the maps section to get something.'

The others immediately turned to look at where Frank was watching Woods fidget. Woods seemed to sense their eyes on him and couldn't resist a nervous look in their direction. At this, Frank got to his feet, making Woods turn and whisper something in the direction in which Emerald had disappeared.

Within a second or two, Emerald emerged from behind the bookcase and strode back up the library, but he crossed to the other side before he got to where Frank and the others were sitting. Without looking in their direction, he and Woods strode out, just avoiding tripping over a long-haired terrier.

'Odd,' said Cas.

Frank certainly thought so too. Perhaps he was right to have his suspicions about Emerald.

20

THE COTTAGE

They all met back in the library after the winter break. Knox had taken Frank home with his usual efficiency and the trip back had seemed to pass in no time at all. Everyone at the farm had welcomed him home enthusiastically. It had only been a few months, but it was like they hadn't seen him in years. They had been eager to hear about his first term at Excelsus. His dad had listened patiently, nodding and looking interested, but not giving much away, whereas Phoebe couldn't wait to hear all about the place and the people he'd met, taking it all in so she could no doubt brag about her cousin's exploits when she was back at school. Even Aunt Rachel had sat at the kitchen table and taken in what he had to say. It had been great to be home.

Frank hadn't said anything about the weirder parts of his stay, especially his apparent supernatural connection to Tweedy. He'd felt it would worry his dad and he'd thought he would see how things developed when he returned to the academy before seeking his dad's wisdom on what had happened. He had been reminded to visit his grandmother, but, with all that had gone on, he'd kind of forgotten about her.

The four week break had passed quickly. Frank had been sad to leave the farm again, but part of him had been eager to get back to his three friends to see if they'd thought of anything over the holidays.

When he returned, however, Gabby had some bad news regarding the little book they'd found in the mews. On the plus side, her mum had confirmed that it was, as Gabby had suspected, written in some enchanted language, but, even though Gabby said her mum had known this instantly, its translation was beyond even her. She had offered to show it to some of her friends, but Gabby and Anya had thought that inappropriate and felt that, if her mum couldn't decipher it, there was little chance that anyone else could. So, Gabby had taken the book back and returned to the academy none the wiser. Frank was pleased that they had taken the decision not to show the book to the wider world; it vindicated his decision to trust them and, even though they were no further forward, it was more important to him that both Gabby and Anya valued the new friendship they had forged with him and Cas. Even so, he wished Gabby's mum might have thrown some light on the book. Frank had no idea how they were going to discover its secret.

* * *

They sat in the library thumbing through their books. Frank and Cas were wrestling with some elementary Wild Creature homework. Professor Furze had asked them to consider the advantages and disadvantages of stumbling across a bear in the woods. Frank had got as far as writing 'run' and had nearly given up when, without warning, a picture shot into his head.

In it, he was looking down on a wooded area. He tried to block it out but found he couldn't. He then realised what was happening. Although it had been a while since his last apparamal, he knew he was seeing the scene through Tweedy again. He felt dizzy. The images he'd seen before had been still and at night when Tweedy was perched, but this was different. The picture swirled round and round, as if the kite was circling above the trees. It then dived down to the tree canopy, causing Frank to take a sharp intake of breath as he thought he was about to collide with a big oak, but the vision took him into the branches and stopped. Tweedy had landed and, through the limbs of the tree, Frank could see a small house; a simple single-storey structure with a thatched roof. The front door was open and, as he tried to concentrate, two figures appeared in the doorway from inside the house. There was no mistaking the tall dark man who emerged first. Dagmar. He was followed by a smaller man who looked like his earlier accomplice in the mews. Dagmar was wielding a pair of gloves. He stopped and hit the other man around the head with them, mouth opening and closing with what looked like a stream of vitriol. He also held a piece of paper which flapped as he whacked the other man. Frank, through Tweedy's keen eyesight, could just make out some markings on it.

The other man cowered and Dagmar started to walk away, but he stopped and looked up into the tree. He stared straight at Tweedy, straight at Frank, snarling. It was like he was staring right into Frank's mind, into his soul. He bent down and, quick as a flash, launched a small rock up to where the bird was perched. It missed, but the effect was to send the bird off and up out of the tree tops, making Frank's head spin all over again.

The image started to fade, but not before Frank could see the two men heading down a path, through the trees and on towards a high wall which stood a good distance away. He recognised it as the wall to the rear of Excelsus; they were headed for the academy once more. The image faded to a pin-prick, and then was gone.

* * *

Frank opened his eyes; he couldn't remember where he was. He was lying on his back, staring up through the exquisite glass dome in the ceiling of the library, breathing heavily. He could hear voices, muffled at first, as his head started to clear.

'Frank, Frank, are you okay?'

It was then that he realised that Anya was kneeling over him, while Cas and Gabby were standing beside her, as was Mr Slater, the young head librarian. Concern filled their faces. He was lying prostrate on the floor; his chair was on its side. He had fallen off it when he started having his vision.

Frank sat up and found that everyone in the library was looking at him, including the sniggering Emerald, sitting a few tables away with Woods, Chetto and De Villiers and laughing about Frank having found his new talent for falling off chairs. Some had stood to get a better view of what was happening.

'Yeah, I'm fine,' said Frank, propping himself up and rubbing his head, although he felt far from it. His mind still swirled with the images and he felt slightly nauseous, not to mention a little self-conscious.

'Good. Will you kindly keep the noise down in future; this is a library after all,' said Slater, irritated.

Gabby glared at the librarian, who noticed and looked awkward.

'So ... er ... if you're okay, Penny, I hope you'll excuse me. Unless you need to go to the sick bay, of course. I ... I can send Dickens, there.'

He pointed to his red setter who was crashed out on a comfy looking cushion under his desk at the front of the room, not looking like he'd enjoy being disturbed to run an errand. Frank shook his head.

'Well then, work to do,' said Slater and scurried off.

So much for the librarian's moment of concern.

The others turned to Frank

'What happened?' said Cas.

'Tweedy. I had a vision.'

'Oh, you're so lucky,' said Anya.' I wish I had—'

'No you don't,' said Frank, rubbing the back of his neck.

'You really must learn to control them,' said Gabby, sympathetically. 'It's not difficult. I meant to ask Mum how to do it. Remind me next time, Anya.'

'Thanks, that might be a good idea.' Frank, feeling a little bruised and not a little embarrassed, picked himself up and rubbed his eyes again.

'I'll write and ask. She was well impressed when I told her you had a familiar, though.'

'Great. I wish I could have picked something that doesn't fly. Perhaps you could ask her if we can swap,' joked Frank.

He sat back at the table and gave the others a full description of what Tweedy had just revealed to him. They all listened intently, looking around to make sure no one else was listening.

'Are you sure it was Dagmar?' said Cas.

'You have to ask?' said Frank, as if he could mistake the man for someone else. 'Not unless he has a twin brother.'

'Ugh, what a thought,' said Cas. 'Any idea where they were?'

Frank explained its proximity to the academy.

'I could use my crystal,' ventured Anya.

The others gave her questioning looks.

'Maybe not, then.'

'Thanks anyway, Anya.'

'It must be Ludlow Hums's cottage,' Cas ventured, 'Blackburn said it was up in the woods.'

'Genius,' said Frank, remembering too what Blackburn had said.

If it was Hums's cottage, it made perfect sense and started to explain why Dagmar would be poking around Rhaedar. Frank began to think that the two must be connected after all. He could feel the pieces starting to fit together.

'I do have my moments,' smiled Cas.

'I wonder how we get there?' said Frank, looking at the others. He was eager to go and see what they could find.

'What? You're not serious?' said a worried looking Cas.

'Where is it exactly?' asked Gabby.

'We're not sure,' said Frank, then, remembering his vision. 'But it's out the back of the academy, up the hill into the woods there. Know it?'

Gabby shrugged.

'Why don't we all go and try to find it?' she said. 'There's a bridge further up the river, outside the north part of town. It leads up into the woods and I'm sure you can get around the back of the academy. Finding a house can't be that difficult.'

Frank remembered that the girls had been in the town for a year longer and that they would know their way around a bit more.

'Okay. We've got a free period at the end of the day, so it'll still be light. What about you?'

'Don't worry about us,' said Gabby, looking over to Anya.

'We'll just bunk off Meditation. Chandra's normally so far gone by the end of the day, he'll never notice.'

* * *

They met up after lessons had finished, or not quite finished in Gabby or Anya's case. Frank had run back to Polly's for a bite to eat and to let her know he was meeting his friends, although he omitted the bit about them heading up into the woods to look for the home of Byeland's most infamous fugitive. He'd grabbed his shoulder bag, putting in a flask of water and his pocket knife, before heading back.

They hurried out of the town's north gate and along the river. The light was still good but it would begin to get dark soon and Frank began to wonder if they should have waited until the weekend.

They came to a bridge which spanned the river as it bent at right angles. The water flowed smoothly beneath them as they crossed. Frank shivered in the winter air as he felt the chill of the river rise up in his bones.

They headed on to an expanse of grass that led to the woods. The ground was crisp under their feet and their breath clouded like a boiling kettle as they walked hurriedly towards the trees. As they entered the woods, it became noticeably darker. The academy was visible away to the left, giving Frank a strong indication as to where he needed to go.

After about ten minutes Frank stopped to get his bearings. The others stopped too, breathing in the silence. Everything was still. Eerie. Frank could still just make out the walls of the academy down the hill, through the boughs of the trees.

'It must be this way,' he said, turning and heading up the hill where the trees grew thicker. Gabby, Anya and Cas followed in silence. There was a tension in the air; none of them felt able to speak. Soon enough they came to a gap in the trees where they noticed the ground had been flattened. Frank looked up and down between the trunks. Gabby followed his gaze.

'It's a path,' she said, looking at the ground. Frank could see that the path headed off down the hill in the direction of the academy.

He turned his head to look up the hill.

'This must be the path up to Hums's cottage,' he said, staring though the trees in an attempt to make out anything that might resemble the shape of a house.

The woods were deathly quiet; Frank noticed Cas shiver and wondered if it was from the chill in the air or the spookiness of their surroundings. He'd been camping in the woods near the farm on many occasions and knew what it was like to feel anxious in the face of nature, but he'd learnt to understand the sounds and silence and was calm in this type of setting.

'You okay?' he asked Cas, who nodded unconvincingly.

'Come on then,' said Gabby, confidently. 'What are we waiting for?'

She took off up the path; Frank and Anya followed. Cas lingered, then realised he was being left on his own and ran to catch up.

They headed deeper into the woods, but it wasn't long before the trees thinned and they came to a clearing, edged with snowdrops and wood hyacinths that were beginning to poke their heads out of the ground. Facing them was a small stone cottage, thatched, with a single chimney. It was the one that Frank had seen through the hawk - Ludlow Hums's house.

They stood on the edge of the glade looking at the building. For somewhere that had been uninhabited for more than two years it looked remarkably fresh, although, here and there, nature had started to reclaim parts of the outside. Some tall weeds and plants grew up the walls in places, but otherwise they would have thought someone might be living there. Frank was hesitant; he'd seen Dagmar and the other man come out earlier that day and was fearful that they might still be inside. Cas just looked terrified. Frank went to lead them across but Anya grabbed his arm.

'Wait.'

'What's wrong?'

'I think I can sense something.'

Cas stiffened. 'Are you sure?'

Anya concentrated for a moment. She pushed her glasses onto her nose.

'No, not really.'

The others let out a collective breath. Anya looked sheepish.

'Then can you stop sensing?' said Cas.

'You really need to practice more,' said Gabby.

She turned back to the house.

'It looks deserted,' she said, sensing their uncertainty.

Frank had to agree. There was no light from inside and the small green door was closed. Hums was long gone, or so they thought. Whatever Anya had said, he was sure there was no one at home.

'Come on then,' he said and led the others over to the house.

Frank cupped his hand to the window and peered in; the others did the same. It was still light enough to see inside. There was no one home. He pushed the door. It swung open so quickly that he thought someone must have pulled it from the other side and he jumped back in surprise, spooking the others, who grabbed hold of him tightly.

'Ouch,' said Frank, as quietly as he could in the circumstances.

'Sorry mate,' said Cas. 'Just thought ...'

They let go and Frank rubbed his arms where they had been pinched. He looked round at them.

'After you,' said Cas.

Gabby huffed and strode in as if she owned the place. The others followed her.

The door led straight into a small living room. What little furniture there was had been turned upside down, the many shelves that adorned the walls were empty and the books that once filled them had been brushed onto the floor. There was a small kitchen area to one side and, towards the other side, a door led off the room. The place had been ransacked. Frank wasn't surprised. Hums may have been long gone, but someone had been here recently and they all knew who that was.

'Guess this is what I expected,' he said. 'I mean, having seen

Dagmar come out of here. I didn't think he was inside collecting the mail or doing the cleaning.'

'If he was, he seems to have missed a bit,' said Anya.

'And I didn't see any laundry hanging on the line,' joked Cas.

They stood amongst the mess. Frank thought it seemed such a shame as he remembered Norris telling him that the older Hums was a tidy and orderly person. He wondered if his brother had been too.

'So, the question is,' said Gabby, 'what on earth were they looking for? Seems they were trying hard to find *something*, looking at all this mess. I wonder if they were successful.'

'I don't think they were,' said Frank, remembering Dagmar's mood as he came out of the cottage earlier. He and Anya moved around the room carefully, occasionally picking something up, irrationally trying not to make more mess. Gabby disappeared through the door to the side. His thoughts turned to Ludlow Hums, the lifelong pilferer.

'If you wanted to conceal something in here, where would you hide it?'

He looked at Cas and raised his eyebrows, thinking that his skills with sleight of hand might give him more of an insight into the mind of someone wanting to do just that. Cas stood there, thinking. Frank could tell he was trying to figure it out. Gabby came back in.

'Same story through there,' she said. 'Just a bedroom, or it looks like it used to be a bedroom. There are a couple of beds but I can't see anything of use. Seems they gave it a thorough going-over.'

Cas still looked thoughtful.

'Now, where would I hide something', he said out loud to himself, 'if I was a sneaky thief like Ludlow Hums?'

He wandered slowly around the small room, touching the walls methodically as he went, looking carefully, his mind working. The others watched him in silence. He paused a few times, pressing and tapping the wall, before moving on. Cas stopped at the small fireplace on the far side of the room, where there was a heavy, free-standing grate sitting in the hearth. Despite the mess in the room, it was empty and clean and had obviously remained unused for some time. Cas dropped to his knees, leaned in and looked up the chimney. He knelt there for a minute, running his hands around the hearth, then raised his hand up into the opening. Frank saw him feeling around inside the flue. He knocked on a few of the bricks. Then he looked back towards Frank with a beaming smile.

'Fancy a fire?' he said, looking devilishly pleased with himself.

The others looked at him with surprise.

'What is it?' asked Frank.

'Just wait and see. Come on then, it won't light itself.'

'There's some matches in the bedroom,' said Gabby, running off to get them.

Frank looked around the room. There was no dry kindling, so, reluctantly, they piled some of Hums's books into the grate and lit them. It wasn't long before the fire was ablaze.

As the flames reached up and began to warm the room, Cas looked once more up the chimney, this time with a degree of difficulty as the flames started to flicker upwards, becoming stronger by the second. Anya and Gabby looked at each other, wondering what was going on.

'Careful, Cas,' warned Frank, still mystified about what he was doing.

'Here we go,' said Cas, staring at the fireplace.

It was then Frank noticed that one of the bricks at the bottom of the flue, just up inside the chimney breast, was beginning to melt. It wasn't made of the same substance as all the others. The hot wax began to drip onto the hearth, slowly at first and then, as the bricks warmed, the liquid spilled in a wide cascade until, suddenly, it stopped.

'Put the fire out,' Cas said to Frank, who was just beginning to get nice and warm in front of the glowing flames.

Frank grabbed the flask of water out of his bag, tipped it onto the fire to extinguish the blaze and stood back, regarding the brick-coloured blob and splatters of wax that had landed on the hearth in front of them. Cas reached up to where the wax brick had once sat and put his hand into the opening. He retracted it quickly as he felt the heat. He tried again and this time pulled out a small, dirty tin box.

'Very clever,' said Gabby.

Frank wasn't sure if she meant the comment for Cas for finding the secret hiding place, or Hums for creating it in the first place.

'I should say,' said Anya. 'Who would have ever thought of creating a false brick out of wax to hide something? No one would have ever found that.'

'Except you,' said Frank to Cas. 'Great job, Cas.'

They all looked impressed.

'So, shall we have a look?'

He handed the box to Frank. It was still warm from the heat of the fire. The four of them sat on the floor. The box, which was covered in grime, had an unusually heavy catch for such a small object and Frank flicked it open.

The interior was lined with rich red velvet; inside was a folded piece of paper, a small spherical object and an odd-shaped piece of stone. They stared at the assortment of objects that sat like uncomfortable companions in the small container. Frank reached in and picked up the small ball. On closer inspection it had a strange appearance. He thought it was a dull brown colour, but, as he studied it, he noticed it turned from brown to turquoise and then to orange. He was mesmerised. He held it in the flat of his hand and, to his amazement, it lifted itself no more than an inch off his palm and just hovered in mid-air, rotating slowly.

'What on earth?' exclaimed Frank, grasping the ball.

He opened his palm once more and, as before, the ball lifted itself into the air and just floated above his hand. He hadn't imagined it. Frank looked at Gabby for an explanation. She just shook her head, looking equally transfixed. Frank placed it carefully back in the box.

Anya had taken the piece of paper and unfolded it, revealing an unusual criss-cross grid.

'I wonder what it's meant to be?' she said.

'It looks like it could be a map of some sort,' said Frank, although he couldn't be certain.

'Maybe,' said Gabby. 'But of what? There are no names on it.'

Frank thought for a moment.

'Wait a minute,' he said, 'I've seen something like that before. Dagmar was holding a piece of paper just like it when he came out of here.'

'Are you sure?'

'I think so, it was certainly similar.'

'Why would someone go to such lengths to conceal a funny looking diagram, a floating ball and this?' asked Cas, inspecting the random piece of stone that he'd found in the box. 'Perhaps it's one of your healing stones,' he said.

'Don't be a dummy,' snapped Gabby, sharply. 'Sano stones are red and black, and shiny. That's just a lump of rock.'

Cas looked deflated.

'They must all be significant in some way,' he said. 'This is Hums's cottage, right? So it must have been him that hid these things. The secret hiding place has all the hallmarks of a clever thief. So why go to such lengths?'

'I don't know,' replied Frank, staring back into the box.

They all looked blank. Anya suddenly took a sharp intake of breath, making the others jump.

'Quiet, I can—'

The sound of footsteps outside made them look up.

'Quick, someone's coming,' said Gabby.

She got up quickly and shut the front door. Frank and Cas stayed low so they wouldn't be seen and edged their way to the rear window.

'Goodness, Anya, ten minutes earlier next time if you don't mind.'

Anya shrugged. 'Sorry, I wasn't really expecting to ... you know.'

Frank looked out carefully and saw a figure emerge from the far side of the clearing behind the cottage. He was small and pale with long limp hair, and wore a shabby cloak. As he walked casually past the house, Frank moved to the other window and watched as the figure ambled past them and disappeared into the woods on the other side, heading down the path that led to the academy, not breaking stride or expressing the slightest interest in the cottage.

Frank felt sure he would have seen the smoke from the chimney, but gave a sigh as he noticed the relief on the faces of the others.

'Who was that?'

'I'm not sure, but whoever it was must have been here before or they wouldn't just have ignored a house like this. Anyone would be bound to have had a look through the window. And he seemed to know his way around. Do you know, it might be the man who I've seen with Dagmar - his accomplice or whatever.'

'Servant, more like,' said Gabby.

Anya nodded. 'So, where's he going?'

They looked at each other, knowing what the others were thinking.

'Let's find out shall we?' said Gabby.

'Sounds like a plan,' agreed Anya.

'What, you think we should just follow him?' said Cas nervously. 'I'm not sure that's such a good idea.'

'Well, we won't find out anything by just standing here, will we?' said Gabby.

'But what about the tin box?' said Cas.

'That can wait,' said Frank. 'I think Gabby's right. Perhaps following that man will lead us to some answers.'

21

ORPHEUS

They quickly put the rest of the items back into the tin box and Frank put it in his bag. His need to follow the stranger who had just walked past the house and into the woods was greater than his desire to learn more about the items they'd just found. He knew they could wait, but the chance to follow this man would only come once.

The four of them went to the cottage door and peered cautiously out. Although it was getting darker, they couldn't risk being spotted. But the man was nowhere to be seen.

'Come on then,' said Gabby, running across the clearing between the cottage and the woods.

The others followed, Cas still looking unsure, as if the forest would eat him. They found their way to the narrow pathway where they had emerged when they first stumbled on the place.

'Careful,' warned Anya. 'We don't want to him know we're following him. If he sees or hears us there's no knowing what might happen.'

They carried on slowly down the hill, treading carefully so as not to make any noise that might alert the man.

The woods closed in around them, darkening their path, but they kept on until, finally, the walls became visible through the trees. They stopped. Still no sign. Cas put his hand on Frank's shoulder, making him jump.

'Flippin' heck, Cas,' he whispered. 'I thought you were someone creeping up on me.'

'Sorry, it's just so creepy.'

Gabby rolled her eyes. Anya looked across to the academy.

'I can't see him,' she said, peering over the short scrubby undergrowth and between the trunks of the trees.

Neither could Frank. He looked around and up. Then he saw what he was looking for.

'Give me a minute,' he said.

'What for?' asked Cas. 'You're not going to leave us here?'

Frank didn't answer. Instead he moved over to a tree on his left and started to climb. He figured that, if he could get up as far as the lower canopy, he might get a better look beyond the tree line to the academy without anyone noticing him. He'd climbed hundreds of trees in the past and this one was a simple task. Up he went, quietly and delicately, sure-footed and leopard-like, until he could see over to the wall.

He stopped and anchored himself comfortably on a branch. Just as he'd hoped, he had a good view across from the woods and over to the grey stone walls of Excelsus. To the right, the walls curved back, in the direction of the cliffs and the waterfall. There were a number of iron gates, set at intervals, leading into the grounds. There was no one there. No Alphaen guards lurking about. He was alerted by movement to his left, over at the wall itself. Two men stood there, leaning against the wall. One was the man who had walked past the cottage, and, even in the failing light, there was no mistaking the tall, dark figure of Dagmar, who towered over the other man. He was holding a piece of paper. By his side was an enormous dog, strong and alert, its studded collar held by a sturdy lead. It sat there obediently. As Frank moved slightly to get a better look he snapped a twig. Its noise was amplified by the quiet of the wood. Both men immediately looked up, searching the trees. The dog's ears pricked up as it turned towards the trees and growled. Frank sat stock still; he held his breath and felt a sweat all over. His heart started pounding. What if Dagmar set his massive hound into the woods? They'd all be found out and then what would happen?

At that moment two pigeons flew out from a bough above him and over the heads of the two men, who relaxed and went back to their conversation. Frank breathed a sigh of relief, then watched as a door in the stone wall opened and the men disappeared through it, dog in tow.

He climbed down quickly and jumped to the floor. The others looked at him expectantly.

'I saw them, two of them, the man we saw and Dagmar,' he said.

'Where?' asked Cas.

'Over there.' He pointed in the direction where he had seen them.

'They've got a very big and nasty-looking dog with them. Goodness, I broke a branch and thought they'd send it after us.'

'We heard,' said Gabby. 'Good job they didn't.'

'Yeah, don't fancy being a dog's dinner,' agreed Cas, relieved that he hadn't had to try and outrun the beast Frank had just mentioned.

'They went through some sort of door in the wall over there. Let's go.'

'Really?' said Cas, anxiously.

Gabby grabbed him by the arm and they headed out onto the clear strip of land that separated the wall from the woods, Frank coming to where the men had been standing.

'Here,' he announced, staring blankly at the stonework of the outer wall of the academy.

'But there isn't a door. It's just the wall,' said Gabby looking confused. 'Are you sure it was here, Frank?'

Frank thought for a moment. He hadn't imagined it, but Gabby was right, there was no door. So where had the two men and their dog gone? Cas walked to the wall and touched it, checking the stonework, moving his hands over the masonry in a pre-meditated pattern.

'There's a door here,' he said, much to the others surprise.

'Where?' asked Anya, slightly disbelieving.

None of them could make out anything against the stone.

'Just here. See, here's the edge.'

Cas slowly traced and retraced an outline against the stone so it became clear exactly what he had discovered.

'Oh, how exciting!' remarked Anya. 'I wish I was that clever.'

'On yeah,' said Gabby. 'Very good, Cas. Seems you are useful after all.'

'All part of the service,' he smiled. 'Give me a minute and I'll get it open.'

Frank and Gabby stood back while Cas felt around. He seemed to be looking for some sort of mechanism.

'Hang on, we haven't thought what we should do. What if they're standing behind it?' said Frank.

'Then we'll have to make a run for it,' said Gabby.

'Don't be daft, they've got a dog,' said Cas. 'A big one, according to Frank.'

'Yeah, but it can only chase one of us, and you look most like a bone, Cas, so it'll go after you,' laughed Frank.

'Thanks very much!'

Cas reached into his bag and pulled out a set of metal levers on a key ring. Using them carefully and proficiently, he teased the door ajar. Collectively, they held their breath, anticipating someone on the other side, but there was no one there. Peering in, they could just make out what appeared to be a long passageway, dimly lit by the glimmer of light from a rusty oil lamp that hung on the wall, but it was difficult to see as it was so dark. Cas pushed the door shut again.

'I'm not going in there,' he declared. 'Much too dark, and that lamp won't be much use.'

Frank silently agreed; dark enclosed spaces were really not his thing. He put the image of the passage out of his mind as he tried to think about what to do and noticed Cas reaching into his bag once more. He produced a small glass flask, exactly like one of those they had seen on the worktop at Blackburn's last term. Frank could see the intense orange liquid and the blue streaks running through it.

'Where did you get that?'

Gabby and Anya looked equally bemused and Cas looked a little guilty.

'You didn't just take it from Blackburn?' asked Frank, annoyed that his friend would have done such a thing.

Cas didn't speak. Frank stood there, waiting for a response.

'Well, he did say the batch didn't work, so I thought I'd keep one,' Cas murmered uncomfortably.

'What for?'

'In case we came across a long, dark, secret passage while following Dagmar and his huge hound, of course, why else?' Cas smiled weakly.

Frank wasn't sure whether to be angry or grateful. The fact that Cas had a bottle of Blackburn's light formula to hand was, he had to admit, extremely handy, given that without it, if they wished to pursue Dagmar, they faced walking down the long corridor in the dark. On the other hand, he had been brought up not to just take things without asking.

'Look, I'm really sorry, Frank. I didn't think he'd miss one, and you have to admit it's an interesting thing.' Frank still looked hacked off. 'Look, I promise I'll go and see Blackburn tomorrow and tell him that I took it, okay.'

'And not do it again.'

'Okay. Not to Blackburn. Sorry guys.'

He opened the door once more, giving the glass bottle a light shake. The liquid immediately lit up, just like magic, emitting a bright glow all around them.

'Come on then, Blackburn said it would last twenty minutes,' said Frank.

He waited for Cas, who was still holding the jar, to move in ahead of him and lead the way. Cas didn't budge; he stood there peering into the darkness of the passage, mulling something over.

'Cas?'

'Okay, but I don't want to be in there when the light goes out,' he said, his tone a little anxious and his body tense.

Frank felt his discomfort. So did Anya.

'Why don't you and I wait here while Frank and Gabby take a look. We can keep guard. That'll be okay, right?'

Anya looked at Frank and Gabby.

'I guess so,' agreed Frank.

Cas visibly relaxed. 'Okay, if you don't mind. I'll stay here with Anya. If you're not back in twenty minutes, we'll go and get help.'

'If you're sure you don't want to come?' teased Gabby. 'Wouldn't want you to miss all the action.'

She turned to Anya.

'If he faints, a good shake and a slap should do it.'

'Go on, get going,' urged Cas. 'Time's running out.'

He handed the light to Gabby. She and Frank entered the passage and they headed down the corridor, Gabby holding the light, which shone so brightly that Frank was worried they would be given away in no time. The cold, dark space was eerily silent and Frank felt his heart begin to thump as he tried hard to keep his breathing from becoming too heavy. They had no idea what was ahead of them and their silence reflected their sense of trepidation. Keeping calm was going to be difficult.

The passage went straight on into the darkness. It could have continued for a hundred yards or more, but it was impossible to see. They moved slowly, desperately trying not to make a sound.

The walls were wet and slimy in places, as was the floor. Gabby held her hand over the flask, dampening the light so they could see about ten yards ahead. Eventually, the corridor turned a right angle to the left. What was this? thought Frank. A secret passage of some kind? Frank remembered Blackburn had said that the academy had its secrets, perhaps this was what he meant.

Rounding the corner, they heard muffled voices. They stopped, straining to hear what was being said, but neither of them could make out the conversation, although, by the level of the sound, they could tell that the men weren't far ahead. Gabby took her hand away from the light to allow its beam to cast itself further down the passage.

'Careful,' whispered Frank. Down the corridor they could see that it took another bend to the right and they could just make out the faint glow of a lantern. Whoever had come in before them was there and now Frank wasn't sure what they would do if they suddenly stumbled on the two men, alone here, underneath the academy.

Then, without any warning, the light in the glass jar went out. They were pitched into complete darkness, save for the pale glimmer of the distant lamp. They both froze. The passage suddenly took on a new dimension, cold and oppressive. Frank was suddenly gripped by a fear, one he held from years ago when he was trapped in the well on the farm. He'd been leaning over, throwing stones in, and had lost his balance. He'd tumbled twenty feet to the bottom and landed, unhurt, in the water. Once he'd regained his wits, he'd felt the cold, dark space close in all around him, causing him to scream in panic. Brigg had quickly rescued him, but the experience had stayed with him for months and now dark enclosed spaces made him feel anxious. He took a deep breath, trying to settle his nerves.

'What happened?' he hissed. 'I can't see a thing.'

'Well, that was rubbish,' said Gabby, looking at the jar which sat dark and lifeless in her hand. Frank calculated they had only been edging their way along the passage for less than five minutes.

'I thought we had a lot longer than that,' said Frank.

'So did I. You wait 'til I see Blackburn next time.'

Frank just hoped there would be a next time and started to think about what they should do now.

'Do you think we should go back?' asked Gabby.,

'Maybe,' said Frank.

'Hold on, I'll give it another shake, see if it lights up again.'

As she gripped the glass jar, Frank remembered what Blackburn had said.

'Okay, but not too—'

Before he could finish, Gabby shook the bottle hard. Too hard. She could feel the liquid bubble in the jar, knocking the sides, causing tiny vibrations. There was a faint popping sound before the jar exploded with a loud bang, sending shards of glass and liquid over the floor. Gabby let out a shriek, then, remembering too late where they were, looked at Frank, eyes wide like a rabbit caught in the lamplight. The muttering from further down the corridor immediately stopped.

'Oops,' said Gabby.

'Run!' hissed Frank.

Luckily, the spilt liquid was emitting a low glow that shone back down the corridor in the direction from which they had come and they could just see the corner they had rounded moments earlier. If they could reach that, it was just a straight run back to the door and the dim oil lamp at the entrance. Frank was fast and he suspected Gabby could shift too. Quickly, they set off at a sprint.

Then Frank heard what he had feared; enormous paws pounding the stone floor behind them and a low level growl - the sound of a dog giving chase. Now the stakes rose, as did their alarm. Frank had seen the hound and knew, from his wide experience of dogs, that this was not one that held up its paw for you to shake. If it licked you, it was probably basting you. They had to do the impossible; they had to outrun it. They had to make it to the door before it caught up with them.

From Gabby's breathing he knew she had heard it too. They rounded the bend and pelted hell-for-leather down the long stretch of passageway. There was no mistake, the dog was gaining fast. Fit, muscular and with the advantage of four legs, its guttural growl, deep and throaty, was getting louder. The pounding of its heavy paws told them it was getting closer by the second. As he ran for his life Frank cast a quick look behind and immediately wished he hadn't. He saw its shadow first, then the dog rounded the corner and bounded after them, its strides three times as long as theirs, teeth bared, eyes focused on one thing and one thing alone - the two of them. They were in its sights. The hunt was on.

They tried to pick up speed but there was only one way this was going to turn out. Still they ran, breath fast, furious, terrified.

Frank could see the dim glow of the oil lamp by the door. Even if they reached it, there was no way they would have time to get it open. How he hoped that Cas and Anya would hear them. The dog was gaining by the second, closer and closer; he could feel it on his heels. Forty yards to go ... thirty ... closer ... closer. He glanced over at Gabby; determination was etched on her face. They weren't going to make it, he knew that for sure. He knew it, and so did the dog.

They could see the wood of the door in the faint glow of the lamp that hung there as some sort of beacon of hope. Hopeless, more like. Then the dog was upon them. Frank could sense its breath. He knew its teeth would sink into his leg any second, bringing him to the ground, bringing the chase to a bloody end. In a last ditch measure, out of sheer desperation, he grabbed Gabby and threw them both to the ground just as the hound bore down on them. They crunched sideways into the wall, awaiting their fate, but, as they did, the dog zipped past them, none of its large paws able to get any purchase on the wet floor, and smacked straight into the door, its head hammering it with a resounding *thunk*. It collapsed on the floor, laid completely spark-out by the impact, tongue hanging out, drool dripping from its mouth, its chest heaving.

Frank and Gabby just sat there for a few seconds, catching their breath and regaining their composure. Frank's heart was bashing into his ribcage. The heavy door swung open, catching for a second on the poleaxed dog. Cas's face appeared.

'I heard a loud—'

He looked down at the unconscious animal, then at Frank and Gabby. The two of them hauled themselves up. 'What the—'

'Don't ask,' puffed Frank.

He turned to Gabby.

'You okay?'

'Yeah, just about, which is more than can be said for old slobber chops here,' she said, apparently none the worse from the experience.

Anya stuck her head round the door, recoiling when she caught sight of the dog.

'It's huge,' gasped Cas. 'I wouldn't like to be chased by that. No way.'

He looked up at the others, who gave him a pointed look back. They heard the sound of heavy feet running quickly towards them from back down the corridor, the sound echoing all around. The glow of a lamp appeared in the distance, getting brighter by the second. Frank sensed they didn't have much time. Dagmar looked strong which meant he would probably be able to run at least as fast as them.

'Time to get out of here,' he said, stepping over the comatose dog.

'Come on, they're not hanging about.'

They hurried out of the door, not sure which way to go. Gabby shoved it firmly closed.

'Why don't we get something to wedge it shut?' she said.

'No time,' said Frank looking left and right. 'This way.'

He headed along the wall towards the rear of the academy building, running as fast as he could, the others following hard on his heels. He hoped that the gates he had seen from up in the tree would be open, or that they would be able to climb over before the men got to them. The wall curved around to the left, away from the woods, and towards the sound of the waterfall. They reached the first gate. Frank grabbed it and pulled. Locked. Damn. He shook it wildly, anxious to get the four of them to safety. It clanked loudly but wouldn't budge. It was no good. There was a gap at the top which he thought they would be able to squeeze through so he started to climb. He'd only taken a few steps up the gate before he felt a heavy hand grab the back of his jacket and pull him down. He fell to the ground in a heap, hurting his leg in the process and letting out a slight gasp. He rolled over; staring back at him was the face of a devil with a sadistic smile, baring his teeth like a shark before the kill. Dagmar.

'Going somewhere?' he sneered.

He pulled Frank to his feet, holding him by the lapels, and pushed him against the gate. Dagmar *was* strong. Frank was terrified. He saw that Dagmar's accomplice was holding both Cas and Gabby by their collars. Anya stood between them and the wall, looking unsure as to what to do. Frank looked at her, indicating that she should try and make a run for it, but then he saw the dog, back to life, seemingly unhurt by its brush with a solid piece of oak.

'Good doggy,' said Anya, trying not to sound scared. She held out her hand. The beast growled, showing its own teeth. Frank wasn't sure, at that moment, which set scared him the most; Dagmar's or the dog's. Any thought of escape quickly evaporated in the darkening, late afternoon air as Anya squashed herself back against the wall in an attempt to put as much distance as possible between her and the menacing animal.

'That's enough, Orpheus,' Dagmar said to the dog, his eyes still on Frank, but it continued to growl.

'*Loose!*' he commanded, raising his voice and making Frank, and the others, jump.

Orpheus shied away and sat a few feet back, still panting, still menacing. Gabby managed to step forward and aimed a kick at Dagmar, her pointed boot hitting his shin hard. He didn't flinch. Instead he just looked at her dismissively, then at his leg.

'Mind my boots,' he said coldly. 'Very expensive, these.'

He sneered at her, finding his own joke funny. The other man sniggered.

'Well now, Percy, what have we here?' He looked at the other man, who seemed particularly jittery, as if not really knowing what to do with his prizes; like he'd gone fishing for mackerel and caught a whale. Percy just smiled wickedly. Frank, still held by the front of his jacket by Dagmar, noticed that Percy's left hand was badly scarred. Dagmar turned back to Frank and looked at him for a few seconds, silent, making Frank feel distinctly unnerved.

'Following me, were you? Snooping around?' Dagmar raised an eyebrow.

Frank didn't speak; he wasn't sure if this was out of fear or because, although he'd always been taught to face down bullies, he was far from convinced that this tactic would work with his current assailant.

'What's the matter, cat got your tongue? Or perhaps I should let the dog have it,' laughed the dark face. Orpheus's ears pricked up, expectant. 'So, are you going to tell me how you came to be over there?' he nodded towards the passage they had just run from. 'When I guess you should be ... in there,' he nodded towards the academy.

Frank stayed silent, mouth dry, unable to speak.

'Leave us alone,' spat Gabby, causing Dagmar to turn his head towards her and raise his eyebrows in surprise.

'Oh,' he said, 'I think leaving you alone is the last thing on my mind, not until you *tell me what you were doing.*'

He raised his voice, causing Cas to recoil. Frank thought Cas might faint out of fear, but Gabby wasn't deterred.

'Seems to us it was you doing the snooping,' she retorted, her eyes fixed on Dagmar, challenging, not wavering.

Dagmar just rolled his eyes and tutted. 'Look, young lady, although I admire your little attempt at being all grown up and plucky, as always, there is an easy way to do this, and a hard way.' In a flash he produced a dagger from his belt and held it by his side. He cocked his head to one side, intent clear.

'We're not scared of you,' said Frank. He was.

Cas looked at him as if to say, 'We're not?'

Dagmar looked back to Frank. His demeanour didn't change. 'Oh dear, that might be the second mistake you make this afternoon,' he growled. 'Orpheus,' he snapped.

The dog came to life with a snarl, up on all fours, muscles tensed, sinews showing, waiting to execute its master's next instruction, which Frank thought might not be particularly pleasant for any of them.

Then, just as Dagmar opened his mouth to speak, whether to the dog or to him Frank wasn't sure, there was a sound from behind him.

'Everything alright here?' came a man's voice.

Dagmar relaxed, quietly put back his dagger and rolled his eyes in disappointment. 'Oh for heaven's sake, what now?' he muttered under his breath and, to Frank's surprise and relief, he let go of his jacket, causing him to stumble slightly.

As he looked around, he was relieved to see two burly Alphaen guards standing on the other side of the iron gate, looking through at them. He looked over to Gabby and Cas, who had been released from Percy's grip. Cas puffed out his cheeks in relief. Gabby pulled herself away from Percy, adjusting her coat from where it had been screwed up in his hand. She gave him hard push and a look of utter disdain, which went unnoticed, and stepped over to Anya. Frank wouldn't have been at all surprised of she'd thumped him.

There was a momentary silence. The guards didn't seem to know what to make of the scene, but they weren't going to budge. One of them produced a set of keys and promptly unlocked the gate.

'Your dog under control, sir?' he asked before opening it. Even Byeland's elite needed to be wary of being overpowered by the frothing jaws of a large dog, it seemed. Dagmar looked as if he was about to explode. His lips tightened and he held his breath for a few seconds. He exhaled.

'*Placo*,' he said to the dog.

At his command, the dog visibly relaxed and sank to the ground, licking its forelimbs. Frank thought how timid and unassuming it now looked, puppyish even, and then how appearances can be deceptive, to say the least. One of the guards came through the gate; the other remained within the grounds of the academy.

'So, what's going on, gentlemen?' he asked, looking first at Dagmar and then to Percy.

Before any of the students could tell him that they were about to be set upon by Dagmar's hound, Dagmar spoke.

'I caught these pupils snooping around the walls out here. They look like they're up to no good, officer,' he said.

The guard looked over to Frank.

'That's not—' Gabby piped up, but, before she could finish her sentence, Dagmar broke in.

'I suggest you take them to Miss Moonhunter immediately, see what she has to say about their roaming around in the woods without permission.'

'You don't need permission to be in the woods,' shot Gabby.

Dagmar gave her an evil look.

'Even so,' he said, still staring at her. 'It's a bit unusual, don't you think, officer? I'm sure the principal would want to know what her students are up to out here, especially if they're involved in some kind of mischief. Wouldn't you agree?'

The guard appeared uncertain as to what to do. Perhaps stumbling across four teenage children and two odd looking men in black cloaks with a vicious looking dog wasn't in the training manual. He nodded at Dagmar.

'Maybe you're right,' he conceded and turned to his colleague. 'I think we should take them to see Miss Moonhunter, right away.'

Frank's heart sank. He had expected rescue, but wondered if being taken to see Aurora Moonhunter was a case of out of the frying pan and into the fire.

The guard turned to Dagmar. 'If you can accompany us too, sir,' he said. Even worse.

The guard moved to one side and the six of them stepped through into the grounds of Excelsus. The guard locked the gate behind them, took out a notepad and a pencil, scribbled a short note and handed it to his colleague, who was holding a guard dog. The other guard read the note then placed it in a pouch that was attached to the dog's collar. He said something inaudible to the dog, which darted off towards the academy building presumably, thought Frank, to warn Aurora Moonhunter of their impending arrival. Frank had hoped they were in relative safety in the academy, but, as they were led across the grounds and into the building, he had an uneasy feeling he might be mistaken.

22

THE OFFICE

The Alphaen guards guided them through the academy towards the west wing where Moonhunter's office was situated. As they passed through the entrance hall, the image of Finestone Lamplight looked down on them disapprovingly, and Frank felt that, although the guards were there, it was Dagmar who was in control of the situation. Worrying indeed.

The guard dog appeared, trotting towards them down the corridor, returning from where it had been sent earlier, message delivered. Moonhunter knew they were coming.

The academy was deserted and ghostly silent. Frank had never imagined it this empty. It was always alive with scholars and learning, the shrill voices of students and the roamings of an assortment of hounds. But not now, not in the late afternoon, after the academic day had finished. Their footsteps echoed around the corridors - a rhythmic beat, like primitive music on the stone floor - as they made their way through the building. Frank felt like a condemned man being led to the gallows as the four students walked ahead of Dagmar and Percy. He sensed the dark man's eyes boring into him but resisted the urge to turn around. He'd already seen enough of that face to last a life time. Dagmar held Orpheus by the lead. The huge hound walked obediently by its master's side, alert and ready to act upon Dagmar's command.

Frank kept glancing over to the others, wondering what was likely to happen once they reached the office. Gabby wore her look of defiance; Anya looked perplexed; Cas looked like he was about to throw up. Frank was still troubled by an odd feeling that he'd had since the guards had intervened at the gate. He was unsettled by the fact that Dagmar had willingly agreed to come along to Moonhunter's office. He thought he would have excused himself and legged it; he was certainly strong and athletic and, with a beast like Orpheus, he was sure the guards wouldn't have given chase. Instead, he was following behind them, now inside Excelsus, in Byeland, a country that, by all accounts, would have him thrown out at the drop of a hat. What was it Blackburn had said? Mark my words, he'll be up to no good. So what type of no good was he up to, exactly?

They headed through the network of corridors and further into the west wing; Frank had not been this way before. It wasn't long before the guard in front turned into a small atrium. In the centre of the wall opposite was a white door with a large image of an eye painted in the centre. It was flanked by two vulture statues. The surrounding walls were ornately decorated in mystic swirls of vivid colours that seemed to move elegantly across the masonry. The whole space had a magical quality and was filled with the heady smell of incense. The four of them were transfixed, while Dagmar, Percy and the guards didn't even appear to notice.

The guard at the front stepped forward and knocked sharply on the door. Frank waited for a voice to summon them in, or for someone to open it, but, rather than simply opening, the door dissolved into thin air, evaporating before his eyes to reveal the inside of the principal's office. Frank wondered how many students actually got to see inside, not that he had envisaged seeing it in exactly these circumstances. The guard led them in and the door reappeared behind them.

She was standing across the room behind a large, round desk, her back turned. Rather than her usual robes, she was dressed in a blue shirt, dark like the night sky. Her trousers were of the same colour. Her rainbow hair was casually tied up.

Frank was startled by a small cat which jumped up onto the desk and eyed them. It circled, like it was stalking its next rodent, and came to a stop. Its coat was orange and patterned with black swirls and its beauty belied its intent. The animal opened its mouth and gave a silent hiss, baring its teeth. Frank wasn't sure if this was in contempt at their arrival, or at the sight of the large dog attached to the end of Dagmar's lead. He considered the relative risk of attack compared to the earlier incident with Orpheus and felt the cat was somewhat less frightening.

He had become slightly circumspect about other people's animals since his first meeting with Gabby in Laskie's when she had said that, although it was as rare as hen's teeth to have a familiar, a person could be partnered with any animal. Although he was happy with Tweedy as his ally, it left open the possibility that, everywhere he looked, there could be someone looking back at him through the eyes of any living thing and this cat was no exception, especially considering its owner.

The room was surprisingly spacious and sparkled with mystery; a reflection, Frank felt, of the principal. He looked up at the ceiling and noticed the image of the night sky. The picture moved - planets rotated on their axes and orbited the sun, and thousands of stars shone across the skyscape. It was mystical and compelling.

The room was scattered with strange-looking objects, unworldly and magical. Jars of coloured powders and liquids stood squarely in cabinets against the walls. Heavy velvet drapes of deep plums and blues hung sumptuously at the windows, giving the whole room a distinctly exotic feel. Frank thought that it looked like a more mysterious and much tidier version of Blackburn's workshop.

The walls were adorned with numerous paintings, all squarely hung and immaculate, in stark contrast, Frank thought, to the jumble and chaos of those that obliquely filled the walls of Jelly's office back in Smithwood. This room would certainly put his to shame. They were mainly portraits of people who were anonymous to Frank as they stared out into the room. He had no idea who any of them were. Judging by the ones he was able to glance at, they could be former professors or students, he couldn't be sure. Anyway, he had more pressing matters on his mind.

In the middle of the desk there was a large crystal ball, within which a swirling cloud constantly changed colour, looking for all the world like it contained a host of secrets and mysteries. It reflected the image that was on on the ceiling, projecting the small stars back out over the room so the office was bathed in starlight and tiny stars danced around them. The ball was cradled in the wings of a glass vulture, guardian of the academy and of the secrets within the office.

'Ma'am,' said one of the Alphaen. 'You received my message?'

Elegant and self-possessed, Moonhunter turned and looked at the assembled gathering without acknowledging them.

'Yes,' she said with a smile to the Alphaen. 'Thank you gentlemen, you're free to return to your duties.'

Without a word, the two guards left the room, followed by their dog, the door magically opening and closing behind them as the rest of them stood there in awkward silence.

Dagmar walked to the side of the room so he could see the faces of both Moonhunter and the students, as if this was some kind of natural reflex for him - strategically repositioning himself so he had everyone in his sights, exactly as he wanted. Orpheus slouched dutifully after him, wary of the cat still sitting on the table, superior and staring down at the dog, watching its every move. It let out another hiss, this time audible. Orpheus, for all his muscle and brutishness, slunk in behind Dagmar, as far away from the feline as his master would allow. Meanwhile, Dagmar unbuttoned his cloak, revealing the black scorpion against his deep red tunic.

'Hello Dagmar,' she said softly, gazing enigmatically at him. It was the sort of look that would have made most people fidget with discomfort; but not him.

He gave the slightest of acknowledgments but said nothing, only turning to glare at the students. Frank was more than a little perturbed. Why wasn't she having him arrested and rushed out of Rhaeder on the next available police transport? Frank knew Dagmar was about as unpopular as a person could get in Byeland, reviled even, so why was Moonhunter so relaxed? It seemed to him that these two knew each other. That would be alarming, the head of Excelsus Academy, chums with Byeland's greatest enemy. Whatever their relationship, it certainly reinforced Frank's opinion that she was not to be trusted.

He glanced at the others and raised his eyebrows, wondering if he should say something. Anya just gazed around the room, oblivious, but Cas got his meaning and shrugged slightly, just as mystified. Gabby scowled at Dagmar and looked like she was about to speak, but Moonhunter appeared to notice and spoke first.

'So, who do we have here?' She looked at the four students, then fixed her gaze on Cas and waited. Cas got the hint.

'Hardcastle Jones,' he said. She nodded.

'You have a brother here? Battersby?'

'Yes, that's right,' he replied nervously.

'Sharp boy, your brother,' she said. 'I believe your family has an interesting flair for, shall we say, sleight of hand.' Cas nodded.

Her eyes moved on to Anya, who gave an audible gulp and shuffled nervously on the spot.

'Anya Wilde,' she just about managed to say. Moonhunter nodded again.

'I love your crystal,' Anya blurted out. 'I wish I had one like—'

Moonhunter held her hand up, indicating to Anya to stop. Dagmar rolled his eyes. Anya gave Moonhunter a nervous smile.

'Thank you Miss Wilde.'

She looked at Gabby, who had turned her attention away from Dagmar and now held her usual angry pout. Moonhunter waited as the silence filled the room. Frank noticed Dagmar staring at Gabby with a sneer on his face, like a predator sensing his prey had been trapped and waiting for his chance for the kill. Gabby breathed deeply, but chose not to say anything. Bad move, thought Frank, recollecting the strange incident on his first day when Moonhunter had somehow known his name just by pointing at him. Moonhunter kept on looking at her as the uncomfortable silence hung in the air. Frank and Cas fidgeted. Dagmar just stood, enjoying every minute of their discomfort. Gabby's will finally broke.

'Gabriella Asaro,' she huffed, looking away.

'Thank you, Miss Asaro,' said Moonhunter. 'I'm not sure I know of your family.' She paused as if trying to recollect, she then placed the fingertips of her right hand on the crystal ball in the middle of the table. There was a brief pause, then the crystal shot out bright green strands from its centre that joined to Moonhunter's fingertips. Anya's eyes widened and she nudged Gabby, who ignored her. Moonhunter removed her fingers and looked back to Gabby.

'Ah, of course,' she said. 'I should have known. hmm, interesting. You don't take your studies here too seriously, do you? Whatever gift you have, Miss Asaro, it needs working on. It needs your commitment, otherwise you will never realise your potential. Whatever your difficulties in the past, remember, it is the past.'

Gabby managed a resentful nod. Moonhunter turned and looked at Frank.

'Ah, Mr Penny,' she said sweetly. 'We meet again.'

She went to continue but there was a knock at the door. A sharp image of a man appeared in the crystal ball. It was Lanks, as if things couldn't get any worse. The image was so sharp it was as if he was already in the room with them.

'Come in, Herbert,' said Moonhunter.

The door disappeared, as it had done when they had arrived, and Lanks entered the room. He stopped when he saw who was there, taking special notice of Dagmar, who watched him menacingly. The two men glared at each other, eyes locked, neither one averting his gaze. Frank thought Lanks hadn't even noticed the four students in the room, such was the attention he gave to Dagmar. His face was full of rage.

Lanks finally broke his stare and looked at Moonhunter.

'I know what you're thinking,' she said.

Frank didn't doubt it, he was thinking it too.

'What's *he* doing here?' said Lanks irritably, with a tone not short of derision.

'Oh, Dagmar was just making sure he returned these students safely; they were out in the woods and seem to have stumbled across each other.'

Lanks gave Moonhunter a doubtful look, then turned to Frank. His moustache bristled with disappointment. Frank looked down to avoid his disapproving eyes and noticed Bertie sitting at his heels, tongue hanging out.

'These students were out in the woods, snooping around,' sneered Dagmar. Lanks just about managed to look back at him.

'Snooping?' said Lanks, barely containing his apparent dislike for Dagmar. 'And what is there to "snoop" at in the woods?'

'You mean you don't know?' was Dagmar's mysterious response.

Lanks went silent and glanced at Moonhunter. Frank sensed some sort of unspoken sparring going on, a silence to keep something secret. Lanks mulled something over in his mind momentarily and then turned to Frank.

'Why *were* you in the woods?' he asked, pointedly.

'I didn't think students were forbidden to go there,' snapped Gabby.

Moonhunter turned to Gabby and, with her usual gentle smile, said 'Miss Asaro. May I suggest that you moderate your tone? I'm not here to reprimand you, but you certainly don't want to get on the wrong side of me.'

Gabby looked at her for a moment and nodded, reluctantly. Moonhunter was difficult to read and Frank didn't know if her smile was that of a friendly hamster or a venomous snake.

'We were just exploring,' Frank cut in.

It wasn't altogether untrue, but he thought by keeping his explanation short and vague he could get away without telling the whole story.

'We saw this man walking through the woods' - he pointed at Percy - 'so we decided to follow him. That's when we came across ... him.'

He looked at Dagmar, who flared his nostrils, his eyes penetrating Frank's. Frank didn't mention Hums's cottage or the corridor down which they had followed Dagmar. He took the chance that Dagmar would want to keep that little secret too. Besides, he wanted to find out much more about where the passage led and, more importantly, what Dagmar was doing down there. However, in keeping quiet and avoiding details about the whole event, he ran the risk that Dagmar would then know he and his friends had something to hide. Even though Dagmar was obviously a malicious and powerful character, he was clearly no fool and the fact that Frank hadn't spilled the beans on his movements would no doubt alert him. Dagmar didn't speak, which confirmed Frank's suspicions. It had become their little secret, which wasn't necessarily a good thing.

Lanks spoke again, flicking his head in Dagmar's direction.

'More to the point, what were you doing in the woods?'

This was a question Frank had had on his mind since the episode in the tunnel, but one he felt Dagmar had absolutely no intention of answering, if he could help it.

'None of your business,' Dagmar spat back, and he looked over to Moonhunter, challenging her to ask the same question. He, apparently, answered to no one. Dangerous, if you were in his hands, as they had been a few minutes ago before the Alphaen had come to their rescue.

Lanks returned Dagmar's glare.

'I would have you arrested and thrown out of Byeland,' he said angrily.

Orpheus stood up on all fours and growled, ready to pounce. Moonhunter's expression changed and she straightened her right arm, palm held out towards the dog. It let out a slight, high-pitched whine as if it had been slapped and immediately sat back down behind Dagmar, who hardly seemed to notice and just looked at Moonhunter, rolling his eyes.

'Arrested, typical,' muttered Dagmar to himself. 'On what charge?' he laughed. 'Strolling through the woods? Birdwatching?

Wearing the leather off my boots?'

Behind him, Percy chuckled, while Lanks looked fit to burst, his usual dry exterior replaced by a look of utter resentment. He glanced at Moonhunter for support.

'I'm afraid Dagmar has a point,' she conceded.

Lanks looked helpless.

'Although he may not be the most popular person, it's not a crime for someone from Kzarlac to stroll around Byeland by themselves. Imagine what would happen to some of our students if that were the case.'

Frank thought of Emerald and his Kzarlac clan and how thoroughly satisfying it would be if they were to be run out of town, along with Dagmar.

'Depends what his intentions are,' huffed Lanks.

'Maybe,' she looked back at Dagmar. 'Though if his intentions are ... improper ... he ought to consider a quick return to Kzarlac.'

Dagmar's expression gave nothing away. Of course his intentions are improper, thought Frank, but he had to admit that proving it without telling Moonhunter the full story of their encounter could be more difficult than it seemed.

'Meanwhile,' continued Moonhunter, 'I believe I should thank you and your manservant, here, for returning these students safely back to the academy. The security and wellbeing of those that attend this school are always my utmost priority.'

Frank noticed Anya and Gabby make strange facial expressions as they considered how safe they had actually been in Dagmar's hands and how he probably had no intention of delivering them securely back through the doors of Excelsus, except inside the stomach of his vicious-looking hound.

'You should search them,' said Dagmar maliciously, eyes narrowing as a smile came across his face.

Frank suddenly remembered the tin box which they'd discovered at Hums's cottage and which was now sitting inside his bag. If he was asked to open it, how on earth would he explain its weird contents and, even worse, how they had come by the box in the first place? He felt a sweat on his brow and resisted the urge to clutch his bag closer, in case it gave him away. The others seemed to realise this too and they exchanged worried looks.

'I don't think that will be necessary,' said Moonhunter in her usual calming tone.

Frank relaxed. He realised he'd been holding his breath and exhaled. Dagmar screwed up his face in anger but chose not to say anything. Frank wondered if he was contemplating pouncing on him and tipping the contents of his bag out for all to see, but then realised that Dagmar had no way of knowing what they had found, otherwise he would have discovered the hiding place himself. Frank thought he must just be acting on a hunch, one that hadn't paid off.

Moonhunter looked at him.

'Thank you, Dagmar. I need to speak to these students. Alone. I won't be needing you anymore.' Clearly she wanted Dagmar to leave. Frank wasn't sure whether to be pleased or not, as being left in Moonhunter's presence might bring its own complications. 'And thank you once again for returning my students to me safely. I know how dangerous it can be out there.'

Dagmar looked fit to snap.

'You have no idea,' he seethed slowly through his teeth, keeping his eyes on Frank.

Even though he had at least learned their names, whatever else Dagmar had hoped to achieve by having them taken to Moonhunter had ended in total disappointment. He hesitated under Moonhunter's stare, obviously not wanting to leave; failure probably wasn't in his vocabulary. If looks could kill.

'Come on, Percy,' he said finally and strode swiftly towards the door and out of the office, dog and manservant close behind.

Frank could hear Dagmar's raised voice, taking things out on Percy as they went down the passageway to the main entrance of the academy.

The office was quiet, but Dagmar's exit hadn't changed the

atmosphere to a more relaxed one. It was still as tense as a string on a fiddle.

'You should be careful. Meeting a man like Dagmar out in the woods is not something I would necessarily recommend,' warned Moonhunter. She stood at the desk and her cat rubbed itself around her arms, giving a soft meow followed by a loud purr. Moonhunter scooped it up and gave it a stroke.

'Well, he's up to no good,' retorted Gabby.

'And what makes you think that?' asked Moonhunter.

Frank willed Gabby to tread carefully. He'd not given them away earlier and hoped she would be discreet as well.

'It's obvious,' exclaimed Gabby. 'You just have to look at him to see what kind of person he is.'

Moonhunter regarded her.

'I would have imagined you would have thought carefully before judging someone by the way they look,' she commented.

Frank knew what she was getting at, but both he and Gabby knew this was different. Gabby had some sort of history with Kzarlac and they knew more about Dagmar than perhaps Moonhunter gave them credit for. Gabby was about to speak again, but Frank interjected.

'I would have thought you would know, or be able to tell, what kind of person Dagmar is. He wouldn't be here unless he wanted something.' He recalled what Blackburn had said to them about Dagmar being up to no good. 'I was thinking you should be concerned that he's sniffing around close to the academy.'

Moonhunter took a few steps forward.

'Oh, I don't need to worry about Dagmar,' she said, but if Frank thought she was about to expand on the reasons why she needn't worry he was to be disappointed.

There was a brief silence.

'I hear you're a natural falconer,' she continued, suddenly changing the subject.

Frank, unsure if this was a question or a statement, nodded.

'I'm not sure if you'd call it natural,' he replied, thinking of Tweedy and the strange relationship he had established with his familiar.

Sensing that Moonhunter was taking the conversation away from the events of the evening, he took a deep breath.

'How do you know Dagmar?'

He blurted it out nervously rather than simply asking the question. His dad had always taught him to not just accept things as they were presented, but to challenge what you didn't accept and to keep going until you got to the truth, and this was one situation where he felt he needed to do just that.

If Moonhunter was taken aback by his question, she didn't show it. Unflustered, she said, 'I'm not sure that's something you need to know.'

'But he must be looking for something and—'

'Enough,' she said, calmly, but firmly.

'But—' Frank tried to continue, knowing that if anyone had some answers to what was going on, Moonhunter certainly did.

'I said that's *enough*,' Moonhunter repeated more sternly, her authority clear.

Cas, Gabby, Anya and even Lanks looked slightly shocked that Frank had tried to continue. The skyscape on the ceiling suddenly turned to a storm; dark clouds churned like a turbulent sea and the room seemed to shudder with imaginary thunder. Suddenly, Frank wanted to be anywhere but in that office. The calm anger of Moonhunter was more menacing than the spite of Dagmar. There was silence.

'I don't know what you've been up to, or what you think you know,' she said, 'but, whatever it is, you need to bring it to an end, and do so immediately. Whatever adventure you might think you're having, believe me, this is not a matter for children. There are things that go on in the world that are both mysterious and dangerous and you really should not be involving yourselves in issues you can't even begin to understand. While you are here at Excelsus, I have the responsibility for your conduct and welfare and, from where I'm standing, you seem to be extremely close to compromising both and I cannot have that. So, whatever you might have begun to get yourselves into, it stops. Now. Before you get into something beyond your control.'

She paused to let her words sink in. Whatever he had said, Frank had obviously just touched a nerve.

Moonhunter continued, 'From now on, I don't want you in the woods unless there is a good educational reason for you to be there, and, by that, I mean it forms part of your studies. Do I make myself clear?'

Her tone left the students in no doubt that she meant what she said. They all nodded. The cat blinked back at them scornfully.

'Good. Now, Herbert, perhaps you would be kind enough to accompany Mr Penny, Miss Asaro, Miss Wilde and Mr Jones to the main entrance, from where they can make their way home for the night.'

Lanks nodded. 'Come on then,' he sighed.

He stepped towards the door and waited for the students as it opened. Moonhunter continued to watch them as they turned to leave. Frank hesitated. He wanted to stay, to ask her what was going on, but her warning had been unmistakable. Perhaps it wasn't such a good idea.

Cas led them out, followed by the girls. Lanks watched them as they filed past and then fixed his stare on Frank. He stopped him as he went past.

'Trouble seems to follow you around, Penny,' he said. 'I'll be keeping an even closer watch on you from now on.'

It was at that moment that Frank noticed Lanks was wearing something around his neck. He'd not noticed it before, probably because Lanks had always been formally dressed with his shirt buttoned up to the top. But now, after the end of the school day, he was more casual and wore it open-necked. As Frank himself wore a locket, he thought there was nothing particularly strange about

Lanks having something similar but, as he glimpsed the odd looking object threaded on the chain around his neck, he thought it looked vaguely familiar, although he couldn't quite place it. Lanks looked down at him and, quickly, Frank averted his gaze, realising he'd been staring at it just a little too long. Lanks's hand made an unconscious move to his neck as Frank moved towards the door. As it closed behind them, Frank sensed that the large eye painted on the door was watching them leave - more than mere decoration.

Lanks led them away from Moonhunter's office to the main entrance in silence, her warning still ringing in their ears like a church bell. Frank couldn't help but think that their brief adventure was over. He also thought that if he never went back into Moonhunter's office, it would be way too soon.

23

THE BOX

Frank spent some weeks licking his wounds after his dressing down from Moonhunter. The enigmatic head, with her calm approach to the most unusual situations, had left him with the feeling that the four of them had let down both themselves and the academy. He thought the episode might have turned out differently had he been able to think more clearly when they were in her office, or had a clearer idea of what he thought he could get away with asking. But she probably still wouldn't have given any answers, anyway. He'd returned to his studies, still trying to discover where his abilities might lie and wondering if Moonhunter would be keeping an extra eye on him.

He'd been intrigued by the inside of her office and the weird nature of the place. After his experience in Jelly's office he knew that Excelsus would be different, but there was something about the rainbow-haired Moonhunter that he couldn't put his finger on. She was difficult to read and he couldn't be certain whose side she was on. That is, if there were sides in all of this in the first place.

Certainly she didn't seem to feel at all troubled by the presence of that embodiment of nastiness that was Dagmar Dag. Why, was another question. Perhaps she held some sort of celestial power over him. That wouldn't be a surprise, given the way she looked and some of the strange abilities she appeared to possess. Perhaps it was all some kind of bluff. But if she and Dagmar were, for some reason, working together, he deduced they had to be looking for Ludlow Hums. Frank knew that she wanted the return of the Liberation Seal, one of the founding objects and talisman of the academy. If

Hums really had it, she might have drafted in the combined talents of the Alphaen and Dagmar to find it. Maybe they'd all been looking across the world for the last two years and this was the next, or last, place to search, finishing where they had begun. She'd also be able put a killer behind bars as a bonus. But was that reason enough to be so severe with them? What 'things' should they not be involving themselves in? Surely looking for an old bloke wasn't such a big deal, so was there something else?

Whatever was happening, they had been warned off in no uncertain terms, but the mere fact that they had been told to stop meddling meant that something important *was* going on, and right underneath their noses.

A few weeks had passed since the episode in the office and their ever-increasing workload had meant that they hadn't had much of a chance to talk about what had happened. They were also afraid that they might talk themselves straight back into a whole world of trouble. Frank knew they'd have to talk about it soon, though, and he also knew that the decision was whether to heed Moonhunter's warning to leave things alone, or find out more. Unfortunately for him, and his friends, he already knew the answer to that question.

* * *

Having just finished his Sorcery homework, Frank was lying on his bed, staring at the ceiling and enjoying the warmth of the late spring sun shining through the window, when he heard a voice from the bottom of the stairs.

'Frank, darlin', you up there?'

He got up and walked to the top of the staircase. Looking up was Polly's friendly face, cutting a broad smile.

'Oh, there you are, gorgeous,' she beamed. 'Got some visitors for you. Young man, thin as a whippet, and a couple of young ladies.'

She lowered her voice.

'One's kind of scary looking, but nice.'

She said the last bit a little more loudly. She glanced down the lower staircase in case Cas, Anya and Gabby were listening.

'Send them up, shall I?'

'That would be great,' smiled Frank.

'Okay,' she said.

She disappeared, then reappeared a moment later, leading his three friends upwards.

'There you are, babes,' said Polly. 'Got him looking all fresh and rosy for you.'

She smiled up at Frank, stopping at the landing as the others continued up towards Frank's bedroom.

'I've got a batch of fruit scones on. Make sure you come down and try them out for me.'

'Thanks, Mrs Quigley,' said Anya.

'They smell delicious,' added Gabby .

'Oh, none of that formality; call me Polly. And it's no trouble at all. Nice to have Frank's friends round. I'll get some tea on too. Now you just come on down to the kitchen when you're ready, my lovelies. Oh, and Frank?'

'Yes Polly.'

'No wild teenage parties now,' she said in a mischievous tone. 'Can't have my poor Norris having a seizure now can I, oh!'

And with that she disappeared once more to tend her baking, laughing loudly to herself as she went down the stairs to the kitchen.

Gabby sat next to Frank on his bed, while Cas flopped on the floor with his back to the wall and his long legs bent up at the knees like a giant tarantula. Anya perched on the window sill.

'She's nice, Polly,' said Cas. Gabby nodded.

'Yeah, I'm really lucky,' nodded Frank. 'She's a friend of my Aunt Rachel. Good job she lives here, otherwise I've no idea where I would have stayed.'

'Nicer than the lot me and Gabby are staying with,' said Anya.

'Yeah, they're a miserable bunch,' agreed Gabby. 'You could have ended up with them.'

She screwed her nose up.

'What are you doing?'

275

'Just finished my Sorcery homework. Tough stuff!'

'Told you so. Anything I can help with?' she grinned. 'I need to take my studies more seriously, don't you know,' she added, recounting Moonhunter's comments.

Frank smiled, got up and shut the door, making sure there was no one down the stairs. He didn't want Maddy walking in on them. Not that she ever came upstairs, but the presence of his visitors might have made her curious, even though she was as scared as a mouse most of the time and just the sight of Gabby would probably have been enough to put her off. He sat back on the bed.

'So what do you make of Dagmar and Moonhunter?'

'Yeah, that's a strange one,' said Cas. 'I got the impression they weren't the best of friends, but then Moonhunter was happy to let him go. I couldn't make it out. Sherbet lemon, anyone?'

He held out a bag of sweets and the others took one each.

'I dunno,' said Anya. 'They looked kind of cosy to me.'

'Huh, I wouldn't waste any of my time on that scumbag,' snarled Gabby. 'She should have just got the Alphaen to take him back to where he came from and dump him there for good. End of story.'

'Exactly, that's what I would have expected her to do, but she didn't. So, do you think they're working together?' said Frank.

'Why would they do that?' said Cas.

'Well, I was thinking, perhaps they're all just looking for one thing.'

'Hums?'

'Yeah, maybe. If you think about it, Moonhunter and Excelsus want the Seal back. Perhaps they've enlisted Dagmar's support to find him. After all, there's no doubt he's thorough and we know he was at Hums's cottage.' said Frank.

'Not to mention snooping around down some secret passage,' said Cas.

'Yeah, right. What I'd give to go back down there,' said Frank, looking at the others to see if they felt the same.

'Are you kidding?' retorted Cas. 'Remember what Moonhunter said. We all agreed to drop it. I wouldn't like to think what might happen if we got caught and who knows if they haven't put Orpheus down there on permanent guard. Yikes!'

Frank had to agree. He thought Moonhunter wasn't the sort who gave warnings twice.

'I guess you're right,' he conceded in resignation. 'But them being in it together would explain why Moonhunter said we didn't need to worry about Dagmar, and why she was okay with letting him go.'

'I think she said that *she* needn't worry about Dagmar. I don't think the same applies to us anymore.'

'So, what I don't get is what's in it for Dagmar?' said Gabby. 'If Hums is really is back in town, which we still don't know is right or not, and they find him, the academy gets the Seal back and Hums goes to jail. Great, but what does Dagmar get?'

It was a good question, one they realised they didn't have an answer to.

'Well, I think it's safe to assume that Mr Nasty isn't the sort just to do someone a kind favour,' said Cas.

None of them could think of why he might be there, but, one thing was for sure, Dagmar was up to something and now he had the four of them in his sights. Not a great place to be.

Gabby spoke again. 'So, the only thing we think we know is that Moonhunter, Dagmar and the Alphaen are all looking for the same thing.'

Frank nodded. 'Well, we know that the Alphaen aren't here to hunt for Dagmar,' he said.

'That's for sure; I didn't notice them rushing to put the handcuffs on him when we were on the way to Moonhunter's office, did you?' said Gabby.

'No.'

'So, the only thing that's missing is Ludlow Hums, along with the Seal.'

'So, Blackburn was right,' said Frank. 'He thought that was the case when he knew the Alphaen were here.'

'Is there anyone not looking for Hums?' laughed Cas.

'Well, we're not,' said Anya. 'Not yet, anyway.'

'Then perhaps we should start,' suggested Frank, looking at Anya. In spite of Moonhunter's warning to stop, he felt they had to try and find out more.

Cas and Gabby exchanged glances. It was a big risk.

'I'm not sure, Frank,' said Cas. 'Moonhunter was pretty clear.' He seemed nervous.

'Oh, come on, Cas, where's your sense of adventure?' coaxed Gabby.

'Stuck between the jaws of a big dog and a scary headmistress,' he laughed.

Frank bent down, reached under the bed and grabbed the small tin box they had found in Hums's cottage. 'Let's start with this,' he said with a gleam in his eye.

Cas looked resigned.

'I'd just about forgotten all about that,' said Gabby as Frank passed her the box.

She flicked the catch and opened it. The three objects they had first seen in Hums cottage sat there as they had before - the small ball, the folded piece of paper and the odd-shaped piece of stone. A most unusual collection of items; why someone would go to such lengths to hide them was puzzling. They seemed bound together, but, at the same time, disconnected and meaningless.

Frank was intrigued by the strange little orb that he'd held when they'd first opened the box, especially the way it had reacted when he'd picked it up. Anya sat on the floor next to Cas, who reached in and took it. He held his hand flat, just as Frank had done in the cottage. He expected the ball to rise and hover as it had done before, but it just sat in his palm, not moving. There was no sign of the animation that had captivated them before. Cas looked thoroughly disappointed. He closed his hand and opened it again.

Nothing. He held it up between his thumb and forefinger. Nothing. They all looked at it. It was just a bland spherical object.

'Do you think it's, er, run out of whatever it had?' said Cas.

Gabby reached over and Cas let her take it between her thumb and forefinger. Again, nothing. She flicked it up in the air and let it come to rest in her palm.

'Don't shake it,' teased Frank wryly.

Gabby laughed. She inspected it more closely, but the sphere remained dull and lifeless. She shrugged, as did Anya, who didn't seem too keen on holding it. 'There you go.' She handed the ball to Frank.

Immediately, it took on a new dimension. As before, it lifted itself above the flat of Frank's palm and hovered there, spinning slowly. It became lustrous and radiating, changing colours as it did so. Frank's eyebrows shot up in amazement. The others gasped and looked at each other, gobsmacked.

'Well, who would've predicted that?' said Anya.

'Probably not you,' said Cas, wryly, the comment earning him a shove.

'Guess it only likes you, Frankie,' declared Gabby, lying back and propping herself up on her hands. She blew the hair from her eyes and watched the ball as it floated easily in mid-air.

'It would seem so,' agreed Frank with more than an element of surprise. He grasped the ball lightly so it stopped spinning and then held it in his fist. He could feel it pulsating slightly, as if there was a certain energy held within. He opened his hand again. The object changed colour, moving from a fiery orange to a vivid meltwater blue, then to a swirling chestnut brown and on to a cloudy white hue. They all looked on in wonder; its appearance was mesmerising.

'What do you think it is?' asked Gabby. 'And, more importantly, what does it do?'

Neither Frank nor Cas had any ideas on both counts.

'I thought you might know,' Frank said to Gabby. 'Looks like it has some sorcery about it, don't you think.'

Gabby had to agree.

'Hey, you don't think that Blackburn invented this too, do you?' laughed Cas.

'Well, he is full of surprises,' replied Frank, still watching the ball which spun on its axis as it continued to change colour.

He grasped it and noticed that whatever material it was made from had a bit of give in it, a slight sponginess that he hadn't felt before, probably because he'd been handling it so carefully. He squeezed it a couple of times before bouncing it hard over towards the opposite wall so that it would rebound back to him. As the ball hit the floor, there was a large flash and a cracking sound. Sparks of all sizes flew out of it and across the room, hitting all of them, as well as the bedroom furniture and the bed. It bounced over to the wall and zoomed between Cas and Anya, just missing Cas's head. They all ducked for cover. Frank managed to dodge as the ball rebounded back to him, hitting the wall he was leaning against and coming to rest on the bed covers. He made a quick grab for it, alarmed and fearful that it would set fire to the bed and everyone would go up in smoke. They all looked around to make sure nothing, or no one, was alight as the aroma of Polly's baking was replaced momentarily with the smell of burning. A voice came from the hallway.

'Frank, you okay darlin'?' It was Polly. She had heard the loud crack as the ball bounced around the room. Frank composed himself.

'Yeah, fine thanks, Polly,' he shouted back.

'What did you just do, Frank?' said Gabby, cowering on the floor, open mouthed.

She'd thrown herself to the ground and covered her head with her arms; her long dark hair hung dishevelled over her face. She brushed it from her cheek and blew the final strands away.

'I ... I ... I really have no idea what just happened,' stammered Frank.

'Look Frank,' said Cas. 'If you're going to let a bomb off in the house, can you please let us know about it beforehand?'

'I thought Dagmar was the only one trying to get us,' quipped

Anya.

'Sorry guys,' he said sheepishly. 'I won't be doing that again in a hurry.' He inspected the sphere more closely, but it failed to yield any clues about itself. He placed it back in the box and its colour drained; it sat there abandoned, nondescript and lifeless. 'There's something strange about that,' he continued, pointing into the box.

'You don't say,' said Cas.

'What do you think we should do with it?' asked Frank.

'I think we should show it to Blackburn,' declared Gabby. 'He's bound to know something about a weird thing like that. Even if he didn't invent it, it has all the hallmarks of something he'd know about, don't you think?'

'Yeah, maybe, perhaps you're right,' conceded Frank, although he thought they should keep their find between themselves. 'I think I'll leave it in there for now.'

'Do you think it's safe in there?' said Cas, nodding towards to box. 'I mean, Polly won't thank you for burning the house down if you keep it under your bed.'

'It's been there a while, so I think it'll be okay, and it only seems to take on a mind of its own when I pick it up, otherwise it just looks like a big marble.'

They turned their attention to the odd looking piece of stone. It had a long, thin stem protruding from a gnarled bulbous end. The stem was about four inches long. At the other end, the stone bent at right angles. It was rough, unpolished and even though it was unusual in its appearance, Frank thought how, at the same time, it was altogether ordinary, like something you would just ignore if you were walking along a stony path and saw it lying there. He picked it up and weighed it in his hands. It was solid, but light. He thought for a moment.

'It looks sort of familiar,' he frowned, racking his brains and trying to place where he might have seen it. He thought about the academy, Laskie's and Polly's and even cast his mind back to the farm in case he'd seen something like it there, although he couldn't think why - he was sure he hadn't.

'I was thinking the same thing,' said Cas, 'but I can't place it either.'

'Uh?' remarked Anya. 'Are you sure?'

'Well I think so.' Frank thought for a moment before an element of doubt set in. 'Maybe not, but it's such an odd shape. It doesn't look natural, if you know what I mean, not like something that's just fallen off a rock face or something. It looks like it's been made.'

Gabby nodded.

Frank inspected the object more closely and saw that the piece of stone looked like it had been worked along its length. There were subtle tool marks on it, indicating that someone had crafted it specifically into that particular shape. He tried to think how such a peculiar object might be useful to a crook, and why was it something they might want to keep hidden?

'Look,' he said, handing the object to Gabby and showing her the crafted section.

She ran her fingers around the edge of the fragment, feeling the indentations, and nodded.

'You're right, someone's made this. I wonder what it's for?'

She held it aloft, in case it sprang into life like the small ball that had given them such a shock a few moments earlier. Nothing happened. She held it in different ways, trying to picture what it might be for, but its purpose remained a mystery. She handed it to Anya who looked at it as they sat on the floor in silence.

'Can we be sure these things really belonged to Hums?' asked Anya, twirling the stone object around in her hand.

'They must have. They were hidden in his house, so I would say the evidence is pretty strong,' said Frank.

Cas picked up the box and dusted off the top of the lid. The grime from within the chimney had made a thin film on the top and as he rubbed the dirt he began to see something. He continued to rub, eventually revealing the shallow engraving of two crossed arrows underneath a flower - a rose. It was an unusual-looking symbol.

'I wonder what this means?' said Cas, showing the image to the others.

They looked blank. It meant nothing and Frank had never seen anything like it before. Cas gave the box the once-over, searching for any secret compartments, just in case. Given how their adventure was unfolding, he wouldn't have been surprised if there was something hidden, lurking in the box. There wasn't. He checked the red velvet lining, but there was nothing.

Gabby opened the piece of paper, revealing, once more, the criss-cross grid of lines they had seen briefly when they had opened the box for the first time. She laid it on the floor. On closer inspection they could see it wasn't just a haphazard pattern, it was less random, and Frank could tell that there was some sort of design, as though the lines were laid out in a definite shape.

'Do you think this is a map of some sort?' suggested Frank.

'Who knows,' said Cas. 'It could just as well be some old language, like the book we found.'

'It's obviously really important for some reason, like the ball thing and the piece of stone,' said Gabby, 'I mean, why would Hums go to such lengths to hide it and these other things? They've been secretly stashed away for at least the last two years and no one hides anything unless it's secret, or they don't want anyone to find it.'

'So why hide them in the first place?' said Anya. 'Why not just get rid of them? Destroy them?'

Frank suddenly had a thought. He thought back to the farm, to his tree house, when he had made a rope ladder that he kept folded high up on the platform itself. You could only get the ladder down by using a specifically shaped stick he had crafted and kept hidden in the trunk of a nearby tree. He had hidden it so that only he could use it when he needed to, and no one else knew it was there.

'Do you know what I think?' he said. 'I reckon the only reason you hide something so no one else can find it, is so it's there if you need to come back for it yourself. I've done exactly that, and think of all the people who hide their spare door key somewhere so it's there if they need it, but not for anyone else to find.'

They all looked at each other. If Frank was right, it could mean only one thing. Hums had planned to come back to the cottage to retrieve the objects and so he'd placed them in his own secret hiding place for himself. It also confirmed what they had thought earlier, that everyone was on the hunt for the elusive Ludlow Hums. They all had an inkling he might return, even though there wasn't any real evidence they could pinpoint that confirmed the missing villain was lurking in the shadows anywhere near the town.

'So, Hums left, but always intended to come back?' concluded Cas.

'I suppose it's possible,' said Frank. 'Maybe everyone thinks he's back now. It makes sense.'

'But you'd think he'd have faked his own death at the time, or something? Made people believe he went into the water after his brother. Then they wouldn't still be looking for him' said Cas.

'Maybe, but no one found anything of his up at the river and Norris said a professor saw him push Wordsworth in.'

'You're right, although have you been up to the waterfall? It sort of drags you in just by looking at it,' said Anya.

There was a knock at the door. They all looked up. Quickly, as it opened, Frank put the stone object into the box with the orb and hid it under the bed. Maddy was standing in the doorway. Her pale features scanned the room and she baulked slightly at the sight of three unfamiliar faces as she hugged the doorframe. Frank thought she would have been forewarned by Polly, but the presence of the strangers still seemed to faze her. She looked uncertain and fingered the doorframe nervously.

'Hello,' she said to Cas, Anya and Gabby, who smiled back at her, at the same time casting looks at each other in the knowledge that the diagram was still on the floor, in plain view.

'Hello, Maddy,' said Frank. He looked at his friends. 'This is Gabby, that's Anya, and this is Cas.'

'I know,' she murmured quietly. 'Mum told me.'

She looked at Gabby.

'What's that on your arms?' she asked, casting her eyes down at Gabby's tattoos.

Gabby glanced down too, then looked back at Maddy, smiling.

'Oh, these,' she said, rubbing her forearms gently, tracing the stems of thorns. 'Where I come from it's a kind of tradition to get yourself ... er... decorated when you're about my age, just a bit older than you. It's an important part of my culture.'

Maddy nodded quickly and nervously, as though she had said something she shouldn't have.

'Do they come off?' she asked.

Gabby chuckled. Frank and Cas looked at Anya and smiled.

'No,' she said sweetly. 'They're part of me for life. We're sort of stuck with each other.'

Maddy nodded quickly again before Gabby held out her arms so that she could get a better look, her face reddened.

'Would you like to touch them?'

'No thanks,' said Maddy quickly, recoiling slightly.

'Okay.' Gabby smiled.

'They look cool.'

'Thanks, babe,' said Gabby, gentle and mild.

Maddy smiled and turned to Frank.

'Anyway, Mum says the scones are ready and said she hoped you and your friends would like to come and have one with some tea.' With that, she turned on her heel, disappeared from the doorway, and ran down the stairs.

'New friend?' said Cas, looking at Gabby with amusement.

'You shut your face.' Gabby looked at Frank. 'She seems nice enough.'

'Yeah, she is,' he said.

The comfortable smell of fresh baking had been wafting up the two flights of stairs ever since Cas, Anya and Gabby had arrived and, while Frank was used to it, the others seemed eager to try the tasty wares that Polly had been knocking up in the kitchen. Cas got to his feet and looked at Frank.

'Come on, best not let some freshly baked scones go cold,' he said. 'That smell makes me feel I haven't eaten for a week.'

He rubbed his stomach in mock hunger. The others laughed and followed him downstairs, Ludlow Hums temporarily forgotten.

Down in the kitchen the smell of warm scones filled the room. Norris was warming himself by the fire and Maddy was sitting on the sofa reading a book, her arm around Tinks. As they came through the door, Maddy looked up and then raised her book to cover her face, her earlier boldness seemingly gone.

'Oh, hello,' said Norris.

'Hi, Norris,' said Frank and he introduced the others.

Norris held up his hand in a meek wave.

'Pleased to meet you all,' he replied.

They all sat at the table as Polly served up a big plate of impressive-looking scones along with a large ceramic pot of her homemade clotted cream and a jar of her blackcurrant jam. It all looked utterly delicious.

'There you go my darlin's, get your chops around those lovelies,' she said as she handed each of them a plate. They tucked in; all the talk and thinking up in Frank's room had given way to sharp appetites.

'Delicious, Polly,' mumbled Cas, his face stuffed full of scone and crumbs dropping from his mouth as he spoke. Anya shook her head as Gabby gave him a disapproving look.

'You're welcome, gorgeous,' beemed Polly. 'You have some more, looks like you could do with putting a bit of weight on.'

Cas needed no second bidding.

'Don't you go having too many, Norris. The children need feeding up but you could do with losing a few pounds.'

Norris huffed. 'You should stop feeding me such delicious cakes then, Pol,' he replied.

'Ignore him,' Polly said to the others. 'He's in a bit of a huff.'

Norris gave Polly a look of irritation. 'Now Pol, you know as well as I do it's been a strange few weeks at the office,' he muttered.

'Oh, Norris, you do make such a fuss.' Polly looked at the students sat around the table. 'I'm sure he just worries that there's not enough paper clips in the cupboard, or that his desk isn't tidy enough, poor man,' she laughed. Polly had such a way with her that the four friends couldn't help but laugh too.

Norris didn't seem amused.

'Enough of your teasing, Pol. If only you all knew the goings-on sometimes.' He nodded his head at each of them in a knowing kind of way.

'Goings-on? Oh, get away with you, Norris, what now? Someone found a stray sheep in the toilets? Anyway, I'm sure these youngsters don't want to hear about that stuffy old council office of yours.'

'No, far more strange than that, a couple of interlopers in the town, that's what, yes, shouldn't say really, no, shouldn't say.'

He huffed and reached over to grab a scone, dislodging the pile and sending them rolling over the table, making Polly tut loudly. Norris quickly grabbed them and placed them back on the plate.

'Norris,' she fussed. 'Set a good example, why don't you.'

Norris ignored her and started cutting the scone in half, reaching for the pot of cream. 'Interlopers, that's what,' he repeated as he slopped a big spoonful of cream onto his scone, getting some on his fingers. He slurped at them loudly, attracting another disapproving look from Polly.

Frank's ears pricked up and he noticed that the other three had also become more attentive.

'What's an interloper, Mr Quigley?' said Cas, feigning ignorance.

'Oh, you know, just people that are here in Rhaeder, er ... uninvited.' He lowered his voice. 'Undesirables,' he said. 'Can you pass the jam, please?' He held a pudgy hand out to Gabby, who picked up the pot of jam and placed it in Norris's outstretched fingers.

'What sort of interlopers would be in this town?' she asked.

'Well, the sort you wouldn't think would be welcome here. People we *know* shouldn't be here. Shouldn't say, really,' repeated

Norris in a disapproving tone, as he spooned a generous dollop of jam onto his scone.

'Surely that's the only sort there is?' asked Anya, appearing puzzled.

'Just saying, even the council knows about them,' said Norris, and he plonked a large piece of jam-and-cream-topped scone into his mouth.

Reading between the lines was easy. So the council, it appeared, knew that Dagmar, one of the sworn enemies of Byeland, was in town. The question was, why weren't they doing anything about it?

'But surely, if you know who they are,' said Frank, 'then why can't you just get rid of them? Send them back to where they came from?'

'Well, that would be the obvious approach, that's what I'd do if I had my way,' nodded Norris, full of self-importance as he swallowed the rest of his scone. 'But, you see, things aren't as easy as that. Or so it would appear.'

'Why not?' asked Cas.

Norris seemed to wrestle in his mind with how much he should be telling the small gathering in his kitchen. He could tell they were keen to learn more. He let out a breath and dropped his shoulders.

'Well, when you get orders from the top ... shouldn't say, really ... but when you get orders from the top, from Governor Jackson himself, then there's a reason why these interlopers are left alone, under close supervision you understand, oh yes, especially on my watch, but left alone all the same and, where I work, you just have to do what you're told and get on with things.' Norris bore a look of disapproval at what he had just said; it was obvious that he wasn't entirely in agreement with what he had been told to do. 'You certainly don't question something when it comes from Mr Jackson, much as I'd like to.'

Frank couldn't believe what he was hearing. If he understood Norris right, now the council, of all things, knew Dagmar was here, but was happy to leave him to do what he wanted. If that was the case, certainly Dagmar would be aware that he was being watched. Perhaps that explained why he'd been happy to have him and the others hauled in front of Moonhunter. He'd have known it would have meant a lot of trouble for him had he dealt with them any differently, in the way he probably really wanted to - the Kzarlac way. Perhaps it was their good luck that Dagmar's moves were being scrutinised, but Norris's disclosure that the council was involved gave Frank a decidedly uneasy feeling.

They ate up. Frank knew they were no further forward with the items in the tin box, but Norris' eye-opening revelation had certainly given them another piece of the puzzle, and more to think about.

So, thought Frank, where was Dagmar now, and how close was he to achieving what he came to Byeland to do, whatever that actually was?

24

THE MAP

Frank was out in the grounds flying Tweedy before classes started, along with an older boy, Leo Wiggis, who was working a kestrel called Ripley. Leo, from intake 819, was an accomplished falconer and Frank found he could help hone his skills. Leo also grew up on a farm, so Frank enjoyed his company. As the weather had grown warmer he'd had more opportunities to exercise the kite and he'd found that it helped to clear his mind.

He'd arranged to meet Cas in the library. Since they'd met at Polly's, they hadn't really decided if they still wanted to find out more about what Dagmar was up to. Moonhunter's warning had been so stern that, although their sense of adventure had been aroused, the potential consequences seemed to outweigh the benefits. Gabby was eager to continue, reminding the boys that she'd been thinking of leaving before she met them for the first time in Laskie's, so getting thrown out of the academy wouldn't be any great issue for her. It might even give her a bit of street cred back home, although her mum might be unhappy. Anya was with Gabby on that score, telling them that she wouldn't mind getting kicked out too, if only to avoid the extra Astronomy lessons she was having to endure. Frank and Cas weren't so sure, but Frank's natural curiosity, together with his new desire to get the better of Dagmar, gave him a strong pull towards Gabby's way of thinking. Given what Norris had said, Frank was even more intrigued about the questionable activities of the council.

Once Frank had finished exercising the hawk, he returned Tweedy to her enclosure in the mews. She always got grumpy when he did this and pecked at the fingers on his gloved hand as he strolled back, giving him an unfriendly squawk. As he placed her on her perch, he gave her a stroke and closed the door. She gave him a brushed-off look and set to preening her feathers after her work out.

Frank turned and looked around the mews, casting his mind back to his vision. He still hadn't figured out where the hooded man had gone, but, now he knew there was some sort of underground passage on the outside wall, he wondered if there was something similar in the mews. He wandered over to the wall on the far side, opposite the gate, and stepped over the row of low shrubs just in front of it. He touched the stonework to see if he could detect anything. The walls were thick and cold and felt damp to the touch. Frank slowly pressed the stones, looking up and down, searching for anything unusual. Nothing. Perhaps, like Cas, you needed a gift for that sort of thing. He sighed and shook his head.

'You okay, Frank?'

It was Leo. Frank had forgotten his falconry companion was also returning Ripley to her enclosure. He looked at Frank and Frank thought how odd he must have seemed, just randomly feeling the wall.

'What are you doing?' He gave Frank a strange look.

'Oh, nothing,' said Frank, giving his friend a shrug.

'But you were ... feeling the wall.'

'Yeah ... I was ... feeling the wall,' said Frank. They looked at each other awkwardly for a moment.

'See yer then,' Frank nodded, and walked past him, heading towards the library.

Before meeting Cas, he first needed to find a book on beginner's chants and incantations for sorcerers, for some homework set by the mysterious Professor Harding, whose classroom always hummed with the fragrance of incense and spice and left him with a dreamy headiness. He knew his way around the library, but, as Mr Slater was there, sitting at his desk at the library entrance, he decided to ask him.

'Up on the mezzanine level, Penny,' he said, not looking up.

He waved his hand in the general direction of upper deck and, in his usual patronising tone, added, 'Over at the far end, section marked "Sorcery", believe it or not.'

'Thanks,' said Frank, not really meaning it.

He walked over to the bottom of the wooden steps and mounted them in a few strides. There were a few students up on the higher level and Frank brushed past them as he made his way along the balcony towards the far end of the mezzanine. A wiry old terrier with two small books in its mouth dodged around his legs.

Frank reached the section he was looking for and ducked in between the bookcases. He searched up and down, looking for the particular book he needed. As he did so, he glanced to his right, over the balustrade, where his eye was taken by two figures on the ground level. He looked more carefully and realised that it was Woods and Chetto. They were standing at the end of a pair of bookcases, like statues, their shoulders together. It didn't look right; they weren't showing any interest in the books and didn't appear to have any work or bags with them. Frank crouched down, pretending to continue to look for his book, but leaned over to get a better look at where they were standing. It would be difficult for them to see him, as the balustrade was shielding him from their view.

Frank realised they were blocking the way into a section of the library and, from his elevated position, he could see why. Emerald was behind them, searching through the books and, by the looks of things, Woods and Chetto were there to make sure he wasn't interrupted. Frank looked at the sign on the bookcase - 'MAPS'. The same section that Emerald had slunk into before. Surely no coincidence.

They hadn't noticed him. They were more interested in the comings and goings of the students, professors and dogs on the lower level, and in making sure that no one disturbed Emerald.

Frank held his position. He could feign looking at the shelves and, at the same time, spy on what they were up to without bringing attention to himself.

As well as two or three open books, Emerald had a piece of unfolded paper laid out on the floor in front of him. He was kneeling over it and flicking through the books, obscuring Frank's view. The way he was acting, looking from the books to the paper on the floor and back again, it was obvious to Frank that he looking for something, comparing the two.

Frank adjusted his angle to see if he could get a better look at the piece of paper on the floor where Emerald knelt. To his amazement, he saw a diagram so similar to the one they had in the tin box that he nearly lost his balance. What on earth was he doing with *that* and where could he possibly have got it from? There was only one thing that Frank could think of. He cast his mind back to the apparamal in which he had seen Dagmar and Percy coming out of Hums's cottage and the sheet of paper that Dagmar was holding. When he first saw the paper in the tin box, Frank had felt that there was a strong similarity between the markings on their own piece and the one Dagmar had. He couldn't be sure that was the same one he now saw on the floor in front of Emerald, but it would have been a real coincidence if it wasn't.

Surely he couldn't be seeing things. But he also thought there was no way he could be right. If he was correct, it could only mean one thing - Emerald was doing some of Dagmar's dirty work, using the academy library to find out what the diagram was meant to represent. Was it Emerald who was helping Dagmar get into the academy? Whatever was going on, Emerald looked worried and a bit frantic. He continuously raked his fingers through his slick hair, eyes darting from paper to book. Frank thought that maybe his research wasn't yielding the results he had hoped for and he was getting anxious. With a taskmaster like Dagmar waiting for nothing less than a positive outcome, he didn't need to wonder why.

As he continued to look at the goings-on below, he felt a firm hand on his shoulder and nearly jumped out of his skin. He thought he would leap right over the balustrade and onto Chetto and Woods below.

'Wotcha,' said Cas, cracking a wide grin at Frank's startled reaction. 'Slater told me you were up here.'

'Get down,' hissed Frank, pulling Cas hard by the sleeve of his shirt.

'What's up?' said Cas, confused.

Frank pointed to the scene below. Emerald had decided to give up on his task for the time being and was starting to fold up the diagram. He had a look of concern on his face and Frank wondered how long he had been given to find out what the picture meant, and what the consequences might be for failure.

'That looks the same as our diagram,' exclaimed Cas, clocking the piece of paper in front of Emerald before he finished folding it and putting it in his bag. 'What's he doing with that?'

'Just what I was thinking,' said Frank. 'But we can't be sure.'

The two boys crept back into the sanctuary of the bookshelves, out of sight from the lower level. They sat opposite each other, backs to the books.

'There's only one way to find out,' said Cas. 'We need to get a closer look at what Emerald has in his bag.' His eyes twinkled and Frank read his mind.

'You mean—'

Frank stopped, mid-sentence, as Meredith appeared at the end of the row. She looked at them oddly and Frank had to admit they looked rather strange just sitting there, like they were up to no good.

'Hello, Meredith,' he said.

'You chaps okay?' she asked.

'Yeah,' said Frank.

'Fine,' said Cas.

Meredith hesitated, still not sure what to make of them. She moved gingerly forward.

'I ... er ... just need to get a copy of Magnus Mavras's *Anthology of Notable Sorcerers*,' she said, awkwardly.

'Okay,' said Frank. He looked up at the shelves. 'I think it's just there'. He pointed to the middle shelf.

Meredith looked. 'Oh, yeah, I see it.'

She went to step over Cas's legs to get to it but hesitated.

'Excuse me,' she said politely, and then stepped over towards the book. She carefully pulled it from the shelf and examined it, making sure it was the right one. She looked at the two boys again. They sat in suspicious silence. 'See yer, then,' she said.

'Yeah, see yer, Meredith,' said Frank.

He watched as the girl disappeared around the corner, taking one last look back at them. Cas looked back to Frank.

'I need to get to his bag,' he said raising his eyebrows and giving Frank a crafty look.

Frank knew exactly what was on his mind.

'We can make a copy and put it back without him even knowing it's gone.'

'We could just take it,' suggested Frank.

'No, that'll make him suspicious, not to mention Dagmar, if that's who he's working for.'

Frank thought for a moment. He felt it was a good idea, but, on the other hand, getting caught would have its problems. Regardless of their intentions, he didn't fancy being hauled up in front of Moonhunter again and could only imagine the punishment for stealing something from another student's bag, as well as having to explain what they were doing and trying to convince her that it had nothing to do with Dagmar. He wondered if they might even get kicked out of the academy, the first students to suffer that fate in the history of the place.

'I'm not sure,' said Frank.

He was surprised to hear himself say it. When he had first learned about his invitation to Excelsus, he really couldn't have cared less whether he attended or not; his life back at the farm had been perfect. But now, having spent the best part of a year there, and having made some new friends and discovered more about himself, he was pleased he had come and was keen to stay to see what would develop for him. So, even though he was eager to check out what

Emerald had, he suddenly felt nervous about losing his place at the academy. Cas seemed to have a different approach, keen to continue to hone his skills as a budding pickpocket.

'Oh, come on Frank, I'm dying to get one over on that bully. I still haven't forgotten the way he tried to relieve me of my liquorice toffees when I first got here. It'll be good practice for me too.'

'Okay then, but we can't get caught, so we'll have to wait for the right moment.'

* * *

They didn't have to wait long for an opportunity to present itself. A few days later they finished their Alchemy class just before lunch and, to their great fortune, Emerald left his bag hanging over the back of his chair and sped off to beat the rush. Frank nudged Cas, indicating to Emerald's empty desk. The room emptied, leaving them pretending to make some last-minute notes. Professor Truelove tidied the books on her desk and made her way out of the room.

'You better hurry,' she said, as she walked past. 'Braised boar and chips today, one of my favourites.'

'We'll just finish off what we're doing, Professor,' said Cas.

'Okay, boys, that's what I like to see, a bit of dedication, good work.'

She left the room, leaving Cas and Frank alone. As soon as she left, they threw down their pencils and made their way to the back of the classroom and to Emerald's chair.

'Come on,' said Frank. 'We need to be quick.'

Frank pushed the door closed as Cas quickly opened Emerald's bag, searched carefully for a second or two and pulled out the sheet of paper from a side pocket. He laid it flat on the floor, placed the thin piece of paper over the top of it and started to trace the image. He worked quickly yet carefully, making sure that he got it completely right. Frank could hear his breathing quicken and he willed Cas to work faster, knowing they only had a limited amount of time. Someone could come in at any minute.

Cas finished. He took one last look to make sure he had

captured every detail and nodded to himself. He folded up both bits of paper, putting their piece into his pocket and Emerald's back into his bag, making sure he put it back in the side pocket where he had found it. Frank breathed easier as Cas put the bag back on Emerald's chair and the two of them sat on the floor smiling at each other.

'What are you doing?'

The voice caught them totally by surprise. Frank swung round quickly to see Lanks staring back at him, a cross look on his face. Cas looked startled. They hadn't noticed him come in. Frank couldn't believe it. It was as if Lanks was stalking them like an invisible snake.

'Well?' said Lanks sternly, sniffing. He seemed to have caught a cold and his red nose twitched as he stared down at them.

'That bag was on the floor,' said Frank calmly, regaining his composure. 'We were just putting it back.'

He hoped that Lanks had only just stumbled upon them and not been standing there the whole time, unseen by the two of them. Lanks took a step closer.

'Don't take me for a fool, Mr Penny,' he said, sniffing again, moving closer still. 'It looks like you're up to no good. Again. I wouldn't like to have to haul you up to Miss Moonhunter's office. Again. As I'm sure she wouldn't appreciate having to have another little chat with you and Jones here. *Again.*'

His voice sounded irked, as well as stuffed with cold.

'No, I guess not,' said Frank.

Lanks looked from Frank to Cas and back to Frank, searching for any sign of wrongdoing on their faces.

'Then I suggest you make yourself scarce,' snapped Lanks, clearly annoyed and making it obvious to Frank that he knew he was up to something.

The boys stood up to leave and Lanks reached into his pocket, pulling out a handkerchief to blow his suffering nose. As he did so, something dropped to the floor, clanking as it hit the ground. Lanks and Frank both looked down. Frank couldn't believe what he saw. It was an odd-shaped piece of stone, exactly the same as the one they had in the box from Hums's cottage. It had fallen by accident from Lanks's pocket when he'd pulled out the handkerchief. Frank's eyes widened momentarily, then he pulled himself back as Lanks looked at him, scanning his face. He bent down, picked up the object and handed it back to Lanks, who took it quickly and, without saying anything, put it back in his pocket. Frank knew that he couldn't possibly know that he recognised it, but, still, Lanks eyed him with suspicion.

Frank quickly walked past Lanks and around Bertie before the professor had time to say anything else. Cas followed. They didn't speak until they were well away from Lanks and heading out towards the canteen, hungry and hoping they might find the girls.

'Did you see—' Cas started to say.

'—the stone thing that that Lanks dropped.' Frank finished his sentence for him.

'Yeah it's—'

'—the same as the one we've got.'

'Yes, so what does that mean? That Lanks is involved in this too?'

'I knew it. I knew he was up to something.' Frank was triumphant. 'He must be in it with Dagmar.'

'This doesn't get any simpler, does it?'

Gabby and Anya weren't in the canteen, so they decided to head to Laskie's as soon as lessons had finished for the day. They ran all the way. There they were, sitting on their own, tucking into doughnuts and orange juice. Anya saw them coming and quickly made room at their table.

'You guys not getting anything?' she asked as they rushed to sit down, breathing heavily from their sprint across town.

'No,' said Frank, 'I've sort of lost my appetite.'

'Why?'

'We know that Lanks has a stone object exactly the same as the one in our tin box.'

'You're absolutely kidding me,' gasped Gabby loudly. 'How do you know that?'

Frank explained what had happened, including that Cas had managed to get a copy of the diagram they had seen in Emerald's possession.

'I knew I'd seen it before,' explained Frank. 'It was hanging around his neck when we were in Moonhunter's office; I saw it when we were leaving. He normally has his shirt done up, but that time he was more casual.'

'Goodness, you have been busy.' Gabby looked impressed. 'So why does our own Mr Lanks have the same thing that we found in Hums's cottage?'

'It's obvious,' said Cas. 'He must have stolen it from Hums, or his cottage. It's as we thought, he's in cahoots with Dagmar. We've always known he was sneaky.'

'I reckon you're right, Cas,' nodded Frank. 'I've always thought there was something fishy about him.'

'But you saw how much he seemed to loathe Dagmar when we were in Moonhunter's office,' Anya reminded them. 'How do you explain that?'

Frank knew Anya had a point; perhaps Lanks's attitude towards Dagmar was just an act. He couldn't be sure.

'Then it could just be a coincidence,' said Cas. 'We have no idea what it is, or does. For all we know, every one of the professors has one.'

'Oh, you're such a dummy, sometimes,' said Gabby. 'Ever seen one before?'

'No.'

'And, seeing as the one we found was cunningly hidden, you have to suppose it's something not everyone has, something secret, and only of use to Hums.'

'Maybe you're right,' conceded Cas. But they still had no idea what it was.

'So what about the diagram?' said Gabby.

'We need to see if it's the same as the one we have,' said Frank. 'How about you all come round to Polly's in the morning and we take a look?'

It was the weekend, so they agreed to meet at Polly's at ten o'clock. Laskie's would be heaving and this wasn't something they could do in full view of all the customers. Also, the weekend was the busiest time in the teashop, so Frank knew that Polly would be run off her feet and too occupied to notice anything they were doing. Maddy usually helped her out and Norris normally went fishing, so he was as sure as he could be that they wouldn't be disturbed.

* * *

The next day they were sitting at the dining table. Frank had initially thought they should go to his room, in case someone thought to ask what they were doing, but, as Frank suspected, the tea shop was full and both Polly and Maddy were busy serving, clearing and making sure the counter was stocked. Frank felt a bit guilty that he hadn't offered to help, but he'd offered in the past and Polly normally politely refused, preferring Frank to have time free to do his own thing. She'd made sure they had a jug of fresh lemonade and some biscuits. Frank grabbed one and took a bite as they laid the diagrams out on the table, side by side, and sat there in silence, looking at them.

'Well, that confirms it,' said Cas.

'Confirms what?' said Anya.

'They're the same.'

Although the two diagrams were identical, what they represented was still a mystery. They both showed a set of lines, laid out in a deliberate pattern, some of them intersecting. Emerald had appeared to be on to something in the library, so Frank tried desperately to figure out the shape.

'Well, Emerald, or rather Dagmar, seems to know that this is some sort of map. That's why he was busy looking through the books in the library. He seemed really desperate to find out what it means.'

'Do you think he's been successful?' asked Gabby.

'No, not yet, but we have to beat him to the secret, whatever it is,' said Frank. 'It must be important, otherwise Dagmar wouldn't have got him to scour the map section.'

'I'd be desperate to find a clue if I had that bloke breathing down my neck,' said Cas. 'I mean, imagine the consequences for failure. Breakfast for Orpheus.'

'Careful, you nearly sound sorry for him.'

'Sorry for Orpheus, more like. Getting all that hair stuck in your throat, ugh!'

They all laughed and Frank went back to the images in front of them. The door through to the tea shop opened and Maddy raced through.

'You okay?' asked Frank.

'Yeah, Mum just needs some more iced buns brought through, and some clean cutlery. Oh, hi ...'

Maddy looked at the four of them seated around the table. Cas gave a wave while Anya smiled at her.

'Hi babe.' Gabby smiled sweetly at the young girl. 'Need a hand?'

Maddy blushed. 'No, I'll be okay,' she said. 'Thanks, Gabby.'

'Knives and forks are here,' said Frank, noticing a tray-load of cutlery on the sideboard next to him.

'Oh, okay,' said Maddy and moved nervously in their direction. She stopped at the table.

'What's that?' she said, looking at the two images, side by side on the top.

'Just a couple of diagrams,' said Frank pleasantly, trying not to rouse any suspicion.

'Something we're doing at the academy,' said Gabby.

'Yeah,' said Cas. 'We've copied this one onto another piece of paper.'

He indicated towards the two diagrams. Maddy moved forward to get a better look. Frank wondered if she was somehow drawn to the activities of older children, trying to appear more grown up. He remembered being just like that, anxious to learn things that should be beyond his age. The things that older people did always seemed much more interesting to him.

'Oh, really?' said Maddy with interest.

'Yes,' said Frank. 'They're the same.'

Maddy paused and inspected the two pictures, as the others had been doing until she came into the room.

'No they're not,' she said, much to Frank's astonishment.

'Not what?'

'They're not the same.' She looked up at Frank, her pale blue eyes twinkled. 'Look, someone's made a mistake on this one and forgotten to rub it out.'

She looked at Cas, as if not wanting to appear rude if he had made a mistake, and pointed to one of the maps. Her finger came to rest on a small line. All of them had missed the difference, not surprising seeing as it was tiny, but Maddy had seen it. Frank looked at the others, wondering if Cas had made an error or, more interestingly, if it wasn't a mistake at all. But the maps *were* different. Only slightly, but different nonetheless.

'Wow, thanks Maddy,' he said, appreciatively. 'Didn't spot that.'

'That's okay,' she said. 'Perhaps whoever copied it should be more careful in future.'

She smiled meekly and picked up the tray of cutlery, her slight frame straining with the weight. She grunted and accidentally knocked over a nearly empty glass of water. What liquid that was left spilled and seeped onto one of the diagrams. Maddy looked mortified and put the tray down, grabbing a cloth that she had tucked into her apron and started to mop the puddle.

'Don't worry Maddy,' said Frank reassuringly, putting a hand on her arm to stop her mopping. 'It's not important.'

She stopped and looked close to tears.

'I'm always knocking things over,' said Anya. 'Born clumsy, that's what my mum says ... er ... not that you're clumsy or anything.'

'It's okay,' said Gabby, stopping Anya from making Maddy feel any worse. 'Accidents happen and, like you just said, we need to recopy it anyway.'

Maddy smiled, apparently comforted. She picked up the tray, once more straining with the weight.

'Are you sure you don't need a hand?' asked Frank.

'Sure,' she said, holding her breath.

She turned and headed awkwardly towards the door. She'd be back for the iced buns.

The four of them looked at each other. Maddy's attentiveness had thrown a new light on things.

'That's weird,' said Cas.

'What is?'

'Two diagrams, maps, whatever, both the same but with a small difference.'

'You mean a mistake,' said Gabby.

Frank shrugged.

'Are you sure you copied Emerald's accurately?'

'I'm sure you would have done,' said Anya.

'Yep, checked it twice, no mistakes.'

'Which one has the extra mark on it?' said Gabby.

Frank looked back at the pictures on the table. 'The one from our tin box. The one Cas copied from Emerald is that one.' He pointed to the other diagram.

'Do you think it means anything?' said Cas.

'I don't know, I mean, I really don't get it. We have two near identical diagrams, which we think are maps of some kind, one from a tin box hidden in Hums's cottage and one that was being carried by Dagmar's lackey. So what's the connection?'

Just then, Frank noticed something peculiar. The wet patch on the corner had started to reveal an image.

'Look at this,' he said, pointing it out to the others. The image was indistinguishable but it was evident that the water had only just started to reveal what was there. 'Wait a sec.'

He sprang up and made his way over to the sink in the kitchen. He grabbed a cloth and ran it under the tap, making it damp. 'Let's see if this works,' he said and rubbed the cloth over the diagram, starting at the corner and carefully working his way across the sheet of paper. Gradually he revealed the full image. The others stared in amazement as the rubbing unveiled a hand drawn vulture emblem of Excelsus, together with the handwritten words 'A friend in the dark is better than being alone in the light'. Next to the writing was a symbol, the same one that they had discovered on top of the tin box: a rose sitting above two crossed arrows, also done by hand. Gabby had seen it too.

'Goodness,' she said, noting the connection.

'What does that mean?' asked Frank. 'A friend in the dark is better than being alone in the light?'

The others shook their heads.

'They must be clues of some sort, the symbol and the writing,' said Gabby. 'They *must* mean something.'

All four were quiet for a moment, thinking. Frank wracked his brains. The same person had drawn both images, meaning Excelsus and the strange cross symbol were connected, which meant they were connected to Hums's box. But how?

'Of course!' he exclaimed. 'It's the academy, it has to be.'

'Huh?'

'Frank's right,' agreed Gabby. 'The lines - it's so obvious I don't know why we didn't think of it before. It's something to do with the academy; why else would the vulture emblem be on it?'

A wave of excitement washed over them. Frank felt they were close to unlocking the diagram's secret. If only he could put his finger on it.

'Are you two sure you didn't knock your heads when you fell in that secret passageway?' Cas shook his head, still not getting it.

Frank looked at his friend. It was then that Frank knew. He stood up and put his hands on Cas's shoulders.

'That's it! Cas, you're a genius.'

'I am?'

'He is?' said Anya.

'Yes, come on.' Frank folded the diagrams and looked ready to leave.

'Where are we going?' said Gabby.

'We have to see Blackburn,' said Frank. 'He's got what we need.'

25

THE BLUEPRINTS

Carefully, Frank put both sheets of paper in his bag.

'Come on.'

He ran out of the kitchen and through the tea shop with Gabby, Anya and Cas close behind. The place was crammed with regular customers.

'See you later, Polly,' he called.

'Have fun, my darlin's,' said Polly, as she poured a smart-looking man a cup of tea.

Maddy was busy clearing tables as they whizzed out of the shop and headed across town.

'Remind me why we're going to Blackburn's?' asked Cas.

'It's the academy,' said Frank.

He looked at Cas and realised he wasn't making any sense. Without breaking stride, he said, 'Remember what he said about his father, the first time I met him?'

'No, I wasn't there.'

'Oh, yeah. Well, the first time I met him he told me that his dad did some of the building work at the academy.'

'So what?'

'So you think he might have an idea what the diagram means?' asked Gabby.

Frank stopped.

'I think *I* know what it means.' He realised he was breathing heavily from the speed they were walking.

'Can we slow down a bit?' complained Cas. 'I've got a stitch.'

They reached the square and headed up Iron Lane. The town

was busy with shoppers and they dodged in and out, avoiding carts and carriages that swept up and down the lane. At last they reached the plaza. Frank felt that the vulture was giving him the evil eye, as if he was about to uncover one of its hidden secrets. He thought it watched him as he rounded the corner and headed to Blackburn's

The door was closed. Frank pushed it hard and the four of them burst into the workshop. Blackburn, wearing a pair of safety glasses, was bent over a side table and he jumped back with a start.

'Hell's teeth!' he said. 'Give an old man a heart attack, why don't you?'

'Sorry,' said Frank.

'Oh, not to worry,' Blackburn smiled. 'Just trying to mix a new venom identification formula for old Naxus Windleham. Not going too well, I'm afraid. Anyway, nice to see you—'

'Blackburn?' said Frank breathlessly.

'Yes Frank.' Blackburn was slightly taken aback at Frank's hasty interruption.

'Sorry, I was wondering if I could look at the blueprints you said you had, the ones your father gave you when he was working on the academy.'

'What, those old things?' Blackburn lifted his safety goggles, revealing bright red marks around his eyes. He looked like a strange sort of panda.

'What d'you want them for?'

'Can I see them?'

Blackburn looked like he didn't know what to say.

'He doesn't mean to be rude. It's just they're kind of important. Apparently,' explained Anya.

'Of course you can.' Blackburn turned and looked up and down the workshop. 'Now, if I can remember where I put them.' He rubbed his chin and continued to look around the room. The others followed his steady gaze for what seemed like an eternity. 'Ah, up there I think.'

He grabbed a stool and placed it next to one of the large dressers at the side of the workshop. Carefully, he stood on it and reached up to the top of the dresser. Frank noticed bundles of rolled up papers, arranged haphazardly, where Blackburn was stretching. They were just out of reach. He was now on tiptoes and huffed as he tried again to grasp the bundle.

'Got 'em,' he puffed.

'Do you need a—' Frank began to say, just as Blackburn managed to get them in his hand. His look of achievement soon turned to one of concern as he rocked on the stool.

They could see what was going to happen, but couldn't do anything about it. Blackburn hung there for a moment, suspended in mid-air, then the stool toppled from underneath him and he fell. He landed in a cloud of dust, backside first, in a large box, sending the rolled up papers across the room. Cicero jumped and ran for cover under a table. The four students watched, open-mouthed, as he sat there, struggling to get out.

'Well give me a hand, then,' Blackburn said, clearly unable to escape the cardboard jaws by himself.

They made their way over to him and tugged him out. Frank had to suppress a chuckle.

'Not my most elegant moment,' Blackburn laughed, brushing himself down. He coughed as the dust he had disturbed settled on and around his face.

'Lesson number one, get a ladder that's man enough for the job,' he muttered to himself. 'Now then, those blueprints.'

Frank collected up the rolls of paper that had tumbled to the ground, as Blackburn rubbed his elbow and winced. He flexed it and winced again.

Gabby reached into her bag and got out the Sano stone. She went over to Blackburn and grabbed him gently by the wrist.

'Looks like it'll bruise up badly.'

She waved the stone back and forth over his elbow. When she let go, Blackburn bent his arm again, this time without discomfort.

'Thank you yet again, Gabby,' he said. 'Making a bit of a habit of this, don't you think?'

'Glad to be of help.' Gabby put the stone back. 'Just be more careful in future.'

Frank handed the rolls to Blackburn. 'Here you are,' he said.

'Oh, thanks, Frank, but it was you who wanted them. Dusty old things, been sitting up there for donkey's years. Can't remember the last time I looked at them; probably never have, and never will. Old bloke like me shouldn't keep so much rubbish, should I?'

He handed the rolls back to Frank, who took them to a large empty table to the side of the workshop. He unrolled the first one, which showed a side elevation of the east wing, the part Blackburn's father had worked on. Frank thumbed through a few more before he found what he was looking for.

'Give us a hand, Cas,' he said.

Cas grabbed one end and Frank unrolled it. He looked around for something to weigh the ends down and stop it rolling back up and found a pile of round metal weights on a shelf, ideal for the job.

'Here,' he said to Cas, handing him a couple from the pile. 'Use these.'

Cas took the weights and placed them on the corners of the paper he was holding. Frank did the same. Once it was flattened, Frank looked at the image. It was a blueprint of the entire academy, drawn from above onto a transparent piece of paper. The picture showed a detailed outline with measurements, including the lengths of walls and various angles. Around the edge were copious notes and complicated equations, showing that this had been a working document in its day. It was just what Frank was hoping to find. He let out a sigh of satisfaction.

'This should do it.'

'Do what?' asked Cas, who had been totally bemused ever since they left Polly's. He looked at Anya, who looked as mystified as him.

Gabby had kept quiet; either she knew what Frank was thinking, or she was just trusting his instincts. Either way, she grabbed Frank's bag and pulled out the diagram, making sure it was the one that had the Excelsus vulture on it.

'I think you need this,' she said, reading Frank's mind and holding out the diagram. He looked at her outstretched hand.

'Thanks, Gabby.'

He carefully unfolded it and turned it so that the vulture was at the bottom, then slid the diagram underneath the blueprint. He moved it carefully so that the lines on the diagram were directly underneath the outline of the academy.

'Bingo!' He stood back from the table triumphantly.

Gabby took a step forward to look at the result. The lines on their mystery picture appeared exactly within the walls of the academy. There was no overlap. It was as if they were part of the same picture.

'What's that then?' said Cas, clearly lost.

'Like you said Cas,' said Frank. 'Secret passages.'

'I did?'

Gabby leaned forward and put her finger on the diagram.

'Look, this is the one we followed Dagmar into.' She pointed to a line that led from the outside wall near the woods and took a left turn then a right turn. 'And this is where we dropped the light.'

'Oh, you are clever,' said Anya, sounding really impressed.

The picture they had revealed showed a warren of tunnels underneath the building. How they got there and where they all led was a mystery in itself, but on Frank's mind was why they were there in the first place. Blackburn stepped forward and leaned over Frank's shoulder. He held his glasses on his nose and inspected the picture.

'Well I never,' he said. 'And to think I was going to throw them out once upon a time.'

'Good job you didn't,' said Frank.

'Hell's teeth,' muttered Blackburn. 'So that's where they all go.' He scanned up and down the lines.

Frank looked round at him. 'You mean you knew there were secret tunnels under the academy?'

'Oh yes, my dad often talked about them. Him and his crew,

they found some of them when they were building there. I remember him coming home and talking about it, how they'd been digging foundations when the earth gave way to reveal a hidden entrance on the north side. Gave them such a shock, I should say. Remember him laughing about it.' He smiled as he reminisced.

'What did he do?' said Anya.

'Not much, I don't think,' said Blackburn. 'I remember he told me that he and his mate, Wally, decided to investigate a bit, so they got a lamp and went down the passage. By all accounts it was well made. Typical of my dad, that, noticing the workmanship of a passage no one had ever seen nor was likely to see. Anyway, after going along for a few minutes, Wally got the creeps and didn't want to go on anymore, thought there was something sinister waiting for him in the dark.'

'Gosh,' said Cas, taking a deep gulp.

'Of course, there wasn't. Scared of his own shadow, was Wally. But my dad didn't go any further. He said that by the smell of the place it felt like it was all blocked up in there, that no one had used the tunnels for centuries.'

'So he never went back in?' asked Gabby.

'Not as far as I know.' Blackburn shrugged his shoulders. 'He wasn't that interested as far as I remember.'

Frank was unconvinced. If he'd found a passage like that, he'd have to know where it went and what it was for. But Blackburn sounded like he was telling the truth and Frank had more urgent matters on his mind.

He turned back to the papers on the table and looked at the image carefully. He ran his finger over the blueprint.

'Look,' he said. 'Here's the mews.'

He pointed on the academy outline to where Tweedy was housed and ran his finger over to the edge of the mews wall. A black line started there and led underneath the academy walls. It confirmed what he had thought.

'That's a passage leading off the mews,' said Gabby.

Frank nodded.

'Well that explains that,' he said. 'Whoever I saw didn't just disappear.'

'No, they managed to get into the passage before he could be seen, which means whoever it is must know all about them.' said Gabby.

'Wowzer,' said Cas.

'So why does Dagmar have a copy of the tunnel map?' said Gabby.

Blackburn flinched at the mention of the name.

'What do you mean, Dagmar?' he said. 'What's that poor excuse for a human being got to do with this?'

'It's a long story,' said Frank. 'But we know that Dagmar has the same diagram as the one we found.'

'Do you think he knows what it means?' said Anya. 'I mean, he knows about the passages, or at least some of them. He must do, seeing as you followed him down one.'

'He might, or he might just know about that one. The fact that he was getting Emerald to try and find out what the diagram meant makes me think he doesn't know everything, but it's probably just a matter of time before he does.'

'But so what?' said Cas. 'So it's a map of a secret network of underground tunnels. I don't see what it actually means, not to mention the other items in the box, oh, and our book full of gobbledygook.'

'Oh come on, dummy,' snapped Gabby sharply.

'Do you have to keep calling me a dummy?'

'Only when you're being one. Look, we know that the man Frank saw in the mews, the one who dropped the book, disappeared into this passage. We know the book is connected to him and, as he knows about the passages, the map must be too. And, if the map's connected, so is the box. We found the box in Hums's cottage so there must be a connection. It all points to Hums.'

She pointed to the map.

'*And,*' she added, 'remember that this plan and Dagmar's are not exactly the same.'

Frank remembered the extra mark on their drawing and looked back to the table. He scanned the diagram once more and found the errant pen stroke.

'What does it mean?' he said out loud, although he meant it for himself.

'You want to know what I think?' said Gabby.

The others turned to her.

'Go on,' said Frank.

'Okay, imagine you're Ludlow Hums,' she began. Her eyes widened at the mention of his name and Blackburn coughed. 'You've stolen the Seal and killed your brother and need a place to hide. Where better to conceal yourself than within the place where your brother, the caretaker, worked for years and years? You'd probably know it inside out. And, if you were that close to the caretaker, and lived near him for years, you might well know some of the academy's secrets, including the secret tunnels. You might even have made a map of the tunnels so you can find your way around. That's what you'd do if you were the sort who liked to sneak about.'

A thick silence filled the room. Frank, Anya and Cas hung on Gabby's words while Blackburn stood back and seemed to be taking particular notice of what Gabby was saying.

'*And,*' she went on, 'if I wanted to keep hidden, especially from the likes of Dagmar, I'd make sure that I had my own little hidey-hole. Somewhere to go until all the fuss had died down. Somewhere only I knew about.' She pointed again to the extra line on the Excelsus plan.

'You're so clever,' said Anya, looking at her friend.

'But it's on the map,' said Cas. 'You wouldn't put it on a map if you wanted to keep hidden.'

'Yes, on *this* map, but it's not on *Dagmar's* map.'

Frank immediately knew she must be right.

'Dagmar doesn't know that this bit here' —Frank put his finger on the map where Gabby was pointing— 'exists. He can't find it. Whoever hid this map didn't want to be found. It was just there for their own benefit, like I said before, that's why this map was so well hidden in Hums's cottage.'

'But we found it,' said Cas.

'Yes, but that's because we had you and your special talents,' said Frank. 'You have the mind of a budding pickpocket, like Ludlow.'

'But why hide it in the first place? If you want to stay hidden surely you just disappear and don't leave clues, like a map? At least that's what I'd do.'

Frank thought Cas had a point.

'Maybe it was put there just in case, as a back-up or something,' suggested Gabby.

'You have to admit it's genius,' said Frank. 'If Gabby's right, maybe Hums has been hiding right under the noses of those who have been looking for him all this time.'

Blackburn shook his head.

'You youngsters sure have got vivid imaginations,' he laughed. 'Old Ludlow Hums hiding in a dark, cold dungeon under Excelsus Academy? Well, I never did hear anything so ridiculous. Sorry, Frank, I don't mean to be rude.'

Frank turned to Blackburn. 'But you said so yourself, when you first learned that the Alphaen were here, you said you thought it might be Hums.'

'Yes, well, er, I might have said that, but I didn't really think so. Everyone thought, or thinks, he's either dead or long gone. The last place he'd be is over there.' He waved his hand in the direction of the academy.

'Exactly,' said Gabby. 'The last place he'd ever be, the last place anyone would look. The first place you'd hide.'

Blackburn screwed up his face in thought. He looked from Frank to Gabby and then to Anya and Cas.

'You haven't got another quaero stick, have you?' Frank asked Blackburn, who shook his head.

'I don't believe it, surely not.' He wandered to the window and looked out through the grease and grime, across the plaza to the doors of the academy. He'd gone from thinking the students' ideas were fanciful and far-fetched, to mulling over the distinct possibility that they were right, all in the space of a few seconds. He continued to stare out of the window. 'Well, well, Ludlow,' he said to himself. 'Have you really been hiding there all the time?'

Frank looked back at the map. Cicero jumped up on to the table and walked over the image. The cat sat down in the middle of the paper, much to Frank's consternation. He was reluctant to move the furry feline; Cicero always carried a look of disdain and Frank often felt the contemptuous cat wouldn't need much of an excuse to launch an unprovoked attack. He looked at Gabby who rolled her eyes and picked Cicero up, giving his tummy a rub. The cat gave out a gratified growl.

'Chicken,' she said, looking at Frank.

Frank smiled and scanned the map. He found the extra mark and traced his finger along the stroke leading to it, following the route. His finger came to rest at the end of a long line.

'There's only one way to find out if we're right.' He tapped his finger on the paper.

Still holding Cicero, Gabby leaned over to take a look, as did Anya. Cas stayed put.

'We need to get in here.'

'Get in where?' said Cas, looking worried. 'Surely you don't mean we're going to look down dark tunnels for ghosts of Excelsus past. Remember what happened the last time we tried that?'

'Now who's the chicken?' laughed Anya.

'We have to, Cas,' said Frank.

'Shouldn't we just tell Moonhunter, or the Alphaen, or someone, what we've found and let them sort it out? I mean, you remember what Moonhunter said about us not going hunting around where we shouldn't? It could mean a lot of trouble if we get caught.'

Frank thought. He really wanted to do the right thing but

couldn't decide whether their efforts so far had dealt them a hand that they needed to play, or if it was time to tell Moonhunter what they knew. He tried to imagine what his dad would do, or what he would tell Frank to do.

'You might have a point,' he sighed.

'What?' snapped Gabby. 'Are you kidding? Hand everything over to Moonhunter? Come on boys, where's your sense of adventure? We've done alright up to now. We've discovered the academy's secret while everyone else seems to be chasing shadows. No way should we stop now, not until we've discovered what *that* means.' She pointed to the map. 'I wouldn't trust any of the adults around here with this stuff.'

Blackburn cleared his throat and raised his eyebrows.

'Oh, present company excepted,' she said. Blackburn nodded.

Frank realised he knew the answer to his own question. His dad wasn't there to help; he was on his own now and needed to make his own decisions, to do what he thought was right, and he knew that Gabby was making sense, even though her obvious disregard for authority might cloud her thinking.

Gabby looked at Frank, who was lost in thought. 'Look,' she said. 'If we don't find anything, or even if we do, we can go to Moonhunter later. Let's just see if our theory's right, yeah?'

Frank looked back at her, then to Anya, who nodded. He looked at Cas who seemed to be contemplating an encounter with something menacing in the dark, below Excelsus. Gabby noticed.

'Don't worry, Cas. When we hear the rattling of chains and ghostly groans, we'll be there to save you.'

Frank laughed. Cas looked even more worried.

'So?' she pushed.

'Let's do it,' said Frank.

26

THE HIDDEN ROOM

They had to wait until Monday. There was no way they were going to try and get into the academy at the weekend; the doors were shut and the Alphaen still lurked ominously along the walls.

When they had left Blackburn's, Frank felt, more than ever, that the guards were watching them even more closely, as if they knew exactly what they were up to. They'd thought about trying the passage where they had run into Dagmar, but, although it was marked on their map, it didn't lead to where they wanted to go and the additional complication of the possibility of running into Kzarlac's chief nasty meant that they'd scrapped that idea very quickly.

They'd left Blackburn pondering quietly. Frank was happy they'd taken him into their confidence and was sure his inventor friend wouldn't let on to anyone about their plans.

That morning Frank's walk to the academy took on a new significance. He now knew that the place that had become his second home over the past months harboured secrets and that made him wonder what else it might reveal during his stay. Norris had been right when he'd said about strange things happening there, but not in his wildest dreams would Frank have imagined that he might get caught up in a mystery such as this.

He walked purposefully up Iron Lane. It was still early, but the street was already busy with shop owners bringing in new deliveries or getting ready to start the week's trade. He knew them all by now and most of them greeted him with smiles and nods as he walked past each morning. There were a few that still ignored him: Mrs

Roberts, who ran one of the art galleries, could barely bring herself to look at him, as was the case with Mr Halberd-Stokes from the jewellers, and some just looked down their noses at him, especially Mr Hook, the upmarket draper, who usually found the time to cast a look of derision in his direction, as if he would have rather cut himself with his oversized scissors than lower himself to a boy from the other side of town. Then there was Mr Rutter, the lantern maker, a small and sinister-looking man who would just peer from behind the curtains in his shop.

As Frank passed Rutter's he stopped and did a double-take. He couldn't be certain, but he felt he was being watched. For no good reason, he found himself with an uneasy feeling. Was it Rutter, or was there someone else in there, spying on him? For a moment he imagined Dagmar, his teeth flashing his evil smile, studying his every move. He stood for a few seconds, looking into the window. The dark curtain cast his reflection in the glass. He decided he must be imagining things and started walking again, continuing on his way up to the academy and putting his misgivings down to the thought of what they might discover.

He crossed the plaza and walked across the bridge and, as arranged, met the others at the bottom of the marble stairs that led up to the door.

'All right?' said Cas.

'Yeah,' said Frank. He turned to Gabby and Anya. 'You okay?'

'You bet,' said Gabby. 'So what's the plan?'

Frank looked around to check that no one was within earshot. A couple of older boys walked past, talking about the weekend's sport.

Once they had gone, Frank said, 'Right, meet us in the library at lunchtime. The passage entrance is just down the corridor from there. I'm sure we'll be able to find it, especially with you, Cas.'

Cas nodded, looking concerned, then said, 'That's close to Lanks's office.'

'Yeah, I know, but he normally takes his lunch early, like most of the professors, so he'll be in the canteen. That's why we need to start as soon as we can. Oh, and we'll need a decent lamp.'

'I could always pop to Blackburn's for a—' Cas began.

'Don't even think about it,' interrupted Frank.

'Leave that with me,' said Anya. 'We've got Archery this morning. Professor Congleton forgets something every time and needs one of us to go to the stores for equipment. I always get asked to run errands like that, so I'll get one.'

'Lucky you. Frank and I have the joy of Ancient Languages this morning, mega yawn.'

'Bad luck,' smiled Gabby.

'Good, that's settled then, let's get going. See you later, girls.'

They set off through the main entrance. Emerald and his entourage were standing just inside the door and, for a moment, Frank wondered if he might have overheard their conversation, but he just gave Frank and the others his usual look of contempt. Gabby and Anya headed off to join the rest of their intake out on the archery field, while Frank and Cas headed down the corridor to their own lesson.

* * *

The morning seemed to drag. Professor Burdock droned on about the ancient dialects of the north and, with ease, made an already uninteresting subject even more boring. Eventually, the lesson ended and Frank and Cas made their way to the library. Gabby and Anya were already waiting, eagerness etched across their faces.

'Did you get the lamp?' asked Frank.

'Yep.' Anya opened her bag to show them. 'I got two actually, just in case. And some matches.'

Frank checked inside his bag for the map. He had brought the tin box, too.

'Okay, let's go,' he said and led them out of the library and down the corridor.

The area around the library was quiet; most students had gone to the canteen for lunch. As they passed Lanks's office they heard the click of a door handle and, unexpectedly, Lanks came out. He turned and locked his office door and saw the four of them loitering. He eyed them suspiciously.

'Can I help you?' he said.

Frank thought quickly. 'No thanks, we're just on our way to the library before lunch. Got some really interesting homework from Professor Burdock. Can't wait to get it done.'

He didn't think he sounded very believable, but Cas nodded enthusiastically. Lanks just looked at them.

'Hm. Well then, the library is ... that way.' He looked back down the corridor from where they had come, turned and headed off toward the canteen. They watched him go.

'That was close,' said Cas.

'Idiot,' scowled Gabby.

Cas gave her a look.

'Not you. Lanks.'

They wandered further down the corridor.

'I make it here,' declared Frank. They were standing outside a small store cupboard, similar to the one where Frank had first met Cas during his encounter with Emerald. The dark, wooden door had a small pane of glass in it. Frank peered in.

'It's a cupboard,' said Cas. 'I've been in there before. It's tiny and full of text books and stationery. Not a secret passage in sight.'

Undeterred, Frank was sure he had the right place.

'It's definitely here,' he said.

He looked up and down the passage. No one was coming and Lanks had disappeared, so he pushed the door and went in. Gabby followed him. Anya and Cas looked at each other and shrugged before they joined them. They shut the door behind them and all four squeezed themselves into the tight space. A shaft of light gave a slight illumination to the inside of the tiny cupboard which was surrounded on all sides by shelves full of stationery, just as Cas had described.

'Well, this is cosy,' giggled Gabby.

'Very,' said Cas.

But Frank was thinking.

'That's strange,' said Anya. 'There's a key on the inside, in the lock. See?'

Frank knew this had to be the place. If someone was able to lock the door from the inside, it meant there had to be another way out.

'There must be an entrance here somewhere,' he said, although he had to admit that being surrounded by shelves did not make for a clear entrance into the elaborate network of tunnels.

He began to feel stupid - maybe he had got it completely wrong. He surveyed the small gloomy room, then looked at the floor and noticed it was covered by a tatty old rug.

'Check the floor,' he said.

With difficulty, they got down and pulled the rug to one side, revealing a large flagstone. There was nothing they could see that was out of the ordinary. As they crouched and scrabbled around the small floor space, Cas lost his balance and fell back against the wall next to the door. His elbow knocked the brickwork heavily, causing one block to move inward as he pushed against it. To their amazement the floor began to drop away. They crammed themselves against the shelves to avoid falling down the hole that had suddenly appeared beneath them.

Gabby gasped as she stared at the stone staircase that led down to a dark passageway below. The whole thing had happened so quickly and silently that, had they not seen it with their own eyes, they would barely have believed it, and no one in the corridor on the other side of the store cupboard would have heard anything but Gabby's gasp.

'Wowzer,' exclaimed Cas.

'Well done, Cas,' said Frank .

'More luck than skill, this time,' said Cas, getting to his feet.

'Come on,' said Frank. 'We'd better get down there before someone comes looking for some pencils or something.'

'Why don't I just ...' said Anya, turning the key to lock the cupboard door.

'Good thinking.'

Quickly, they walked down the staircase and into the dark passageway below. Although a faint shaft of light filtered down from the store cupboard above, they could barely see anything. Anya rummaged in her bag and produced the lamps, which they lit, with difficulty, in the gloom. She handed one to Cas. The passage was illuminated. Strange, angry shadows were cast in all directions; fierce silhouettes caused them to look carefully around in case something, or someone, had been lurking, unseen, in the darkness.

'That's better,' she whispered.

'Why are you whispering?' said Cas, himself lowering his voice, for no apparent reason.

'I don't know,' she said, still whispering.

Their eyes gradually adjusted to their new surroundings. The passage was wide, wider than the one they had followed Dagmar into before, so Frank was relieved as he stood in the middle of the corridor. It was so spacious that he felt satisfyingly non-claustrophobic. Strangely, it was dry and quite warm, probably because they were well inside the academy walls and the heat from the floor above must have had a drying effect. But Frank had the feeling that someone had been using it, and recently.

Without warning, the staircase lifted back up, cutting them off from the room above. The movement made them all stand back, pressing themselves against the walls. As the trapdoor shut, they all looked at each other, knowing now that there was no going back. They would need to continue on, to try and solve the puzzle.

Frank pulled out the map. He put his finger on the place where they had entered. He'd taken the trouble to trace the blueprint onto the paper so that he could pinpoint exactly where the passageways ran, underneath the academy.

'This is where we are. We need to go down there to this junction.' He traced his finger on the map to a point where their passage met another. 'We go right here, and around this corner. The place we're looking for is just here.' His finger came to rest on the mark that Maddy had spotted when they'd met at Polly's. Frank had gone over and over the route in his mind many times since then, but he had to do it one last time, just to make sure. The others nodded in agreement.

They set off, slowly and deliberately, down the passage. It wasn't long before they came to the T-junction. This new passage had the same dimensions as the one they had just come down. Frank was about to turn right, in the direction of their target, when Gabby pulled him back.

'Did you hear that?' she said, her voice hushed.

Frank hadn't heard anything, but was suddenly on edge.

'What?' he said, his voice low.

Cas grabbed Frank's sleeve, his eyes wide.

'I thought I heard something,' she said.

They all went deathly quiet for a moment, ears strained for the faintest sound. Nothing. The passage was eerily silent.

'Maybe I imagined it,' Gabby said, after a few moments.

'Well try not to imagine it again,' said Cas. 'You scared the life out of me.'

'Like it takes much,' laughed Gabby.

They gathered themselves and went on.

'This way,' said Frank, leading them to the right and down the passage, where the corridor then turned to the left. The walls narrowed slightly. Frank noticed that there were iron torch holders on each side at regular intervals, indicating that, at some point in the past, these passageways had actually been used often. A long time ago by the look of things, although he still couldn't shake the feeling that someone had been here recently.

They went about twenty yards. Frank stopped and looked at the map again, Cas shone his lamp onto the diagram, so they could all see more clearly.

'Here,' he said looking up and around. The lamps illuminated a short stretch of the passage where they stood. 'It's here.'

The others looked blank. All they could see were the dark grey stone walls.

'There's nothing here,' said Cas.

Frank looked down to the map again and then around to the stone that enclosed them. 'But it's here, on the map.' He turned to the left hand wall and put the palms of both hands against it. 'Here,' he repeated.

Cas put his lamp down and started to feel around the blockwork, just like he'd done on the outside wall of the academy when they were following Dagmar, when he had discovered the door in the wall. He stepped back and shrugged at the others. Nothing.

'Perhaps it's not here,' he said. 'Are you sure it's not further down?'

Frank looked down the corridor. He knew from the map that it took another bend a little farther down, but that would be too far. It had to be here.

Anya raised her lamp, peering myopically through her glasses, looking for some sort of clue. It was then that she saw it; a small hole in the stonework, just above head height. It was less than an inch square, tiny, and no one would ever have noticed it unless they had stopped and looked specifically at the wall. Even then, it would be difficult unless you shone a lamp directly onto it.

'Look,' she said, suddenly full of excitement. 'There's a hole, just there.'

Anya pointed to the aperture. Certainly it was strange. The stones that the passage was made from were large and heavy and they hadn't noticed any blemishes like this during the walk from underneath the store cupboard. Frank reached up and pushed his fingers into it.

'That's odd,' he said. It was especially odd as it was in the exact place where he had expected to find the small turning on their map.

Then Gabby spoke. 'Frank! Your bag, the tin box.'

Then Frank understood. He knelt down and opened his bag.

'Quick, Cas, shine your lamp down here.'

Cas duly obliged, looking perplexed. Frank rummaged for a moment and fished out the tin box. He opened it and pulled out the odd-shaped stone object that had mystified them ever since they had first laid eyes on it. He brandished it like a short sword.

'D'you reckon ... ' Gabby began.

'I reckon,' smiled Frank.

'Reckon what?' said Cas.

'It's a key of some sort,' said Frank.

'Not just some sort,' said Gabby. 'Try it, Frank.'

'Shh,' said Anya, making them all stop.

'What?'

'Someone's coming. I just got a feeling that—'

But, before she could finish, they were startled by a distant clanking sound, like something being dropped, from back down the corridor they'd followed. Gabby grabbed Anya's lamp, leapt forward and walked quickly and quietly to the corner at the turning they had rounded minutes earlier. She peered carefully around. If there was anyone coming they wouldn't have been able to see her in the darkness. She could make out movement and the glow of a lamp a long way down the corridor. Whoever it was, was coming in their direction, and quickly. She watched a little longer, but then she saw him. Dagmar. And Percy was with him. She let out a gasp. Her heart started to race. She turned and ran back to Anya and the boys.

'Guess who?' she said.

'Not Dagmar,' said Cas.

'Got it in one,' she said. 'They'll be here any minute.'

Cas turned a shade paler.

'If he finds us here, we're dead,' said Frank.

He was still holding the stone object. Gabby snuffed out one of the lamps and shielded the other to damp the light down.

'What are we waiting for, Frank?' she said as her eyes flashed towards the long stone thing in his hand.

He turned back to the wall, adjusted his grip, reached up and thrust it into the hole in the wall. It fitted exactly.

'Bingo!'

Frank pushed it in right up to the hilt, the round end stopping it from going in any further. They waited expectantly. Nothing happened. The voices from around the corner were getting louder. Cas and Anya looked alarmed. They looked at each other, then down the corridor, then to the wall where Frank had just inserted the stone key. Even Gabby's expression had an element of panic setting in.

The glow of a lantern appeared at the corner. Frank could feel himself getting hot and his breathing becoming more rapid. The thought of coming face to face with Dagmar again, but with no Alphaen guards around, suddenly filled him with dread. No one even knew that any of them were down there. What were they thinking of? Why hadn't they told someone?

'Do something,' hissed Gabby in a whisper, her voice quavering slightly.

Frank reached back up to the knot of stone that now protruded from the wall. He twisted it frantically, first one way then the other, praying that something would happen. The lamp light grew brighter and Frank was sure the men would turn the corner any minute and discover them. Perhaps they should run.

He gave the stone one last, hard twist and, to his astonishment, not to mention utter relief, a section of the wall in front of them simply vanished, revealing a small, polished wooden door set back in an alcove. There was a little gap between the corridor and the door and the four of them leapt in, needing no encouragement. They stood there as the two men rounded the corner.

'That stupid Emerald boy. Wait 'til I see his father. We've been this way before, you idiot,' came the unmistakable hiss of Dagmar. He was about to walk right in front of them, there was no way the men could possibly miss them. They were done for.

Then, as quickly as it had disappeared, silent as a hunting owl, the false wall reappeared, blocking them off from the passageway just as Dagmar and Percy walked past. They were thrown into darkness, but for the faint glow of their lamp, not that any of them minded.

They stood there looking at one another, thanking their lucky stars.

Once he was sure that Dagmar had passed and was out of earshot, Frank spoke.

'That was close,' he whispered, still breathing heavily.

'Too close,' said Cas, exhaling. He'd forgotten that he'd been holding his breath for what seemed like minutes.

'You can say that again,' said Gabby.

She unscreened the lamp and the cramped recess lit up. The closeness of the space made the light seem brighter than it really was and there was barely enough room for them to move. They managed to turn to face the door that had just revealed itself to them. Neatly carved in the middle was a familiar symbol: the two arrows and the rose. Frank shivered.

'What *is* this?' said Cas.

'I guess it's what we've been looking for,' said Frank.

'What, a hidden door, behind a disappearing wall, in a network of secret passages? Yeah, like, where have you been all my life?' joked Anya.

Frank had to smile, so did Cas.

'I have to admit this is all *really* weird,' said Frank.

When he had twigged about the map showing secret tunnels, and had then had an inkling about the extra mark, he hadn't visualised the scene that had unfolded, but here they were, standing in a space no bigger than a bath tub, blocked on one side by a magical wall of some kind and facing a sturdy oak door on the other.

Frank grasped the ornate iron ring handle and looked at the others. They all nodded. Frank nodded back and turned it. He had expected the door to be locked, but the latch snapped upward and, as he pushed, it slowly heaved its way open. He led them through and they stood at the entrance to a spacious square room. It was lit from one end by a large, diamond-shaped skylight, allowing the sun to cast a glorious yellow beam across the room, which was immaculate, as tidy as anything Frank had ever seen. Books filled the shelves that lined the walls. Flames leapt up from a large fireplace on the far side of the room, around which were situated a large, battered sofa and a rickety-looking, wooden rocking chair. To one side was a small bed and in the middle was a large wooden desk.

As they stood there, the man at the desk slowly turned his head. He lowered his spoon, from which he had just taken a sip of hot broth. His brow creased and the huge white eyebrows met in the middle. Frank immediately recognised the diminutive old man with the wild white hair.

Wordsworth Hums.

27

THE DROWNED MAN

The students stood there in stunned silence, staring at the man staring back at them. Except for the crackling of the fire as it split the logs in the grate, the room was quiet. Although it was large, it was warm and cosy and had obviously been lived in for some time. It was immaculate, tidy and ordered, with not a thing out of place and as clean as a whistle. A doormat inviting visitors to 'Please Wipe Your Feet' sat just over the threshold.

No one knew what to say. Wordsworth Hums was the last person they had expected to find. After all, the last time anyone had seen him he was falling head first into the fast-flowing torrents just ahead of the waterfall. Even the strongest swimmer wouldn't have been able to escape, let alone the ancient caretaker. For a drowned man he looked remarkably healthy.

Although Frank and his three friends had thought they might be on the trail of the old man's brother, they hadn't really thought about what they would do in the event that they actually discovered anyone. Frank wondered if Hums might just keel over at the sight of the four strangers that had just entered the room.

'Well, bless my ten toes,' said the old man, breaking the silence, his voice high-pitched and husky. He wiped his mouth with a bright white napkin and pushed himself slowly to his feet, his ancient and frail-looking frame seeming to creak with the effort. 'Well, don't just stand there, come on in.' He beckoned them into the room. 'I've some soup on, if you want some.'

He looked at them in turn. They all shook their heads. Food was the last thing on their minds.

Frank edged slowly into the room, moving like a boxer does in wariness of his opponent, although in this case the adversary was a wizened old man who looked as if he might expire at any moment. Cas, Anya and Gabby followed him. Frank looked around, checking to see if Ludlow was there. No sign.

'That's it,' beckoned Hums, waving them across the room. 'Come on in. Why don't we sit over by the fire?'

'We?' thought Frank. They hadn't even been introduced and the man was inviting them in like old friends.

They moved further into the room and, as they headed over to the sofa, Frank noticed a dog lying on the rug in front of the hearth. It looked as old as Hums himself and didn't move as they approached. Not exactly a guard dog, thought Frank, but then why would Hums need a canine sentry, hidden away so securely down here?

The four of them sat down. Hums followed and dropped into the rickety old rocking chair which seemed fittingly reserved for him by the fireside. It creaked sympathetically as he sat. The old bloodhound raised its head gently, as if aware of his master's presence.

'It's okay, Cedric. Just some visitors,' said Hums, his lived-in face creasing into a smile.

The dog slumped its head back to the floor and fell into a deep sleep once more. They sat there awkwardly. Finally, Frank plucked up the courage to speak.

'Are you Wordsworth Hums?' he asked. Hums looked aghast.

'Oh, my, where are my manners? Here I am, inviting you in, and I haven't even properly introduced myself. Well I am sorry. You'll have to accept the apologies of a poor old man. You see, I'm a bit out of practice. Don't get many visitors down here and, well, it's been quite a while since I ... er ... well, yes, quite a while.'

'Nearly three years,' said Frank.

Hums looked at him. Melancholy filled his hollow eyes.

'Is it really that long?' he said. He turned his head and gazed through the fire, deep in thought. 'Three years,' he muttered. 'Three years. Oh well, it's not like I was looking forward to an exhilarating retirement travelling the world!'

A beaming smile filled his face, as did a multitude of lines and his skin creased like an antique squeezebox.

'Welcome to my room, and, you're quite right, I am Wordsworth Hums.' He looked at his visitors, hands on his knees. 'And who, may I ask, are you?'

'I'm Frank,' said Frank. 'And this is Gabby, Anya and Cas.'

'Pleased to meet you,' said Gabby.

'Hello Mr Hums,' said Anya.

Cas nodded.

'Oh, and pleased to meet all of you,' said Hums. 'As I said, Cedric and I don't get to see many folks in here, so it's nice of you all to call in.'

It was an odd use of words. He appeared to be treating them as idle passers-by who happened to notice he was at home and felt like a chat.

'And to what do I owe the pleasure?' continued Hums.

They just looked back, not sure what to say.

'We're not really sure,' said Anya.

'You're meant to be ... well ... ' Cas's voice trailed off.

'Dead?' said Hums, knowingly.

'Yes.'

Hums smiled.

'I don't get it,' said Frank.

'And what is it you don't understand, Frank?' said Hums softly.

'We thought everyone was looking for your brother, Ludlow. He stole the Liberation Seal and pushed you into the river, someone saw him do it, saw him kill you, then he disappeared, so how come ... '

Frank stopped. He just couldn't believe that everyone had been looking for the wrong man and that the caretaker hadn't met his doom at the hands of his brother, but was alive and well and living in a secret room under the academy where he had spent his entire life.

'Then, quite evidently, they are very mistaken,' chuckled Hums.

'In fact, I believe they're not looking for Ludlow at all.'

'So if they're not searching for your brother, then—'

'They must be looking for me,' Hums chuckled some more.

There was a silence. None of this made any sense.

'So where's Ludlow Hums?' asked Gabby.

Hums looked momentarily sad. He shrugged his shoulders but didn't answer. More silence.

'Why is everyone looking for you?' asked Frank.

Now that they had actually found the supposedly drowned caretaker, now that he was getting used to the surprise that Hums actually existed and was alive and well within the academy walls, he was eager to get some answers.

'Are you looking for me?' said Hums, his deep-set eyes wide.

'Not really. Well, perhaps ... we just know that lots of others are,' said Frank. 'But, like I said, we thought they were looking for Ludlow Hums, not you.'

'Well, they can keep on looking, can't they? Three years and counting, eh?' he mused. 'But you found me. How on earth did you manage that?'

Frank told him how Cas had found the tin box in the chimney, what they had found inside and how the map had led them to his door.

'Bravo!' Hums clapped his hands together. 'You are clever, finding my sneaky hiding place. I thought when I first came down here I'd better keep a map and a spare key somewhere, you can't be quite sure if you won't need something like that, especially as I'm getting old and a bit forgetful. Good job I did.'

Frank was even more confused.

'So Ludlow didn't hide it?'

'Oh no, he wasn't the sort to keep things. He would always rather just sell his ill-gotten gains. Not really a planner, my brother.' Hums smiled to himself. 'I couldn't have hidden it in my rooms. Too obvious. Ludlow's cottage seemed like a better place. Have you got it with you, the box?'

Frank pulled it out of his bag and opened it. It was now empty, apart from the mysterious small ball. As Frank picked it up, it took on its usual radiance and hovered just above his palm. Hums looked pleasantly surprised. He waggled his eyebrows and Frank thought he might take off.

'What's this?' Frank asked, taking his eyes off the sphere and looking at the old man.

'Oh that? Good heavens, I only put that in the box at the last minute, didn't want anyone else to get it. Should've brought it with me,' he muttered.

'Anyway, never mind. What this is,' he said, 'is an Elemental Ball.'

'Right,' said Frank, none the wiser. 'What's that, then?'

'Oh, clever little thing, given to me years ago by a particularly clever friend of mine, ex-student here.'

'What does it do?'

'Do? Well, Frank, as the name suggests, it allows you to command the elements.' Hums pointed to the ball as it hovered. 'You see the colours – orange, brown, blue, white?'

Frank nodded, enrapt.

'They are fire, earth, water and air - the four elements. They live within the sphere. You can feel their energy and, if you wish...'

He reached over to Frank's hand.

'May I?'

Frank nodded. Hums took the sphere and it continued to dance above his hand. He grasped it, drew his hand back and threw the ball towards the fire.

'Water!' he shouted in a hoarse voice.

The students watched as a huge plume of water flushed through the fire where the ball had landed, then shot up the chimney and out of the hearth, soaking them and the poor dog, who had been enjoying some fine dream until he was showered. The hound jumped up and shook itself, further showering all five of them. The fire went out immediately and the ball returned to Hums's hand. He let out a cackle.

'You see?' he said plainly, unaffected and dripping, as if he had just buttered a piece of bread.

Frank, as well as being wet, was stunned.

'Clever little thing. Could come in very handy in the right situation, don't you think?' He held the ball out to Frank, who wiped water from his face and took it back.

'It'll only respond to certain people. Seems it quite likes the look of you, Frank. Why don't you try and relight the fire, hmm?'

Hums raised his enormous eyebrows, a mischievous look on his face. Frank got the hint. He took the ball, gripped it, feeling it pulsating in his hand, he tossed it a couple of times in the air, looked at the others, who stared back in wonder, then he launched it at the hearth.

'*Fire!*' he shouted.

As the ball hit the sodden ashes, a towering flame consumed the fireplace, sending a jet of hot air out into the room. The ball returned to Frank's hand, leaving them all staring in wonder at the newly-ignited fire, the heat nearly drying them off in the process.

'Wowzer,' said Cas.

'Wowzer,' said Gabby.

'Wowzer,' said Anya.

'That's better. Gets a bit chilly down here at times. I do like my fire, reminds me of home,' chuckled Hums. 'Not bad, Frank, not bad at all.'

Frank held the ball out to him. 'You should have it back,' he said, indicating for the old man to take it from him. 'It is yours after all.'

Hums took the ball and smiled, apparently touched by Frank's gesture. He looked back to Frank.

'You know, I have no need of it anymore. You should keep it. You never know, it might come in handy someday. I suspect it might. You all seem the sort who have a sense of adventure, otherwise I guess you wouldn't be here.'

He held the orb out to Frank, who hesitated, and then took it.

'Thanks, Mr Hums,' he said. It was a generous gesture, and to own an object that could do such things was like a dream.

'And Frank, don't let it out of your sight or give it to anyone else, ever,' said Hums enigmatically.

'Okay.'

Hums looked back to Gabby.

'So, who else, in particular, is looking for me?'

Gabby hesitated, not sure if she should start talking about what they knew, but the old man seemed so ordinary and self-effacing. He was also kindly and, having let Frank keep the ball, seemed so generous.

'A man called Dagmar and, we think, Aurora Moonhunter, she's the principal—'

'Oh, I know who they are,' Hums cut in. 'And, yes, I believe you're right, they are looking for me. Even brought in the big guns. Got the Alphaen searching and everything, so I hear.'

Frank thought it was odd that he knew, seeing as he seemed to be stuck here, in his underground room.

Hums went on. 'I can't be sure, but it wouldn't surprise me one bit if Miss Moonhunter has been creative in getting Dagmar to help her. Very clever, that woman, don't you forget it. Perhaps she cast a spell on him,' he chuckled. 'They might be working together, but they're far from best friends.'

'And Professor Lanks,' said Cas. 'He's in on it too. He's got one of those stone key thingies, we've seen it. If he finds the keyhole, like we did, you'll be found, no messing, then he'll turn you over to Dagmar.'

'And what makes you think he has reason to look for me?'

'We just don't trust him. He's had it in for Frank since he got here and he always seems to be keeping an eye on us,' said Cas.

'I admit Herbert has a certain way about him. I keep telling him he's too serious. Needs to lighten up a bit if you ask me. Even so, I'm not sure what I would have done without him these last ... three years, you say?'

'You mean he's on your side? Lanks?' said Anya, clearly amazed. 'Who'd have thought it?'

'I'm not sure there are any sides to be on, but, if you put it like that, yes. Professor Lanks has been my eyes and ears since I've been here.' He looked around the room. 'He looks out for me, checks that no one is on my trail, so I can see why you might think he's got his eye on you, but he has my interests at heart.'

Frank didn't find Hums's endorsement of Lanks any comfort. It did, however, explain how Hums knew what was going on outside his four walls.

'And, seeing as you found me, perhaps he has a good instinct for that sort of thing.'

'So why are the others looking for you?' asked Gabby.

'Ah.'

Hums smiled, got to his feet and paced slowly across to his desk. There was a small, box-shaped object covered with a dirty-looking sack, sitting on the floor by the side, unnoticed until now.

'Well, they might tell you that they're looking for this,' he said, and he pulled the cloth off, revealing what was underneath.

The object shone brilliant gold as it caught the rays of the sun shining through the skylight. Frank looked at it, open-mouthed. He knew exactly what it was. It was the stolen casket. It was open, and an ornate object was in plain view inside. The Liberation Seal.

'So, everyone was right,' said Cas. Hums looked at him.

'What do you mean?'

'You stole that, or your brother did,' said Cas, pointing to the casket. 'The Seal, that's why you're on the run.'

'Hmm,' said Hums. 'Seems that the more someone tells a story, the more folks believe it.'

'But you do have it,' said Frank.

'Yes,' chuckled Hums. 'Caught red-handed,' he raised his arms in mock surrender and he laughed. 'Searching for the Seal? That old thing? Don't you believe it. Don't you believe *them*!'

'Why not?' said Anya.

'I mean things aren't always what they seem, young lady,' said Hums, lowering his tone. 'They don't want to get the Seal back, that's just a diversion.'

'But I don't understand ... you've got the Seal, you took it,' said Cas.

'No,' said Hums shaking his head. 'I never took it. Neither did Ludlow.'

'Uh? So who did?'

'Dagmar, of course.'

'Dagmar?' said Frank. 'But I still don't get it.'

'Of course you don't,' said Hums. 'There's no reason why you should. Dagmar took the Seal so that he could put the blame for its disappearance on Ludlow. Typical of that rascal.'

'You mean he set him up?' Frank sounded surprised, although he hardly should have been, knowing what he did about Dagmar.

'Oh yes, well, he certainly intended to set my brother up - and me. I don't know how much you know about Dagmar?'

'Enough.'

'Well then, you'll know he's a ruthless, self-serving individual.' Frank nodded.

'It was the only way he could get us away from the academy, where I had been safe all these years,' continued Hums. 'Well, safe when Hector was there. Hector Baggus, that is. Then that Moonhunter comes along and things change. Dagmar managed to steal the casket containing the Seal. The theft was going to be pinned on Ludlow and they all expected us both to be marched off to prison, with me as his accomplice in the theft. After all, Ludlow would need me to get to the Seal in the first place, what with my access to all parts of the academy. Fortunately for me, though, Dagmar has a weakness.' Hums gave a wry smile, one that indicated he'd outsmarted the villain.

'He does?'

'Yes, like most power-crazy so-and-so's, he made a schoolboy error. He underestimated me - a bent old codger like Wordsworth Hums couldn't possibly outsmart someone like that. Vanity! That's his downfall. He couldn't possibly have thought that I had an escape plan, not that I thought he would go to such lengths to get his hands on me. Stole the Seal from right under the academy's nose. Now, although I have nothing but dislike for the fellow, I have to take my hat off to someone who can pull that off.' He paused. 'Unfortunately, Ludlow wasn't so lucky.'

'So how come you've got it now?' asked Gabby.

Hums made his way slowly back to his rocking chair.

'Ha! I stole it back, stole it from Dagmar. Oh and doesn't he know it,' he said, as he plonked himself back down. The rocking chair groaned.

'How did you do that?' asked Cas.

'Too easily,' said Hums. 'The thing is, he doesn't trust anyone - another frailty of his, for who are we if we are unable to put our trust in others, especially those we love, eh? Including our friends. You should all remember that. So he kept it with him. I just had to find out where he was staying, which wasn't difficult. Kzarlac only has a few sympathisers in Rhaeder, so I'd pop out here and there to search. Eventually I found it, I knew I would, and his fingerprints are all over it. I bet he's hopping mad. One nil to Hums don't you think? Shame his original plan backfired. Now he has two reasons to look for me.'

'So, you said they're not after the Seal?' said Frank.

'No,' replied Hums, shaking his head. 'It's *me* they're after.'

'Why?' asked Gabby. 'What have you done that's so bad?'

Hums thought for a moment, mulling something over.

'Well, there's another story, *the* story.'

He paused.

'Perhaps some tea? I have a pot on, could do with a cup.'

He waved towards the pot that sat on top of a small stove behind the sofa. On a shelf to the side were six neatly arranged mugs.

'If one of you would be so kind.'

He rocked gently in his chair and patted his leg.

'Gammy knee,' he said with a smile.

Frank got up, poured five mugs full, and took them back to the others. They sat clasping their drinks with great anticipation.

'So?' asked Frank.

Hums paused as if burdened with the decision as to whether or not to tell them what he knew. He nodded to himself.

'Look, I'm an old man and I expect I don't have much time left in this life,' he said. 'I have no family of my own, not anymore, so I must choose who to tell. I suppose it's time that I should pass on what I know to younger folks like you - resourceful, good people, people who seem to care - especially because I know Dagmar won't rest until he finds me.'

Frank didn't think Hums would be that easy to find.

'You haven't come here with weapons, you must be bright to have found me and you're showing an old man some respect. I guess I can trust you.'

'Pass on what?' said Frank.

'Perhaps I should start at the beginning. How much do you know about the history of Byeland and Kzarlac?'

Frank recounted their meeting with Halnaker in Blackburn's workshop. How the divide between Byeland and Kzarlac had come about centuries ago and how the antipathy between them still existed.

'You are well informed,' said Hums, impressed by what they knew. 'Halnaker does know his stuff. Good chap, even if he does dress like a birthday present. So, as you know, while Byeland lives in harmony, there is nothing that those who rule Kzarlac wouldn't give to conquer its peace loving neighbour.'

Gabby snorted. Hums looked at her and noticed her arms for the first time.

'Oh,' he said. 'You're from Prismia?'

'Yes.'

'Hmm, annexed by Kzarlac oh, five or six years ago.'

'Invaded, you mean, and its people slaughtered,' said Gabby, tears springing to her eyes.

Frank and Cas gave each other surprised looks. Anya put a comforting hand on Gabby's arm.

'Yes, terrible business. You got out, though.'

'Just.'

'My sympathies, Gabby,' he said sincerely. 'And, mark my words, many people think that the invasion of Prismia was just a prelude to the main event.'

They all looked at him, knowing exactly what he meant.

'Kzarlac's overthrow of Byeland?' said Frank.

Hums nodded gloomily.

'But why haven't they done that before?'

'Ah, good question, the answer to which lies at the root of all this. The simple fact is that they haven't been able to.'

'Why not?'

'Because of me, and those like me.'

The students looked blank. Hums noticed and went on.

'You remember when the land was divided by Kester, the sovereign at the time? Yes, but what Halnaker didn't tell you, because he didn't know, was that Kester took out an insurance policy. One that was sure to keep the peace, forever.'

'How did he do that?'

'Not easily, by all accounts. He gathered the very best minds from across from the lands - sorcerers, knights, clerics and more, all of them ex-students - and, using their combined talents and expertise, asked them to create a binding power, an energy, to keep things in equilibrium so that the two lands could never conquer each other. An impossible task you might think, but remember - these were Excelsus' finest scholars and create it they did. It was called the Simbrian, and, once it was created, all the time it was in existence there was no possible way that either side could overthrow the other. The power would not let them. It somehow acted as an obstruction, an impediment to tyranny and war. I dare say some have tried, but over all these years - centuries - neither side could hope to rule the other because a greater power stopped them. Shrewd move if you ask me, especially when it came to Kester and the conundrum with his twins. Of course, there was no issue with his son, Joleyon, but it seems that he wasn't such a fool after all, like some think. Seems he knew that his daughter, his own flesh and blood, was a bad egg and that she would harbour venomous and brutal thoughts of power to reunite the lands and rule over them with a fist of iron - thoughts that exist to this day in Kzarlac. But that's not all. He also feared that someone might try and seize the Simbrian and claim it as their own. Own it and yield it in the wrong way. So, as an extra precaution, it was fragmented, split into several elements and given to a number of keepers to act as guardians. Their identity was kept a closely guarded secret so it could never be seized or fall into the wrong hands. The guardianship would also pass down through the generations. With these precautions in place, there was no chance of there being a war, an invasion, or anything like that. Peace and harmony prevailed. Hurrah!'

Hums raised his hand in the air, momentarily, in a gesture of triumph, then his expression changed to one of resignation.

'Until things changed,' he said.

'Changed? Why, what happened?' said Gabby.

'Someone achieved what no one thought was possible.'

'What?'

'Someone actually discovered a way to create and possess the Simbrian. Impossible, but they did.'

'Possess it?'

'Why yes. Imagine if you could actually have it for yourself, own it, control it. Now, imagine if that power fell into the wrong hands - dark, vengeful hands. This is what Kester had feared at the beginning and why he'd taken such extreme precautions. He thought they'd be fail-safe, but didn't bargain on someone *extremely* gifted coming along hundreds of years later and achieving the unachievable.'

'You mean Dagmar had it?'

'No, oh my goodness, what a thought. No, lucky for everyone that wasn't the case.'

'Then who?'

'I'm afraid I don't know who it was. You'd think I would, hmm. But one thing's for sure, Kzarlac found out who it was and Dagmar took it upon himself to get it.'

'So what happened?'

'Well, about, hmm, let me think, about twelve years ago - my goodness how time flies - yes, twelve years ago, more or less, whoever managed to possess it, knowing that Dagmar was on to them, and realising the potential consequences, managed to' - Hums swallowed - 'destroy it.'

'Destroy it? The Simbrian?' said Frank.

'Yes, completely. Bang. Gone. Goodness knows how. Apparently, whoever they were found out that Dagmar and Kzarlac were intent on taking it, to hunt it down at all costs. Story goes that Dagmar's men chased them for miles and were about to seize it, so, rather than let that happen, they decided to destroy it. Imagine possessing the key to the greatest power known to man, and then deciding to obliterate it, and yourself, to keep us all safe. Now, that takes *real* courage.'

Hums sat there looking vacantly into the fire. A silence fell over the room.

Anya spoke. 'What, so it doesn't exist anymore?'

'Not exactly,' said Hums.

'So, why doesn't Kzarlac just try and invade Byeland, if there's no power or magical force to stop them?'

'Because they can only do so *if* they have the Simbrian, not without it. With no power, the two lands are in a kind of limbo.'

'Then surely that's a good thing.'

'You might think, but for one small point.'

'What?'

'Well, some people, some very prominent individuals, eminent scholars, believe that destruction isn't the end of the story; that

342

the Simbrian can be, will be, recreated, and that this was foretold by one of the original creators, a powerful psychic called Mildred Everbleed. She made a prophecy, several in fact. My goodness, she liked a prophecy, that woman, by all accounts. One in particular told that the Simbrian would one day be destroyed, but that it would also be restored, and that those who brought it back would be the bearers of an even greater might, a power that would bring total dominance, forever.' He paused. 'So, imagine for a moment that the prophecy is true - certainly the first part has happened - and that those who seek to restore the Simbrian - the power - are from Kzarlac.'

'The ultimate power in the hands of Dagmar ... wow!' said Frank.

Hums raised his eyebrows.

'Not just Dagmar, but the fearsome Etamin. Ruthless woman, the ruler of Kzarlac.'

'What, you mean Dagmar isn't Kzarlac's leader?' Frank had thought all along that Dagmar would answer to no one, so he was surprised to learn there was someone else above him.

'No, he serves his despotic leader, or appears to,' said Hums. 'But I imagine he actually serves no one but himself and it wouldn't surprise me if he has designs on a higher position. One that possessing the Simbrian would give him.'

'So he's working for her, this Etamin?'

'Yes, for now, anyway, and it appears that Dagmar and only a handful of others are aware of the prophecy. You see, he was part of a select group of really talented individuals who formed a sort of secret club when they were students at the academy. I remember him well - good student, focused. And those few individuals were taught about the prophecy back then. He believes it, one hundred percent, so no wonder he's putting all his efforts in working out how to rebuild it. But some refuse to accept it to this day. Governor Jackson knows about it and, apparently, he thinks it's a load of old nonsense. But I'm not so sure.'

Frank was amazed. He'd never even considered Dagmar as

having been a student at Excelsus, but, now he thought of it, he wasn't at all surprised. It also explained why the council was keeping a close eye on events.

'But what's all this got to do with you?' said Gabby. 'Why did you run away?'

'Oh,' chuckled Hums. 'I'm afraid a man can run away from anything' —he leaned forward in his chair— 'except his past.'

Gabby shook her head.

'What do you mean?'

'I mean, they're looking for me because I'm one of the guardians.'

He let the words sink in. The revelation caught Frank by surprise. He hadn't expected this old man to harbour such a secret.

'You're kidding?' said Cas incredulously.

Frank couldn't help but agree.

'I admit I don't look like I should be the custodian of something so important. At my age I'm becoming a bit forgetful. But the secret, its energy, or at least part of it, resides with me, and Dagmar thinks I'm part of the key to rebuilding the Simbrian, along with the other guardians.'

'So how many of you are there?' asked Frank.

'Seven, I believe.'

'Who are the others?'

'Oh, I have no idea, Frank. None of us knows who the others are. That was always how it was, right from the very first day the Simbrian was created. Security you might say, the secret passed down through the generations, but the problem I have is that Dagmar knows about me. He somehow found out that I am one of the guardians. Goodness knows how, but he did. I went to Hector, just in case this happened, and he made sure I was protected all the time I was at the academy. So was Ludlow. But then he stepped down and Moonhunter became principal and that's when Dagmar stole the Seal.'

'But that doesn't explain about your brother, Ludlow,' said

Gabby.

'No, it doesn't,' said Hums. He looked vacant for a moment. 'My poor brother. He was in the wrong place at the wrong time, with the wrong person as his brother'. He lowered his voice. 'Dagmar.'

'Dagmar?' said Frank. 'I knew he would be involved. How did he find out about you in the first place?'

'I have no idea, my dear boy, but I was certainly betrayed. Someone gave up the secret, *my* secret. ' He paused. 'You see, Dagmar wasn't entirely sure if it was me or Ludlow; he couldn't figure which Hums he was after. He had the choice between the secretive, sneaky, villain or the old, unassuming, caretaker. I think he got it wrong - he thought it was my brother and went after him first. It took the attention away from me for a while, but he still hatched his plan to get his hands on the both of us. We were both under the protection of the academy, but Ludlow had the misfortune of seeing Dagmar as he was stealing the Seal. You see, he'd sometimes take to walking around the academy at night - kept him out of mischief, away from other temptations, if you get my drift. Oh, I knew what my brother was, all right. Couldn't help himself. But he was my flesh and blood, after all. So, instead of having him walk around the town, I'd give him my keys. Then, on that fateful night, he saw Dagmar coming out of Moonhunter's office, with the casket.'

'What did he do?'

'What most people would do, faced with Dagmar. He ran - legged it all the way back to the cottage to collect some things. Then he came and told me what was happening, that he feared he was being set up. After all, having a notorious thief in the academy when the Seal goes missing seems like an open-and-shut case. And, once he was hauled off to prison, there would have been no knowing what would have happened, and I'd have followed close behind him. It was then that I knew Dagmar was on to me, so that's when I made my escape and I told Ludlow to get as far away as he could.'

'Do you think Moonhunter had something to do with it?' asked Frank.

'I can't be sure,' Hums replied. 'Maybe, maybe not, I thought that was why Hector might have been replaced - that they'd discovered my identity and needed to get me out of the academy. Anyway, I didn't feel safe anymore. I knew that when Moonhunter and the authorities found out that the casket had gone missing we'd both be blamed. I knew I couldn't stay.'

'But someone saw you and Ludlow by the river ... he pushed you in, killed you,' said Cas. 'Or not, obviously.'

'Ah yes, I have Herbert to thank for that. Of course, if Dagmar was on to me, I couldn't have anyone thinking I was still alive now, could I? A bit of honest dishonesty. Herbert took some of my things and left them by the river and told the authorities what he'd seen. Or not seen, as the case may be. I thought it would take the heat right off me. Being dead has its advantages, you know.'

'And you've been here ever since?'

'More or less, yes, although I do venture out now and then.'

'So, what happened to Ludlow?' said Anya. 'Is he still on the run?'

Hums shook his head. 'My poor brother. He went on the run all right, but I heard that Dagmar caught up with him. It wouldn't have taken him long to find out he'd got the wrong brother. I can't imagine what he did to Ludlow before turning his attention to me. You see, Ludlow didn't know anything about my secret, the Simbrian. I always thought it best not to tell him. Keep him in blissful ignorance. Protect him, so to speak. But once Dagmar had found out he knew absolutely nothing about any of this he'd have no further use for him. So I can only think he killed him, or had him put in some filthy Kzarlac dungeon. My poor brother. Dishonest, yes, but no one deserves that. It should have been me.' He shook his head, his voice full of regrets.

'Naturally, everyone else thought that Ludlow stole the Seal and ran. No one even knew Dagmar had been anywhere near the place, except me, of course. Luckily, they all believed Herbert's story, but, believe me, Dagmar is smarter than that. He knew I hadn't gone over the waterfall. He knew that I knew he'd found me out and escaped, and he's been looking for me ever since. Still looking, but I sense he's getting closer.'

Frank suddenly felt sorry for the old man. He'd kept his secret for goodness knows how many years and a case of mistaken identity had caused his brother to fall into Dagmar's hands.

Hums reached over to a book on the fireside table. He opened the cover and pulled out a tatty-looking loose leaf of paper.

'If I needed any further confirmation that I'd been rumbled, I found this,' He held it up so the four of them could see. 'Dagmar had it. I found it with the Seal.'

Frank stared at it. He couldn't believe his eyes. He recognised it instantly - the missing page from the book. It simply showed a single image - a rose and two arrows - the same as the one on the box and on the diagram. Frank reached into his bag and pulled out the book.

Hums face became animated. 'Well, bless my soul, where did you get that?'

'Someone dropped it in the mews, running from Dagmar.' Hums looked at Frank quizzically.

'I did?'

'Yes, Cas found it.'

Then he realised what Hums had said.

'You? No, someone else ... the man I saw was young and fast, er, no disrespect Mr Hums.'

Hums chuckled to himself. 'That's because you only see with your eyes,' he said enigmatically, looking at Frank, who pondered the comment.

Hums looked back to the book. 'I thought I'd lost it, feared it had fallen into Dagmar's hands. I can't begin to tell you what a relief it is, knowing that he hasn't got it.'

Frank opened the book and turned a few pages, looking at the lines and shapes.

'I don't suppose you know what it says?' said Gabby. 'It's just that my mum couldn't decipher it and she's really, really good at that sort of thing.'

'Sorceress?' said Hums.

'Yeah.'

'You too?'

'Maybe.'

'Excellent. And I can guess what your special talent is,' he said, looking at Cas. 'Finding secret hiding places, dropped books and more I don't doubt. Ah yes, I always tried to figure out what the talents of the new entrants were; became a bit of a hobby, got quite good at it.' Cas smiled. 'And you, Anya?'

'I'm meant to be a seer, but I'm not very good.'

'Nonsense, you stick at it. I'm sure you're better than you think. Some of the most talented students are slow starters. Take it from one who's spent years here.' His kind remark made Anya smile.

'And Frank, what about you?' Frank shrugged.

'No idea,' he said.

'Nonsense, everyone who comes to Excelsus has something. There's *always* a reason.'

'So everyone keeps telling me,' said Frank, rolling his eyes.

'Then you would be wise to believe them. Even those unpalatable individuals whose parents pay have something, even if it's small. Baggus was so against them, but the academy *never* makes mistakes. I take it you're all meritters?' They nodded. 'Thought so, I can tell a mile off. A lifetime at Excelsus teaches you to sniff out these things.' He tapped his nose and looked back to Frank. 'And most of the rich kids at the academy will no doubt let you think they are somehow superior.'

An image of Emerald immediately sprang into Frank's mind.

'Now, Frank, remember, an average person sometimes thinks he isn't, if you get my drift.' Frank looked confused. 'You might not be able to see it, but, take it from one who knows, some talents are not as obvious as others. You don't have to have any particular skill to possess the greatest gifts known to man. The gifts of kindness, compassion, patience, friendship, trust and more. They're all worth a thousand able swordsmen.'

Frank thought about it. What Hums was saying made sense, although he couldn't help thinking he was being kind.

'You'll find out in time,' Hums continued, smiling kindly. 'Believe me.'

Their attention turned back to the book. Hums held out his hand and Frank passed it to him.

'So what does this mean?' said Gabby, pointing to the book.

'I haven't got a clue,' said Hums. They all looked disappointed. 'But I know it's important.'

'So, if you don't know, how come you've got it?'

'It was sent to me. Just arrived at Ludlow's cottage one day, not long before the Simbrian was destroyed. No note or anything. I don't know to this day from whom, or where, it came, but the first page was already torn out and it appears that Dagmar had it. A strange coincidence, don't you think?'

'The symbol,' said Frank. 'The one on the page that was missing.' He pointed to the sheet of paper that Hums still held in his hand. 'That page, it has something to do with you, doesn't it?'

'Very astute,' said Hums. 'And, yes, it does. In fact the symbol *is* me, or rather it represents me, and my ancestors.' He ran his fingers over the image on the page, a rueful look etched on his face. 'The crossed arrows and the yellow rose, the symbol of friendship. My dynasty, of sorts. A clue to my identity, for sure. Dagmar knew that.'

A friend in the dark, thought Frank.

As Hums opened the front cover, his expression changed to one of alarm. 'My goodness,' he said. 'I didn't expect this.'

'What is it?' asked Anya, as Hums continued to stare at the book.

He didn't speak for a moment.

'What is it, Mr Hums?' she asked, again.

'I hope I'm wrong.' He looked up at them. 'But it looks like you may have set off a chain of events, one you might not be able to stop.' He held up the book, showing them the second page, which had always been blank when they had looked at it before. Etched on the paper was now another symbol - a pair of stag's antlers that cradled a star.

Frank studied it intently. 'What does that mean?' he asked.

'I can't be sure,' said Hums. 'But, if I was a betting man, I'd say this is the identity to the next guardian.'

Frank looked at the others. If what Hums was saying was right, the fact they had found him meant the trail to the next person, the second protector of the Simbrian, had been revealed to them. Quite what it meant they should do about it was another matter altogether. Hums snapped the book shut and handed it back to Frank.

'I just hope my telling you all of this is a wise choice,' he said. 'Because we all have choices. I mine and you yours. Choices to seek power and conquer, or to be peaceful and use the talents we have for the good of all.'

He leaned back in his chair and rubbed his wrinkled face with his hands. 'The world is getting too fast for me. When I first arrived at the academy it was all about finding out who you were, taking time to smell the flowers, listen to the birds. Where what you were mattered more than what you wore. The world is a beautiful place and we often overlook what is important. In later years I saw people more obsessed with what they had, rather than what they did; like having a bigger carriage somehow makes you a better person. As I said, you youngsters have choices to make - make them wisely. There is so much more in a scent of a daisy than in a pocketful of crowns'

Frank thought the words sounded like they could have come straight from his dad. 'What should we do?' he said.

'You must stop him, of course,' said Hums, quickly.

'Dagmar?'

'Yes. Dagmar, those behind him and those he serves. Stop him from getting the Simbrian. For if he accomplishes that, there is nothing to look forward to but darkness. You must succeed, you have to.' His tone had changed; he was deadly serious. 'And you must find the next guardian. Make sure they're kept safe.' He patted the book. 'If you don't, he will. He'll find out who it is, if he doesn't know already, and then he'll be a step closer to the power he craves and the destruction of Byeland.'

'But surely there are people much more able to do that?' said Cas. 'We're just a bunch of kids. Why don't you just tell the council? They'll be able to do something about it ... help you, I mean.'

Hums thought for a moment. 'Don't underestimate the power and innocence of youth. There is much in the adult world that is good, people who can guide you and from whom you can learn an immense amount about how to live your lives, if you choose wisely. But power, the taste of it, the elixir, the persuasion ... Any man can stand adversity, but, if you really want to test a man's character, then give him power. The road to ruin is littered with a thousand good souls and many well-meaning grown men have succumbed to its romance, while these are things that do not trouble the young. Time has yet to corrupt you. That is, if you choose to tread the right path. Perhaps this is your destiny calling?'

They drank their tea; the weight of what they'd learned hadn't fully sunk in. Whatever they had thought they were getting into, it certainly wasn't this. Frank reflected on Moonhunter's words not to get involved and wished they had heeded them.

'Now you must go, and take this.'

Hums got to his feet and walked over to the casket. He flipped the lid shut and, with a grunt, picked it up and handed it to Frank.

'I trust you to keep my secret and not to tell anyone that you've found my hiding place.'

They all nodded.

'We won't, Mr Hums. That's a promise.'

They got to their feet; Cedric didn't disturb.

'There's a safe way out behind the fireplace,' Hums continued, ushering them to a small alcove behind the hearth.

'Will you be okay?' Frank asked the old caretaker, who looked tired from the unburdening of their conversation. 'Down here, I mean. And what if Dagmar finds you?'

Hums looked touched by the comment. He put a gentle hand on Frank's shoulder.

'My boy, I'm as tough as old boots,' he smiled. 'Cedric and I will be fine. We have each other and there are others looking out for me too, but thank you for your concern.' Hums shrugged. 'Perhaps it's time to move on?' Frank nodded. Hums went on. 'And remember what I said; you *must* stop Dagmar from rebuilding the Simbrian. Do it for my brother, for Ludlow Hums.'

As Hums showed them the way out, Frank wondered how on earth he and his friends had any chance of doing that, and how they had got themselves into this. All he knew was that they had to try - the future of Byeland and the battle to stop the tyranny of Kzarlac had, somehow, found its way into their young hands.

28

THE BEGINNING

After they left Hums, Frank took the casket containing the Liberation Seal back to Polly's and kept it hidden in his room. While letting the enormity of their discovery sink in, he discussed with the others what to do with it and their first thought was that they should just leave it somewhere with a note, or that he should give it to Norris and tell him they found it in the woods. In the end, he thought the least they could do was to return it to the academy and, eventually, he made the decision to leave it outside Moonhunter's office, thinking that would be the right thing to do. Arriving at the academy early one morning, before anyone else was there, he placed it in front of her office door and made off before anyone could see him.

News of the return of the Seal spread quickly, although no one knew how it had turned up out of the blue. Moonhunter arranged a special assembly of the whole academy and made a long speech, saying how it was a defining day in the history of Excelsus. Rumours abounded. Some said it hadn't really been stolen at all and been found by one of the masters in a cupboard, hidden behind a box of chalk where it had been all along. Others, that it had been used as a door stop in the kit store and Mrs O'Flynn hadn't realised what it was. It even made the front page of the *Broadsword*. 'Liberation Seal Returned' read the headline, sporting a picture of Moonhunter and the academy, with more guesswork about where the Seal had been and how it had turned up. It was only Frank, Cas, Anya and Gabby who knew the secret.

Despite finding Hums, they hadn't mentioned it to anyone. They had promised the old man, after all. Even though they had unlocked the secret of the missing caretaker and discovered the man who had eluded capture for nearly three years, none of them felt particularly happy with what they had done. It was as if Hums had placed a huge burden on them that they hadn't expected and it was now up to them to try and fathom what to do with what he had told them about the Simbrian, the quest to recreate the power that would bring total dominance, and how to stop Dagmar from doing just that.

As the end of the academic year approached, Frank found it difficult to concentrate during any lessons and had to stop himself thinking constantly of what they would do.

* * *

It was the last day of term and he woke early. He'd packed his bag the night before in readiness for the journey home. His ride was from the academy so, after a farewell breakfast, he slung his bag over his shoulder, ready to make his way across town for the last time, until the new term started in September.

Polly gave him a hug so tight he thought his ribs would be crushed, tears rolling down her cheeks as she packed some buns into his bag and said goodbye.

'I'll be back in September,' he said.

Maddy gave him an awkward hug, reminiscent of the one Phoebe had given him when he had left the farm months before. Even Norris left for work late so that he could say goodbye.

'Damn paperwork can wait,' he said, drawing a telling off from Polly.

It was a warm farewell, completely in keeping with his time there, and he knew he would be welcomed back in the same way in a couple of months' time.

He walked quickly through the town. Although he was going to miss his friends, he was excited about going home to see everyone at the farm and he needed a break from all that had happened back at the relative normality of his home. As he thought about his family he realised he hadn't gone to see his grandmother, even though he'd promised his dad. A feeling of guilt struck him. He'd make an extra effort next year. He had yet to work out what to tell his dad about the encounter with Hums. They'd promised the old man they wouldn't tell anyone about his secret, so he wasn't sure how much to disclose. He hoped his dad would know what to do, but something like this might even stretch the wisdom of Lawrence Penny. He and his friends had done nothing but talk about what they now should do with their newly acquired information, and the revelation of the second image in the book. It was a lot to take in. They just found the whole thing both frightening and daunting and had agreed to wait to decide what they should do until they returned after the summer.

Frank reached Iron Lane, which was busier than normal due to the traffic heading towards the academy. He kept to the inside of the footpath to avoid the large carriages, some of which mounted the pavement as they rushed up to the plaza. He'd arranged to meet the others at the entrance to say goodbye. With all that had gone on, it was important for him to see his friends before they all went their separate ways. Thoughts of Hums, the Simbrian and ghostly guardians filled his mind and he wasn't paying much attention to the goings-on around him as he headed up the lane.

As he approached Rutter's shop, he was suddenly aware of someone behind him. He spun around to see only a hooded figure. The door to the shop opened and, before he could react, he was bundled through the door. Rutter, the shopkeeper, was standing there, apparently in readiness. He put his hand on Frank's shoulder, gripping him firmly and spinning him around. There was no need to guess who the other man was as he slammed the door shut and pushed his hood down - Dagmar. As Dagmar pulled himself up to his full height and stared down at him, Frank felt his knees go weak.

'Ah, Frank Penny,' said Dagmar, with his usual menacing smile. 'What a pleasant surprise. So glad you could join us for a little chat on your way to the academy.'

'Let me go,' said Frank, barely able to disguise the fear in his voice.

'Well, Frank, if you cooperate, then perhaps I can oblige,' replied Dagmar.

Frank went to move, but Rutter held him tight. He looked around the room seeking an escape route. For a lantern maker's it was notably dark. Lamps of all shapes and sizes filled the room, all unlit.

'I'm not scared of you,' said Frank.

He was. He thought of Ludlow Hums. Had Dagmar killed him just because he was the wrong brother? If so, what might he do to Frank?

'Perhaps you should be,' said Dagmar casually. 'I would be ... if I were you.'

'What do you want?' said Frank. Dagmar's eyes darkened and they burned into him.

'You know what I want,' he said, his tone threatening. 'You found him, didn't you?'

'Who?' said Frank, too quickly. Dagmar ignored him.

'I really have no idea how you did it. I've been searching for ... well, let's say some considerable time ... but you, a snivelling little good-for-nothing student, an uneducated rat-bag, got there ahead of me. I can't deny that even I am more than a little impressed and even more intrigued. Now, you peasant, perhaps you'd like to enlighten me as to how you did it and, more to the point, where he is?'

'Did what?' said Frank, anxious to buy himself time, to think of how to get away.

'Don't play games with me, boy,' he grabbed Frank by the shirtfront. '*Where is he?*'

'I don't know what you're talking about.'

Dagmar let out a sigh. 'Give me strength,' he muttered under his breath. 'You're going to tell me—'

'Don't tell me,' Frank interrupted. 'There's an easy way and a hard way.'

'You pick things up very quickly, for a farm boy.' He loosened his grip and flashed his evil smile once more. 'So, let me tell you how this is going to go.' Frank didn't think it was going to go well at all. 'I'm going to ask you one more time, just once, and you're going to tell me, okay?'

Frank's eyes darted around the room again. There was nowhere to run. Rutter had him firmly by the shoulder, no lanterns lit a route through the shop and Dagmar was blocking the way out to the street. Dagmar bent forward and put his hand on Frank's other shoulder.

'So, Frank, where is he? Where is Wordsworth Hums?'

Dagmar's grip tightened, his eyes locked on Frank's, who found he couldn't look away, no matter how much he tried. At that moment the door to the shop was flung open and in strode the familiar figure of Lanks. Frank never thought he would ever be so relieved to see him, but there was no doubt he was to be his saviour. Dagmar released his grip and swung around, quick as lightning. Frank noticed his hand instinctively go to where his sword would have been, had he been wearing one. He made a gesture as if pulling it out of its sheath, ready to strike, until he realised he was gripping thin air. He shook his head in annoyance.

'What do you want?' he spat, giving Lanks a look of derision. 'Shop's closed - can't you read?' Dagmar nodded towards the sign that hung on the door.

'Oh, I'm not looking for a lamp, I just thought I'd join your little gathering,' said Lanks.

'Oh, sod off. Can't you see Frank and I are having a little chat here ... in private?'

'That's what worries me. Good job I was walking down the lane when I saw you accost young Penny, here,' said Lanks.

Dagmar seethed.

'So, perhaps you'd like to explain what you're doing?'

'Pah! You expect me to answer to a deadbeat like you, you weak Byelander?'

'No, I don't, so, if you'd excuse us, gentlemen.' He looked over at Frank. 'Come on, Penny, you're wanted up at the academy.' He beckoned him with his hand to move towards the door. Frank needed no second bidding; the safety of the street was but a few quick strides away. He moved forward and Rutter reluctantly let go his grasp. Unexpectedly, Lanks put a kind hand around Frank's shoulder as he pushed past Dagmar, who look fit to burst, as he had done in Moonhunter's office.

'Bad move,' hissed Dagmar.

Without another word, Lanks ushered Frank out of the door.

'You haven't seen the last of me, Penny,' seethed Dagmar as Lanks slammed the door behind them.

Frank didn't doubt it. Whatever he had now got himself into, his path was now entwined with that of one of the meanest individuals around. Not a good place to be. He knew that, whatever was going to happen after his encounter with Hums, Dagmar would inevitably be involved.

Once out of Rutter's, he and Lanks strode up Iron Lane towards the plaza.

'You okay?' said Lanks.

'Yeah, thanks,' said Frank. 'And thanks for saving me back there.'

'Don't mention it,' said Lanks. 'If that man knows what's good for him he'll head back to Kzarlac right now - and stay there.' He stopped and looked at Frank. 'He's a very dangerous person, Penny, the sort who would run you through with his sword as soon as look at you, even a schoolboy such as yourself. Whatever it is he has in for you, it will bring you no good, mark my words.'

As Lanks spoke, Frank realised that he seemed unaware of their meeting with Hums, otherwise he would know why Dagmar had grabbed him. Hums couldn't have told him. The old man had kept their secret too.

'Let's hope he does go back to Kzarlac then.'

'Yes, for your sake, for all our sakes.'

'You said I was wanted up at the academy,' said Frank, not knowing if Lanks had meant it back in Rutter's shop, or if it was just an excuse to get him out of there.

'Oh, yes,' said Lanks. 'Miss Moonhunter would like to see you before you go. She sent me to look for you. Good job she did, eh? I've told Knox that you'll be a little delayed.'

They entered the plaza to be confronted with the mayhem of large carriages, vying for position so they could cross the bridge to pick up the throng of students who were congregating at the entrance. Frank cast his mind back to his first day and smiled as he thought how ludicrous the whole scene was. Big wheels crashed against each other as drivers struggled to keep control of their charges. Expletives were exchanged and Frank narrowly avoided being run over by a particularly aggressive driver.

'You go ahead,' he said to Lanks. 'There's someone I need to say goodbye to.'

'Okay, Penny, but don't forget,' said Lanks, and he made his way across the plaza.

Frank pushed open the door of Blackburn's workshop. The bell tinkled. Blackburn was over at the forge, eating a sandwich. He was watching a flask full of purple liquid as it bubbled over a burner on the workbench. He looked up as Frank came in. Cicero snoozed on a chair.

'Come to say cheerio?' he said, as Frank made his way across.

'Yeah, and to say thanks for all you've done,' said Frank.

'Quite an eventful year, all things considered,' mused Blackburn, raising his eyebrows.

'Yeah, see you in September,' said Frank.

'Not stopping for some tea?'

'Sorry, Moonhunter wants to see me, and my ride's waiting.'

'Oh, well, best not keep her waiting then,' said Blackburn. 'You take care.'

He gave Frank a hug. Frank breathed in the oil and spirit fumes of his overalls.

'And say goodbye to Cas, Gabby and Anya.'

'I will.' Frank turned and left the ramshackle shop, knowing that he'd miss it, but he'd soon be back.

As he hurried across on the footpath to the front of the building, he cast a last look at the vulture and wondered if it knew it had given up one of its mysteries, even though he felt there were bound to be more. He saw Cas, Anya and Gabby chatting at the top of the stairs and bounded up to greet them. They returned his beam with smiles of their own.

'Ready to go home?' he said.

'I guess so,' said Gabby.

'Can't wait,' said Anya.

'Me too,' said Cas. 'After all that's happened, I need a break, clear my head a bit.'

'Then we need to think about what to do next,' said Gabby. 'Hums put his trust in us and, if what he says is right, we should have a plan to stop Dagmar.'

'I'm with Gabby on that one,' agreed Anya.' Although it's all a bit scary.'

Frank knew they were right, even though he didn't exactly relish the prospect. He nodded. 'We'd best all think about that,' he said. 'And by the way, not wishing to spoil your holiday, but Dagmar's on to us. He knows we found Hums,' said Frank. 'I had a near miss with him just now in Rutter's and Lanks came to my rescue.' He recounted to episode to them.

'Blimey,' said Cas. 'You okay?'

'Yeah, but I agree with Gabby, and it just makes me think we need to do what Hums said.'

'Stop him, you mean?' said Cas, looking distinctly worried.

An older boy called him from the bottom of the stairs. It was Battersby, Cas's older brother.

'Ready to go, Cas?' he called as a small clapped-out carriage that looked like it had seen better days pulled up.

Frank saw Emerald laughing. He gave Cas a hug.

'See you in September, mate, and thanks for everything, for being a good friend,' said Cas.

'You too,' said Frank.

'Here, take these for the journey.' Cas handed him a brown paper bag.

Frank looked in to see it was filled with liquorice toffees. 'Thanks,' he said.

Cas said goodbye to Gabby and Anya and they watched as Cas walked down the stairs to the waiting vehicle.

'Come on, Gabby, our ride's waiting too,' said Anya. She turned to Frank. 'See you, Frank. Keep out of trouble.'

'Bye, Anya.'

Frank turned to Gabby, not sure whether to give her a hug or not.

'See you too,' he said.

'Sure, Frankie. And to think I was going to leave before I met you guys. Now my life will never be the same, in a good way, I think.'

Frank felt she meant it, despite what had happened. They smiled at each other.

'Gotta go, our ride's on the other side of the bridge, can't stand all this stuff.' She hesitated. 'Have a good break.' She gave him a squeeze and both she and Anya ran off down the stairs. Frank watched them all go and knew he'd found three unlikely, but wonderful, friends.

He noticed Knox approaching him, and then he saw the gleaming academy transport parked over to the side of the building. Knox had a cloth in his hand.

'Hello, Mr Knox,' said Frank.

'Mr Penny,' said Knox, touching his forehead in acknowledgment.

'I have to go and see Miss Moonhunter before I go,' said Frank.

'So I've been told. It'll give me a chance to give the wagon a quick clean before we set off.'

Frank grinned and Knox raised his eyebrows in response. Frank liked the man.

'I'll just wait by the carriage for you,' he said, wiping his hands on the cloth.

Frank set off into the academy and headed to the west wing, retracing the route by which he had been led by the Alphaen guards a few months before. The place was deserted and it wasn't long before he reached the atrium in front of the office. The walls swirled with the colours of summer and the eye on the door seemed to be watching him. He stood in front of it, hesitating. He raised his hand to knock but something made him take his locket in his hand, flick it open and look at the picture of his mother, as if he might need her with him for his meeting with Moonhunter. He gave the image a kiss, took a deep breath and knocked softly.

As it had done before, the door melted away, revealing the inside of the office. The night skyscape that adorned the ceiling previously had been replaced by a dazzling sun that lit the whole room. Moonhunter was seated at her desk, writing a letter. Her cat sat upright on the corner, watching him carefully as he entered the room.

'Hello, Frank,' she said disarmingly. 'It's alright, Star,' she said to the cat, who still stared at him suspiciously.

'Hello, Professor,' Frank said, easing into the room. 'You wanted to see me?'

Moonhunter got to her feet and walked slowly toward him, watching him with interest.

'Yes,' she said. She paused and Frank shifted uncomfortably on his feet. 'I wanted to know what you thought of your first year here.'

Frank wondered if she really did, although, given their previous encounter, it could well be she had a particular interest in his progress.

'It's been good, thanks. I've made some good friends and, er, learned a lot about myself, I think,' he said, honestly.

'Good,' said Moonhunter. 'An important part of the journey here is to learn not just about new subjects or skills, but also about ourselves.'

Frank nodded. Moonhunter paused.

'And I see that things about yourself aren't all you've discovered.'

She looked at the wall behind Frank, an action designed to make him look round. He did, and saw the small casket, now residing in its cabinet. Back where it belonged. She knew he'd returned it.

'How—'

'Frank, there is little that escapes my attention here.' He didn't doubt it. He thought of the eye on the door. 'And I have a feeling that a certain Mr Dagmar may have had something to do with its disappearance in the first place, judging by what an analysis of the Seal and the casket has turned up.'

'I ... I wouldn't know.'

Moonhunter paused and gave him a knowing look. He still hadn't figured out her relationship with Dagmar and he wasn't going to ask her about it again, not after last time.

'No, I don't suspect you could have known. How could you possibly have?' Frank felt himself start to go red. Moonhunter continued, 'I would ask where you found it, but I'm not sure I would get a wholly truthful answer.' It was a question more than a statement.

Frank thought. He could tell that Moonhunter was weighing him up. His dad had always told him to tell the truth and he had always abided by this, even if it got him into trouble. But somehow he wasn't sure that the need to be honest covered every set of circumstances. Moonhunter paused, as if waiting for an answer. He kept silent.

'Quite so,' she said, perching herself on the edge of her desk as she continued to look at him. 'And I must therefore draw my own conclusions and consider if there are other things you may have learned, people you may have come across.'

She was obviously waiting for Frank to reveal their discovery of Hums. She knew, he was sure of it, but he wasn't sure what 'other things' she was referring to. Did she know about the Simbrian and, if so, how much of the story was she aware of, and how did she know?

'I'm not sure what you mean,' he said, aware that he sounded unconvincing.

'Frank, you have nothing to fear from me, but let me tell you this. I said to you and your friends earlier in the year that there are things that children should not get involved with, things way beyond your comprehension and ability, things that could put not just you, but your family, in danger. I'm speaking of issues that not even the most capable of scholars or knights are able to master, let alone yourself, and it is my responsibility to keep you out of harm's way while you are here; a duty I take very seriously. Perhaps you have learned things that excite your natural taste for adventure. If so, then you need to consider the consequences, very carefully, before embarking on a quest that might cost you more than you think. Concentrate on your learning, on finding your abilities - for undoubtedly you have some - and not on other distractions.'

She paused. Frank could feel his heart beating hard inside his ribcage. Still he wasn't sure how much Moonhunter knew, but her meaning was crystal clear. She continued.

'You can probably guess that I possess certain abilities, some of which are beyond your imagination, so, if there is anything you feel you want to tell me, remember, I can help you.'

Frank wasn't sure what to say.

'Think about it, Frank. Think about it over the summer and we'll talk again when you return.'

'Thanks,' said Frank, nodding. 'I'll bear that in mind if I think of anything.'

Moonhunter smiled and he thought he detected a slight look of irritation on her face. The room fell silent. Frank felt he should leave but wasn't quite sure of how to excuse himself. Then she spoke again.

'I understand you've been wondering how you ended up receiving your invitation to be here,' she said.

Frank was surprised at the statement. She had apparently ended her attempt to elicit some information from him but, even so, she now had his full attention.

'Yes I have, ever since I got the invitation. I mean, I've never quite known how that happened,' said Frank. 'I wanted to ask you on my first day here.'

Although he still mulled the question over from time to time, he had cemented his place at Excelsus over the year and thought about it less often.

'So I remember,' said Moonhunter.

'The academy's meant for the gallant and gifted,' said Frank. 'And I'm neither. I mean, I grew up on my dad's farm, that's it. I can round up sheep, nothing special.'

'Well, perhaps I can shed a bit of light on that for you, if you wish?'

'That would be great.' Perhaps he could find out enough to close the issue in his mind. Even though he'd acquired a familiar in the form of Tweedy, this still didn't explain to him how he came to be invited in the first place and he was still none the wiser as to what his actual gifts were, if he had any at all.

'It's quite simple, really,' said Moonhunter. 'The Department for Education here in Byeland has been getting increasingly concerned that places at the academy are becoming more and more filled by those who pay, rather than those who, shall we say, deserve to be here.'

Frank remembered what Hums had said and nodded.

'The academy was set up by Finestone Lamplight to enhance the skills of anyone who had the necessary talents to become great - those who can serve their countries and work to preserve the peace we have all enjoyed for generations - and that ethos appears to have become a little lost. So the Department for Education asked the New Entrants Committee to invite children from different backgrounds this year, including giving consideration to home educated individuals, like you.'

She paused.

'But I still don't understand,' said Frank.

Moonhunter gave him a quizzical look.

'I mean, from what I understand, the authorities don't know, or didn't know, about me. I've never been to school, so how could they know to invite me?'

'Oh, believe me, Frank, minor details like that are no barrier to Excelsus, or to someone like me.'

Frank was astonished. It was as if Moonhunter was saying she could pinpoint his existence even though no one officially knew about him.

'But that still doesn't explain why me. I mean there are probably, what, thousands of home educated kids out there, ones who are cleverer than me, gifted, and would be much easier to track down. They would be much more deserving of a place here above a farm boy like me.'

'And what makes you think that?' Although she spoke softly, Frank had an inexplicably uncomfortable feeling about where the conversation was leading.

'Because there's nothing special about me. I'm just ... ordinary,' he said, his mind starting to race.

'Not so, Frank.'

'What?' he said, uneasy.

'I said, that isn't the case.' Moonhunter allowed the words to sink in. Frank couldn't grasp what she was getting at.

'Let me tell you,' she continued. 'When the committee gave me the list of names, the names of children that were to be considered, I saw your name and instantly knew, without hesitation, you were the one who must be invited.'

'Why?' Frank knew he was missing something.

'Well, because of your name, of course,' she smiled.

'My name?' He felt the hairs on the back of his neck stand up.

'That's right. Frank Penny.'

Frank still didn't understand. Moonhunter continued.

'You're Lawrence Penny's son, aren't you?'

'Y ... y ... yes. So what?'

'There you are then. Your dad, Lawrence Penny. He was a student here. One of the finest the academy has ever had.'

The story continues with ...

Frank Penny and the Kzarlac Spy